Baker City Testament

Baker City Testament

Kathleen McColloch

Thank you to Elerina Aldamar, Reference Specialist at the Oregon Historical Society, who helped me research their archives specific to the "McColloch Family Papers."

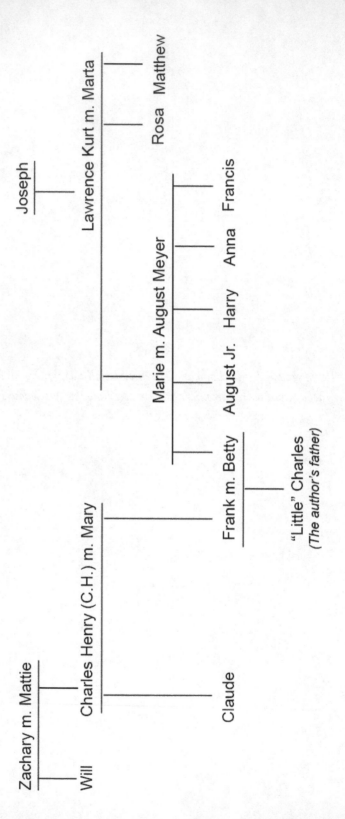

Prologue

Baker City, Oregon in 1980 looked much like so many Western towns suffering the slow death of an economy that once depended on the land's abundance. The rich gold, silver and copper mines responsible for her nickname, "Queen City of Mines," had long been played-out and shuttered, so the sturdy, self-reliant men of the West turned to timber for their daily bread. Too soon, Americans began to mourn the inevitable loss of their lush, green playgrounds and demanded government policies to restrict logging. Baker City's humming sawmills fell silent and those who had worked there moved away.

The town that had once been the epicenter of a gold rush boom looked tired. Many of its citizens worried that the glory days were dead and gone, and the grandeur of the town that had once been the largest city between Salt Lake City and Portland had disappeared forever.

Some knew a secret, however. They knew that the grandeur hat had once been was not gone at all. It was just hiding. It had remained hidden for decades under false facades of plaster and metal applied in a time when 1950s America believed nothing was beautiful unless it was sleekly modern. It was no longer sleek and had never matched the Victorian beauty that had once graced Main Street. These citizens took steps to change things. They formed a small passionate group, Historic Baker City Inc. They applied for grants and appealed to investors. Change began to happen. In 1993 The Oregon Trail Interpretive Center brought in tourists and the vintage Geiser Grand Hotel reopened.

Still, restoration was expensive and many merchants were slow to restore their buildings. Historic Baker City Inc. applied for more grants. They took votes and more votes over what other steps might be taken to convince the hold-outs to complete the job and return the downtown to its original charm. Then on June 20, 2002 a final vote came in, a vote no-one could argue with.

As Tabor Clark told it, the sound was like a train coming down Main Street. He ran outside to see the sheet metal façade on his building, J. Tabor Jewelers, begin to separate from the original brick store front as a terrific gust of freak wind tore it lose and sent it crashing to the street. He later reported that he had meant to restore the building but had never gotten to it.

"It makes sense to try to renovate," he laughed. "This is historic renovation by divine intervention."

Now the work is nearly complete and the ghosts of the past are finally freed to tell their story.

1.
McColloch

A baby cannot pick the date and place of his birth. If such self-se-lection was a possibility, the infant Charles Henry McColloch could never have picked a worse time and place in which to be born than the one selected for him by fate. The event took place in a two room farmhouse near Monticello, Arkansas. The date, October 6, 1861, was neatly sandwiched between a day six months earlier when Con-federate forces opened fire on the federal garrison at Fort Sumter in Charleston Harbor beginning the Civil War in the United States and a date just four months later when the Union Army brought that war to the Confederate state of Arkansas.

Zachary McColloch, the father of little Charles Henry and his mother, Mathilda (Mattie) McColloch had been relieved that there had been no fighting in their state for the first months of war, though theirs was a state that had seceded from the Union shortly after Fort Sumter. In actuality, their small farm was well south of the border with Missouri where Arkansas was most vulnerable because of clashes be-tween Union and Confederate forces just across the state line. How-ever, the couple would soon learn the sad fact that in a civil conflict, everyone, the civilian populace as well as the combatants, pay a ter-rible price. The family's intimate involvement with the war began on a summer day in June, 1861 when Zachary's oldest son, Jeremy, brought a notice home from his trip to town for supplies.

"Pa, this here says that General Ben McCulloch is travelin' around the state to put together an army to fight the Yankees and keep 'em out of Arkansas," Jeremy had breathlessly reported," He'll be in Monticello next week! Is this the same guy who is the Texas Ranger related to us?"

"Yep, he's a cousin. He's from Tennessee, and the family spells their name that way over there. We would too, except my granddaddy never could spell very well," Zachary shrugged with a laugh. "I did hear Ben was sent to Little Rock by Jefferson Davis, himself, to get up an army out here in the West."

It was easy for Jeremy to talk his father into attending the meeting in town to gather news of the war, hear the speeches, but mostly to see their illustrious relative in the flesh for the first time. Jeremy for one, was very impressed by the sight of the Texas Rangers turned Confederate soldiers traveling with the newly minted general who had been a friend to Davey Crockett and a member of Crockett's "Tennessee Boys," the men who fought and died at the Alamo, a battle Ben McCulloch had missed by a week due to a bout of measles.

The sight of his Rangers with their distinctive long hair and even longer mustaches wearing their signature slouched hats with a brace of pistols around their waists would have impressed any youth raised among farmers. But Zachary was unnerved by his son's excitement knowing that young men so easily allow their emotions to override good sense. He reminded himself that this was a recruitment drive, and that his own son was the target for these men building their "Army of the West."

In growing panic, Zachary began mumbling to an unhearing Jeremy that it looked like General Ben wasn't coming after all and that they should be heading home. But his words were lost when a cheer went up from the crowd as a horse and rider pushed through the gathering, and one of the Rangers announced the arrival of the awaited celebrity.

When the crowd quieted, Zachary heard one of his neighbors turn to a nearby Texan and ask, "What's he wearin'?" waving in the direction of the General who was clad head to toe in black velvet.

"That's his fightin' suit. It's what he wears for battle!" the Ranger shot back with obvious pride.

"Well, that's a fool for ya!" the farmer commented in low tones to a friend standing near Zachary. "He'll be shot for sure goin' around dressed like that!"

Suddenly, Zachary was very glad that his granddaddy couldn't spell and that he might never have to admit that this ridiculous dandy was related to him. He, of course, did not know the meaning that the color black held for many Confederate officers. He was unaware the color signaled the wearer was a leader of Southern fighting men who favored a "Black Flag Policy" under which any Yankee captured while fighting alongside black soldiers would not be taken prisoner, but would be shot on the spot. Many Union sharpshooters were well aware of this policy, however, and made it a practice to seek out and shoot any enemy officer wearing a black arm band or black hat feather. Certainly, few such Confederates chose to be as conspicuous about their politics as General Ben whose Civil War career would end at the hands of Union sharpshooter, Peter Pelican, on the first day of Pea Ridge, which was only his second major battle in the war.

Unfortunately, before he could again suggest they leave, the speeches extolling the glories of war that await any lucky recruit ended and Jeremy ran forward along with several age mates to eagerly sign up for the chance to help "… turn back the Union hoards and save the great state of Arkansas for the Confederacy!"

"I just can't spare you, son." Zachary argued with Jeremy on the trip home. "If you leave, I won't have any help here on the farm. Your mother is with child and Will is too young. He tries, but he's only four and really can't do much but carry water now and then."

It was true that Zachary had worried about his lack of harvest help especially when he and Mattie had lost another son to the small pox. That son, Robert, had been just a year younger than Jeremy. It had been two years ago, but the pain at remembering was still so bad Zachary could not yet talk about it.

"You still have Jake and Red for help," Jeremy countered, referring to the deal his father had made with their neighbor, Ronald Patterson, after Robert's death.

These two trusted field hands were ex-slaves that Ronald, a Quaker and a pacifist, had bought five years before and immediately freed once his own harvest was in. They had both stayed on and worked side by side both Zachary and Ronald to bring in the crops from their back to back acreage for a share of the proceeds. Most everyone in the county thought the father and son were slaves co-owned by the two farmers, and once Zachary had asked Jake why he had never left them or even made his freed status known.

"It's just not safe for me and my boy to wander around a slave state alone," Jake had answered, shaking his head. "Besides, I 'spect I have it as good as any white farmer, maybe better, 'cause I don't have to worry none about gettin' me enough money to buy me some land," he chuckled.

. . .

In the end, Zachary lost his bid to keep Jeremy safe from war and the boy marched off when the Army of the West moved on toward the north to engage the Union in Missouri. By summer's end, news came that the Confederates under Brigadier General Ben McCulloch had gloriously won the Battle of Wilson's Creek Southeast of Springfield, Missouri. Neither Zachary nor Mattie joined the celebration for the "Hero of Wilson's Creek" since a paper nailed to the outside wall of the Monticello General Store carried the names of the casualties and they found Jeremy's name on the list headed "Men Killed."

Several months later, one of Jeremy's friends, Joshua Duncan, who had signed up with Jeremy, returned to Drew County on furlough and stopped by to give his condolences to Zachary and Mattie for the loss of their son. After dinner, Mattie left the room to feed her new baby, and Joshua related to Zachary the chilling story of what had happened at Wilson's Creek and why he was no longer anxious to follow Ben Mc-Culloch into battle again.

"We was camped on the low ground by Wilson's Creek when the Federals attacked and drove our cavalry off the high ground above the creek. We infantry was ordered to charge up the hill to engage the enemy and three times we tried. By the second charge, though, most all of us was plum out of bullets 'cause they only gave us twenty rounds each to begin with! Now, how in hell can a man fight a battle with only twenty bullets? By the third charge, hardly nobody had any fire power left and we jus' had to smash at 'em with our gun butts. That's when we lost the most men. All of us thought we was goners for sure. But glory be! The enemy had to be even worse off than we was. Damned if most of them Yankees didn't jus' up and leave ahead of our last charge! When the dust settled, we all stood lookin' around at each other. When it sunk in what happened and that we'd won the battle, we jus', started laughing like fools, then we stopped when we saw that so many died in that last charge."

Zachary could see the boy was truly shaken by the telling of this account, so he leaned forward and spoke in low tones, "We all know you boys were true heroes in that fight."

"All I know is that all the glory went to that jackass, Ben McCulloch! He's the one the Confederacy hails as the 'Hero of Wilson's Creek'! Some hero! What kind of man gives his soldiers only twenty rounds and then orders three charges up the hill they now call 'Bloody Hill'?" Joshua exclaimed and then looked stricken remembering that he was speaking about his host's relative.

"A jackass to be sure. How could I feel any differently about a man who treated the life of my son so casually?" Zachary agreed to the boy's relief.

Joshua finished his story explaining that the Confederates had been too disorganized and ill-equipped to chase the retreating Union forces. He warned Zachary, however, that the Yankees sorely wanted to take Arkansas away from the Confederacy and would gather their strength and return since they knew Confederate Arkansas was too weak to defend itself very long. This warning set Zachary to thinking about how to best protect his wife and two small children when the Yankees drove south as far as Drew County.

...

At this time, long before the invention of modern refrigeration, every farmhouse in Arkansas had a root cellar consisting of a cool, earthen vault dug into the ground where fresh vegetables could be kept for long periods without rotting. However, not every farm had two root cellars. Years before, Zachary's father had dug such a cellar next to their barn. It had only been in use for one season because the family realized that the composition of the ground in that spot was too dry which caused the vegetables to soon wither and became inedible.

They tested several alternate areas on the property and had finally settled on a new site nearer the house that maintained the desired level of humidity and proved to be very suitable.

Now that he was most concerned with the family's safety, Zachary envisioned a new use for the first cellar that had for so long been empty. He began by tearing down the old wooden doors that covered the opening and, with the help of Jake and his son, set about digging a larger room below ground. They would be able to use the wooden shelving that had been built for the original root cellar to store supplies; blankets, lanterns, dried meat, and jars of fruit and vegetables that Mattie had canned during that spring. The men finished this well-stocked hiding place with new flat wooden doors onto which they placed layers of earth and grassy sod. Once the doors were lowered shut, the opening was invisible above ground. Now, should the war bring the Union enemy close enough to them to become of concern, all of them including the Patterson's could safely wait out any nearby battle beneath ground. And so they waited and worked the farm in relative peace for the remainder of 1862 though always alert to any approaching danger.

There were no newspapers or even letters delivered from relatives outside Southern Arkansas that could have informed the little farm's inhabitants of what was happening beyond their small world. The shadow of a great evil was indeed approaching as Zachary had believed, but the source and nature of it would not prove to be from the battles he had imagined might take place near their homestead.

The family had no way to know that the institutions supporting civilization in their state, namely the political and military leadership of Confederate Arkansas had completely broken down. As a result, the Confederate high command sent a Thomas Hindman to Arkansas to try to revive the Confederate forces in that state. What he actually found upon arrival in Little Rock was that there was no government or military; no law and order of any kind. In response to this crisis, Hindman declared harsh martial law, and began forcibly removing men from their farms and pressing them into service. He created bands of "partisan rangers", guerrillas charged with summarily executing deserters, staging hit and run raids on detached Federal troops, and burning any crops that could be seized by the Federals. Though some of these fighters were dedicated to defending their state against the Union invaders, many were merely armed bandits whose only cause was themselves. They roamed the countryside and indiscriminately preyed on the Yankees and helpless civilians alike. This complete disruption of civil society replaced by rampant murder, rape, theft and mindless destruction in Arkansas would last for another two and a half years. All concerns over states' rights and the continuation of the Old South that had led to secession and war with the North was replaced by daily horror and a grim struggle to survive.

Zachary's clever plan to wait out the conflict, provided the clan some protection from whatever danger might arrive. In their isolation, the family lived quietly without knowing their greatest threat was from marauding Confederate guerillas bent on thievery and other mayhem that would usually attack small defenseless farms at night. Still, Zachary knew that at any time the war could find them and that their safety depended on their keeping a constant vigil for any approaching danger. The family settled into a routine where any work to be done would occur in the daylight hours with one of the men standing guard near the road in a tree between their farm and that of the Pattersons.

At night, Mattie and the boys would descend into the root cellar compound while Zachary, Jake and Red slept and rotated guard in the hay loft which offered a clear view of the empty house. All the family's belongings had been stowed in either the root cellar or the hay loft and the men had left a few smashed dishes and other broken items of little value inside the house, hoping that anyone up to no good would conclude that the farm no longer held anything of value and just pass them by.

...

Months passed as Arkansas citizens continued to suffer the ravages of war made worse by a particularly hard winter. By March, it became evident that someone would have to leave the farm to try to find fresh supplies and more importantly to seek news from the outside world. Zachary suspected that he would need something to trade for food, so he gathered what little jewelry the couple had which consisted of their wedding rings, Mattie's gold earrings, a gold locket and her mother's cameo broach. He decided to take Old Jake with him in the wagon to ride shot gun. They would travel at night and reach the town by daybreak. They hoped to find what they needed and return the next night and be home by daybreak the second day. Red would stay behind to stand guard in the loft while Mattie and the boys would stay hidden in the root cellar. In truth, Zachary was afraid of the possibility that he and Jake might not make it back, and he wanted to make sure Mattie was left with at least one man to help and protect her.

Red took his assignment very seriously and stayed watchful guard from his perch in the barn for the entire night and all the next day. By nightfall, however, he could no longer shake himself from an over-whelming need to sleep. Soon, Red was awakened by the sound of horses approaching and men's voices calling to one another. In the light of a full moon, Red counted four men on horseback and two men driving a wagon and another man lying down in the wagon. At first he was relieved to see that they wore Confederate uniforms though some of them only wore the uniform hats. He would not welcome them until he could ascertain what they were up to. He clutched his rifle tighter as the group stopped in front of the cabin.

One man riding in front of the group spoke to the two men on horseback, "Gabe and Sid, you two check the house. If it's empty we'll stay here for the night. If it's not, shoot 'em an' then we'll stay here for the night." He snorted a laugh then waved his hand at the last man on horseback, "You go an' check out that pump and if the well ain't dry, water them horses."

"The cabin's empty. Nuthin's in there at all!" reported one of the men sent inside.

"Well, OK then," answered the one in charge. "Gabe, now go tell Rudy to take the bitch inside. He wanted to bring 'er along so he can just take care of 'er. That is, after the rest of us get our share."

"Yassir, Cap'n! I sure do want a little of that myself!" cried Gabe running toward the wagon.

Red watched as all the men dismounted and appeared to prepare to spend the night. The man named Gabe talked in low tones to the one driving the wagon who then reached into the back and forced the person in the back to sit up then climb down. For the first time, Red could see that this was not a man, but a woman. Her hands were tied behind her with a tight gag on her mouth. His heart beat even faster when he realized that he knew her. She was Rachel Patterson the wife of Ronald Patterson, the man who had given him and his father their freedom! He instinctively looked in the direction of the Patterson farm and for the first time noticed a red glow of a large fire behind the trees. He surmised that this group had torched the Patterson farm and no doubt killed Mr. Patterson but not his wife who they had brought along for their pleasure. He watched in sorrow as the bound woman stumbled toward the cabin. He grasped the sweat-slicked rifle closer to his chest when he saw one of the men walking toward the barn and he hastily withdrew into the shadows.

"Oh no you don't. Damn it, Ned! Ain't you had enough burnin' for one night!?" It was the Captain who had quickly dismounted to run after the man advancing on the barn. "If you wasn't so quick with a match we'd be restin' easy at the last place after hangin' that no good deserter! You can do what ya want when we get ready to leave here. Now go help the guys with the horses!"

So there it was. All laid out for him. Red realized that he had come close to burning alive inside the barn. Now he had a reprieve at least until dawn. But he had to act before then. He had to do something to help Mrs. Patterson, but if he tried to save her alone he would surely be killed in the attempt. Then there was Mr. Zach and his father to think about. He couldn't let them ride in the next morning without warning them about these murdering men. Then a new threat…

"Say what the hell?! I think this here ground is hallow. Come on back here, Ned. See if you don't think this ain't no solid ground!" called the Captain to the other man when he started to walk away as ordered. They both stood stamping their boots right on top of the root cellar where Mattie and her boys were hiding. "Let's go see if we can't find us a shovel or somethin' to dig with in the barn. Some of these farmers hide their valuables before they leave thinkin' they'll come back later for 'em."

Now Red knew his hand had been forced. He would never let these men find Mattie and her boys! He had to wait for the best possible moment to act. There were six of them and only one of him. He had to pick the right moment for a clear shot. He knew that he was fairly accurate with a gun from all the game he and his father had brought home on their hunts in the nearby woods. But at that moment his hands shook so much that he was deathly afraid of a miss. Then, in the time it took to reload, one of them would surely take him down. The two men began to rummage about in the darkened barn while Red crept closer to the edge of the loft.

Suddenly, a shot rang out from the vicinity of the cabin and the two men turned and ran to the barn door just as the cabin door flew open and Rachel Patterson dressed only in a torn camisole and naked from the waist down ran into the yard holding a hand gun. Men ran toward her from all sides; three from the horse trough and two from the barn. They circled the hysterical woman with their own guns drawn eyeing the hand gun she waved wildly about. "Come on lady. Hand over the gun. Ya caint shoot all of us," reasoned the man closest to her.

At that, Rachel sobbed and seemed to lower her weapon and the man sprang forward to take it. As he quickly closed the distance between them, Rachel took aim and put a bullet in the center of his chest. Then she turned the gun on herself and took her own life.

The others appeared dazed by this sudden turn of events and just stood staring at the two dead bodies on the ground. Then, the Captain shrugged and turned to the man called Ned and told him to go pick up the shovel he had thrown down when the two first spotted Rachel in the yard. "Let's see if we can find us some treasure over there," he said waving his arm in the general direction of the hidden root cellar. Then he pointed to the two men still staring at Rachel. "You two go see if Rudy's dead in there. Stupid fool shot with his own gun! An' if he is dead get him out. I ain't sleepin' with no dead body."

Red watched as the Captain and Ned bent to examine the area where they intended to dig. Just as Ned started to use the shovel, Mattie claimed the advantage of surprise and threw open the cellar door. The stunned Ned gaped stupidly at her as she raised a shot gun and gave him a deadly blast at short range. The Captain came to his senses and went for his side arm, but as he turned to use it on Mattie, Red shot him between the shoulder blades. Then, with shaking hands, Red immediately began to reload for he already saw the last two men running from the cabin toward Mattie who was struggling to close the cellar door. As they closed the distance between the cabin and barn, Red took careful aim and shot the man in front and then started to reload without even watching to see if the hit man stayed down or what the second man was doing. When Red looked up again, he saw the second man was running toward the tethered horses where he jumped on the nearest and galloped away down the road.

Red called to Mattie to close the door and wait for him to check all the dead to make sure it was safe. Then, he set about surveying the carnage after carefully covering Rachel with a blanket he'd brought from the barn.

His only worry concerned the man who got away and the possibility he might return with more fire-power. Their secret hiding place had been compromised as long as that man was alive. As Red finished establishing that, in fact, all the bodies were dead ones, he returned to the cellar just as Zachary drove his wagon into the yard at top speed. Both he and Jake jumped from the wagon and ran directly to where Red stood. The anxiety etched in the face of each man relaxed when they realized that the family was all safe and miraculously unhurt. Even Red's worry was resolved when Jake showed him the body of the man who tried to get away in the back of their wagon. Jake and Zachary had seen the burning Patterson farm and the body of Ron Patterson hanging from a tree and were trying to return home as fast as they could. Then they saw this man riding toward them at break neck speed, and Jake shot when the rider pulled his own gun and aimed it in their direction.

That night the men drove their wagon loaded with the bodies of six men deep into the woods and buried all of them in unmarked graves. Mattie carefully dressed and prepared the bodies of Rachel and Ronald Patterson and the family prayed over them as they buried each beside the other on their own land.

Mattie was surprised and pleased when Zachary returned all her jewelry but was suddenly very frightened when he told her that they had found the store empty and abandoned and that many buildings in town had been burned to the ground. There was no food or supplies to barter for. As he finished this awful story, Jake and Red called the two over to the wagon left by the guerrilla band. Jake swept his arm over the contents with a loud chuckle. "Looks like them fellas done brought the store to us!" he laughed.

Inside, they found many jars of canned goods, bags of dried meat and cornmeal that would easily last until their own vegetable garden bloomed again. In addition, they now had several new horses and an arsenal of guns that would all remain cleaned and loaded in the hay loft for the rest of the war.

• • •

As the war raged on into 1864, the baby, Charles Henry, was nearing his fourth birthday and his brother, Will, was already eight years old. Neither child really remembered a time that did not end each day in a bunker below ground. Incredibly, they were very happy, well-adjusted children since, in fact, they were provided everything a child needs in life. They were kept warm and safe from harm and surrounded by loving adults. Their parents understood that children, especially ones in the situation the family now faced, needed mental stimulation as well as affection in order to grow up healthy in mind and body. Their mother, Mattie, had always loved to read and had been taught early by her minister father to love books. She had inherited a small library of American literature which she brought down to the bunker placing it on the shelf with their canned goods. Both parents agreed that the sustenance provided by the books was as important as food.

Every evening, before Zachary joined the men in the hay loft, the family ate their meager dinner together in the root cellar, after which the children greatly enjoyed and looked forward to their mother reading stories from one of her books. Mattie would sit in the soft lantern light reading from the works of Washington Irving or James Fenimore Cooper with little Charles Henry sitting on her lap following her finger as she read, performing the magic of turning the print on each page into wonderful stories. They especially loved to hear chapters from Cooper's Last of the Mohicans and Irving's Life of George Washington or Legend of Sleepy Hollow.

While Mattie read to the boys, Zachary would sit quietly reading his well-worn Bible. Before war came to Arkansas, he had been known as something of an expert on the Bible who could be counted on to provide an appropriate Biblical quote pertaining to any subject. Because of this ability, he had been a source of local entertainment for the community citizens who liked to test him, and he had even been asked, on occasion, to fill in for the local church's pastor. In their hideout, Zachary and his sons often played "the Bible game." The boys would pick a passage and then read along as their father attempted to recite from memory. Points were given the boys if they could catch their father in a mistake and, if they could not, points were awarded Zachary. At first, it was assumed that little Charles Henry was too young to play, though he always watched the page along with Will. One night he surprised his parents when he pointed out a mistake that Will had missed. Everyone broke into startled laughter hugging and patting the proud, grinning child. It was evident that the four year old could read!

• • •

The little group on the McColloch farm continued to live in hiding for the remainder of the War Between the States. By 1865, the Confederacy in Arkansas had ceased to exist after the state had lost more than 10,000 of its citizens leaving many additional thousands with grievous wounds of war. The battered populous now had to begin the bitter agony of rebuilding their state that had suffered such widespread devastation. The Reconstruction continued in fits and starts for another decade due to the constant political struggles for power between the old planter elites who wanted to regain their prewar economic status and those citizens who supported "Radical" Reconstruction passed by the U.S. Congress that would allow Southern states to return to the Union only after passing new state constitutions that embraced universal, male suffrage and also ratified the Fourteenth Amendment to the U.S. Constitution giving ex-slaves full rights as U.S. citizens.

In 1868 delegates met in Little Rock to draft a new constitution. A group representing the old planter ruling class called "the Conservatives" was against Radical Reconstruction and the requirements laid down by Congress. Their seventeen members were far outnumbered by the twenty-three white Southern delegates they called "scalawags" because of their support for the "Radical" cause. To make the rift even more bitter for the planter group, the "scalawags" voted with eight black delegates and seventeen white delegates from outside the South that many people referred to as "Carpetbaggers" for the cloth suitcases they carried. The state of Arkansas was officially readmitted to

the Union on June 22, 1868 after a popular vote of the people ratified the new constitution and elected a new state legislature controlled
by Radicals who had joined the Republican Party of Lincoln and then
gave most positions of power in the state to like-minded Republicans.
The old planter class would have to wait until the state elections of
1874 before they regained any share in state government. Many of
these men were not about to just quietly step aside and let their hope
for a return to the old ways vanish. They were ready to employ any
means including violence to reestablish for themselves their prewar
economic and social status.

• • •v

During this period between the end of the war and Arkansas' readmission to the Union, Zachary and Mattie gradually dismantled their
carefully constructed fortress of isolation. They quickly realized that,
if they were to rebuild their own farm and effectively address the devastation to the infrastructure of their community, they would need to
band with neighbors in this effort. They began to reach out and establish contact with other families and to socialize with a few neighbors
in nearby farms.

They became especially close with Martin and Abigail Shaw who
owned a farm just down the road from theirs. The Shaws had been
brought from England several years before the War by one of the areas richest Arkansas planters who hired Martin as his personal butler
and Abigail to serve as his children's governess and tutor. The two had
managed to save enough to buy their own farm when their employer could no longer afford to have any servants who were not unpaid
slaves.

Zachary and Mattie took to the Shaws immediately after their first
meeting and were particularly grateful to finally have other adults to
talk with who shared much of their own thinking and concerns about
what was happening in the wider world around them. The two little
boys were fascinated by the Shaws whose clipped English accents made
them seem to be very exotic creatures indeed. Both were a little afraid
of Martin who had a rather formal, courtly manner from his years as
a butler in homes of the wealthy. However, they were entranced and

completely won over by Abigail who always spoke directly to the children and appeared to be very interested in everything they had to say. But, for Charles Henry, the best thing about Abigail was her personal library! She had so many more books than his mother and seemed quite excited to share them with the boys. The children spent hours talking with Abigail about what they read and what it meant to them, and she never tired of their questions. In short, she was the perfect teacher.

For his part, Zachary had begun to leave the farm regularly. He traveled several times a month to Monticello, the town closest to the farm, and to other small towns farther away serving as a circuit riding preacher. These churches paid him items such as food, tools, live chickens, or seeds for planting; all things that made life during the barren aftermath of war more bearable. Once he returned with a sack of white flour and a small crock of freshly churned butter and Mattie served the boys their very first white flour, buttered biscuits that evening.

Another advantage to these preaching trips was that Zachary was able to bring back news from the outside world. In this way, his family learned about the tumult of Reconstruction and the remarkable events that would change the social and economic life of Arkansas forever. They learned, too, that all of them would play a part in establishing this new direction, not only for their state but for the nation.

Following the readmission of Arkansas to the Union, ex-slaves were promised full rights of citizenship including voting rights for freed male slaves. The new Republican state government pushed hard for voter registration of all ex-slaves. Zachary and Mattie saw to it that both Old Jake and Red were well informed about their new citizen status and discussed with them their rights and responsibilities as voters. Zachary and Martin proposed they all go together to town to lend moral support to the two new citizens during voter registration. At this suggestion, Jake, at first seemed unable even to speak, his lips trembling and moving in wordless anxiety. "Naw, Mr. Zach. I ain't never been one to care 'bout politikin' an' such. I'm fine goin' on the way I am," finally came his unsteady answer.

But, when Zachary and Martin turned toward the old man's son, they saw in his eyes an intensity of burning desire. "So, are you ready for citizenship, Red?" Martin quietly questioned.

"Yep, I am fer sure!" and they all noted that the young man seemed to be standing taller than before.

A week later, the determined group of men, trekked to town for the registration event. Even Old Jake had finally conceded to try voting at least once. Zachary and Martin had solemnly promised to explain all issues and the stand of any future candidates, so that Jake and Red would be well prepared when the time came to caste a vote in a real election.

Outside the tiny registration office, they took their places in a long line to sign up. The almost party atmosphere with men shouting greetings, joking, laughing and slapping each other on the back seemed to quell any misgivings they might have had over participation in this momentous occasion. Suddenly, loud gun shots startled the crowd to silence, and a dozen riders on horseback thundered down the road reining up in front of the group. Each horseman carried a shotgun and wore, what looked to be, a fluttering white bedsheet with eyeholes apparently meant to hide their identity.

"Well looky here!" yelled one near the front, "If it ain't a bunch of Union traitors and their little black friends. Do ya'll love 'em so much yer ready to die for 'em?" growled the masked man sweeping his gun in an arc at the crowd.

The crowd seemed paralyzed, incapable of speech or movement. Martin who was in back of the group, but standing next to Old Jake who was visibly shaking in fear, sensed some quick movement as an obviously enraged Red began to walk forward. Martin reached out to restrain him, "Wait, I will address this," he whispered hoarsely into the young man's ear.

As Martin pushed through the silent and frightened men toward the gun-waving horseman, Zachary shouted in alarm, "No, Martin. No!"

Martin paid no mind to his friend and continued to walk forward, stopping just under the lead horse and rider. For long moments it seemed like time was halted. Then Martin spoke in a tone of quiet determination, still loud enough that all could hear. "I know who you are, Mr. Leeds." He began. "Twelve years as your personal butler, and I would know your voice barking orders anywhere. And you, too,

Mr. Walker and Mr. Gordon and Mr. Morrow. I polished those boots enough on your many visits to my employer at Elm Haven, I recognize each of you too," he added pointing at each of the front riders in turn.

Then Martin's voice grew louder. "So this is what has become of planter aristocracy! Now desperate cowards all! These men, I am proud to have joined, are the new South, and this is a new beginning that will not be stopped by the likes of you, hiding behind your guns and hoods! Every man in this nation now has the power to decide its direction. One man, one vote! It is the new order. Did the war teach you nothing?! Will you stand tall and vote beside these good men, or will you forever be shamed by your own violent actions?"

A long period of tense silence hung in the air. Then, unbelievably, the riders in front of the group, the apparent leaders Martin had called out and named, began to turn their horses and without a word, rode back down the path from which they came. After a confused moment or two, the others followed them silently down the road, away from the new voters and the new South.

2.
Krann

"**M**arie! Will you for once make haste? We will be late for the beginning!" As always, Rosa was impatient with her sister's care for details when the two had a schedule to meet. Rosa was well aware that her sister had been busy giving lunch to their mother who soon expected her fourth child. Due to this difficult pregnancy, she had been "laying in" under strict doctor's orders. Just now, her sister would be worried about properly turning down the gas lamps framing the heavy front door of the family's townhouse that stood only blocks from Vienna's Ringstrasse. Marie would then fiddle with securing the lock and carefully alighting the high stone steps without a fall, whereas Rosa had fairly flown down the same steps minutes before, thinking only of making it to the Theater an der Wien before the curtain rose on the newest Franz von Suppe operetta.

"We have plenty of time," cautioned the older girl as she ducked her head through the small carriage door.

"Grossvater!" responded Rosa through clenched teeth, "Please remind my sister that we will be denied entrance until the second act if we are late!"

"Calm yourself" replied the older gentleman, "Marie is correct. We have plenty of time to take our seats before the first act," their grandfather, Joseph Krann, assured the fuming girl. He was well used to these squabbles between loving sisters so close in age but so different in personality. Rosa, only a year younger than Marie, was constantly full of passionate energy that seemed well matched by her dark beauty, flashing green eyes and luxurious mane of unruly curls. Marie, on the other hand, was often called "the Dresden doll" by her grandfather who marveled that their family had produced this ethereal creature with her pale, almost translucent complexion, punctuated by eyes the color of sea-glass and framed by soft waves of white-blonde hair.

Both girls, however, loved these outings with their grandfather who delighted in opening for them the constant, cultural gift that was Vienna in the late 19th century. Since they were nearly twelve and thirteen years old, they could begin to appreciate the music, art and theater that was so much a part of Viennese life, though at their young age, they would naturally prefer operetta to opera and pastry to high cuisine. He would remain patient until the day they were ready to appreciate Mozart and Brahms as much as they did the lively operettas composed by Suppe and Johann Strauss Jr. He was happy to slowly introduce the magnificent art in the Belvedere Palace and the rest of Vienna's Museum Quarter as well as the Imperial Opera when the girls became mature enough to appreciate and respect what was offered every citizen of this golden city during its "Golden Age."

Joseph especially enjoyed a slow carriage ride down Vienna's great boulevard, The Ringstrasse and even more so when his granddaughters were with him as they were that morning. As a much younger man, Joseph could well remember 1857 when Austria's Emperor Franz Joseph I decreed the demolition of the walls and moats that encircled Vienna, and in their place he laid out his plan for a wide "Ring Road" that would become the city's crown jewel. The boulevard plan included the placement of many parks and monuments as well as impressive public buildings that would be a showcase for the glory of the Hapsburg Empire.

The Emperor's edict had had special meaning for Joseph and his father because they owned a brick making business near the Lastenstrasse, a cargo road that paralleled the Ringstrasse and on which the commerce needed to maintain the inner city took place. During the following years, the Kranns greatly profited from the booming construction of opulent public and private buildings that lined the great street. In their frequent trips through the city, Joseph was careful to point out to his granddaughters which public edifice or which luxurious mansion had in part been constructed using bricks produced in their brickyard.

Joseph also felt a great responsibility to become the "cultural guide" for his granddaughters, especially because he knew that their father would never take on such a role. His own son, Lawrence Kurt Krann (Kurt), did not share his father's love for their city and its cultural heritage. Though they worked side by side in the daily job of running their brick business on land they leased from the government, the two men were as different as Joseph's two granddaughters. Where Joseph was constantly mindful of their incredible luck at living in such a wondrous place and time in history that made it possible to live in peace and enjoy the prosperity that came with being part of Vienna's burgeoning middle class, his son dreamed of nothing but leaving for a wider world he believed offered so much more. Where Joseph felt a constant sense of pride in his role providing the basic building blocks of Emperor Franz Joseph's "dual monarchy", his son saw their brickyard as only a way to make a living and a borrowed one at that. The Austria-Hungarian Empire offered much of civilization's greatest riches, but it did not, nor would it ever, offer the one thing that Kurt wanted most, property of his own. In addition, Kurt felt stifled by the very civilized nature of this place and time. He felt as though all the excitement and adventure that is possible in a life where the future is unknowable had been wrung out of Austria. Every citizen in Vienna knew what the next day and the next and the next would bring. Kurt wanted out and the freedom to find his own destiny, a destiny he just knew was out there across the wild Atlantic waiting for him to make the move.

Kurt successfully hid these unhappy feelings from his family, for it seemed to him that fate worked solidly against his desires for free adventure. When he had been unencumbered by wife and children, the America he so desired to be part of was consumed by a great Civil War. He could not risk going there and becoming involved in a conflict the issues of which he did not understand nor care about. By the end of that great conflict, Kurt had met and married Marta, a woman of such exotic beauty that, upon first meeting her, his father had wondered if she had a drop of gypsy blood. Almost immediately, the two girls were born and then Mathew, their younger brother, a few years later.

Though Joseph had been dimly aware of his son's earlier discontent, he had believed that the joys and the responsibilities of marriage and family had matured him. In addition, after the civil conflict in America wound to a close, the revived union was involved in a convulsive era of reconstruction and rapid westward expansion. To aid in this process of national rebirth, the government reached out to the great cities of Europe encouraging private investment. When this activity reached Vienna, the coffeehouses buzzed with speculative excitement. One day, Kurt returned from his luncheon waving a flier that promoted investment in a gold mine newly discovered in the fledgling American state of Oregon. Though Joseph had some misgivings about the wisdom of such speculation, he agreed to part with some of the company's profits hoping that this move would act to satisfy once and for all Kurt's cravings for property ownership. This had been years ago, and Joseph noted with satisfaction that Kurt seemed more settled and had never mentioned the mining stock since that time. Now Marta was pregnant again and Kurt, who dearly loved his wife, felt he was finally and forever stuck in this predictable present with its equally predictable future.

However, just as men feel they understand the workings of fate, inevitably there comes a surprising turn. As Joseph and his granddaughters enjoyed the lively music of the operetta, Marta, home alone and resting on their parlor divan, experienced a sharp pain in the vicinity of her unborn baby. Then came another and another, so intense she was thrown to the floor. As Kurt worked over accounts in the brickyard office and Joseph and his granddaughters enjoyed an after theater meal of crisp schnitzel and the tiny buttered dumplings called spatzel, Marta lay on the parlor floor hemorrhaging away her life and that of her unborn infant son.

• • •

In the months that followed Marta's death, a pall fell over the family. They were all in deep mourning, but no-one felt the black despair Kurt suffered. His entire being was poisoned by a toxic brew of darkest grief laced with a grinding guilt. He could not shake the feeling that he had failed Marta. He had not been the husband he should have been because of his persistent, selfish, adolescent longings for a life other than the one he had with her and their children. Now he felt his life had become overnight an empty shell, a dry, lifeless husk that had once been so full and rich, but had been so foolishly unappreciated. He could hardly look at her picture without a bitter gorge rising in his throat, yet he was constantly drawn to the small oval likeness of that dear face. Had she known how trapped he had allowed himself to feel? Had she been lonely, always hoping for him to show the love she deserved? Why, he wondered, had he so completely wasted their precious time together? Now he would never know. Now he could never make amends. His busy mind circled again and again to these hellish questions for which there were no answers and no peace. He suffered this mental inquisition day and night and with each guilty examination, his self-loathing grew.

As the months passed, Joseph noted, with increasing concern, how withdrawn Kurt had become. He rarely ate and spent the long hours at night pacing the floor of his room rather than in healing sleep. Kurt was alarmingly thin and his normally ruddy complexion was now a frightening gray. Kurt seemed to be sleepwalking through his days. He had always been a hard-worker, but now, seemed completely distracted by some inner turmoil. He would sit for hours at his desk in the brickyard office just staring ahead. Sometimes his lips moved as if in some silent conversation. Should Joseph or another person speak to him, he answered in monosyllables which often indicated that he had not really even heard the question directed to him.

Joseph was desperate to help his son. He had known people who had lost a loved one and very soon after had died themselves, it was said, of a "broken heart." He greatly feared that if Kurt did not come to terms with his loss soon, he would surely die from its pain.

Because he was a lifelong citizen of Vienna and took pride in keeping abreast of any social or political news in the empire, Joseph was aware of some radical new theories concerning the treatment of mental disturbance that were widely discussed, not only by medical practitioners, but had captured the interest of the Viennese public at large.

In fact, on a day a year before Marta's tragic death, Joseph had taken his lunch far from the brickyard in order to supervise a large delivery for construction of a new wing for the Vienna General Hospital. He had wandered into the Café Landtmann to try their luncheon menu. As he sat quietly sipping his sweetened black coffee, he was disturbed by a crowd of men engaged in a very loud and lively discussion. He noted that they had apparently come to lunch from the hospital nearby since some still wore the typical physician's white lab coat. One bearded man, well dressed in a tweed suit, seemed to dominate the discussion that had become increasingly heated. His voice grew loud enough for Joseph to hear quite plainly. With each word, Joseph became more and more appalled by what the man was saying. The subject at hand involved ideas about the cause of mental disturbance and this man talked of things that no gentleman should ever say in public, perhaps not even in private. He talked of man's "aggressive sexual urges" and how "unresolved erotic attachments to one's own mother" can cause mental problems in adult men. Disgusting! This was certainly no fit subject to entertain over lunch in a public café or anywhere short of a church confessional. When the waiter brought the check, Joseph quietly asked who the man in the tweed suit was.

"Why, that is Dr. Freud. He lectures at the hospital. He is famous!" whispered the grinning waiter, apparently very proud that such a man would come to his café.

"Famous?! For what, pray tell, is he famous?" questioned the astonished Joseph.

"Why, it is said that he can cure people with mental troubles just by talking to them," had been the even more astonishing answer.

...

Now, in his search for help and meaningful advice, Joseph turned to his foreman Gustav Haber. Gustav was much older than Joseph and had been with their firm even when Joseph's father had run it. Joseph greatly respected Gustav's quiet intelligence. He had often noted that the older man never treated employees with arrogance, but always with respect and appreciation for their efforts. Both men knew, from long experience, that a company only thrives if its employees also thrive. Because of this shared wisdom, their company made solid profits year after year which rewarded their loyal workforce as well as its leaders.

Since Gustav surely had noticed Kurt's obvious distress, Joseph asked to talk to him in private. As they talked, Gustav waved off any suggestion that the new mental therapies espoused by people like this Dr. Freud would prove to be a cure for Kurt.

"Joseph, you are not a man who believes that science holds the answer for our spiritual trials. You have always turned to God and our holy Church when dealing with issues of the soul. You and Kurt need a priest not a doctor," the older man had quietly answered.

Joseph immediately sensed the truth of this wisdom and decided to see Father Duchene, the family's parish priest, at once.

• • •

Joseph decided to give his own confession upon entering the Cathedral St. Augustine where he attended weekly mass. When he had completed the prescribed prayers for penance, the priest, Father Duchene, quietly approached and slid into the pew next to Joseph.

"Forgive me, Joseph," whispered the kindly priest, "But I must ask how you and your family have adjusted to the passing of your son's dear wife, Marta. I could not help but notice during your confession a certain, shall we say, emotional tension most unlike your usual calm demeanor. I have also noticed and meant to ask you about the unusual absence of your son, Kurt, at mass. For weeks you have attended without him. Can I offer you or your family spiritual guidance you might well need at this time?"

This statement and the kindness in the eyes of his confessor affected Joseph in a way he had not at all anticipated. He began to weep, at first silently. But soon, to his chagrin, he wept openly in huge, gulping sobs. It seemed as though his own grief in losing Marta combined with his growing fear that his beloved son might soon follow her in death now poured from every cell in his body in the form of these unexpected tears. When he finally regained some control, he told the listening priest of his fears and of his seeming inability to help his son himself.

When he had finished, the priest turned to him and said, "It is indeed evident that you and your family are afflicted and in need of spiritual comfort. As you must be aware, the Blessed Virgin appeared to the young girl Bernadette Soubirous at the little village of Lourdes, France thirty years ago. Many miraculous happenings occurred there at that time including a spring of waters that gushed from the ground near the Grotto of Massabieille. Since then, these waters have been responsible for many cures of physical and spiritual malady that have been validated and confirmed by the Church fathers in Rome."

"Are you saying, father, that I should take my family to this place and hope for a miracle?" asked the incredulous Joseph.

"That may not be necessary. As you know, I belong to the Society of Mary. We Marianist priests and brothers have long believed that the mother of Our Lord Jesus Christ, like her son, represents God's love for mankind and will, when petitioned, intercede on our behalf. We believe that her visitations to the peasant girl and the miraculous waters of Lourdes act as proof of this. I will pray with you and your family and we, together, will make a special novena to Our Lady of Lourdes."

· · ·

The following day, Joseph returned together with his three grandchildren. Kurt was not with them and Joseph had been bitterly disappointed in his son's refusal to pray with them. He could not know that the true reason was that Kurt felt that his sin against Marta was too great to ever gain forgiveness. He felt that he did not deserve God's grace but greatly deserved the hell in which he presently lived.

For nine days the family lit the novena candles and prayed with Father Duchene. Joseph prayed for an end to Kurt's particular misery and for some peace for his son. At the end of the ninth day, Joseph turned to his grandchildren and admitted his own fear that they had not helped their father.

"Perhaps we should take your father to France, to Lourdes, where he can drink or bathe in the healing waters." He had sighed in desperation.

"But, Grandfather, Papa wants to go to America." Marie interjected.

The old man turned slowly toward his little granddaughter. At that moment, as he looked into those innocent, questioning blue eyes, he was struck by how much Marie resembled the face of the Madonna statue behind her. He felt an awed chill as he realized that perhaps this was indeed the answer to their prayers after all.

3.
McColloch

Martin Shaw's momentary success in turning back a group belonging to the Ku Klux Klan, certainly did not stop the terror tactics employed by this group bent on bringing a halt to the changes the new post-war constitution and Republican state government in Arkansas were attempting to implement. The Klan's campaign of destruction and murder continued throughout 1868 and into 1869 until Arkansas' Republican governor, Powell Clayton, organized a state militia to put it down. Once order was reestablished, Clayton's administration began programs to help rebuild the state's economy. As part of this effort, free public schools were set up statewide for the first time in 1869.

Between 1869 and 1874 the family of Zachary McColloch also experienced marked changes. When the elderly minister of the Drew County Baptist Church passed on, the congregation petitioned Zachary, who was well known as a circuit riding preacher, to take over their pulpit. Zachary had a gift for delivering sermons that intimately connected Biblical teachings with the very concerns that most weighed on the minds of his parishioners. He was no "fire and brimstone" preacher but instead expertly wove humor and optimism into the fabric of every message. He understood well how thirsty the people were for hope after they had suffered for so long from the grim realities of war. He proved to be so popular that, in his first year, the congregation doubled in size and brought in the funds needed for an extension to the church building.

Old Jake's son, Red, met a pretty girl from St. Louis who was visiting nearby relatives for the summer. They married in the fall of 1870 and moved north back to her hometown. Old Jake was thrilled that Red then landed a really good job at one of the many breweries there and was able to send some money every month to his father. For his part, Jake continued, as he always had, working the little vegetable garden with Mattie on the farm. The two, shared the purchase of a number of chickens and shortly had a small egg business. As their business grew, the demand for eggs extended beyond Drew County, so Martin Shaw began a delivery service for the eggs and other local farm products to towns farther away. At first, Mattie's son, Will, helped with deliveries but later traveled to Hot Springs Arkansas to take part in a lucrative building boom of the many hotels and bath houses that would serve the post-war bathing industry in that town.

...

By the time Charles Henry turned thirteen, his father and mother thought it was high time for him to have some formal schooling. The boy was no longer needed to help with what had always only amounted to subsistence farming. He was very excited by the idea of school and what he pictured would be a great adventure in learning more about the world. What a luxury it would be to spend his day in uninterrupted reading and study! He imagined long conversations with a skilled teacher who would be much like Abigail Shaw.

Early on the first day of the public school winter term, Mattie and Charles Henry presented themselves to the school master of the one room school house outside Monticello. Mattie nervously introduced the boy to the teacher, a very tall, reed thin, rather sour looking man by the name of Mr. Brian Ferguson who stared at mother and son with milky, pale blue eyes and not once smiled as Mattie explained that her son was thirteen and had never attended school though the family had done its best to educate him at home. She added that he was very smart and quick to learn. She was about to list some of Charles Henry's specific academic accomplishments when, without a word, Mr. Ferguson placed two fingers in the middle of the boy's back, pushing him forward into the empty classroom and firmly closed the school-house door behind them. Mattie was shocked to find herself cut off in mid-sentence and alone on the small, outside porch.

Once inside, the frowning teacher looked Charles Henry slowly up and down. He judged that here was just another farm boy too old and too stupid to learn and forced on him by his equally stupid mother who could not see that this was a lost cause. Finally, to the boy's relief, the man spoke. "You are much older than the rest of the boys. Kind of late to be just starting, I would say. What does your mother expect me to do with you, I wonder?"

Charles Henry opened his mouth to answer but was cut off when the man added with a sigh, "Oh well, you can sit over there." He waved an arm in the general direction of a small table and bench pushed against the far wall next to an iron, pot- bellied stove. "You can make yourself useful and bring in some wood. You'll be responsible for feeding the stove today."

Perplexed, the boy looked at the isolated table and bench next to the stove and then surveyed the rest of the room filled with long tables and equally long benches where evidently the rest of the class would sit. "Won't I be sitting with the rest of the boys?" he finally questioned.

"You! Do not speak unless I ask you to!" thundered the teacher shoving a forefinger into the chest of a suddenly very frightened Charles Henry. "Now, bring in that wood or you'll feel the sting of me rod!"

As it turned out, this unhappy start to his public school experience taught Charles Henry an important lesson about how he would survive it. He realized, rather quickly, that the less interaction he had with Mr. Ferguson the better. He decided that he would just sit quietly in his assigned corner and then tell his parents that he was not going to return the next day. He would also keep the wood stove filled so as not to bring any dangerous attention to himself. After the other students filed in and took their seats, the teacher seemed much too busy to take much further notice of his newest pupil. Charles Henry was left alone to sit and wonder about this volatile person who was so unlike any other adult he knew.

Mr. Ferguson was indeed an entirely different breed of person than Charles Henry had ever met. He had been born into privilege, the son of a landowner in England. His father had moved his family to Southern Arkansas to escape the taxes English landowners were required to pay the crown and to enjoy additional savings from owning black slaves rather than paid servants.

As is true of many bullies, young Brian learned brutality and violence from the example set by his father, a man of quick temper and a complete sense of aristocratic entitlement. Brian knew that his father had, for example, instructed his overseer to use the lash on fieldhands, not only for punishment but also as a frequent incentive to work harder. His father was no more kind to the house servants. Brian had witnessed many instances of his father's explosive temper, such as the time he had dumped an entire terrine of scalding hot soup over the head of a server who had accidently spilled a little of the hot liquid on his master's hand while ladling out a portion.

Brian Ferguson stood to one day inherit the land, the slaves and his father's kingly existence but for the coming of war. After Fort Sumter, the old man sent his wife and son back to England to stay with relatives. By the time it was safe for their return, Brian's father was dead, some said from a revolt of his own slaves, and the plantation house and fields had been destroyed by fires set either by Union sympathizers or Union troops. This outcome required Brian to face the fact that he was destitute and would have to make his own way in the world. He had no real skills other than the ability to read and write, and he had never had to develop a work ethic. However, the powers in Little Rock saw in Brian Ferguson the makings of a school master for its new public system.

Mr. Ferguson's teacher training took just under an hour. A representative from the state department of education came from Little Rock to instruct him in teaching methods in preparation for his new position. The first fifteen minutes were spent showing the new hire the various primers that students would learn from. Then came a short lesson in the "recitation and memorization" method where students would repeat aloud and in unison words and phrases in their primers until each lesson was pounded into their "thick heads." Finally, an entire half hour was spent on the subject of discipline. Mr. Ferguson was handed a stout hickory stick and admonished to use it "with a strong arm and often" in order to maintain order and to aid learning. This idea suited the new teacher, and he proved to be absolutely gifted in its use.

Charles Henry did not have to know Mr. Ferguson's background to know, with certainty, that this was a man a wise person should give a wide berth. As that first day wore on, the boy saw enough to solidify his first impression. He saw that the teacher walked among the rows of boys, either as they recited their lessons or as they copied letters or numbers on their individual slate tablets, and, without warning, he would reach out and cuff a boy for no reason that Charles Henry could ascertain. The school master frequently called his students "fool" or "stupid" or singled out someone to embarrass in front of the room. The boy also noted that whenever the teacher returned to his own desk, he opened a drawer and took out a bottle of brown liquid and drank what Charles Henry suspected was whiskey. Finally, the long morning of sitting idle, broken only by occasionally fetching more wood for the stove, ended with a break for lunch. All the boys rushed out into the brisk, clean air to eat whatever they brought from home and then to run and play freely.

They played rough and tumble games like Red Rover and Capture the Flag which Charles Henry had never played, since he had never had a group of friends to play with. The other boys, were friendly and seemed to immediately accept him. The "lunch hour" actually lasted over two hours since this was the time of day that Mr. Ferguson slept off his morning libations at his desk. These hours at raucous play with new friends proved to be some of the most joyous of Charles Henry's young life, and he was beginning to mentally amend his first plan to refuse to return to school.

Charles Henry, dubbed "C.H." by the other boys, did return to school and continued to return for most of that winter term. He loved the comradery with the other students who began to see him as something of a leader. This was not only because he was a bit older than they, but also he had a way of noticing the humor in any situation. He pointed out the foibles of their school master which rendered Mr. Ferguson ridiculous in their eyes and thus nullified the teacher's ability to humiliate. He often had the other boys doubled over with laughter over the events of the morning which acted as a tonic for any boy who had recently been the subject of the teacher's venom.

For a while, these new friendships were enough to make continued school attendance bearable. Then, one day, as Charles Henry returned to his usual spot after bringing more wood for the stove. He noticed a few new books on the shelf with the student primers. He saw immediately that they were beautifully bound and had titles stamped in gold on the side. Upon closer inspection, he saw that they were Homer's Iliad and Odyssey. He knew that occasionally wealthy donors from the town brought nice books to the school, but that usually Mr. Ferguson whisked them away to add to his own library. Impulsively, the boy picked up one of them for closer inspection. He was so engrossed in the book that he failed to notice that Mr. Ferguson was watching him.

"What do you think you are doing there, boy?!" the man bellowed from across the room. "You'd better not even think of stealing that book"

"I just wanted to read it a little." answered the surprised boy.

"Read it? OK, ignorant, hick. Go ahead and show us how you can read!." snarled the school master, sensing a prime opportunity to humiliate another victim.

Forced to comply or risk a beating, Charles Henry carefully opened the Odyssey to the first page and began reading Homer's tale of the Greek hero, Odysseus and his epic return from the Battle of Troy.

"Sing in me, Muse, and through me tell the story
Of that man skilled in all ways of contending,
The wanderer, harried for years on end,
After he plundered the stronghold
On the proud height of Troy ..."

As Charles Henry continued smoothly reading the classic poetry, the other students began to snicker and then to openly laugh especially hard as they saw their teacher's face flush bright red from being so skillfully shown up by the "ignorant hick." Unable to bear it longer, the man roared, "Why you insolent little whelp!" and advanced on Charles Henry swinging his hickory rod.

Thinking quickly, the boy grabbed a nearby stick of firewood and threw it side arm toward the enraged teacher. The last thing Charles Henry heard as he escaped out of the school door, was a great howl of pain when the firewood smashed solidly into the school master's kneecap.

That evening, after he had told his parents the story of the day's events, they easily decided that he would not return to school. In fact, they had only just that day received a letter from Will, who was working construction in Hot Springs. He wrote that the grandest and newest hotel in the area, the Arlington, was advertising for young men to help carry guest luggage and that these jobs paid well. This new adventure definitely appealed to Charles Henry and he agreed that his father should take him by wagon as soon as possible.

• • •

In the summer of 1875, young Charles Henry McColloch felt that his life was finally beginning. His parents had agreed not to send him back to Mr. Ferguson's "tender" care, but instead would allow his older brother, Will, to introduce the boy to an adult world of work and life in Hot Spring, Arkansas. Charles had dreamed and planned for the day when he would ride in the wagon with his father toward an exciting world of sophisticated, educated people who came from all over the world to sample the pleasures and the storied mineral waters of this booming resort. He did not believe that he would "make his mark" or stand out in any way, but he had faith that these glittering strangers would accept him as long as he was cheerful and polite and worked hard. He did decide that he would change himself just a little to appear more grown up in their eyes. He would hence forth introduce himself as "C.H. McColloch" rather than by his full name which seemed to always end up as some childish nickname like "Charlie" or, God forbid, "Chuck."

The second day of their trip took C.H. and his father to Malvern a town a mere twenty miles from Hot Springs. C. H. wondered why his father opted to pay for a room in one of the town's boarding houses rather than proceed on the short way to Hot Springs. When he questioned Zachary about the stop, his father explained, "I thought that it would be nice on what will probably be our last night together for a while to enjoy a good meal in a restaurant and a time to chat together like two old friends."

C.H. was entranced by this sign that his father was accepting him as an adult and almost a peer. However, Zachary had held back his true reason for not wanting to proceed on after dark to their destination. He had been warned about the road between Malvern and Hot Springs as a favorite of roving gangs who preyed on the many travelers flush with plenty of cash to spend on luxury hotels, spa treatments, gaming and expensive restaurants. If they were going to travel that perilous road, they would do it in the full light of day and with a loaded shotgun under the seat.

The next day was so softly warmed by summer sun and the roadway so beautifully dappled whenever a breeze brushed the silvery leaves on arching branches overhead that Zachary almost forgot his concerns over the dangerous last leg of their trip. He had so enjoyed his evening meal with his son where C.H. had him convulsed in laughter over the story of the boy's narrow escape from the horrors of public education. He had also been surprised at his son's ability to converse in a way that entertained on a very adult level, but also offered a refreshing view of the world seen through the eyes of someone who was experiencing so much for the first time.

Suddenly, Zachary's reverie was cut short by shots fired into the air and the appearance of five armed and masked men on horseback who surrounded the small wagon so quickly that Zachary had no time to retrieve his hidden shotgun. There would be no way to resist this gang bent on robbery, and putting up a fight would only lead to an even worse outcome.

"So where you two headed on this fine day?" asked one of the men who dismounted apparently feeling there was little to fear from the men in the wagon.

"I'm taking my son to a new job in Hot Springs. It's his first job, actually." Zachary added easily as though informing a friend of his family's news.

"Oh, let 'em go! These guy's don't have no money worth takin'," shouted another gang member as the first began to rummage through the parcels in the back of the wagon.

"Oh yeah? Let's just see 'bout that! Well, yer so smart. Looky here!" cried the first man holding up a small pouch of bills and gold coins meant to tide C.H. over until his first pay check. "I'll just relieve you two of this here burden."

"Hold up on that" warned the mounted man. "I want to know what their sympathies are first. These guys ain't no rich Unionists. I want to know what they really are. Which side was you on in the fight, mister?"

"Why I would have to say I was and still am on the side of the great state of Arkansas enough to give the life of a son who died a hero at Wilson's Creek," answered Zachary who could not quell a catch in his voice at this memory.

"It's okay. Leave 'em their money," ordered the man on horseback. "There's plenty a rich Yankees for us to be more interested in. Good day to you, mister and good luck, son, in the new job." With that the group turned their horses and galloped away from the wagon and its two dumbfounded riders.

...

Times of war are always times of great deprivation for the citizens of any country spending its resources on some foreign campaign. Civil War, however, not only deprives a country of any pleasures enjoyed in peacetime but exacts the most extreme toll possible when all of war's horrors are brought right to the doorstep of a helpless citizenry. The people of Arkansas, so whiplashed by both sides of the civil conflict, had suffered war as an immediate, tangible, daily terror. It is little wonder that in the decade following the end of hostilities, a place like Hot Springs drew thousands of visitors from around the state and also the rest of a war weary country, and so satisfied their pent up desire for all the enjoyments long denied them, most returned over and over again. This once small town not only offered physical succor in the form of warm, soothing mineral baths but also surrounded any visitors having a few dollars to spend with the kind of luxuriant experiences that had only been enjoyed by the landed gentry before the war.

For C.H., a boy who had spent much of his life in a hole underground, the first glimpse of Hot Springs convinced him that heaven might actually exist on earth. As their wagon rolled slowly down the main boulevard, the boy counted twelve hotels, each seemingly grander than the last. As they drew up in front of the Arlington, C.H. was truly astounded by the multi-storied edifice with its great mahogany double doors flanked by glittering cut glass side lights. Almost immediately, two men in splendid red uniforms adorned with gold braid and epaulettes jumped down the marble steps. One grabbed the bags from the back of the wagon and the other bowed and took hold of their horse's halter to lead the wagon to a place for parking so that Zachary was free to go inside with his son.

C.H. had read many stories set in the palaces of Europe, but the reality before the boy's wide eyes in the form of the Arlington's courtyard lobby convinced him that no palace could possibly compare in grandeur. The room was huge and fairly sparkled from every gleaming surface due to the many sources of reflected light; scores of gas lamps burning inside cut-glass globes, a wall of windows that framed a multicolored inner garden and a dazzling overhead chandelier measuring six feet in diameter and made entirely of tiny glass crystals.

As father and son stood gaping at this magnificence, a tall, silver-haired gentleman approached and introduced himself as Mr. Mathews, the hotel concierge. Zachary explained that his son, Charles Henry, was there seeking employment in response to the flier offering young men jobs at this hotel.

"Oh, that is very good, we are in great need of eager young men with strong backs to handle guest baggage and even perhaps learn enough about our establishment and about the hotel business in general to consider a long-term career with us!" explained Mr. Mathews to the delight of C.H. who felt immediately welcomed and valued by this obviously important person. "Now, young man", continued Mr. Mathews turning to speak directly to C.H., "Before you start with us, we have a few days of training that always begin with a day-long tour of every department. We require employees to learn about the function of every other employee and to know how to use each as a resource for making our guests happy and comfortable. So, you will start today to learn by watching and listening on your tour while we will excuse your father to take his leave. From this moment on, young Charles, you will be on your own."

Taking the hint, Zachary whispered to his son that he was off to find Will at his construction site and that both would return that evening to have dinner with C.H. and to hear how his first day went. Then C.H. followed Mr. Mathews' lead on the first leg of his "hotel education." Because the day was just beginning, the concierge explained that this was a good time to see the workings of the front desk as new arrivals would be greeted, registered and dispatched with their baggage boy to their assigned room. He indicated a tall stool in a corner out of the way of busy front desk clerks but close enough so the boy could see and hear clearly how they handled the registration process.

It was still early in the day and most of those manning the front desk busied themselves with review of new reservations and what special requests had been made by those important personages who would soon be arriving. Then, at ten o'clock, as the large brass clock over the front desk struck the hour, the front doors burst open and a small group of well-dressed travelers entered led by a dust covered man pushing a cart loaded with baggage.

The dusty man leaned over the desk and announced breathlessly, "We were just held up by the James boys! Take special care of these people. They have already had quite a day! The Malvern Road again! I wish to God that railroad would hurry up and get built!"

Of course, even in the relative isolation of their tiny Arkansas farm, C.H. had heard of Jesse and Frank James and their gang. Occasionally, Zachary had returned home from preaching up north with the Kansas City Times where their editor Thomas Crittenden usually included an editorial in praise of this gang of modern day "Robin Hoods." Once he had read a letter in that paper from Jesse James himself in which he claimed the gang's innocence of the many crimes attributed to them.

C.H. leaned forward to be better able to hear the comments from the newly arriving guests about their experience. The first couple to register was a man and woman who introduced themselves as Mr. and Mrs. Cooper who had requested the "Presidential Suite." They seemed flushed with excitement and fairly gushed with the story of their recent adventure. "They were all gentlemen and very kind to us, I must say." Explained Mrs. Cooper. When the clerk asked her husband if they would need a change of room, he answered that that was not necessary.

"They didn't rob us. They asked everyone what side they fought on in the war. I said 'Confederate and proud of it. I served under the finest commander on either side, General Sterling Price! That stirred up a real hornet's nest. Some of our fellow passengers suddenly didn't like the fact that they were riding with 'Confederate scum' and let everyone know it. That's when the gang took every penny they had! I heard one couple say they'd be returning home right away."

"They were so nice to us," put in Mrs. Cooper, "I insisted they take my broach as a token of our appreciation. After all, if we weren't robbed of something it wouldn't be as good a story to tell my lady friends in St. Louis!"

That night at dinner, C.H. informed his father and brother of this interesting event. He had them howling when he added, "Pa, we shoulda let those fellas on the road take our money. I didn't know what an honor it was to be robbed by them!"

4.
Krann

Kurt Krann stood with the other first class passengers of the luxury Oceanic steamship gazing over the rail at the crowds of tattered, steerage passengers from the decks below as they were loaded onto huge barges to be ferried across New York's harbor to Castle Gardens, the immigration processing center located on a tiny island near the tip of Manhattan. He wondered at the courage of these people who had taken such a long, perilous journey seemingly without the resources needed to make a new home half way across the globe. Yet, he saw no sign of fear or dread, but rather what could only be described as a party atmosphere with people all smiling and laughing and calling to each other. He could only believe that what these poor souls had left behind was far worse than facing any unknown new life.

As a prosperous Austrian of German decent, Kurt had always been a privileged member of his country's ethnic majority. He had never experienced the grinding poverty or governmental oppression the people on the barges desperately hoped to escape by seeking America's promise of freedom. Yet, it was indeed freedom that he was seeking, freedom from oppressive family responsibility and a life of crushing boredom where every outcome was preordained. He had been tied by invisible tethers of love for his father, wife and children and for most of his adult life had truly believed that nothing would ever change.

Then, he had lost his beloved Marta and suddenly realized what a gift providence had given him when she became his wife, a gift he had never fully appreciated. Wrapped in guilt and despair, Kurt had sunk into the blackest of depressions. It was at the moment when Kurt was most convinced that he was and always would be worthless to himself and worthless to his family that his father, Joseph, came to him with a proposition.

Holding in his hands the stock certificate in the gold mine located in America, Joseph reminded his son of the large investment they had made and the promises that had been made for regular dividend payments that had never materialized. His voice filled with urgency, Joseph convinced Kurt that it was imperative that someone should investigate since it was quite possible a great deal of money was at stake! Furthermore, Joseph stressed that the one to investigate should be Kurt, because he was young enough to take such a journey and he was "family" and therefore could be trusted! This new proof of Kurt's value to the family, along with the shift in focus that planning the trip required, began the "cure" that Joseph and his grandchildren had prayed for at the feet of the Madonna.

· · ·

A bell sounded to call the remaining passengers into the first class salon. Kurt was grateful that first class passengers would not have to travel to Castle Gardens and endure the "processing" that often took days to complete. Instead, it was assumed that the wealthier passengers were in good health and already had the resources to insure that they would not become a social burden to their new country. They would only have a short interview with an immigration official before being allowed to go ashore. In Kurt's case, he explained to the official that his father had made arrangements through his business contacts for Kurt to be met by a German speaking guide, a "Herr Schneider" who would take him to the train station where he was to purchase a ticket and continue on to Oregon. Within minutes, Kurt was alone with his baggage on the pier.

After a short wait, Kurt realized that he did not know how exactly he would make contact with his "guide." He noted that there were several men holding signs that attracted some of the passengers who then went with them to waiting coaches. He did not see a sign with his name on it, so he would just have to introduce himself until the right man was identified. He began at one end of the line of men who appeared to be waiting to meet someone. "Ich heisse Kurt Krann. Sind Sie Herr Schneider?"

...

These questions were met by blank stares but no sign of recognition. Finally, a well-dressed gentleman tapped Kurt on the shoulder and in perfect German said, "I am Herr Schneider. You must be Kurt Krann. I have been waiting for you. I had asked the ship's people to point you out, but they just now indicated who you were. I am so very sorry for your inconvenience!" explained the man with a courtly bow.

"I am so happy to make your acquaintance! I had almost lost hope and began to think I would have to find the railroad station on my own!" Kurt gushed in relief.

"Oh no, I am here to take you myself. I will carry some of these bags to my coach since I had to leave it down the street, because these stalls were all taken when I arrived." Herr Schneider explained apologetically. "Follow me, it is not far to walk."

Gratefully, Kurt followed the kind gentleman down the street where they turned the corner into a narrow alleyway. "Here is my coach. My man will help me load your things while you rest inside a moment," Herr Schneider politely suggested directing Kurt to the open coach door.

As Kurt bent to climb the narrow steps, he felt a sharp blow to the back of his head and immediately lost all consciousness. When he awakened, "Herr Schneider," his coach and his man servant were gone as well as all of Kurt's luggage and the money belt he had worn under his waistcoat. Slowly, Kurt realized that he had been robbed and that he had foolishly brought this sad event upon himself when he had so loudly proclaimed to every stranger on the pier his own name and the name of the man he was waiting for. When the world around him ceased to tilt and swirl, Kurt staggered to his feet and returned to the pier where the ship remained docked. A few first class passengers were still disembarking the gangway near a uniformed officer who dropped the clipboard he had been holding as Kurt, covered in his own blood, approached.

The officer quickly regained his composure enough to help his bleeding passenger up the gangway and back to the first class salon where it was quickly decided that Kurt must be taken to the doctors who awaited arriving passengers to be processed at Castle Gardens. It was explained that at the processing center there were services available for those who arrived in the U.S. without the resources needed to establish a home in their new country. Unfortunately, this now described Kurt's situation!

...

During the two days of complete rest at Castle Gardens, Kurt had a chance to reevaluate his plight. His head wound was healing with no apparent permanent damage, and his gold mine stock contract was still sewn safely inside the lining of his waistcoat together with a small amount of his remaining money. The people in charge of immigrant processing at Castle Gardens provided him with the work and travel options available to steerage level passengers which were assumed that first class passengers did not need to know. Once it was established that Kurt fully intended to continue his travel plans to Oregon country, he was informed of the low cost "Immigrant Trains" that carried foreign passengers to their final destinations even as far West as Oregon. He would take the ferry across the Hudson River to board such a train the very next day. Kurt could hardly believe his great luck in this turn of events when his greatest worry had been that he would have to wire his father for money and then return to Vienna, a failure.

In the half-light of dawn, Kurt, carrying his only possessions which consisted of a bed roll and a few cheap toiletries he had purchased at Castle Gardens, joined the bedraggled crowd of recent immigrant arrivals for a gloomy, rain-soaked trip in an open barge across the Hudson to board the Immigrant Train. It did not seem to Kurt that it would be possible to jam such a huge group into the few miserable boxcars that awaited them on the tracks, but almost immediately family groups were called to board. Women and their children were directed to board the first cars, then the men in the remaining cars. Even though the railroad employees tried to make the directions clear, it was evident that many of the passengers did not understand what they were being directed to do. This created a kind of chaotic panic where husbands attempted to board with their family groups and sometimes had to be physically ejected from the "women's cars." When finally the passengers had all climbed aboard the correct cars, the train creaked and jolted out of the station.

Once inside his assigned car, Kurt took in his miserable surroundings. The "room" was only a long box made of wooden slats with a small stove at one end and a convenience at the other, which explained the need to separate passengers by gender. Along each wall were placed wooden benches that were so narrow it was impossible for a grown man to sit comfortably. At least, Kurt realized, he and the other men were spared the unceasing crying and screaming of the many infants and young children jammed with their harried mothers in the first few cars.

The men's car was far from comfortable. Only a glimmer from one oil lamp offered any light at all. In addition, the hot, dark interior was rank with wet, dripping clothing and sweat. One man, swearing loudly, jumped up and forced open a high wooden window hoping for some fresh air. Instead, a plume of thick, black smoke from the train's engine filled the cabin. With that, a hulking, giant of a man sporting unusually bushy side burns and mustaches at the other end of the car stood and shouted, "Gott im Himmel! Schliessen Sie das Fenster!"

Kurt, so surprised and excited to hear his native tongue spoken, jumped up and immediately closed the window. As he turned to regain his seat on the unforgiving bench, the stranger grabbed him in a muscular bear-hug and slapped him solidly on the back, "Danke, danke schoen, mein Freund!" cried the fearsome giant, "Ich heisse August Meyer! Wie heissen Sie?"

• • •

It was only natural that the only two German-speaking men in the car would choose to sit together and converse as the creaking, lumbering train journeyed west from New York where many of the new immigrants would disembark in other cities that offered employment opportunities. With each stop, the car became less crowded and the men no longer had to sleep sitting up on the wooden benches. After a stop at Council Bluff, Iowa, the depot officials furnished each car with "cushions" of straw wrapped in burlap sacking that could be placed at night on every two benches pushed together to make a crude bed. The fully clothed passengers could lie on these straw mattresses in relative comfort though there were not enough bench-beds to go around. Therefore, the men were encouraged to "chum up" as sleep-mates so that everyone could recline for the night. By the time this system was put in place, Kurt and August Meyer were well acquainted and felt fairly comfortable sharing one of these makeshift beds.

...

If it had not been for the forced intimacy of this peculiar mode of travel, it was very unlikely that Kurt Krann and August Meyer would ever have become friends, for in many ways they were complete opposites.

Kurt's unremarkable features were pleasant but not handsome. His pale complexion and thin, rather stooped physique was that of a man who had never done anything more strenuous than sit at a desk. For most of his adult life, even his own dinner had been prepared and delivered by servants. He stood out from the other men in the car due to his well-tailored suit and his mustache and beard which were neatly trimmed in the current Viennese fashion. Unlike them, he had never done any work with his hands and his skill set was similar only to men raised to work and live in the civilized society of an established European city. He had no idea how unprepared he was for the world he was about to enter where survival required the practical skills necessary to build one's own shelter, kill or grow one's own food and prevail against the myriad physical threats the "wild" American West could throw at a man.

August Meyer, on the other hand, was a man who always stood out in a crowd. His huge size, outlandish facial hair, and booming voice made him impossible to ignore. He was taller than average but it was his massive frame built of great muscular cords that convinced anyone upon first meeting him that he was a man to be reckoned with. He had fought on the Union side in the Great Civil War as a lowly infantryman involved in some of its bloodiest battles. The fact that he had never even been wounded was evidence of his agility and skill in close hand to hand combat. In peace time, he had worked New York's loading docks, spent time as a lumberjack, but was most proud of his abilities as a hard rock miner. While Kurt had never spent much time with any man but his own father, August or "Gus" as he was most often called, had learned early to value and develop male friendships. He was well aware that, whether in the army or in the mines, a man's survival often meant being surrounded by people who cared enough to come to one's aid.

Kurt, initially cowed by his new friend's size and overwhelming personality, had been completely won over within an hour's time. He was so intrigued by the man's stories that he happily sat for hours in awed attention. They only spoke German to each other, and Kurt wondered why the bilingual Gus never once spoke English to the other passengers. August explained that it was to his advantage to let strangers think he could not understand what they said. Anyone up to no good might then let down his guard and say something that would give away his evil intentions. Kurt was impressed by this common sense and embarrassed by his own foolishness when he remembered how easily a stranger had taken nearly everything he had of value within minutes of his landing in New York.

• • •

The western region of the U.S. was dotted with small towns that seemed to fairly sprout from the earth like fast growing plants wherever the railroad tracks had been originally laid. While the railroad brought the people to populate the country west of the Mississippi River, it continued thereafter to provide a sustaining lifeblood of commerce with the cities of the East.

At Council Bluffs there was a last "Immigrant Hotel" where those riding the trains could eat and rest for a night before moving on. Once the train crossed the Missouri River, however, passengers stayed on the train to eat and sleep for the remainder of their journey. At each stop, passengers would hurry onto the platform to buy food and other needed items from vendors selling such goods. Occasionally, new passengers would board as well.

Close to evening on the second day of the new sleeping arrangements, two new men boarded and were assigned to the car Kurt occupied since there was still room for additional passengers. These two immediately introduced themselves around to the other men as "Joe and Vernon." They also offered to pass a bottle of whiskey, and the man named Vernon said, "As long as we're ridin all the way to California with you fellers we brought this as a little icebreaker."

"Well, thank you kindly and welcome. I'm Clem and this here is my brother, Nate," shouted one man near the door as he happily drank from the offered flask. "We don't know the names of anyone else. That group over there are Italians and they don't speak no English. They're okay, though," explained Clem and, to demonstrate his point, he walked over to the group to offer them some liquor which they all accepted with much nodding and laughing.

"And those two over there," Clem continued indicating Kurt and August, "they're a couple a Krauts and don't speak no English neither. They mostly keep to themselves. Only talk to each other. They seem nice enough. Just kinda quiet." Clem added as he gestured with the bottled toward August who was also nodding and grinning.

As Clem walked toward them to share in the whiskey, August bent close to Kurt and said in German, "Pretend to drink. There's something funny about this."

As the hours passed, the car of drinking, laughing men continued its journey toward the setting western sun. At dusk and with the whiskey finished, the passengers began to push their benches together in preparation for the night. Clem explained the system to the newcomers who were given the two free benches closest to Kurt and August for sleeping. The car was soon filled with the snores of drunken, sleeping men, though Kurt and August lay wide awake on their bench.

After an hour had passed, August sensed movement and then could hear one of the new men say, "It's almost time. The train will slow soon for the water tower. We'll start with the Germans and work toward the door."

August could see in the dim light two bent figures rummaging in the bag that held Kurt's few possessions and the one that held his own money. He gave Kurt some whispered instructions and then with a deafening roar, rose up and caught each surprised man by the coat-collar as Kurt threw open the side car door. Then with a second roar, August pushed the two men out of the door and clear of the slow moving train.

By the time the would-be thieves had been ejected from their car, all the other passengers were fully awake and clamoring with astonished questions about what had happened. They were equally astonished when August turned to them and said in perfect English, "I figured they were up to no good. They said they were headed to California, but they got on without baggage!"

5.
McColloch

Charles Henry's first paid employment at age fourteen with the luxurious Hotel Arlington in Hot Springs, Arkansas introduced the boy to an amazing array of worldly enjoyments not the least of which was the opportunity to interact with the political, literary and industrial titans of the post war "Gilded Age." As a lowly baggage boy, he was true to his personal vow to cheerfully work hard which made him well thought of by his supervisors.

It was also evident that he enjoyed his work mainly because he truly enjoyed people. His own father was a popular preacher primarily because he was not a Puritanical scold as were some who occupied a pulpit. Charles' father accepted people as they came to him, warts and all. Zachary had imparted to his son his personal philosophy that human foibles were the source of great humor. He often told his son of his suspicion that, if our flaws as human beings were totally erased, all humor would go with them.

In addition to the many interesting and accomplished people who visited The Arlington, the hotel's extensive library furnished C.H. with a seemingly inexhaustible supply of books to devour during his free time. He especially enjoyed reading the essays, short stories and novels by the very popular humorist, Samuel Clemens known to most by his pen name, Mark Twain. Twain's own brand of humor reinforced the boy's belief in the boundless hilarity of human nature. Though

C.H. read everything from Thomas Aquinas and Plato to Ivanhoe and The Three Musketeers, it was Twain that provided him with the kind of humorous response that could be counted on to lighten any tense moment in his many dealings with the public.

Certainly, Charles' work ethic and his evident enjoyment of the colorful hotel guests who flocked to Hot Springs and The Arlington helped him succeed at his new job. It is unlikely that he would have risen in the ranks of hotel employees had he not had an important mentor and friend in the hotel's "Chief Butler," by the name of Jackson. This former slave wielded considerable influence since he was in charge of all the Arlington's wait and room steward staff. Like Jackson, most of those who tended to the immediate needs of the hotel's guests had at one time been "house slaves" on the South's largest plantations, since these men and women were trained from childhood in the finer graces required of those who directly served their owners.

Jackson, named for the Mississippi city where his master purchased him as a child, had lived most of his life prior to the war on the land of a planter who believed that it was the white man's duty to take care of black slaves, because they were little more than perpetual children who could never survive on their own. The planter's wife, as a kind of hobby, took it upon herself to teach a few of the house help, including Jackson, to read and write. Neither of them worried that such teaching was illegal, privately congratulating themselves on their enlightened and decidedly "Christian" treatment of these needy, dependent creatures.

The war turned such thinking on its head when many freed slaves left the ruined plantations for gainful employment elsewhere. Those who stayed to farm the land as free men and women got to keep some of the profit from crops raised while giving a share to the landowner for use of his land. Jackson's own children had stayed to work the land of his former owner since they only had field experience.

Unfortunately, as was the case in most share-cropping situations, the amount of profit from sold crops provided only subsistence for them, the old planter and his wife. However, since Jackson earned an exceptionally high salary in his position and his meals and room were also provided cost-free, he traveled once a year to see his children and give them enough additional money to live in comfort. He was also slowly buying up the old plantation acre by acre. Ironically, it was this money from the sale of land to their former slave that kept the once wealthy land owners from extreme poverty. Jackson usually felt saddened by the pathetic circumstances of his former master who invariably broke down in sobbing gratitude when given cash for more of his land.

As Charles Henry and Jackson worked together, the two with so many obvious differences began to see how much they actually had in common. They were both self- educated and well read, both had a keen sense of humor, both enjoyed their work and did not shrink from long work hours. Both had been raised outside mainstream American society and therefore had built for themselves a moral code unencumbered by the many Victorian era prejudices and hypocrisies.

All the while Jackson was teaching C.H. about the inner workings of the hotel, the younger man was unaware that he was giving his mentor his first white friend. By year's end, the two recognized their closeness and mutually valued this special relationship. Whenever they were alone, Jackson dropped his stiff "butler" persona and reveled in the relaxed give and take of true friends. On these occasions, they enjoyed the freedom to exchange personal secrets as well as humorous observations about the antics of their hotel guests.

Jackson so trusted his young friend that he confided his plan to slowly purchase the plantation on which he had once been a slave. While C.H. helped the older man pack for one of his annual journeys south, Jackson explained his method for safely transporting the large amount of money used to buy more land.

"The first time I went, I asked myself, 'How in hell will I get this money down there without bein' robbed?'" Jackson explained. "I was actually straightenin' the books in the library while I was worryin' over that question when my eye was caught up by this here book, and I knew that was my answer!" He said holding up a copy of Dante's Divine Comedy .

"Why was that your answer?" wondered C.H.

"Why I just put my big bills in the pages of the first part about the guy's travels through the inferno of hell. I ain't never been robbed in all these years, and I figure that was my 'divine intervention' and the answer to 'where in hell I should hide my money'. Course it probably helps that I dress like some old guy without a penny to his name!" Jackson chuckled shaking his head.

• • •

Since Jackson had a good eye for workers who could be trusted to follow his instruction to the letter, he began to assign C.H. to positions that paid more and required more responsibility than carrying baggage. Jackson had noted that return patrons often asked for C.H. by name, so he decided to try the boy as a room steward to serve the needs of guests in the more expensive suites.

Dressed in a starched white shirt and a fine woolen morning coat, C.H. thought he cut quite a figure. At first, he tried to adopt the formal mannerisms that came so naturally to Martin Shaw who had long served as an English Butler. However, C.H. eventually became a much more relaxed version of Martin who would never have engaged in casual banter or, heaven forbid, joke with those he served. Luckily, C.H. remained true to his own instincts and always seemed to know the best time to employ humor when dealing with the hotel guests. These important people were used to being surrounded either by mute, cringing servants or falsely, flattering sycophants. Invariably, they found C.H. refreshing, and often reported to Jackson how pleased they were with him.

One such older gentleman, a well-known Eastern industrialist, was to give his grandniece away at her wedding held at the Arlington one spring. This lavish event had been covered by the society sections of all the local papers and most of the big-city Eastern papers as well. All the guest rooms had been reserved for the wedding party guests and the suites C.H. served held the bride's closest family.

On the afternoon of the event, C.H. made his way to his assigned floor to deliver newly polished shoes belonging to the industrialist. He knocked softly, but there was no answer. After a moment, C.H. entered the room to find the man sitting in a chair slumped in a posture of defeat. The young butler also saw that every small drawer in the man's armoire had been pulled open and various pieces of clothing were scattered about the floor of the room. When he noticed that one of the old man's feet was bare, he concluded that the gentleman must have been looking for his other dress sock. He may have been some-what distracted with the coming wedding ceremony or with some oth-er business concern as he dressed, because C.H. could see that both socks were on the other foot.

"Here sir, let me help you with these laces," C.H. offered as he knelt and removed one of the socks and quickly put it on the man's one bare foot. "Very good, sir," added C.H. in a hearty tone of congratulations, "I use this system myself! Keeps the socks warm until you need them!" At this, the old man broke into peals of relieved laughter. He loved that joke so much that he told many friends the "sock story" at the rehearsal dinner.

...

In their off hours, Jackson and C.H. dined together in the staff din-ing room connected to the hotel kitchen, or spent time talking over the events of the day in Jackson's lovely book-lined parlor. This had to be the extent of their socializing since, as a black man, Jackson would not have been welcome inside the town's restaurants or bars as a patron, though segregation of the races had not yet been codified into law.

Arkansas law had allowed former slaves to enter into legal con-tracts and to own property ever since just after the war, and enter-prising men like Jackson became part of a rising black middle-class. Some even became rich like Wiley Jones of Pine Bluff who, by the early 1890s, owned the city's race track, two streetcar systems and extensive rental properties. The white population, many of whom faced worsen-ing economic circumstances, resented any evidence of black success and had no desire to mix socially with former slaves. As time went on, white resentment would spawn a virulent and dangerous bigotry. Nei-ther Jackson nor C.H. wanted to test how accepting the society outside the hotel would be of their very unusual friendship.

Both men had overheard many conversations in the hotel dining room that proved to them that even members of what was considered to be the "refined" upper class, were as likely as anyone to be riddled with ugly notions. In fact, some members of high society seemed to believe that their superior station allowed behavior that could only be described as basely corrupt. C.H. noted that the worst of these seemed to hold public office. He stopped being surprised by how open, even proud, some of these men were about their dishonest dealings. Paraphrasing another Twain quip, C.H. told Jackson one night, "I would say that all politicians are jackasses, but that would be unfair to the jackass."

Though both men were well used to the craven behavior of politicians, they could still be taken by surprise by that of other "respectable" guests. One day, over their private dinner together, Jackson told his young friend that, when he counted the silver from the main dining room each evening, he had noticed for some days that some of it was missing, so he had been closely watching the wait staff in order to catch the culprit. After a few days, he spied a woman slip some of the silver cutlery into her large purse. He was amazed because this woman was a St. Louis socialite known for her many lavish parties and who brought, at her personal expense, several lady friends to enjoy Hot Spring's spa amenities and to play cards away from their husbands.

"Why would a rich woman like that want to steal?" Jackson wondered aloud. "People say she's so refined and the newspapers always talk about all her big parties. Her friends must know she's a thief?! Why a bunch of them were sitting right there when she did it! Why would those other women just look the other way?"

"Well, as Mark Twain would say," C.H. laughed, "'Virtue never has been as respectable as money.'" Then he added, "I assure you, old friend, her bags will be a lot lighter when I deliver them to her coach."

After this incident, Jackson made C.H. his maître d in the main dining room. The new position suited the young man, for it provided him with unlimited opportunity to meet and converse with all the hotel's important and colorful guests. During the course of a typical day he might greet, seat and converse with P. Lorillard, the tobacco king, "Diamond Joe" Reynolds, the man who brought the railroad to Hot Springs, or the actor Frederick Ward, who was to play the leading role in the first production of the new Central Avenue Opera House. Many of New York's glitterati made yearly migrations to Hot Springs "for the waters" and the comforts offered by the Arlington. One such person was Chauncey Depew, general counsel to Cornelius Vanderbilt, who C.H. could count on to provide some hilarious nugget to later share with Jackson over dinner.

On the first morning of one stay, Mr. Depew entered the dining room unaccompanied. "Will there be anyone joining you, sir?" C.H. inquired.

"I rather enjoy a solitary breakfast," answered the distinguished lawyer, "which is a good thing since all my friends skip breakfast to take in a bracing morning walk instead. In my opinion, walking downstairs is exercise enough for any gentleman." Then he added, "After their walk they will go to the baths and later will down a pint of whisky, then dine on half a cow all the while congratulating themselves for all they do to maintain their good health. In truth, half my friends are digging their graves with their teeth. I suppose I should thank them, since I get my most strenuous exercise by acting as pallbearer for my friends who exercise!"

Many years later, C.H. was unhappy to read a piece in a William Randolph Hearst publication by a David Graham Phillips who was known as a muckraking journalist trying to make a name for himself. The focus of the article, "The Treason of the Senate," was Chauncey Depew who was serving a term as U.S. Senator from New York. The article claimed that Depew was owned "mentally and morally" by Vanderbilt. C.H. was relieved to later read letters expressing outrage over this "libel" from both Senator Henry Cabot Lodge and President Theodore Roosevelt.

* * *

Though it was true that, by his nineteenth birthday, C.H. had developed a deep dislike for politicians especially the blowhard types who populated state and local politics in Arkansas, he was soon to meet a man whose friendship would act to temper the young man's negativity toward anyone engaged in politics.

In the spring of 1881, Jackson asked C. H. to temporarily act as personal room steward during the stay of just one special guest, James G. Blaine, the Secretary of State recently appointed by the new President, James Garfield. Jackson explained that Mr. Blaine was coming to relax after the pressure of the recent campaign and had requested one of the executive suites far from the bustle of the lower floors in order to reflect and prepare for his new post. Of course, C.H. was impressed and excited about his new assignment and took pains to make sure the suite was perfectly in order and that the cleaning staff was aware that they could only enter these rooms when he signaled that Mr. Blaine was out for a spa treatment or a meal.

C.H. was prepared to do his best to please this important man who was sure to be especially demanding. However, within days of his arrival, the young room steward realized he had been wrong in the belief that Blaine would be a difficult guest. He was not at all haughty or coldly superior as C.H. had expected him to be. Instead, Blaine was warmly approachable and appeared to be eager to share some of his plans for his new post. C.H. was especially impressed by Blaine's hopes for establishing stronger ties with other countries in the Americas through a system of arbitration to prevent wars in the Western Hemisphere.

"We cannot possibly fend off European aggression unless all the countries of North and South America are committed to mutual cooperation and peaceful arbitration of our differences," Blaine explained to his young friend who was beginning to see that a political career could actually lead to more than craven self-promotion.

Blaine continued to work many hours each day on his proposal for a Pan-American conference where nations might make legal agreements to support and strengthen each other. However, Blaine was eager to talk about his plans and he found in C.H. a willing listener and even someone, young as he was, who through wide reading and personal experience had much to bring to their conversations.

During one of their discussions about the way of the world, Blaine turned to his room steward and said, "You know, Charlie, you would make a fine politician." Then he had to laugh when he saw the young man's horrified expression. "Well, maybe you would prefer a career as a diplomat. There are many good things that government can do. You should not discount its power to make the world a better place. Why, if it were not for the direction our government chose to take a decade ago, your good friend, Jackson, might still be enslaved."

Later, in a discussion connected to Blaine's beliefs pertaining to strengthening the country, the Secretary referred to the potential of Western expansion. "The new Western states are experiencing the violence that always seems to come with the birth of nations. The railroad is the umbilical that will feed civilization to the wild new lands. But they need more than anything else men like yourself, Charlie, who will lend their youth and strength to this expansion and in return reap the blessings of opportunity only available in the West."

For his part, C.H. quietly thought about what Blaine seemed to be challenging him to consider. It had never occurred to him that he might make his home anywhere other than in Arkansas. Then, he thought of all he had right where he was: friends, family, and work that was more a career than a mere job. No, he decided, his life was "on track" and he had no interest in changing its direction. Like so many of the very young, he was blissfully unaware of how often fate deals out life-changing surprises.

6.
Krann

After nearly two weeks of travel on the immigrant train, Kurt Krann and August Meyer knew each other as well as do most life-long friends. By the time they were finally freed from the confines of their closed boxcar in San Francisco, both men were convinced that theirs would prove to be a profitable partnership. Kurt's admiration of August had grown daily as his new friend shared fascinating stories about his wartime army exploits and his peacetime adventures freely working wherever his travels took him. August had lived the kind of life Kurt had only dreamed of and now was on the brink of living himself. As for August, he was very happy to finally have a friend who could be fully trusted as a true confidante. In addition, August was sure that Kurt was the perfect person to aid him in carrying out the next step in a secret plan.

August had some money that could take them north into Oregon more comfortably by rail as coach passengers. Finally, Kurt could view from his window seat the kaleidoscope of natural beauty that is the American West. He gaped in awe as the train first passed rolling hills turned golden by the late summer sun. Then would come a sudden flash of some diamond-clear lake or a dark green stand of ancient oaks brushing the glass inches from his startled gaze. The sunlit valleys and forests of Northern California gave way to the great shadows cast by glacier-topped mountains slowly turning dark against a flaming sunset.

Late the next day, the train slowed to a stop before a depot sign reading "Jacksonville." August reached over and shook a sleeping Kurt awake. "Come on! This is where we get off. I only bought tickets to get us this far. I have plans for this place," he announced to a bewildered Kurt who followed his friend down the platform, through a thriving town and across a meadow with a short stop in front of a road-side farm stand where they purchased two large baking potatoes and some ears of sweet corn.

The two friends continued down a dirt track until they reached a forested area where they could put down their bedrolls, knapsacks and provisions next to a small, clear creek. Kurt was filled with a childlike excitement at the thought of camping under the stars. He realized that the air was redolent with the sweet aroma of nearby campfires which made him feel as though he had stepped into a new world shared with fellow adventurers. Soon, August managed to bring life to their own cooking fire and placed their food to cook near an outer ring of hot rocks. As they ate their meager fare, Kurt could not imagine any food tasting better than the roasted corn or the buttery soft baked potatoes.

They ate in hungry silence until August turned to Kurt and began to explain that he had planned all along to travel to this part of Southern Oregon. He told Kurt that this was the first area prospectors had discovered gold in the Oregon Territory. He said that a couple of mule packers named John Poole and James Cluggage were on their way to Sacramento, California when they stopped to camp for the night. While watering their mules, they noticed some gold glints in the debris next to the creek. They had accidentally discovered a gold strike to rival that of California's American River.

"Because of it, those two both became rich and that town we just walked through was started by them and is now the biggest town north of San Francisco! There have been many more discoveries in all the mountains around here. At first, it was possible to get rich just panning the rivers and creeks for gold mixed in with sand and gravel. Most of that easy pickings is gone, so now the large operations are digging deep lode mines and they use men who know how to do hard rock work." August explained and paused to stir the fire a bit.

"And you're a hard rock miner. Do you plan to go to work with one of those outfits?" Kurt put in with some trepidation.

"That's making money the hard way," replied August shaking his head. "I would never work for someone else in this business. That's for sure. The owners don't give a rat's ass for a miner. They say that miners are worth less than timber, so they skimp on the timber and next thing you know you're under a twenty ton cave in!"

"So why are we here and why did you plan to come here in the first place?" wondered Kurt.

"This is why," his friend answered as he pulled from his pocket a well-creased paper. "I found this in a newspaper back East last month. It's an article about this place. I read they were looking for hard rock men and that the Beekman Bank in Jacksonville was offering thousand dollar purses for the winners of drilling contests held every month all summer. The article said that the Beekman Bank is the only bank in America that doesn't charge its clients for banking with them. Doesn't have to since their scales have weighed in over ten million dollars in gold! Think of it, Kurt! A guy could make more in one contest than working over a year in the mines!"

"And you want that guy to be you," Kurt finished for him.

"Not just me. The biggest purse is two thousand dollars for 'double-jacking' and that takes two guys."

"You and who else?" wondered Kurt. Then he gasped as August continue to stare at him. "I have never even heard of 'double-jacking' before this very minute. I have never even seen a 'double-jack.' Whatever that is."

"It's not a thing. It's a process, and I can teach you your part. We'll get some sleep and we'll start tomorrow to become the best damn double-jacking team in Oregon!"

...

August didn't have to wake Kurt the next morning, for Kurt had lain wide awake all night fearing that he would let his friend down and ruin August's plan to win the big purse. He had never done any physical work in his life, and he knew he was soft; not a strong man in any way.

Nonetheless, when August kicked aside his blanket and bedroll, then bounded to his feet with a broad grin, Kurt did his best to hide his own growing dread. "I have some dried meat here in my sack we can chew on while I explain about double-jacking," August fairly shouted, then he unrolled another blanket that held some tools, a large sledge hammer and a series of different sized spikes.

"Kurt, these tools are used by hard rock miners to drill holes in rock large enough to put enough black powder in to blast the rock apart. Then they shovel the rock pieces into mine cars and send the cars to the surface. Once on top, other men sort any ore they find from the rock," August began. "The most efficient way to hand drill these holes is to use a team if two men, one to hold the spike and the other to hammer it into the rock. That is what is called 'double-jacking'. The man holding the spike is called the 'shaker'. He must hold the steel spike in position and then rotate it 90 degrees with each blow of the hammer, and he also needs to know when to change to longer spikes as the hole gets deeper.

The other man is called the 'driller'. His job is to swing the 12 pound sledge hammer at the rock spike being held in the shaker's hands. He must strike a firm blow, and never miss. Most teams change places because no one man is strong enough to hammer accurately for ten or fifteen minutes at a competitive rate of at least 50 blows a minute. The switching can eat up their time. But, I average more than 60 blows a minute and I can keep it up the whole time in a ten minute contest which this is going to be. That way we could get a very competitive hole-depth of at least 24 inches in the allotted time. In the end, the men with the deepest hole wins. And that's about it. Simple, huh?!"

"Gus, what if you miss with that hammer?" Kurt whispered, and August noted his friend's suddenly ashen complexion.

"Put that out of your mind. I never miss. Haven't missed in years."

"How many years has that been?" Kurt ventured in that same strained whisper.

"Say, the best way to put your worry to rest is for us to start right in now to practice! We have lots of time to get our rhythm down. The contest is in five days." This did not sound like enough time to Kurt. Not enough time at all.

...

That first day, the two would-be contestants practiced for hours. After August had demonstrated just how the shaker had to hold and turn the "steel," he had Kurt do it as he watched. Kurt seemed to catch on quickly, so August took up his hammer for the two to practice a rhythmic pattern of having Kurt turn the steel between hammer blows. After a few minutes, August laid down his hammer to praise Kurt's "technique" though he thought privately that he had never before seen a shaker who actually shook! He also noted that his teammate spent the entire first practice session with his eyes squeezed shut. August did not want to make Kurt's fear worse by telling him that his trembling hands made it harder for him to deliver a firm and accurate hammer blow.

By the end of the second day, Kurt had grown to trust that his friend would not accidentally split his head open like a melon with his murderous-looking hammer. August judged that their timing was getting so good that they should go to town and sign up for the contest.

"You can't wear those clothes to town today." He told Kurt indicating the work clothes he had purchased in San Francisco before their trip north. "I want you to wear your good suit."

"If I am in my suit, I will be more conspicuous than I already am. As it is, no-one would take me for an experienced miner even in my work clothes. I just won't fit in at all."

"Exactly," August nodded with a wide grin.

...

By the day of the contest, August said he was confident that they could hold their own in the competition. Their rhythm was smooth and they had a considerable edge as August explained. He told Kurt that miners were a hard drinking crowd and that any big contest, like the one they had entered, would draw a crowd of on-lookers who already knew the men who made up the best teams. Inevitably, those men were treated to drinks by their fans in the days before the event even took place. He speculated that the two of them might easily be the only sober team in the contest, a definite plus for them.

Kurt admitted that August had been right about miners and their drinking. In town, throngs of people spilled out of the bars and saloons that lined the main street, many of them held a glass in one hand and a pint of whiskey in the other. Most were just on-lookers there for the entertainment. Kurt wondered why a long line had formed outside the Beekman Bank's doors and snaked down the side street and around the corner. August explained that those men were waiting to make bets on one team or another

Finally, August and Kurt managed to push their way toward the high platform that had been constructed for the contest in the street that was an intersection of two wide boulevards that met in front of the Beekman Bank. They wormed their way to a spot where an official with a clipboard stood checking off various teams as they arrived. Another official stood on the platform with a megaphone announcing teams to the crowd. Most of the teams had chosen to register with made-up team names like "The Butte Boys", "Cornwall Kings." and "Montana Might." Loud cheers from their supporters accompanied each announcement. However, when August and Kurt were announced as "Gritty Gus and The Gentleman," the crowd broke into hoots and laughter. Kurt heard someone say, "'Gritty Gus and the Tinhorn' is more like it"

"See, I knew it. Because of me, they think we're a joke," whispered Kurt mournfully.

"Yes, they call you the 'tinhorn.' Meaning you are an inexperienced pretender. They think you won't be much help to me, and that is very, very good!" returned August without any concern that they would be overheard since they always spoke to each other in German. "I think it's about time we made a little side bet." And he winked and joined the line at the bank leaving an astonished Kurt alone on the street.

By the time the contest was officially announced, the streets on either side of the contest platform were packed with hundreds of onlookers. Many were drunk and quite unruly. The jostling for position led to several actual fist fights. Some enterprising souls had climbed streetlamps for a better view. The contestants themselves stood just below the platform in a roped off area. August watched intently as each team finished and water was poured into their drill-hole to wash away any loose rock chips in order to make a clean measurement. He watched for any sign from the officials that one team or another had drilled a winning hole. He knew that no measurement would be announced until the final contestants were finished competing. Kurt, on the other hand, chose to look only at his shoes and pray that he would not make a complete fool of himself.

At one point, August spoke more to himself than to Kurt. "Everyone is using three inch steels."

"What does that mean?" Kurt anxiously questioned.

August bent closer and, in low tones, explained, "I decided to use two and a half inchers instead of the usual three inch spikes. We have to change 'em more often, but they won't dull out as much as the ones that have to go another half inch in hard rock before changes. I also tempered 'em for extra strength, and I brought extras just in case they're needed."

"Oh, good thinking," responded Kurt with no clue what any of that meant.

When their turn finally came, Kurt was nearly faint with anxiety but made an effort to hide it by sprinting up the stairs, then stumbled on the top step bringing great guffaws from the crowd. Once in position, the crowd quieted and their timing began.

August swung his hammer and delivered a solid blow once every second while Kurt quickly made his 90 degree turns after each blow. Kurt could actually feel August's competitive nature kick in as each successive hammer blow was harder and more deliberate than the last. Each steel spike throbbed in Kurt's frantic clutch and sweat ran down his cheeks with his efforts to hold onto them.

Since each powerful hit of the hammer seemed to deepen the hole, it was hard for Kurt to know for sure when it was time to switch to a sharper spike. In practice, August had suggested he exchange spikes once a minute which was around sixty blows. He had instructed Kurt to count to sixty then shout "change" as a cue to pause in the hammering. In this way, Kurt kept his concentration and was able to smoothly make the necessary exchanges for sharper spikes to replace the dulled ones.

Their hours of practice paid off as they continued in perfect rhythm for the entire allotted time period. August could see that theirs was surely a competitive hole once he stepped back to watch the water clean the debris from the small opening. For his part, Kurt was just glad the whole awful thing was over. He nearly fell over trying to stand while his heart beat a wild tempo, and he gasped for air since he had held his breath for much of the prior ten minutes.

Once they resumed a place in the audience, Kurt found watching the contest quite entertaining. Of course, he had a team he was rooting for, so he enjoyed any sign of weakness in other teams. One driller was so drunk by the time his team was called that he accidentally stepped backwards off the platform, knocked himself out as he hit the cobblestones head first and had to be carried away by his friends. When another team, "The Cornwall Kings," was called, August explained that they were a team that would probably make a good showing. "All those guys from Cornwall are great miners with really good skills," he said.

Finally, in the fifth hour of the competition, the officials announced the winning measurements. They started with third place for a $200 prize. That team was a couple of guys from Colorado who had drilled a 29 inch hole. Kurt remembered with worry that, according to August, a 24 inch hole in ten minutes was really good. Apparently not good enough to even win third place.

Next, the second place winners for a prize of $400 was a California team that had drilled a 32 inch hole. Kurt took a quick sidelong glance at August who, for the first time all day, looked concerned. Now, his heart began again to thump a steady drumbeat as the officials seemed to be in some kind of discussion. Why, he thought, couldn't they just make the announcement of which team won the grand prize of $2,000! After what seemed like an interminable pause, one official stepped forward. The crowd stood in breathless silence.

"We have an unusual situation today. We must announce that the Cornwall Kings have drilled a depth that breaks records for any contest held in this county for a ten minute drill. Their measurement was an astounding 34 inches!" A huge cheer went up from the crowd while the official waved for quiet.

"We must also announce that, as amazing as that accomplishment is, we have a second team with an identical measurement. That team is Gritty Gus and the Gentleman! Will both teams please come up for a conference."

August, Kurt and the two men from Cornwall all walked up the steps to discuss the situation with the officials. One of the Beekman Bank executives turned to the two anxious teams and spoke softly.

"Well, you men have certainly astounded us. We have determined that there is only one way to resolve this tie. That would be is to hold a run-off contest where each team drills for another ten minutes."

"We can't do that! Our steels're plumb wore out. They're too dull to be any good to us for another ten minutes!" cried one member of the Cornwall team.

Kurt looked anxiously at August to see what he would say to this. August seemed to be thinking the situation over, and by this time the crowd had begun to chant "Run-off! Run-off!"

August took Kurt aside who was very relieved to hear him say in German, "We have plenty of sharp spikes left, but I know you don't want to go again, so we won't." Then Kurt was sure August had completely lost his mind when the big man turned to the others holding his still-sharp spikes in his open palm. "We agree to a run-off which is the only way to decide who wins first place at this point." He paused while he let the other team clearly see the sharp spikes he held so casually in one hand.

"No, no, no!" shouted both members of the other team at once. "We agree to a tie! Let it just be a tie!" they yelled, as the crowd continued they're deafening chant for a "run-off"

At this, the officials seemed stymied. Then August leaned into their huddle drawing the other team in too. "We will agree to share the first place prize money with this team, but only if we are named the first place team due to their refusal to a run-off." He calmly suggested to the group.

"We agree," announced the officials in unison eager to end the stalemate. Then the officials, with August and Kurt turned to stare at the men from Cornwall who turned away to conference.

"All right, that's fair enough. We agree to share with them, and they can claim first place." They reported after a short conversation.

The Beekman Bank executive then took up the megaphone and shouted, "The first place team is officially Gritty Gus and the Gentleman! The Cornwall Kings must default to a run-off due to insufficient drilling tools."

With that final announcement, all the prize winners followed the officials through the noisy throng and entered the Beekman Bank to collect their prizes. Once a prize was given out, the winners all immediately left to celebrate in the nearest saloon leaving August and Kurt alone with just one of the officials who was, in fact, the bank's president. He spoke directly to August. "I'm sorry your prize envelop is so light. You two put on quite a show, and your generous offer to the other team really took us off the hook for a solution in the end. This second envelop should help you forget the prize money you gave up."

With that, August quickly pocketed the money envelop and pulled Kurt out the door where they collected their bedrolls that they had earlier stuffed under the contest platform. Then August led his confused friend at a run to the railway depot. There, he purchased first class coach tickets on the next train north.

It was only when the two were seated and the train was pulling safely out of the station, that Kurt turned to August and said solemnly, "I am so sorry you had to give up that money because you knew I didn't want to go through a run-off with that other team. You lost out on a thousand dollars because of me! I let you down when you have proven to be a better friend than I deserve."

Kurt was startled when August broke into such loud, long gulping laughter that tears sprouted from both eyes. When he regained a little composure, August said to his confused friend, "Oh, no little tinhorn. Because of you, not one person but me bet on our team to win, and win we did! Because of you, we benefitted from very, very good odds!" As he spoke, he opened the second envelope that had been presented by the bank president. Inside was the pay-off for August's "little side-bet," seven, thousand-dollar bills!

7.
McColloch

A very young man just shy of his twentieth birthday can be forgiven for believing that he is able to control his own destiny. At such a young age, a man usually lacks the kind of hard experience that teaches humility and a proper respect for the vicissitudes of fate. Additionally, young men make an understandable mistake when they foolishly equate their seemingly boundless good health with abilities and traits older men have learned belong only to mythical creatures and are forever denied mere mortals. This kind of thinking leads many youth to ignore the laws of nature at their peril. Older men who seek power and privilege have always understood and capitalized on this fatal flaw that drives the young toward patently dangerous acts. For this reason, those in power have historically found it easy to convince young men to go to war. With the wave of a flag and a stirring song, the young eagerly agree risk all in order to win more glory, land and treasure for their leaders.

However, if a young man is very lucky, he will respect some older man, a father or a mentor, and will then listen to their words of caution and advice. Charles Henry was particularly blessed by having been surrounded since birth by men who were models of sober reflection and careful action, habits of thought that improve one's chances of survival in a chaotic and perilous world. Even in the early summer of 1881 when Charles Henry lived and worked in Hot Springs away from his boyhood home and family, he still had an older man in whom he could safely confide. However, when he told Jackson one evening of his plan to always remain in the same place, working at the same job and surrounded by the same friends in order to insure a life of happy satisfaction, he did not receive the congratulatory response he had expected from his friend and mentor. Instead, he would later admit he had received some very wise advice.

"That kinda plan worries me some, son," Jackson sighed as the two sat together having their usual evening brandy. "That's the kind of "plan" every ruined Southern planter once had. They thought they had the power to turn back all the political, social and economic changes that the country was going through. To control their future and to stop "change" in its tracks, they went off to war cock sure of glorious success. Why, they had no backup plan at all it seems! Now they sit in their crumbling houses dreaming of the day life will go back to the way things were."

"Do you think things here will change like that? Do you know something I don't know?" C.H. wondered with some concern since Jackson was in a position to know something about the future of the hotel.

"No I don't have any inside knowledge about how things will change. Only, experience shows me that change will happen, it always does. We can't stop it, but we can prepare ourselves. We can make a plan. And, if we're smart, we will make a backup plan for when the first idea doesn't work out. In the meantime, learn new skills and sharpen the ones you have so when "change" hits you between the eyes, you just might survive it."

Nineteen-year-old C.H. could not have known how soon the winds of change would begin to blow away his own "Plan A." In fact, within a month's time an event would occur which would be a harbinger of things to come.

...

On July 2, 1881 Mr. Reynolds, the manager of the Hot Springs telegraph office ran wildly down the town's main street waving a newly received telegram. Red-faced and gasping for breath, he finally regained enough composure to shout to a gathering crowd, "The President's been shot! Garfield's been shot!"

The terrible news reached the Arlington Hotel within minutes, just as C.H. and Jackson were reviewing the day's work assignments with the front desk clerks. For the next 80 days America waited and prayed for the life of the man who had only been in office a few short months before Charles J. Guiteau stepped onto the Baltimore and Potomac Railroad Station platform and shot Garfield just as he was about to address a crowd.

It would not be fully reported until much later that Garfield's death should be contributed more to the arrogance and ineptitude of his doctors than to the assassin's bullet. Though European doctors had used antiseptics since the 1860's due to the Listerian Theory that germs, invisible to the naked eye, were the cause of infection and illness. Many American doctors including Dr. Willard Bliss who took charge of Garfield's medical treatment after the shooting, rejected the idea that something that could not be seen could cause illness or that "germs" even existed. From the time he was shot until he died, the President was poked and prodded with the dirty fingers of doctors vainly hoping to find the bullet Bliss very publicly stated was lodged somewhere in the man's right side. Bliss would not allow any second opinions to prevail over his own and even went so far as to refuse to let anyone examine Garfield's left side where the bullet actually was. On September 19, 1881, riddled with infection, his body filled with abscesses, President Garfield mercifully died.

Nine months after Garfield's death, his assassin, Charles Guiteau, would be hanged for his crime. During his trial, Guiteau had often claimed that he had actually deserved to be rewarded with a diplomatic position in Garfield's administration, because he had been such a loyal supporter of the Republican. The proof of this delusional contention was that he had written and distributed a letter in support of Garfield.

The assassin's family reported their attempts over the years to have Guiteau committed as his delusional behavior had become increasingly worrisome. In the clutches of his growing mania, he had told anyone within earshot that he should have been rewarded with a diplomatic consulship in Vienna or, at the very least, in Paris.

Members of Garfield's administration also testified about the increasingly strange behavior of the man accused of assassination. On March 8, 1881, just four days after Garfield's inauguration, Guiteau obtained entrance to the White House and spoke to the new president long enough to give him a copy of the speech that the deluded man announced had won Garfield the election. When he later scanned the speech, Garfield found it humorous that in some original form, the speech was in support of Ulysses S. Grant who had lost the primary to Garfield. In his rush to rewrite, Guiteau had left many references to Grant in this rambling diatribe that had never been publicly delivered.

Since the long trial was covered in every daily newspaper in the country, C.H. was well aware of the prominent part James Blaine, as Garfield's Secretary of State, played in the unfolding drama. The papers covered all the testimony that recreated the assassin's movements for the two months leading up to the shooting. During that time period, Guiteau spent his days stalking Garfield and shuffling between the State Department and the White House where he accosted any prominent Republican with his incessant demands for a diplomatic post. He was destitute, unshaven and filthy since he wore the same suit every day and was banned from the White House waiting room on May 13, 1881.

He then focused his attention on speaking to Secretary of State Blaine who finally told him, "Never speak to me again of the Paris consulship..." For this slight, Guiteau wrote a letter to Garfield demanding that Blaine be fired and that if this action was not taken both the President and the Republican Party would "come to grief."

As he read these accounts, C.H. remembered that, when he had met Blaine only a few months before the assassination, Blaine had been so optimistic about forming a cooperative body of Western Hemisphere countries that could have done much to ensure peace and prosperity for the entire continent. He worried that the madman Guiteau had not only ended the life of a potentially great president but had also derailed Blaine's dream for the country. "Well," he thought to himself, "So much for anyone's ability to control destiny!"

The nation healed some with the closure that Guiteau's execution provided, but C.H. could not seem to shake a feeling of profound insecurity that sometimes even darkened into dread of a future no man can control or even accurately predict. He finally told Jackson one evening when they were alone, of these black feelings that seemed to stalk his every moment and even haunted his dreams.

"Why you're way too young to be a pessimist!" the older man exclaimed.

"How can I be anything else when wicked men can so easily destroy the good men!? When I think back on my life, I realize how sheltered I was, living out the war in a safe little hole while evil swirled all around us. That was the real world where good men like our neighbor was hanged just for trying to protect his family. I grew up, I think, to be a naïve fool. But now I know the truth! I will not hold onto the illusions that humanity is basically good and all things turn out well in the end!"

"Now hold on a minute, Charlie. Remember what your favorite writer would say. 'Don't part with your illusions. When they are gone you may still exist, but you have ceased to live.' Mr. Twain has lived longer than you have, so I think you would be smart to wait awhile before you pass judgement on the whole human race."

"Yeah?! He also said, 'Such is the human race. Often it does seem such a pity that Noah didn't miss the boat.' " C.H, countered.

"True, true." Jackson put in. "He also stated once, 'Damn these human beings; if I had invented them I would go hide my head in a bag.'" Jackson chuckled as he noted that his friend was also laughing. "I think, Charlie, that the best tonic for pessimism is humor. Now, I know I said that it's dangerous for anyone to think they can control or even predict the future. But, I also said that the only thing you can be sure of is that nothing stays the same. I warned you to prepare yourself for the worst. That is exactly what your daddy did when he built that underground shelter to hide his family in. Sometimes you have to fight the bad things and sometimes you just have to wait things out, just wait for the good things to come along. As bad as things seem right now, this won't last. The next good thing is just around the corner. You'll see I'm right."

...

C.H. was later surprised by how right Jackson had been when a few months after their conversation he would literally turn a corner that would most profoundly change his life. It happened one morning when C.H. was at his usual morning station reviewing the day's tasks with the front desk staff. As the young man finished, Jackson drew him aside and said. "Charlie, the manager and I hired a new seamstress yesterday, and we have her hemming new drapes for the library. The woman is in there now but could really use a man's help in taking down the old curtains."

When he first rounded the corner and entered the dimly lit library, C.H. saw no-one since the curtains had not yet been drawn to let in the morning light. Then he sensed movement near one of the windows and, as his eyes adjusted to the darkness, he could make out a woman leaning from a ladder and struggling with the heavy velvet drapery. C.H. turned up the gas sconce adjacent to the doorway which startled the woman who turned so quickly toward the light that she nearly fell from her perch. To keep from tumbling to the ground, she grasped the heavy fabric with both hands as the awkwardly placed ladder began a wild wobble. C.H. managed to close the distance between the door and the falling ladder in time to catch the seamstress around the waist and convey her safely to the ground.

At first neither person spoke, both being out of breath and somewhat embarrassed. Finally, C.H. managed a small laugh and stated the obvious, "Looks like I arrived just in time. You appear to be in one piece."

Then, in the better light, he could see that this person was not at all what he had expected. She was not some work-weary matron with red hands as he had first visualized when he was sent to help. Instead, she was a slim, wisp of a girl who looked to be younger than himself. As she slowly regained some composure, she managed a furtive sideways peek at him with what seemed to him to be the most arresting, dark gray eyes he had ever seen. They were large and made to look even larger since they were set in a very small, pale heart-shaped face. Then she blushed and looked away, and he was mortified to realize that he had been staring at her. "Please sit for a moment while I, I fetch some water for you." He stammered and ran from the room.

Returning with the promised water, C.H. saw that the girl had removed the white linen cap she had been wearing to work in, and sat primly in the center of a leather sofa with cascades of impossibly lustrous, red hair falling about her narrow shoulders. The vision before him affected the young man in a way nothing ever had before. His tongue felt swollen and his mouth was dry, but even if he, himself drank the water he had brought the girl, he could not have uttered a word. For the first time in his life, he had been struck speechless. Mercifully, she spoke first. "Thank you" she said taking the glass he held in a trembling hand. "You have been most kind. Now, I must get back to work."

• • •

In the weeks that followed, C.H. managed to regain his power of speech and also manipulate his schedule to allow daily contact with the girl, who he soon learned was Mary Wooddy. The two talked constantly in the way that men and women do when thirsting for deeper knowledge about the person with whom they are falling in love.

The two soon found that they had much in common in terms of background. They had both been touched by the war from almost the moment of birth. Mary's folks had moved from Tennessee to northwest Arkansas several years before the conflict to make their home in Rhea's Mill a small, prosperous township a few miles west of Fayetteville. Mary's mother had been a Rhea before marrying William Wooddy, a poor circuit riding Baptist preacher. The newlyweds were invited to come and live at Rhea's Mill by William H. Rhea, Mary's uncle and owner of the three stores, a mill and the surrounding farms that made up the thriving township. It was there in 1859 that Mary was born. By then, her father had made enough money to buy a house in Fayetteville just three miles from Rhea's Mill where he worked as the local Baptist preacher and her mother took in sewing. The family enjoyed peace and prosperity for three short years before war came to northeast Arkansas.

The next part of her story astonished C.H. with its irony. By 1862 Fayetteville had become an important supply center for the Confederate army. In February of that year, at the very time C.H.'s father and brother were being enticed to join the fight and march north to reinforce the army under General Ben McCulloch, the troops they were to join were running wild through the streets of Fayetteville looting stores and private homes. After his troops had plundered all they could take with them, General McCulloch, with no apparent concern for the Confederate citizens of the town, ordered his troops to burn Fayetteville so as to leave no supplies for the advancing Union Army.

Three year old Mary and her parents lived in one of the few untouched houses in the area, though once the two great armies had their battle at Pea Ridge just north of town, there was little left for the remaining civilians who had not actually died inside their burning houses. For the next two years, the family would lay low and occasionally, Mary's father would ride to Rhea's Mill for supplies. Mary's mother begged her husband to move them back to Rhea's Mill where they would surely be safer than living in an exposed house surrounded by parched, bare land. She was mortally afraid of his trips to the mill on a road they both knew was targeted by "bushwhacking" thieves who preyed on people leaving Rhea's Mill with fresh supplies. Her husband refused to listen to his wife's pleas or even consider her growing fears.

As she recounted this part of her story, Mary's huge eyes burned with a terrible fury. "My father refused to do what would have kept us safe, because he was a stubborn, prideful man who hated the idea of being further beholden to the Rheas! He told my mother to never ask him again to move to her family. She had to swallow her fears that seemed to grow with each passing day, because she was only a woman after all, and like all women she had no power even in her own home."

In 1864 just months before the war's end, William Wooddy did not return from one of his supply trips. His body was found beside the Fayetteville road but his supplies, horse and even his boots had been taken by thieves. "So, way too late, my mother was proven right. We finally got to move to safety, but by then my mother had ceased to feel safe anywhere!"

Mary and her mother lived at Rhea's Mill for the next years, a time when Mary recounted that her mother barely existed inside a shell of dark depression. When Mary was thirteen, the two women moved to Hot Springs to work in a laundry serving the hotels. Like C.H. and his brother, they too realized that living in Hot Springs afforded them the benefits of one of the few economically thriving communities in postwar Arkansas. William Rhea had arranged for the women to live with a Methodist minister and his wife who ran a school where Mary could attend every morning and work in the afternoons.

Mary had already learned to read the Bible, but for the first time she also read about the kinder, happier world that existed outside of the horror that plagued her childhood. C.H. showed her that this world could even bring her love. But the war had taught a lasting lesson that would never leave her about cruelty and injustice and how innocents guilty of no wrong-doing can be made to suffer because they have no power to fight the evil in the hearts of some godless men.

...

In the months to come, C.H. was to discover that Mary was not like any woman he had ever met. He had met many women in his work at the hotel. Many of them had been pretty in the way pampered, wealthy women usually are. They wore lovely dresses, were perfumed and powdered, their lips were rouged rose petals and their elaborate hairdos were never out of place. Their soft skin and white hands were never chapped from hard work, and their smooth complexions were not flawed by crow's feet from years spent bending to difficult tasks. He had heard their conversations in the hotel dining room and had even been occasionally paired with some socialite left without an escort for a debutante ball. He had found them rather shallow. Their interests seemed to begin and end with the latest fashions, the latest gossip and the latest grand parties to take place in the latest "social season." Ask any of them their opinion about literature, history, political or social issues and one was invariably met with a blank stare. In short, he found them boring and much preferred an evening with Jackson as company.

But Mary was something else entirely. They had known right away that they had much in common. Both had endured an artificially restricted childhood with their formative years spent under the cloud of war. But both were resilient young people who, once released from their wartime bunkers, had a great desire to learn and experience all the wonderful things the world had to offer.

Their early experiences contained some notable formative differences as well. C.H. had enjoyed a close-knit family life filled with a love for great literature that he wished to share with her. Mary's childhood home had only one book, The Holy Bible. C.H. had parents who regularly and lovingly engaged their children in adult conversation to make up for the deprivation their isolation imposed. Mary's home was a grim place where her father's word was law and children and wives were to live furtively and quietly in the background so as not to disturb his study of their one book.

However, once Mary came to live with the Methodist minister, Mr. Caldwell and his wife, she also came to know the magic of reading and its ability to open the world and transport the reader beyond the present moment. She was also very intrigued by the forward thinking of the Methodist clergy and congregation who met regularly at the Caldwell's home. They read the Bible in these meetings to be sure, but they also related this reading to current social-justice issues. Most of these discussions involved the ideas that women should finally be given the vote along with all the rights and responsibilities of citizenship enjoyed by men such as serving on juries, freely engaging in commerce and holding public office. These meetings and the articles she read regularly in the Methodist newspaper, Arkansas Methodist, gave shape and direction to Mary's smoldering anger first ignited by her father's stubborn refusal to consider her mother's need for simple security. Methodists also supported the temperance movement along with women's suffrage since they believed that males-only saloons fed the alcoholism that destroyed families.

Mary and C.H. both recognized that while physical attraction had initially drawn them together, the intellectual stimulation provided by their nightly literary and political debates was a new and heady experience neither had ever experienced before. C.H., however, realized that he had to tread lightly when the subject involved some of Mary's most fervent beliefs. For this reason, he was especially careful in 1884 when conversation turned to the Presidential election that year. He, of course, planned to vote for James G. Blaine, the Republican candidate, over the Democrat, Grover Cleveland. Mary supported Samuel Pomeroy representing the American Prohibition Party. C.H. listened quietly and supportively whenever Mary expounded about the many reasons he should vote for her candidate.

All the while, he was silently glad that she did not yet have the vote. He was well aware that those advocating for "the vote" for women were usually also advocating for national prohibition and he rather relished his evening brandy after a long day's work. He thought that the world without champagne would be sad indeed.

• • •

C.H. had often heard the contention of older folks that "bad luck comes in threes" or "accidents come in threes." He had once even witnessed such thinking in play when one of the hotel's wait staff accidently allowed two large soup tureens to slip off a tray and break to pieces upon hitting the dining room floor. The hotel's chef immediately insisted on smashing a third tureen in order to "break the spell" and to insure that the coming "third accident" wasn't a worse catastrophe. C.H. had considered such superstitious antics just more proof of human nature's seemingly inexhaustible well of humorous foibles. However, two more events that followed closely on his first meeting Mary Wooddy would convince the young man that in the case of "life-changing events" there might be something to this "rule of three."

C.H. was well aware that gambling, though illegal in Arkansas, was nevertheless an entertainment staple in Hot Springs. He also knew that his beloved Mary, who lived in the home of Reverend Caldwell, had been influenced by the pastor's many Sunday sermons railing against the twin evils of alcohol and gambling. His church, like that of most Methodist congregations, supported the idea of prohibition, and Mary had embraced membership in their local chapter of the Woman's Christian Temperance Union.

After every meeting she seemed to become more and more fervent in her belief that drinking and gambling destroyed families just as readily as the violence of war. She was horrified to learn at one of those meetings that Frank Flynn, the man who controlled all the illegal gambling in Hot Springs paid regular bribes to the Hot Springs Police Department to prevent any intervention by local law enforcement. Mr. Caldwell included in many a Sunday sermon the warning that the corruption had spread to the Sheriff's Office which was in the pay of a newcomer to the illegal gambling scene in Hot Springs, one Alexander S. Doran.

C.H. thought it was endearing that Mary took such an interest in the happenings of the world around her. Whenever she expounded about what was wrong with the world and what should be done about it, he was struck by how her beauty seemed to always glow brighter when the girl was in the grip of fiery passion. He knew that he was helplessly in love and that the only course of action he could take about it was to get her to marry him. He decided to ask her, just as soon as he had the courage to do it. But, he would have to do it right. The timing and the setting would have to be planned perfectly.

C.H. finally decided to "pop the question" on Mary's birthday since he had already promised to take her to luncheon at a lavish new restaurant a few blocks from the hotel to celebrate. They decided to walk since the weather had created a day of cloudless perfection. C.H. was gratified that the meal they shared was also perfection and he had arranged for a small cake to be delivered to their table. Mary was entranced by this elaborate dessert with its several lit candles, each encircled by a sugar rosebud. C.H. was entranced by her beautiful eyes shining in reflected candlelight. "Happy birthday, dear heart." He murmured and even more softly added, "Would you marry me?"

The startled girl looked up from the cake to see a tiny, open box that held a gold ring with one small, glittering diamond at its center. "Oh, yes," she breathed as he pushed the box closer to her across the table.

"Perfect, perfect, perfect!" C.H. thought happily. "Everything had gone exactly as planned," he congratulated himself, while taking Mary's arm for their slow walk back to the hotel. He could see in a quick sideways glimpse that the girl radiated the pleasure he felt himself.

Then, the lovers were shaken from their private bliss by pistol shots, shouting and a crowd of men running in their direction followed by more shots. C.H. pulled Mary out of the way as some of the men passed them. Then more shots echoed down the street, while the two hurried in the opposite direction toward the hotel's entrance.

By evening everyone in town knew that a major gun battle had taken place on the city's main streets between the two gambling bosses, Flynn and Doran, and some of their gangs of corrupt lawmen. The final body count was reported to be higher than the famous Tombstone fight at the OK Corral in 1881.

Mary insisted on C.H. joining her at Mr. Caldwell's church for a prayer meeting and a sermon denouncing these terrible events. After-wards, the tearful girl turned to C.H. and said, "I promised to marry you, and I will, but only if you promise me we will leave and live far away from this evil town!"

···

Throughout the following weeks, C.H. felt the misery of being stuck between the proverbial rock and a hard place. Any decision he would consider carried with it a formidable downside. He could not lose Mary, but he was just as convinced that his happiness was depen-dent on continuing his life and career in Hot Springs. He was not con-vinced that the place was any worse than other towns. People being what they are, every place would have similar problems. He was sure of that. However, during many heated arguments he had with Mary, he finally realized that he would not be able to convince her to stay and make her home with him in Hot Springs. She would not back down, and he realized that she was tough-minded enough to leave there, with or without him.

Just as he was despairing of finding an answer to this dilemma, Jackson gave him his answer. As the two sat together on a night Mary was attending one of her many WCTU meetings, Jackson sighed and turned to interrupt C.H.'s silent, gloomy brooding over his glass of brandy.

"I have been meaning to talk with you about something, son," he began as the younger man looked up and saw that Jackson held some papers in both hands. "Awhile back I got word that the old planter, my old master, had passed away. It came in a letter, from his wife, Miss Caroline Meacham. She is in terrible distress, because she is afraid that she might be forced to give up her home. Seems that she was told soon after the old man was buried that he had not paid the taxes on their house and on what little land I hadn't already bought from them. Well, sir, this gave me an idea about what I could do to help her and myself in the bargain."

As he could see that he now had his listener's full attention, Jack-son continued. "I wrote back to her with a proposal. I explained to her that it would not be enough for me to pay the taxes for her because in another year, there would just be another round owed to the county. No, what she needs is some way to make money to support herself and keep the house too. I told her I would buy her place and that, with some work, I could turn it into a first class lodging for overnight guests passing through. Folks could enjoy a taste of a bygone era, a time before the war changed everything. I would run it, of course, and I could bring in some of my children to learn the hotel business. We would call it 'Miss Caroline's Place' or 'Miss Caroline Meacham's'. It's an old family name around there and has been connected to that plantation for nearly a hundred years. No one need know that a colored man is the owner which could risk some interest on the part of the little bit of Klan that still makes some trouble around those parts."

"I don't understand," questioned C.H. as the full import of what Jackson was telling him slowly took hold. "Are you saying you're leaving here?"

"Well, I got this letter back from Miss Caroline today. She has spoken to an attorney who is a friend and a Quaker to boot. Both she and I can trust him to keep the sale transfer quiet. He will do the paper work and file it with the state. Then Miss Caroline will have her home and I will have my own hotel! That's a dream I never dared to have before. Really, I have to say that the only one I will miss around here is you, Charlie," Jackson finished.

"It seems cruel that you will always have to pretend that you are just a servant rather than the actual owner of a hotel. At least here people know about your accomplishments. Wouldn't you be better off staying here where people respect what you have made of yourself?" C.H. argued hopefully.

"Respect me? It's not difficult to understand that a young white man like yourself has not fully noticed how the social climate is changing for my people. Oh, right after the war when the only staff in most places like this hotel was colored, it was fine for someone like me to be handing out orders. I can still do that, but only if that staff person is also colored. As more white folks get jobs here, I won't be able to do my job. I just think I am better off leaving before they ask me to leave," Jackson answered as he took a slow drink of his brandy.

While listening to his friend explain a world the younger man did not fully comprehend, it occurred to C.H. that, for some time, Jackson had routinely given any orders directed at white staff to C.H. to deliver to them. He felt sudden, hot shame over his own naiveté and profound sadness that Jackson had been forced to hand the authority of his butler's position over to an upstart kid like himself. Even worse, Jackson had to give his authority to him, not because he had earned it, but only because he had the "right" skin color.

•••

It didn't take C.H. long to realize that Jackson's leaving changed everything. He saw clearly for the first time that it was the people in any place, not the place itself that made it special. This job and this place would be empty without Jackson in it. Once he recognized that truth, he could hardly wait to tell Mary that they would be leaving just as she had hoped they would.

The wedding of Mary Wooddy and Charles Henry McColloch was a small, joyful affair that took place in The Arlington. Only Mary's mother and C.H.'s mother Mattie, brother Will and friend Jackson attended with his father, Zachary, officiating.

The next day three wagons piled high with belongings left Hot Springs. One, driven by Jackson headed south for a new start as the owner/manager of Caroline Meacham's Place near the Arkansas border with Louisiana. For this good man, a life of careful planning and prudent investing would pay off with final years surrounded by family and immersed in fulfilling work.

Two others, one driven by C.H. with Mary beside him and the other driven by his brother, Will, headed northwest. Their first stop would be to deliver Mary's mother to the only home where she had ever felt safe, Rhea's Mill. After that, the three planned to drive on to Council Bluffs where they would sell their wagons and horses, stow belongings in rented boxcar space and board the Union Pacific headed west. It would be at that point that their definite plans would end. They would then be guided only by a dream shared by so many others willing to take a chance on a newer, shining world far from the tired, war-weary place they left behind.

8.
Krann

August Meyer watched from a window of the Baker City railroad depot as his friend and partner, Kurt Krann, paced the length of the outside platform occasionally stopping to mop beads of sweat from his brow or to peer up the tracks for the train that was not due for another hour. It was nearly five years since Kurt had seen his family, and very soon he would finally be able to again throw his arms around his dear father, Joseph, and his children Rosa, Marie and Mathew. This would be a happy moment, but also one mixed with anxiety born from concern that his family was so used to the refined culture of Vienna, Austria that they would find the unruly tumult of an Eastern Oregon mining town appalling.

At least the place had managed to add a thin veneer of civilization since he and August had arrived five years before. Back then, the two men had arrived to a town that was little more than a row of all-night saloons and gambling houses backed by another row of dance halls and brothels that served the appetites of a mostly male populace made up of prospectors, ranchers, cowboys and assorted con-artists. But five years ago, Kurt and August were just two more visitors who dreamed of sharing in the vast wealth waiting in the streams, rivers and under the surrounding hills of Baker City, the supply center for the over one hundred gold mines operating in a sixty mile radius of the town. They had planned to strike it rich and then move on to a more civilized city where they could enjoy their new wealth.

The first item of business for the two partners had been to check on the mine Kurt had purchased stock in. The night before he had carefully removed the stock certificate from the lining of his coat, so they could take it to the small building in town where the record of any mining claim was kept in a locked vault. August would have to do all the talking since Kurt still only knew a few English words and phrases. They planned to go to the claims office early in the morning hoping that they would be alone and could talk privately with the registrar. When they arrived in the morning, they were in luck as they entered an empty office and rang a small bell for service.

August had explained that the mining stock represented by the certificate he pushed forward for the claims officer to examine was actually owned by his partner standing beside him who had purchased the stock shares in Austria. He further explained that he was there to act as a translator since Kurt did not speak much English.

For several tense minutes the man behind the counter spoke not a word as he looked over the certificate with a small magnifying glass. Finally, he sighed and looked at August while avoiding Kurt's anxious stare. "This here's a fake, mister," he said in low tones while sliding the paper back across the counter to August. "We know a lot of these fakes are bein' sold to marks back East. Why, the governor of Pennsylvania wants to make a law against buyin' Oregon gold mine stock 'cause of all the scams! Now I see the hucksters are goin' to Europe, too! Guess they figure that guys like your friend will never actually come here to check it out."

"Well, how do you know it's fake? My friend told me they checked into it and there is a Baisley-Elkhorn mine operating here," countered August.

"Oh yeah. There is. That's true. It's a little ways northeast a here near the town a Sumpter. They're still quartz mining over there. They've sunk several shafts that are still goin' strong for gold. The con artists know that even guys way over in Europe can check to see if a mine is real. But that's not the thing. These here signatures are fakes. No-one by these names has ever been the secretary or president of Baisley-Elkhorn, I guarantee it! I know. I been here a doin' this job for near on twenty years now. But I have a book back here an' I can show you who the real men are who have been officers of that company."

After August had checked the man's book and verified what he had been told, he folded the stock certificate and gave it back to Kurt once they were alone and back on the street.

"What happened in there? What did the man say about my mine and the stock?" questioned Kurt in a loud whisper, though it was clear that he suspected the worst. His greatest fear was that he had been taken. That he had once more been made a fool. Unlike the time he was robbed in New York, this time he would have to tell his father about how stupid he had been.

"It seems." August began slowly and in German. "When you bought your stock, the mining company had great hopes, because they had struck a vein of gold. But that vein had run out right away and those men had to close the mine. Later, the mine was sold to some other fellas who started mining the same spot for other minerals like quartz. They're doing 'quartz mining' now." Finished August who was confident that Kurt would not know or, with his limited English, ever know that "quartz mining" was the miners' term for the underground mining of gold-bearing quartz deposits.

"You mean I didn't buy a fake? I wasn't fooled?"

"No, no you weren't fooled." August answered softly as Kurt began to visibly relax. "You just had bad luck with that investment. It happens all the time, and it can happen to anybody. Now, I think we need to put our contest money to work on a new investment that we can work together!"

. . .

In the days that followed, August explained to Kurt how they would proceed in their search for golden riches. Since there was only the two of them, they would stick to simple "placer" or above-ground methods of separating gold from gravel. August further explained that his past experience with underground hard rock mining had convinced him that he never again wanted anything to do with it.

He told Kurt that he had seen men lose a hand, a leg or even killed from a poorly loaded charge. And then there were the frequent cave-ins because owners hired green men who did not know how to properly place timber. Air quality underground was another constant danger. The new carbide lamps that had replaced candles used for lighting did not give the miners warning as did a flickering candle when oxygen content in the air was dangerously low. The carbide lamps continued to burn long after a man was dead from affixation. The worst thing was what happened to a man after a lifetime in the mines breathing silicon laden dust. These razor sharp particles lodged in a man's lungs and eventually caused a horrendous death. A man dying from silicosis would actually cough up pieces of his own lungs in his last days. August was happy to confine the use of his hard rock skills to winning contests that offered a large purse and to do all his actual gold mining above ground in the fresh air.

He told Kurt that they would start investigating areas reported through word of mouth to be yielding gold. According to the General Mining Law, they could pay a $100 holding fee for an area to be tested. If they made a mineral discovery, they could make a $500 investment for development and actually buy the land for $2.50 an acre. Initially, they would start close to town and investigate areas like Griffin Gulch on Elk Creek.

Once their camp site was set up, August began teaching Kurt simple panning and rocker methods for extracting gold from dirt near the creek. August first showed Kurt how to use a shallow pan into which river gravel was poured along with a scoop of clear water. The trick then was to very carefully swirl the mixture allowing the water and light material to spill over the side of the pan leaving behind heavier gold nuggets or gold dust at the bottom of the pan. They would also employ a rocker which was a transportable, rectangular wooden box set at a downward angle with a sieve at the top and mounted on a rocking mechanism. Dirt and rock was to be dumped into the top, followed by a bucket of water, then the mixture was rocked by hand. The big rocks were caught in the sieve and heavy gold fell to the bottom of the box. August suggested that they employ both methods because they had different advantages. The rocker could process more material than a pan, but only the pan would be able to trap the smallest particles of gold called "flour."

The two men worked for a year at Griffin Gulch where they did find some gold remaining from an earlier gold rush. August finally decided that they would be better off moving farther from town to Cracker Creek where placers had reported better results. Their results were so much better that they decided to invest in a more elaborate "long tom" system featuring a downward slanted 20 foot long trough where at least two men would shovel rocks and gravel into the top and fast moving water from the creek would move the material along while another man would throw out the bigger rocks. Twice a day, the sand caught at the bottom of the box would be removed and panned.

The new process required at least three or four men, so August went to the encampment of Chinese miners in the nearby mining town of Granite. He explained to Kurt that the Chinese were skilled at above-ground mining techniques, therefore, they would not need instruction which would be quite impossible given their obvious language barrier. He added that he preferred working with the Chinese, because they were very rugged, hard workers, and unlike other miners, could be trusted to show up sober. Additionally, these workers were highly motivated to keep their jobs and even continue working claims during those times when gold was scarce, since they all worked to send money back to families in China. For them, changing jobs as often as white miners frequently did was unthinkable because such behavior might mean hardship for loved ones back home.

August had returned from Granite with two Chinese men who had been introduced by their agent as "Lo" and "Ping." Neither spoke a word of English, but were exactly as August had described. They needed no direction and appeared to be eager self-starters and tireless workers used to long hours of hard labor. They also proved to be trustworthy and could be relied on to guard the claim when August and Kurt had to go into town for supplies.

...

Five years later, Kurt received word from his father that it was high time for them to be reunited as a family. Joseph explained in his letter that he was too old to run the brickyard alone and so had sold the lease and the factory for a goodly sum. He also wrote that he had already bought passage for himself and the children, and they would all arrive by rail within the month.

Kurt felt confident that his father would be impressed by his mining success which would be proven by his swelling bank account. He was less sure that Baker City would live up to the standards of a cultured man like Joseph.

Thankfully, Baker City had grown beyond being just another squalid mining town. In fact, the city had completed a building project that transformed the central commercial district to replace the ramshackle, wooden buildings which had been lost to a catastrophic fire. This fire had wiped out a saloon, a general store, a butcher shop, jewelry store and a hotel. By 1895, most of Main Street was lined with similar multi-story stone buildings housing all the diverse businesses a stable citizenry requires. The town had six newspapers, several hotels, restaurants, department stores, groceries, druggists, and fine ladies and men's specialty shops. Kurt was especially glad that these shops included several milliners who provided the creative embellishment that no woman would think of leaving home without. His own daughter, Rosa, had written to him that she was beginning to work after school for one of Vienna's finest hat makers, Frau Mannheim, who had told her that she had artistic talent.

As Baker City slowly changed from a vulgar mining camp to become a more respectable place suitable for men with families, its habitants saw to it that schools and churches were built. Kurt knew that his family's spiritual needs would be met by the town's Catholic Church which ran two parochial schools and was in the midst of planning to build a cathedral.

• • •

Kurt mentally ticked off the structures that his family would see along the wide boulevard that led to their rented house. Among them were particular buildings that he knew would help make a good first impression. There was Carl Adler's Crystal Palace marked by its large pedestal clock rising over a story high on the outer edge of the sidewalk where one could purchase luxuries such as fine musical instruments, china, cut glass goblets, and a range of diamond jewelry. Farther north, the family was sure to notice the three story Heilners Department Store that was crowned with a fabulous cupola and the commanding

First National Bank building right next to it. Across the street and a block beyond the bank he would point out the distinctive tower decorated with huge granite lion heads belonging to the new Warshauer Hotel. Kurt planned to direct their attention to these edifices and away from the nearby mansion that was Jenny Duffy's bordello.

Kurt's reverie was interrupted by a loud whistle that announced that the train would soon pull into the station. With that, August joined his friend on the platform but stood a few steps back to wait until the family had finished with their initial greetings. As the many passengers began to leave the rail carriage, Kurt nervously watched on tiptoe until he finally spotted his father and a young man alight from the car then turn to offer a helping hand to a lovely, young woman beautifully attired in a fashionable traveling suit and matching hat set at a becoming angle atop a lustrous pile of dark, well-coifed curls. As she stepped onto the platform the woman looked up to see Kurt and with a wide grin, called "Papa, oh Papa!" while running with arms open in his direction then stopped when she saw Kurt's startled look of total confusion.

"Why father! You do not recognize me. I'm Rosa!" cried the laughing girl.

"Rosa! You are all grown. I, I did hardly recognize you," stammered Kurt as the girl flew into his arms.

"Then you probably don't recognize Mathew, either" called a smiling Joseph as he approached with a tall young man at his side. "Five years is a long time for children. It is certainly enough time for them to grow up!"

Kurt's first confusion quickly gave way to overwhelming emotion as the group hugged and kissed. He almost forgot August standing some feet away, but finally remembered his manners and turned to introduce his friend. "But, where is Marie?" he wondered after realizing that someone was missing.

"Oh, you know Marie. She is probably still checking to make sure we got off with all our belongings. Truly, if she didn't take care of all of us, we would probably have lost most of our things along the way here. We would have left a trail all the way back to New York!" laughed Rosa. "There she is and with Mathew's sweater!"

The group turned at once to see another young woman standing in the coach doorway. Kurt stared at the girl with open mouth. He had almost forgotten how his older daughter's flawless, porcelain complexion seemed always to glow with some inner light and how her white blonde hair could shine as it was now when touched by sunlight. He caught his breath when he realized that on the high lace collar of her silk blouse, she was wearing her mother's cameo broach.

As Mathew took his sister's offered hand to help her down the narrow steps, Kurt heard August behind him mutter under his breath, "wonderschoner Engel." The family had always jokingly called Marie "the Dresden doll", but now Kurt silently agreed with his friend. The girl did indeed look more like a beautiful angel.

...

By the next year, the Krann family had settled into a routine that defined the roles each needed to assume in order to live comfortably in their new home. The men, Kurt and August, continued to travel the miles into the mountains where they worked their claim all week and returned to the family's rented house in town on the weekends. Mathew Krann, at fourteen years, was too young yet to go with them to the claim, and it was determined that he should be enrolled in the Catholic school to continue his interrupted education. His two sisters, Marie and Rosa, worked to set up house; arranging their new furnishings, cleaning and polishing everything in the house that they determined had long been neglected by prior tenants. Grandfather Joseph accompanied the women whenever they needed to go into town to provide male protection in a place where unescorted women were usually employed in one of the many brothels.

Once the house was in order, Marie took over most of the usual duties of an Austrian "Hausfrau", for she enjoyed cooking elaborate meals, and even enjoyed doing the mundane shopping, cleaning and laundry tasks necessary to maintain a smoothly running home-life.

Rosa, for her part, had never enjoyed such a homebound existence. She longed for the excitement of city life left behind in Vienna. Rosa very much missed working in Frau Mannheim's fine millinery shop where her artistic talents for creating beautiful hats had been so appreciated by her employer and by the shop's fashionable clientele.

Joseph could not help but notice that whenever someone mentioned a need to go into town, Rosa was quick to volunteer. Since he always accompanied her, Joseph also noticed how his granddaughter lingered in front of any storefront window display of women's fashion, especially slowing for any milliner's window.

On one such outing, Rosa turned away from a store window with a heavy sigh, "The hats here are so old fashioned. Look at that bonnet! They haven't seen a 'Bavolette' like that in Vienna since the 1860s!" the girl whispered in disgust while pointing out the ribbon frill at the back of the bonnet meant to modestly cover a woman's bare neck. "Why really, these hats are divided into social classes! See, the ones with the big floppy brims covered with ribbons, feathers, flowers and anything else it seems someone found on the cutting room floor! I see those hats on the women who walk in pairs and only come out of the buildings over there", she waved a hand indicating the side of the street where two story saloons usually housed an upstairs 'bawdy parlor'.

"Then, there are these awful bonnets!" she continued. "Most are plain as bread, all straw and no grace. Like little straw helmets! And they're all so matronly! The only reason a woman would wear one is so no-one would take her for a prostitute. It certainly wouldn't be to look pretty," she finished in a lower tone.

"It is evident that the women of this town need you to save them from fashion ruin, Rosa." Joseph chuckled. "Seriously, you should inquire about a position in one of the better shops. Most of the merchants in the bigger stores here, like Baer Dry Goods, the Heilner-Neuberger Department Store or Adler's Crystal Palace, are Jewish men from Germany who still speak the language. I have spoken with many of them, and I find them very outgoing and friendly. I am sure they would be glad to help you."

Within the week, Joseph's inquiries yielded Rosa an interview with the town's leading milliner, Frau Weber, a German-speaking lady from Catholic Bavaria. It had been Carl Adler's wife, Laura, who had arranged this. She had lost a dear sister to illness. Since that girl was also named "Rosa" she was eager to help another Rosa.

Frau Weber was a hard-headed businesswoman who had a reputation to protect, so when Rosa presented herself, she insisted on testing the girl's level of hat-making skill. She handed Rosa a large piece of moss green velvet and showed her into a back workroom, well stocked with tools and trimmings. The woman instructed the girl to make a hat and have it finished by closing time. Rosa returned in half the allotted time carrying her creation which she shyly presented.

Frau Weber sternly and silently inspected the hat. She saw immediately that this was unlike any hat sold anywhere in Baker City. Rosa had folded the lovely velvet into narrow pleats which were tacked down by perfect and nearly invisible stitching on the underside. This gave the hat some height but allowed it to softly and lightly cover a woman's hair without matting it down. She had fashioned a band covered with moss-green ribbon with a large flat bow at the side which was embellished by a fanciful, tiny fan made from a length of cream colored lace stiffened by glue and folded into shape. The fan was pinned on the ribbon by a row of small, faux pearl buttons. Without being told to, Rosa turned to a large wall mirror and put the hat on her own head, carefully placing it at a flattering angle so that her own curls could peek out from the pretty band. As she slowly turned toward Frau Weber, this business woman who rarely gave her employees compliments, clapped her hands exclaiming "Wunderbar! Marvelous!" as though she had just enjoyed a great opera. "Liebchen, please agree to start tomorrow!"

• • •

While Rosa was finally and happily immersed in daily exercise of her considerable artistic talent, her sister, Marie, enjoyed continuing in the role she had taken after her mother's untimely death. The girl was a born nurturer and loved doing all the little things that make a house warm and comfortable for its lucky inhabitants. She was an adept seamstress and had magically produced lovely furniture coverings, decorative pillows and draperies at her little treadle machine which had transformed their tired, drab rental house into what her father called "a true home" and August Meyer, with his usual bombast, dubbed " an amazing showplace!"

However, it was in the kitchen that Marie truly excelled. She loved cooking and had learned from her mother the culinary secrets to producing all the marvelous dishes that grace the best German tables. Of course, Joseph, Kurt and Mathew were used to such cooking and had no way of knowing how heavenly Marie's fork tender roasts, crisp fried potato pancakes and schnitzels, cloud-light dumplings, sweet-tart red cabbage and buttery stollens would taste to a man like August raised on an unvaried diet of boiled chicken, boiled potatoes and cornbread. It is true that his parents were first generation German immigrants, but his mother was a decidedly uninspired cook who worked hard all day as a laundress and wanted only to throw together the same white and yellow fare every evening and be done with it. For August, every bite of every meal was a treat worthy of high praise. Though Marie found his constant exclamations of pleasure somewhat embarrassing, she was also pleased and missed this show of appreciation whenever he was not present.

What most pleased Marie was August's evident interest in the culinary craft that she herself so loved. When it was clear to both of them that the other men preferred to hear August tell of his war time exploits or about his experiences logging the Wisconsin forests rather than hear an in-depth explanation of how to best prepare sauerbraten with noodles, August began to visit the kitchen before meals to watch as Marie prepared what he considered to be wondrous miracles of taste. He became, in effect, her sous chef happily chopping and stirring as she directed.

Marie was not the only Krann who was intrigued by August. Mathew had become smitten with a serious case of hero worship. The boy had only known men like his father and grandfather who sat all day hunched over a desk in some tiny office. Mathew had always been a mediocre student in school but had excelled in any sport. Most days he would stare, unseeing at his books while counting the hours when he was released from that boredom to run to the soccer field. For him, August was a revelation, a man whose formidable, physical skills had brought him a continuous livelihood as well as fantastic adventure. Mathew realized for the first time in his young life, that one did not have to be a scholar to succeed and that he, himself, possessed special talents that would serve him well in this new home.

...

By the end of the second year in Baker City, it seemed to Joseph

Krann that everyone in his family had found a comfortable place in the fabric of their new home. Both Rosa and Marie loved their work and felt a sense of accomplishment at the end of every day. His son, Kurt, had become a very different and much happier person from the sad and confused man who had left Vienna six years prior. He even looked different. Where he had once been pale and thin with a rather timid air about him, he had developed a miner's muscular physique and now walked with the confidence of a man who had proven to himself that he had what it takes to survive the many challenges of the American frontier.

Though his family was contented, Joseph feared that more was needed to ensure their futures. When they lived in Vienna, he had never worried what would happen when he passed on. They had the brickyard and, by law, this business could be passed indefinitely from father to son. Joseph was a businessman who believed in the impor- tance of investing in the future. They now lived in the epicenter of an economic boom, and they had money from their brick business to put into play. However, he knew he had to proceed with caution and fully research any investment opportunity.

The family had already lost money investing in mining, and though Baker City was widely known as the "Queen City of Mines," Joseph decided to look into other areas of economic activity. Certainly, by 1900, the merchants who owned the many downtown stores had be- come Baker City's wealthy civic leaders. In addition, money was to be made in the timber needed for the massive amount of building tak- ing place and in raising the cattle and crops to feed the rapidly grow- ing populace. It was evident that while most men were employed in mining for gold, the few who provided for people's basic needs had and would continue to prosper. Joseph was convinced that these busi- nesses would provide far more prudent investment opportunities than would mining. Yet, events soon proved that even a man as wise and careful as Joseph Krann could fall victim to gold's siren song promising untold riches.

...

One summer weekend when Kurt and August returned to the

Krann home from working their placer claim, Joseph waited in the parlor for the two to finish washing up. Both men first noticed an undercurrent of impatient excitement in the older man when he abruptly stopped August on his usual immediate trip to the kitchen in order to help Marie prepare that evening's culinary treats.

"I have something extraordinary to show the both of you." He explained as he waved them to take seats around a central table. " I have received this correspondence from my old friend, Franz Schneider. He is a man I went to university with in Vienna and now lives in New York. Kurt, he is the man who was to meet you when you first arrived there. Of course, you never actually met him, because he was delayed that day, and by the time he arrived on the dock, you had apparently already procured a ride to the railroad on your own."

Joseph did not notice Kurt's suddenly flushed face at remembering his foolish behavior on the dock that day. Nor did he notice August's fleeting smile. Instead he continued, "The children and I stayed for a few days with Herr Schneider in his lovely home when we first landed in New York. At that time, my friend expressed some interest in our new adventure. As a savvy businessman, he was especially interested in the financial opportunities that have opened up in the Western United States."

"Why is it that you mention this man?" asked Kurt. August could not suppress a wider smile of amusement since Kurt's question came out as an odd, whispered croak.

"It is to explain why I have just today received this packet from Herr Schneider who is inquiring about a very interesting business opportunity for us to look into for him, and also for ourselves, I might add!" Joseph continued as he opened the large envelop he had set on the table before them.

"First, I want you both to read this news article from the town of Bourne that I understand is only a few miles north of Sumpter and only a day's journey from here. You will see that it tells of an entrepreneur, F. Wallace White, who has formed a corporation to buy up the lode mines in the Bourne area. This newspaper is the local Bourne paper and they report that these mines have already been producing well for individual prospectors for many years, but individuals can't afford the new technologies such as stamp milling that can produce millions. In fact, according to this article, he has already tripled gold production in the area with just one stamp mill! He needs investors in order to finish buying up properties and for building more stamp mills like the very productive mills owned by corporations in the Sumpter area. His operation should easily return handsome profits to those who buy stock. This corporation has offices in New York City and London and is selling stock on the exchanges in London, New York, Boston, Chicago and Salt Lake City to pay for the properties and the stamp mill. Herr Schneider also sent this with the newspaper." Joseph added with evident enthusiasm, as he withdrew a slick, gilt-edged prospectus from the packet and laid it out on the table for Kurt and August to inspect.

"I was not aware that all this was going on in Bourne which is not far from our claim," said August after reading the material Joseph had presented. "But, I have not been personally interested in lode mining, and Kurt and I never go to Bourne. It is Sumpter where we take our gold to be weighed and where we get our supplies. I thought that there are only a few hundred miners who still live in Bourne. Most have moved up the hill to Granite, I was told. But, things can change quickly in the mining business. Whenever there is some new find, everyone rushes to where the action is to try to cash in too. This is interesting, and it would not be hard for all of us to personally check it out."

• • •

A week later, August and Kurt returned to the Baker City house with a plan to investigate F. Wallace White and the situation in Bourne. Their first step would be to have Herr Schneider send a telegram from New York to Mr. White explaining that three very wealthy investors from Austria were touring the West and had expressed an interest in mining and, in particular, in the Sampson Company Ltd., the name of White's Bourne-based operation. The telegram also stated that they would arrive in Baker City in a week's time and asked for an appointment to visit with White in Bourne.

"It is important that we remain skeptical about this man and his promises." August warned, " If he is dishonest, he will have worked out ways to cleverly hide his deceit and to appear to be honest and successful. We must employ the same methods and hide our true identities. If we appear to be gullible marks who naively expect business on the Western frontier to operate much as it does in the great cities of Europe, he may let down his guard enough for us to see through his ploys."

By the end of the next week, the three men received word from Herr Schneider that Mr. White was anxious to meet them and have them for dinner at his home in Bourne with a tour of his mining operation. Of course, it was easy for Joseph and Kurt to play the part of Europeans on tour. All they had to do was to take their good suits from the closet to wear. Even Mathew, who begged to go along on this adventure, had the correct outfit to put on for the occasion. For August, the transformation took a little more effort.

In the morning of the Bourne appointment, Marie stood in her kitchen quietly peeling apples for one of her strudels. She sensed movement behind her and a shadow over her worktable and turned with a startled gasp to see a well-dressed gentleman standing in the kitchen doorway.

"Are you here to see my grandfather?" she asked the stranger who answered with a shake of his head. "How did you get in, then?" she asked with growing trepidation.

"The same way I always do, dear girl. With my key."

"Herr Meyer?" Marie whispered, gaping in total wonder at the man in a fashionable suit and cutaway jacket, vest and holding a black, felt bowler hat in gloved hands. Gone was the wild hair, trademark bushy sideburns and over-long mustaches that had been expertly shaved, trimmed and styled by a talented barber. "You, you are so … so handsome!" whispered the girl.

"I thought I looked pretty good, before," August joked.

"Oh no, this is so much better! Oh my! That was so rude of me! I, I am so sorry to have said such a thing," stammered the girl in confused embarrassment.

"I may never get over it. I may just have to keep this look," teased August with a laugh as he crossed the room to give the girl a consolatory hug.

As he began to pull away, Marie encircled his waist with one thin arm and looked him square in eyes. He stared mesmerized into those pools of blue, while the girl laid one soft, delicate hand on his cheek and murmured, "To me, you have always been beautiful." Then, she turned shyly away to once again take up her knife and apple as August silently floated out of the room.

• • •

That afternoon, the men assembled in the front parlor for their trip to Bourne. August was to give them their final instructions. "Vee vill now begin zee trip," he began in English with a heavy German accent, making the usual substitutions and expertly rolling his "r" sound as do Germans who first learn the language. Mathew, who had attended enough American schooling to know English, erupted in hearty laughter.

"Nein! You vill nicht do zis!" August shouted at the boy who immediately reddened and chocked off his laughter. "Matt, we must convince this man, White, that we are who we present ourselves to be." He said more softly and in German so everyone would understand. "This will be easy for your grandfather and for your father who speak little English and for whom it will be natural to constantly look to me, their translator, to tell them what White says in English. I will be speaking with this accent to show him I am unused to speaking in English. This will add to his comfort with us as a bunch of rich foreigners who know nothing about mines and mining, but are greedy enough to jump in with little proof that this is a good investment. If he is for real, there will be plenty of proof that this is, in fact, a good investment. But, if he is a huckster, there will be proof of that too, especially if he lets down his guard due to his belief in our ignorance."

"I, I understand. I will say nothing while we are there just in case I slip up and say something that will wise him up to us. I promise," Matt vowed, with head hanging.

"I know you to be a man of your word, Matt." August agreed patting the boy on his slumped shoulder, "Now, I only have to worry about your father slipping up!" he added with a wide grin.

• • •

The home of F. Wallace White outside the hamlet of Bourne was no mere house. It was an impressive structure standing high above the road atop row upon row of terraced gardens that was more "Versailles" than "Eastern Oregon."

The bell was answered by a uniformed maid-servant who showed the men down a wide carpeted hallway and into an elegant living room filled with softly upholstered furnishings, flanked by polished side tables and anchored by a massive stone fireplace where a huge log burned brightly behind a pair of brass, lion-head andirons. To the right of the fireplace was a staircase that curved up six feet to an open landing where the men could see a long dining table lit by soft candlelight from a glittering, overhead crystal chandelier.

"Welcome, welcome friends!" boomed a voice from above, as a man dressed in soft felt trousers, cream silk shirt and a red satin smoking jacket appeared above and then stepped down the stairway to their level. August, who was struggling not to show how impressed he was by these opulent surroundings, stole a sideways glance at the others before he turned to make the introductions in English. He was relieved that the three Kranns were so used to living in a fine house, themselves, that their demeanor was only that of polite gentility. As Joseph was first to be introduced, White stepped forward to shake hands but quickly withdrew the gesture as the older man made a deep bow. The other two made the same gesture in turn.

"Good touch. Worthy of Austrian nobility!" thought August.

"Gentlemen," White nearly shouted at the group. "I propose that we enjoy some fine Kentucky whiskey by the fire and get to know one another. And then, while we still have the light, I want to show you what you came to see. I want to show you the road to yellow riches beyond your every dream!"

...

August had to admit that the man gave quite a show. The house, the hospitality, White's own engaging affect. It was hard to resist and hard to remain neutrally skeptical. It was also evident that the Kranns were actually impressed by the tour of operations made by open carriage to see White's various holdings.

They were shown one gaping mineshaft after another, each guarded by armed men. White also took the group to a hill down which they could see a large stamp mill building connected to a mine above by a tramway of inch-thick cable where there hung 200 buckets. White explained that each bucket had the capacity to hold 250 pounds of gold-bearing rock to be crushed so that the ore could be extracted and later turned into bullion. At this point, White made a move that August saw as stellar salesmanship. He brought out a bar of solid gold for the men to pass around, so that each could hold it briefly, just long enough to catch a bad case of "gold fever."

Over drinks and dinner, F. Wallace White regaled the men with stories of his many past business dealings and successes in Colorado and California. He talked constantly, ate little and drank copious amounts of wine, pausing only to wave an arm in the direction where Joseph and Kurt were seated across from August and Mathew and bellow, "Tell them! Tell them!"

After each translation, both Joseph and Kurt would nod eagerly laughing and making congratulatory comments to each other in German about how lucky they were to meet this wonderful American businessman. Though August doubted that White understood their words, their expressions of eager acceptance were entirely convincing.

They enjoyed after-dinner brandy again by the fire where White gave each of them another copy of the prospectus, and then showed them regretfully to the door so that they could make the trip back to Baker City before it got too late.

"The moon is full and bright tonight which will make your trip back so much easier!" he announced, waving them on as their buggy traveled down the hill to the road below and turned right in the direction of Baker City.

After a short way, August stopped the horses and turned them around. "I think it would be wise for us to spend the night at the hotel in Bourne rather than go back tonight. We'll head back tomorrow morning after breakfast when it's light."

After the Krann men got their room keys and retired to the upper floors of the small hotel on the only road running through Bourne, August stayed to talk with the desk clerk. As the two made banal pleasantries, the door opened with a bell signal that made both men turn to see a woman begin to enter and, then with a startled look, back out the door and rush away.

"That's funny. Was it something I said?" asked August of the amiable clerk. "Say, isn't that the maid who works over at the F. Wallace White's house?"

"Naw, she's no maid. Why that's Moll Brandt. She's the German woman who runs the cat house over yonder. Comes in ever' night around now for a spell to chew the fat and share a whiskey away from work. Why'd ya think she was someone's maid?" asked the man.

"I was just over there for dinner and thought the maid over there looked a lot like that woman."

"Why was you guys there for dinner? You all some news reporters or somethin'?"

"Why do you ask?"

"Cause of him bein' the owner of our newspaper. That's why. He's a real nice fella for a rich guy." The man ran on, glad for the company. "He don't make no money with that little ole paper, so folks figure he inherited a fortune to afford that house a his. But, he's no smart business fella, that's for sure. Why, he's been buyin' up all the played out mines 'round here an' also that run down North Pole stamp mill. A big waste a money. I'd say. If it weren't for him throwin' his dough around, this place would be a ghost town by now. All the regular miners already moved on to Sumpter or Granite where the gold action really is."

The next morning over breakfast, August told the men of the run-in with the "maid" and the very interesting conversation with the desk clerk. Then, he went on to explain that his subsequent trip to the outside privy before bed was even more informative.

"How was a trip to the privy more informative?" Kurt wanted to know.

"Well, because of this. It was part of a pile of old newspapers put out for guests of that particular privy to use for their, ya know, 'comfort'" August answered with a wink, as he spread out the front page of the newspaper. "Note the date." He added, thumping the date at the top of the page. "It's the same date as the Bourne newspaper Joseph got from his friend in New York. Also, note that this one has no mention of all the fabulous gold strikes being made by the Sampson Company Ltd. right here in Bourne. It does mention a local turkey shoot and a list of Bourne citizens that were arrested for drunk and disorderly conduct over in Sumpter. Wouldn't the good citizens of Bourne think that all the gold strikes going on around here are newsworthy? The clerk also told me that it is our friend and host, F. Wallace himself who runs this paper. Looks like he prints up two different ones every day. One is for the locals and one is for rich marks out of state!"

"Too bad, that guy really had me going for awhile." Kurt put in with a sigh.

"I was also impressed with his operation." Joseph nodded. "But now that I think about it, nothing was really happening over there. Guess that's why he wanted to entertain us in the evening, so we would assume that it was just 'after hours' quiet," Joseph realized. "August, I owe you a debt of gratitude. If it were not for your detective work, I would have really been taken in! I'll never be able to repay you for protecting my life's savings."

"Repay me?" August questioned as the group stood to leave the restaurant. "Actually, now that you mention it, I do want you and Kurt to consider something that has been on my mind. I want you to consider allowing me to ask Marie to be my wife," he said as he handed their hats to each dumbfounded man.

9.
McColloch

C.H. and his new bride did not enjoy a private honeymoon until their visit to Rhea's Mill where Mary's mother was welcomed back into her birth family home with a great show of familial love and celebration. Both C.H. and Will were impressed by the prosperous little township that had been founded by Mary's uncle who was her mother's brother, William H. Rhea. William had died in 1884, leaving his widow Elizabeth and son Robert, Mary's cousin, to run the three stores, mill and several farms surrounding the hamlet.

Before the war, William Rhea had supplied the region with goods imported by wagon from St. Louis, New York and Philadelphia. His merchant stores were always well stocked with shoes, glassware, household items, drugs, clothing, hardware, and dry goods needed by the citizenry of nearby Fayetteville and by the farmers of the area. In addition, he offered such luxuries as fine wine, jewelry and firearms which were quickly sold, adding to his personal wealth.

When the war came to northwestern Arkansas, Rhea's stores were frequently hit by the foraging Union armies that looted the towns there. However, Union commanders did not order their troops to burn Rhea's buildings as they usually did. The family's salvation rested with their huge grist mill where grain could be ground into flour to feed the troops whenever supplies ran low.

From 1862 until the end of the war, federal troops foraged goods from Rhea's property. Every time he was hit, Rhea recorded in a ledger the amount of material that was taken by the men, including goods stolen by entire regiments after the major battles at Prairie Grove and Pea Ridge. When the conflict finally ended, Rhea sued the federal government for damages. Supported by the proof in his ledger, he was awarded the full amount he had recorded as a loss. Because of William Rhea's cool-headed business acumen, Rhea's Mill became a major commercial center and played an important role in the post-war revitalization of Washington County, Arkansas.

...

When they first arrived and Mary's mother explained to Elizabeth Rhea that her daughter and C.H. had only been married a few days, the newlyweds were shown to a lovely chalet detached from the large family home. William had built it to house dignitaries who regularly visited him from Little Rock and even Washington D.C.

The couple was entranced by the opulence of the chalet with its fine furnishings, artwork, leaded windows and a brightly burning fire in the hearth of a great stone fireplace. A beautiful canopied bed stood at the room's center. It had been made with fresh linens and a creamy satin coverlet. When she saw it, Mary turned to C.H. with eyes full of tears. "Now you see what comforts my father refused his family to enjoy!"

"Your father was a proud man. He must have felt it was his duty to provide for his own family", C.H. tried to console her.

But she shook him off as he attempted to put his arms around her shoulders, "Well, pride goeth before a fall!" she scoffed with a hoarse, humorless laugh. "His precious pride cost my father his wife's sanity and his daughter's love! In the end, it even cost him his life! Wherever he is now, I hope he's satisfied!", the girl continued to rail between clenched teeth.

Then, as quickly as Mary's fury had begun, it was over, and she wilted into her husband's embrace. "I love you, Charles. I love you most because you will never be a man like that. You always seem to know what I need and always try to provide it. For most of my life, I thought all men were the same. All like my father. But you are truly different. I can really trust you with my heart and I trust that you will always make me happy!"

As glad as he was that Mary had shaken off her anger, C.H. felt a small twinge of foreboding. It seemed to him that no one was able to provide everything someone else needs and that the individual really needs to provide their own happiness.

As the days passed at Rhea's Mill, the three travelers were in no rush to leave that idyllic place made especially lovely by an unusually soft Arkansas spring season. Mary was amazed at the sudden change in her own usually dour mother. She could not remember when she had last seen her mother smile, and she was sure she had never heard her mother laugh. Since coming back to her family home, it was like the woman had been released from an emotional prison, where she had served a long sentence in dark, fearful depression. Mary noticed that her mother, who had only ventured beyond the confines of her bedroom for meals in Rev. Caldwell's house, was suddenly taking daily walks into the meadows and along the forest paths near the Rhea hamlet. The old woman would later report with evident pleasure about all she saw and experienced on these ramblings.

...

C.H. and Will enjoyed the company of Robert Rhea who had taken over running the family's many enterprises after his father's death. The two younger men were eager to learn all they could about what is required to be successful as a merchant, since they entertained a partially formed notion that they would go into business together as shopkeepers in some newly established western town. Robert enjoyed opening his father's ledger so C.H. and Will could see exactly how important it is for any business to keep careful account of all profits and losses.

Besides explaining the mechanics of running a business, Robert also shared his inside knowledge of Arkansas politics with C.H. and Will.

"My father learned just how important it is for any man in business to understand the political climate of the times," Robert explained to his eager listeners. "He knew that soon after the war ended the Republican leadership wanted to promote national unity and that is why they objected to the idea of any reconstruction laws meant to punish the South. He also figured that it was likely that the radical crowd would get their way sooner or later. That is why he pressed Washington very soon after the conflict ended and received just compensation for all the Union foraging that went on. If he'd waited even a few months he might not have gotten anything!"

Robert also introduced C.H. and Will to business friends who had many dealings with Little Rock. One of these visitors explained to the two young men how much of the economic and social change that took place with emancipation and the end of the war meant life improved for both black and white urbanites.

"Living in Hot Springs you probably saw that for yourselves. For the rural folks, the picture hasn't been that pretty," Robert's associate noted. "Most of the farms are now run by landless tenants. These 'croppers' only get a small share of the profits from any farm and that share has steadily decreased with economic pressures from white landlords in the form of new crop liens and the use of free convict labor that cuts into the tenants' pay. The thing folks in the cities don't always realize is that more than half of these sharecroppers are white. In their eyes, they not only returned from war to grinding poverty, but even their social position has slipped below that of men who were former slaves! They see this as completely intolerable. Many have taken to criminal behavior and violent resistance to social change typical of the Ku Klux Klan. This group is also actively involved in politics and is already putting huge pressure on Little Rock and the Democrats in power now."

At this point, the business man's voice rose with very obvious and deeply felt anger. "Unfortunately, the craven pols in the state capital do not want to do the hard work it takes to lift all economic and social boats. No! They only have plans meant to undercut black advancement. They use the promise of "Jim Crow" racial segregation laws and laws to limit black voting. Why, they are even planning to institute a 'white primary' law to bar blacks from voting at all in any Democratic primary. All this to make a show of restoring the old prewar caste lines in the hopes of appeasing their white constituents and keep them from voting for Republicans or a third party. They're too lazy or too stupid to understand that when you take away the ability of a huge part of the population to contribute to the public and economic good of the state, you end up hurting everyone!"

Even this politically astute businessman could not have predicted the devastating effect new laws segregating the races along with measures aimed at limiting black voting rights would have on black political participation in Arkansas. It would be a short three years until black politicians were swept from most local and county offices, and another eighty years before a single black lawmaker would again serve in the Arkansas legislature.

Later, when he had the time to think over what Robert and his friend had said about the future of Arkansas, C.H. connected it to what Jackson had told him about his awareness of the problems that most probably lay ahead for a black man in his high profile "Butler's" position at the hotel. Jackson had evidently been very wise to leave Hot Springs when he did. C.H. also realized that Robert was right. A man ignores the political and social climate of wherever he lives at his peril.

. . .

When C.H., Mary and Will finally took their leave from Rhea's Mill, they headed west into Oklahoma Indian Territory. Will had taken a job with the Singer Sewing Company to sell their sewing machines on commission to the enterprising tribes living in the region. They would move slowly from village to village demonstrating the wonders of this technology and take orders to send back to Singer's main office. They also had permission to forge new sales territory farther west as they traveled toward California, the place where most in the U. S. considered to be the true "land of opportunity."

Will had looked forward to travel with his younger brother, because C.H.'s outgoing personality and ability to see humor in most situations along with his brother's constant interest in learning more about the world had always made him very good company.

However, Will had failed to factor in the effect his brother's new marriage might have on C.H. who suddenly seemed to be consumed by marital bliss and completely focused on Mary. Will, himself, was married with a child, but had left them in comfort back in Hot Springs with the promise of sending for them once he was settled somewhere. He did not remember ever behaving like his brother even when he had been courting.

All day, as they jogged along the rough Oklahoma roads, C.H. and Mary sat in their wagon with their heads together talking in whispers and constantly touching one another as though, if they did not hold onto a hand or an arm, the other might suddenly disappear in a puff of smoke. Will was closed out of their little world, which made for boring travel and also made him a bit nauseous.

Evenings were even worse, since the happy couple continued to communicate in low tones, private jokes and long looks into each other's eyes. Will could not know that his travel companions had discovered in each other a physical passion that surprised them both and seemed to be growing with each night together.

Like most women raised with a mix of Puritanical and Victorian admonishments about how "nice" women were supposed to feel and behave even in a marriage, Mary had not expected to like sex. Her own mother had mumbled something about "a wife's duty to her husband," on the day before the wedding, then fled to another room in mortified embarrassment. However, these two came to marriage with a fierce physical attraction the consummation of which seemed to only build the fire rather than extinguish it.

On the first night that the three travelers had to camp under the stars, the brothers decided that C.H. and Mary should sleep in the wagon rather than make Mary endure the cold, hard ground. In the morning, C.H. rose to stir the fire and make coffee.

He had expected to find Will up or possibly still sleeping by the dying embers, but he was nowhere in sight. He was not near the fire or in an adjoining meadow, so C.H. walked farther from the fire ring into a stand of trees. Still, no Will.

"Will? Will? Where are you?" he called sotto voce trying not to disturb the sleeping Mary. When he got no answer, he walked further into the trees to call again.

Finally, he heard a slight cough and his brother's low voice, "I'm over here."

"What are you doing in the trees? Why didn't you stay by the fire where it's warm?"

"Well," responded Will, as he stood in order to be seen. "I was actually afraid for my life over there. The way you two were moving in that wagon, I was afraid you'd pop the brake with all the rocking and send it rolling over me in my sleep! I figured these trees could stop a runaway wagon."

"Oh, sorry. I guess that we will have to try a new arrangement tonight."

"Does that mean I get to sleep with Mary in the wagon?" suggested Will with a grin.

"Naw, that won't work at all"

"I think it's a fine idea," countered Will.

"No, for one thing, she thinks your ugly!" C.H. laughed and turned to run.

"Does she also know I'm mean?!" shouted Will as he sent a few pinecone missiles flying past his brother's head.

That night, C.H. and Mary slept under the wagon with a tarp tacked on one side for privacy.

. . .

By midsummer, the Oklahoma weather had turned hot and the land became ever drier with a constant wind as the travelers moved farther to the west to reach tribal groups that had yet to witness the magical technology of Singer sewing machines. Finally, the group grew tired of the heat, the wind and the incessantly blowing dust and decided to move north as originally planned toward the Iowa/Nebraska border where they would sell their teams and board railcars headed west to California.

C.H. and Will had arranged for any mail family might want to send them to be collected and held at the post office in Council Bluffs near the rail station there. When they arrived at that location, there were two letters waiting to be retrieved.

One was to Mary from her mother that informed her daughter how happy she was to be living with family in her new home. She loved the quiet and beauty of the place, and had begun to garden in a small plot near the side of the main house where her own room and parlor opened directly to it. Every morning, she could open her door to enjoy the fresh air, or perhaps take her tea outside in her own garden This was happy news for Mary who could not remember a time when her mother would leave her room without being forced either by Mary's insistence or by Mary's father when he was alive. Though her mother had begun to walk around the Rhea township properties before Mary had left on their travels, Mary had feared that her mother might again retreat into her shell once her daughter was no longer near. Finally, Mary felt truly free to look forward, without worry for her mother's welfare, to a new life far away from Arkansas, a place she always equated with the horrors of war, sin and corruption.

The other letter was addressed to Will and C.H. from their mother. Will was first to read it while C.H. went to reserve rooms for them for one night's lodging. He was immediately alarmed by his mother's account of Zachary's recent bout with pneumonia. She explained that after the wedding, their father had succumbed to a cold that had settled in his chest, so that they were unable to travel home to the Monticello farm. Instead, they stayed with Will's family in Hot springs, and after Zachary had regained his health, he and Mattie decided that they no longer wanted to deal with the farm and really preferred the comforts of Hot Springs. They explained that Jake had also planned to move to St. Louis to be near Red and his wife and children. They would sell the farm and split the proceeds with Jake as they had agreed years ago. This would allow all concerned to enjoy a more comfortable retirement. Mattie ended quoting Zachary as saying, "I'm at an age, now, when I have to think about where I will spend my last days. I do not want to be buried in the low lands where sooner or later water will always rise in one's grave."

As Will finished reading the letter, he suddenly felt a clarity of thought for an idea that had been slowly growing in the back of his mind for many days. He realized that he no longer wanted to continue to California. He understood that what he really wanted was to go home and that he missed his wife and child. His mother's letter provided him with a reason to return home since his parents would need help from at least one of their sons to make their desired move.

Once C.H. had also read the letter, he folded it and handed it back to Will. "We need to go back home as soon as we can," he agreed. "The folks will certainly need help packing and moving." With that, he turned toward the hotel where Mary waited for them to check into their reserved rooms.

C.H. knew how Mary felt about Hot Springs and he knew he should prepare for her inevitable resistance to the idea of returning there, even if only for a visit. It often occurred to him that dealing with Mary was a bit like playing chess with a shrewd opponent. It was important that he anticipate how she would counter his arguments and also plan ever more compelling reasons to hopefully convince her to see things his way.

After he had related the news about his parents, C.H. saw a look he had seen in Mary's eyes before. It was not just mere anger or disappointment, but more like a determined fury that never failed to make him want to run the other way. He would just have to fight the urge to retreat or give in. He had responsibilities to his parents and he thought it only right that he not put it all on Will.

Finally, Mary spoke and in a barely controlled voice said, "I will not have the baby I am carrying in Arkansas!"

It was as though C.H. felt a seismic shift beneath his feet as he stared stupidly at his wife. "Baby? Baby?" was all he could manage to say, but he thought, "Checkmate, game over!"

The next day, C.H. and Mary boarded a train headed to California.

10.
Krann

The Krann family gaped in wonder as they surveyed the fantastic lobby and dining room of the recently reopened Geiser Grand Hotel hailed as Baker City's finest establishment. Though this same building formerly known as the Warshauer Hotel had been where the family had held a celebration dinner following the wedding of Marie and August Meyer seven years prior, they had to agree that the refinements added by its new owner, mining magnate Albert Geiser, were unbelievably luxurious. Newspapers from all over Oregon trumpeted that this hotel along with the new, magnificent Baker City Opera House with its metropolitan proportions and world class entertainment made this prosperous town one that truly offered elegant living.

"Close your mouth, Gus, before a bird flies into it," whispered August into his four year old's ear as the youngster stared in wonder at the massive, lighted stained glass ceiling overhead. As the little boy began to giggle with understanding at his father's joke, August picked him up and whirled around to take in the full view of the hotel's opulence. "I have to agree, though, this place is truly amazing. What a palace!" he exclaimed waving one arm at the many crystal chandeliers, the brilliant polished brass fixtures and wax-rubbed wains coating, the wide stairway and the new "birdcage" elevator that could carry guests to an open mezzanine that encircled one story above the dining room below.

Once seated at a large table set for eight with August at one end, he could enjoy the sight of his two older children sitting in their best clothes on either side of their aunt, Rosa. His oldest, Elizabeth, who everyone called "Betty" ever since the quiet girl had forcefully explained to her family that at six years old she would no longer respond to the nickname "Lizzie," sat primly with her linen napkin in her lap. August smiled and gave the girl a slight nod which made her blush in delight over this sign of fatherly approval.

Little August Jr. sat abnormally still as Rosa smoothed a napkin in the boy's lap and leaned to explain to him items on the menu he might enjoy. August then turned his attention to his lovely Marie seated on his other side who was busy placing small biscuits on a highchair tray for their youngest, two year old Harry. He noted that her figure was still slim and her recently announced pregnancy was barely noticeable. When she turned and caught him beaming at her, Marie beamed back. She was proud of her beautiful children and of her husband who she thought looked particularly sartorial in a new suit bought specially for this evening that would end with a performance by Austrian-born contralto, Madam Schumann-Heink at the Opera House. She thought he looked like a prince and had always been pleased that, though he was still a miner, every week when the men returned to town August headed straight for his barber for a hair trim and shave.

After their white gloved waiter poured wine for the adults, August indicated that twenty year old Matthew, seated at the other end of the table next to Kurt, was old enough to also enjoy a glass of wine. He then raised his own glass in a toast.

"It is only fitting that we celebrate in this beautiful place the fact that our Rosa will soon open her own store! This toast is to Rosa who has done so much to bring beauty and sophistication to the lucky women of our city."

"Thank you, August," Rosa replied with a wide smile that almost immediately faded. "I only wish that Grandfather Joseph were here to see the opening of my store that he was so much responsible for," she finished, referring to one of the provisions that had been made by Joseph in his will just before that good man died peacefully in his sleep the year before.

Besides bequests to each family member, Joseph had added that in

Rosa he was making his final business investment. He wrote, "I have learned that the best and safest investment is in one's own family. I have seen how Rosa has coupled her natural talent with business sense to produce a wildly successful product. She should not continue to work for someone else, but instead must have her own place of business."

"We must add a prayer for our dear grandfather in our prayer of thanksgiving for this wonderful meal and Rosa's new venture," Marie murmured as she put down her glass and crossed herself. With that, the others, even the children, immediately followed suite and all bowed their heads, and in unison began, "Bless us O Lord and these Thy gifts..."

· · ·

In the seven years since Rosa began working for the milliner, Frau Weber, she had made quite a name for herself as someone women flocked to for a custom hat that drew praise whenever it was worn. She had taken pains to keep abreast of the latest millinery fashions shown in the salons of Europe and New York. She was fortunate that her grandfather and father subscribed to several newspapers mailed to them from Austria and a German language paper from New York. Whenever a new one arrived, they had allowed Rosa to remove all the fashion and society news where wealthy socialites were pictured wearing the latest styles. In addition, Rosa had written to her former employer in Vienna, Frau Mannheim, about her new position in a millinery shop and the kind woman had begun to send the girl hat-making industry publications that not only featured pictured hat styles but also provided step by step directions for reproduction.

Frau Weber's store was the only one in town that had banished the matronly straw bonnet that so offended Rosa's fashion taste. Instead, the shop's window featured hats meant to be an essential element to a woman's overall "look." At this time, it was fashionable for a lady's silhouette to resemble an S-shape. For this reason, Rosa's hats featured a brim that cantilevered over a woman's face which added to the desired curvaceous form that was completed by a ruffled bodice blousing over the waist and ending in the folds of a floor-length, trained skirt.

Rosa made sure that any featured hat was accompanied by one of her full fashion drawings showing exactly how the hat would complete a woman's entire ensemble.

Rosa kept a growing scrapbook for women to look over whenever she needed to consult with a customer about creating a custom hat. She also used her book as source material and inspiration for her own special touches. If a customer indicated an interest in a certain style, Rosa would sketch it and add any trim and color accents she and the customer agreed on. The girl seemed to have an unerring eye for how to create a hat that best suited a particular woman's hair style, facial proportions and coloring. Whenever a hat was completed, Rosa would work with the customer before a large mirror to demonstrate various ways to wear the new creation until the new owner was certain how to make the most pleasing presentation.

Another trick that helped Rosa make any of her hats truly one of a kind was her suggestion that customers provide some adornment from home to incorporate as part of the trim. This could be anything the customer thought was pretty; a faux pearl necklace, a silver belt buckle, a favorite broach or a decorative button. Sometimes a lady might present Rosa with an assortment of possible objects and the two could play with each until they could agree on what looked especially pleasing.

Within the first year with Frau Weber, Baker City women began to refer to Rosa's work as "Rosie hats" and a local paper remarked that, "Every Baker City woman wants to own a Rosie hat." Frau Weber was wise enough to incorporate that quote in all her advertisements. She also suggested that Rosa design her own artist's mark to be sewn inside all her hats to prove authenticity. With Marie's sewing help, Rosa came up with a small embroidered red rose surrounded by a circle of gold thread. The first time Mrs. Weber pointed out the tiny rose inside a customer's hat the woman cried, "How wonderful! But I want it sewn outside on the band, so everyone who sees me will know that I own a Rosie hat!"

Rosa had always enjoyed working for Frau Weber over the years. The older woman had encouraged and supported every idea the girl suggested to enhance and promote the shop. Frau Weber had also been the person most responsible for Rosa's command of English. When the girl was first hired, she spoke almost no English and, therefore, could only work behind the scenes as a trimmer. However, Frau Weber could see potential in Rosa becoming active in sales as well. Since the older woman was born in Bavaria and was brought to the U.S. as a young child, she was fluent in both German and English which made her the perfect person to teach Rosa how to speak to customers.

A first, Rosa learned only a few phrases to use in short interactions with customers. She quickly mastered common polite greetings such as' "Good morning, please be seated while I call Frau Weber." In addition, she kept a small German/English dictionary to look up unfamiliar words. At home, she insisted that both Mathew and August speak only English to her, so she could practice and become more fluent in conversation. August was particularly helpful because he had lived all his life immersed in American culture and could explain the meaning of the many slang phrases Americans were prone to use.

August was also careful not to laugh as Mathew often did over Rosa's confusions with idiom. Once, Rosa reported that the husband of one of their customer's came to the shop and yelled loudly at Frau Weber. Later, her employer explained that his wife bought an expensive hat which made the man "hot under the collar." Furthermore, Mrs. Weber had said that the man was "off his trolley" if he thought she would give him his money back. She also said that he was lucky he had a wife at all, because "his face would stop a clock."

Mathew could not hold back a loud guffaw when Rosa asked, "August, why would the wife's hat make his collar hot and how can a face do anything to a clock? Also, why would Mrs. Weber say he fell off a trolley when we have no trolley here?"

• • •

Rosa was not the only Krann to learn new skills. The day of his high school graduation, Mathew announced that he was ready to go to work and earn some money of his own. Kurt suggested he try to get a job in one of the shops or work at a factory like the lumber mill or Sam O Bottling Works. None of these ideas suited the boy who longed only to do physical work out of doors. More than anything, he wanted to be a miner and wanted to learn from August the skills that had made him well known throughout the county for winning so many contests. Since neither August nor Kurt wanted Mathew to go anywhere near a lode mine, August promised to teach Matt double-jacking with the proviso that he use the skill only in contests and always work for real above ground as a placer.

August was happy to have Mathew join their crew. He was impressed with how easily the boy learned to be the second man on a double-jacking team. Matt proved to be strong, tireless and fearless which was a good thing since August, himself, had lost some of his own youthful strength and Kurt still hated taking part in the high pressure contests that paid the biggest prizes which were held several times yearly in the town square of nearby Sumpter.

August was also glad to have the boy work with them, because he had fears he had shared with Kurt concerning their two Chinese workers. He worried that sooner or later the two would want to return to China where they had family. They might also want to escape the constant pressures created by white prejudice.

In fact, life for the Chinese in the U.S. had become steadily more dangerous. Since the time the first wave of Chinese workers came to California during the 1849 gold rush followed by wave after wave of Chinese to do the hardest work building the transcontinental railroad, white workers complained about the "yellow horde." They claimed that the influx of Chinese was the reason for declining wages and any other economic ill. Finally, though the Chinese were only .002 percent of the U.S. population, in response to growing pressure on Congress, President Chester Arthur signed The Chinese Exclusion Act of 1882 which suspended Chinese immigration for ten years and also declared illegal their naturalization. The act was so popular that it had been renewed in 1892, and by then many Chinese had returned to their native country.

Those that remained, like Lo and Ping, were increasingly in danger of violence against them. In most work situations, the Chinese were given the most dangerous and difficult jobs. Chinese workers were the ones sent into mines to ignite dynamite fuses, and while building the railroad through mountainous areas, Chinese workers were lowered on ropes over the side of cliffs to ignite dynamite charges in the rock face. Many died as result of being pulled up too slowly.

Even Chinese who did not work on a white mining crew were in danger. In 1888, August told Kurt of a rumor that over thirty Chinese miners had been massacred while working their placer claim deep in Hells Canyon on the Snake River. They had probably felt safe mining in such a remote area. However, the unlucky crew had been spotted from above by a gang of white cattle rustlers. The gang figured that the Chinese had probably been working that spot in good weather for many months since it was early autumn. They would have hidden their gold for safekeeping until they could again climb out of the canyon and either cash it in or send the gold to China.

August had met a man in a Sumpter saloon who had lived in Enterprise north of Baker City in the Wallowa Mountains and had mined along the Snake River. He said that miners were finding Chinese bodies for months washed up along the river. He also said that the authorities had arrested three men who had confessed to being involved.

"They had a trial in Enterprise but it was over in a day and they were let go." The miner finished.

"Weren't they guilty?" August had wondered.

"Oh probably. But no-one is going to hang a man for killing a Chinaman." August was nauseated and appalled that this statement rang true.

Because of this kind of thinking, most Chinese were forced for their own safety to live together in crowded camps outside the various towns in the West that invariably were dubbed "Chinatown" by the locals. Most of the larger mining towns, like Sumpter, Granite and Baker City had a Chinatown section located somewhat away from the main city population. This satisfied the desire of the local citizenry to keep the Chinese segregated and also afforded the Chinese a sense of safety and a measure of economic freedom.

The Eastern Oregon cattle town of Pendleton voted in a curfew that required all Chinese to be off the streets by sundown. It was said that any Chinese that showed his face after dark "didn't stand a Chinaman's chance in hell" and would most likely be shot by some liquored up cowboy. The clever Chinese of that town dealt with their lot by building large dens below street level and tunnels connecting them until they had created a virtual underground city of apartments, stores of various types, laundries and even bawdy houses frequented by those same drunken cowboys.

Knowing all this about the treatment of the Chinese, August had two main worries. He thought, of course, that their two hardworking, loyal crewmen might one day sail for home. Also, He feared that some white miner down on his luck or a drifter might see Lo and Ping and decide they were safe to steal from and maybe even kill. For this reason, he was particularly glad to have Mathew join their outfit which made it less likely that a thief would mistake their camp for a vulnerable Chinese camp.

With the addition of Mathew to the crew, August instituted some extra security measures for the group. Since they needed more in the way of sleeping quarters anyway, he had them build two more of the kind of sturdy housing favored by most miners. These log structures topped by a tent of thick canvas provided satisfactory shelter most of the year with the exception of the two deepest winter months. With four such "houses," the group now, not only had the quarters that already housed August and Kurt and the other for Lo and Ping, but now a third for Mathew and the fourth for supplies and tools. They also purchased a second wagon and team that they had needed for some time. This produced the effect that theirs was a large camp of many men and therefore, less attractive to anyone up to no good.

In addition, he also decided that, whenever he, Kurt and Mathew, returned for the weekend to their home in Baker City, Lo and Ping should take their second wagon back to the Chinatown in Granite for their safety. He added that they would not keep any amount of gold in the camp, but would routinely deposit it regularly in the Sumpter bank. Whenever it was necessary to make that short trip, two would go so one could ride shotgun, and they would never pause even to enjoy a cold beer before returning. The one to stay back would provide the "white presence" that afforded some protection.

• • •

As months passed, August and Kurt were satisfied that their precautions worked. They were especially pleased that on one trip to Sumpter when they engaged in some polite banter with the bank teller who they usually dealt with, the teller asked when the rest of the crew would visit town.

"Some of the local fellas were talking about how big your crew was gettin' with all the new hires you guys have. They said your camp takes up one side of a hill on Cracker Creek," the teller remarked.

"Yeah, we've been at it so long that the two of us just needed some younger help, so we brought in some strong young guys from Baker City," explained August to reinforce the idea that their camp was well protected.

...

By December and the first heavy snow, the men decided that they would pack up and return home for the Christmas season and watch for a break in the weather for a chance to begin work again. August and Mathew would take the last of their gold to Sumpter and return with cash to pay Lo and Ping for their share before they took the second wagon to Granite. Kurt and the two Chinese men would tear down the long tom and equipment that had to be left behind and pack it into the tool shed for storage out of the weather.

As Kurt worked inside the shed to organize tools to make room for the rest of their equipment, Lo and Ping busied themselves with crowbars disassembling the series of wooden troughs where flowing water helped miners separate gold from gravel. The two didn't hear the approach of two men on horseback behind them until one man called out, "You men have some drinking water handy?"

The two Chinese did not understand what was said, though they looked up squinting into the sun reflected brightly off the new snow in the direction of where the two men sat on their horses. But, then they ducked their heads and continued to work silently.

"Say there, I was talkin' to you. Don't you have no manners?" said the man who had first spoken. "Stan, I think these fellas need a lesson in manners." He growled at his companion.

"Yeah, you're right about that. They do need to be taught some manners," said the second man as he pulled out a hand gun and pointed it at the two silent workers who stopped all activity at the sight of the brandished gun.

"Well, I'll tell ya what we'll do for you fellas," continued the man with the gun. "We know you Chinamen hide your gold. You never take it to no bank. That's for sure. So, you just give it to us and we'll be on our way," he told the obviously frightened men who made no move or sign that they were about to obey the order.

"OK, that's the way you want it! Maybe if I just shoot me one of you yellow bastards I'll get the one left to hand over the gold!" he cried louder and cocked his gun to make good on the threat.

Just then, Kurt holding a shotgun appeared behind them having heard the shouted threat.

"What's going on here!?" he cried.

Before he could even shoulder his own rifle, the startled man with the cocked gun whirled and shot blindly in Kurt's direction hitting him in the upper leg. Just as quickly, the second man pulled at the gun arm of the first man shouting, "Ya stupid fool! Ya just shot a white man! C'mon les get outta here!"

The would-be thieves reigned their horses and took off over a hill and disappeared from sight as Lo and Ping ran to Kurt's side. The men acted quickly to move Kurt into his cabin and place him on his cot. Beyond that, they did not know what best to do next as they eyed, with panic, the massive bloodstain spreading across Kurt's trousers from the leg wound.

· · ·

At the same time, Mathew and August were bumping along the wagon road to their camp from Sumpter. "Say, Gus, where do ya suppose those guys are goin' in such a hurry?" Mathew wondered as he pointed out two riders galloping away from them on a ridge just over Cracker Creek.

With an immediate sense of dread, August prodded the team into a faster pace though mindful that the road's rocky surface posed the danger of a broken wheel or axel. Once they pulled into the camp, they could see that something was terribly wrong. No man was in sight, but they could hear loud Chinese chatter coming from the cabin and noticed a dark, wet trail leading to the canvas door. Inside, August could barely see in the crowded, gloomy space that Kurt was on his bed and a blanket had been thrown over him. He turned just as Mathew also tried to enter the tiny room.

"Matt, I think your dad's been hurt. Can you take these men out so I can look at what is wrong?"

"Wh ... what's wrong with him? Is it serious, Gus?" questioned the frightened boy.

"It must only be his leg. There is some blood there. I need you to relax and give me room to help him. Can you go outside for a minute?" August answered while gently guiding all three men out the door.

He turned his attention to Kurt who lay still under the blanket, though his eyes were open and watching as August lifted the edge to survey what he feared would be a bullet wound beneath. What he saw, made him wince and draw in one long, shuddering breath. Kurt had evidently been shot and the bullet had hit his femoral artery which accounted for the blood that pumped from the savage wound in spurts with each beat of his friend's heart.

As August tore a length of cloth to use as a tourniquet with the hopes of stopping the fountain of blood, Kurt muttered, "Two guys... wanted gold ... threatened the men with a gun. I, I tried to stop..."

"Shhh! Don't try to talk. Save your strength, Kurt. This will stop the bleeding and then we'll get you out of here, old buddy!" August promised with false heartiness.

"Want... water, Gus" Kurt responded weakly. And as Gus raised his friend's head slightly to drink, Kurt said, "I really messed things up this time."

"Messed up? Why, you saved those men's lives! They would have shot them, for sure." August countered softly while holding Kurt's face close to his. "You're sure no tinhorn any more, guy. Kurt, no one could have handled the situation better than you did."

Kurt's only answer was a brief smile.

"Gus? Gus? Is he all right?" Mathew's voice questioned shakily from the doorway while August still bent over Kurt.

"We have to take your father to Baker City, Matt," August answered without turning around.

"No! Gus no! That's too far! We have to go to Sumpter! There's a doctor in Sumpter! We have to take him there!" cried the nearly hysterical boy.

Then August turned and stood as Mathew walked toward him.

"No, Matt … He needs to go home."

And Mathew saw the streaming tears, and finally, he knew.

11.
McColloch

It was a slow day at the Portland Oregon Justice Court of the Albina District and by noon Justice of the Peace, C.H. McColloch, was hearing the final case of a typical morning's series of traffic violations, small claims disputes, and the occasional public drunkenness or minor assault case. Just as he was calling for a lunch break, C.H. noticed a familiar uniformed police officer approach his bench from the side and begin to speak in soft tones.

"Say Charlie, I need to talk with you in private. It's about one of your boys."

Once inside the judge's chambers and alone the man continued. "I wanted you to know that we have your boy in custody down at the station house along with some of his pals who caused some serious trouble this morning. I went to your house to talk with Mary, but no one was home, or I wouldn't bother you in court. As an old friend, I figured you needed to be told right away."

"Jack, what kind of trouble are you talking about?" C.H. wondered in total disbelief.

"Seems these boys got the idea to soap the commuter train tracks at the Killingsworth Avenue Station. It's the station right before that steep downhill grade. When the train tried to brake for the station, it slid right by and down that hill, halfway to Greeley Avenue! Well, I guess some of the working stiffs on the train didn't take kindly to being made late for their jobs and took off running after the scamps. Now we have the ones they caught and your boy is one of them."

"That's just not possible. My son is at school," C.H. calmly explained. "And I know Claude would never be mixed up in such a thing."

"It's not your older boy, Claude. It's the younger one we have. I've seen him plenty a times at your butcher shop to know."

"That just can't be. Frank is only seven years old." C.H. protested less sure that the officer was mistaken.

"Yeah, he is a lot younger than the rest of the crowd. The others are nine or ten, so we asked those boys why the little guy was with them. They said he is a friend in their class at school. They said he is real smart, so the school put him in their grade last month. They even have a nickname for him. They call him 'Gopher' because he's good at burrowing under the fence at the railyard where they like to go when they cut school."

"Dear God!" C.H. breathed. "Well, I'd better go down there and retrieve 'Gopher' from the pokey!

...

That night after dinner, C.H. excused Claude to start his homework while he had a word with Frank about his day time activities. "You know, if I had ever done anything like the things you've been up to, my daddy would have beaten me with a very big stick," he began, gazing sternly at his penitent son. "Do I need to beat you with a stick to get through to you the need to change your wild ways?"

"No, sir. I don't think that would do the trick," the boy answered with a slow shake of his head which sent Claude working at the big parlor desk across the room into a fit of giggles.

"Well then, I'm going to have to do some thinking about what will do the trick!" was all the worried father could think of to say before sending both boys to bed.

He would just have to wait until Mary came home from whatever meeting she was attending as she did nearly every night of the week. He could not keep up with her many activities. There were four different committees to promote the vote for women alone. She had continued her membership in the Women's Christian Temperance Union by joining a local chapter when they first moved to Oregon and was now it's very vocal president. Finally, she was also active with her church, Albina Presbyterian, whose flamboyant pastor considered himself a disciple of the fiery evangelist, J. Wilber Chapman.

He could not help but think that they both had neglected their children. Mary was far too involved with activities that took her away from her home and children. As for his part, he had always worked long days, first as a butcher and then as a Justice of the Peace elected to a six year term. Whenever he was not at work, his nose was buried in a law book in preparation for the bar exam he would soon take.

Of course, their first born, Claude was a quiet, studious boy who did well in school and had never gotten into any trouble. He was far more likely to be found reading quietly in his room, than running wild with other boys in the neighborhood. They were just not prepared for their second son, Frank, whip-smart but constantly moving and into everything as though he believed that the only way to learn about the world was to throw himself at every experience without a thought to any possible danger. They would have to be together on this. Clearly, Frank needed to be more closely monitored, and he greatly needed his parents to act as a united front.

...

As the parlor mantel clock struck midnight, C.H. awoke from an exhausted sleep in his "reading chair." Troubled, he noted the late hour when he heard Mary's key jingle in their front door lock. As she entered removing her hat and coat and placing an armload of papers on the small hallway table, she did not see her husband sitting in the gloom across the room until he stood from the chair where he had been sleeping.

"Goodness! You gave me a start. Why are you still up at this hour?" she wondered. "Is there something wrong?"

"I would say there is something we need to discuss that can't wait until morning, Mary. But first, where on earth were you until midnight, might I ask?"

Her husband's unusually accusatory tone and grave expression put Mary on her guard, so she strove to try some light, newsy banter to lighten his apparent mood. "I was at an Oregon Suffrage Association strategy meeting Abigail called to plan our ballot initiative to present to the legislature this year. She finally wants to include the WCTU in the planning, so it was very important for me to attend."

"I thought Abigail Duniway doesn't want to be associated with you temperance folks. I thought she believes that male voters and the state's liquor interests will kill the women's vote every time if her suffrage movement is seen as also pushing for prohibition." C.H. noted.

"That's true enough. She got the idea from that back stabbing brother of hers. It was Harvey Scott who filled her head with worry about being involved with the Temperance Union before the last vote. He promised her the support of his paper, then he turned right around and threw the full weight of *The Oregonian* against her! It was because of him that suffrage went down with only 28% of the vote. I think she's beginning to see that we are an important constituency. She just can't afford to go on alienating us!" Mary finished.

"Important work, I agree. But, Mary, you have another important job right here." C.H. began to provide an opening for the discussion he really wanted to have with her. Then he told her about Frank's troublesome activities ending by saying, "...so I can check on his school attendance every day, but I think you need to be home in the afternoon to make sure he is here and not running wild as he has been doing."

With this statement, C.H. could see the familiar thunder clouds gathering behind his wife's eyes, and he knew that he would have to somehow break through Mary's angry resistance to any suggestion that her duty as a wife and mother was to stay home and take care of the needs of her family. He was well used to this particular fight, but as usual, he completely missed the stark fear that was behind her dread of having to take up this wifely role.

...

Mary had not always thought that the role of "wife and mother" was tantamount to a prison sentence. Even as a child, Mary understood that her own mother was most comfortable within the confines of her home and chose to rarely leave it. As she grew older, though, Mary began to understand that home was a prison of her mother's own making and that the poor woman's fear of the outside world was more a symptom of her depressive mental state than it was a happy embrace of society's preferred role for women.

As an outgoing young woman with many interests and social contacts, Mary had never suffered from the kind of fears that drove her mother to hide from the world. Mary also understood that her own happiness depended on making sure that she never married a man like her father, a cold authoritarian male who did not think of women as the intellectual equal of men and so was not at all interested in any kind of social interaction with females, even with his own wife and daughter. In C.H. she found a man who was in every way the opposite of her father, a man who was certainly a safe bet to take as a husband.

Everything about their early courtship and marriage was a joyous affirmation that her choice in a husband had been a wise one and that this alone was all the insurance she needed for having a happy, fulfilled life. She firmly believed that by having a husband who valued her as an equal and who was as stimulated by their discourse as he was by her physical attractions, she would forever escape the restrictions society so often imposed on women. Mary well understood that both the law and Victorian social mores dictated that men were in charge and would set the tone in and out of the home. The choice of the wrong man would mean a wrong life, and Mary congratulated herself on avoiding such a terrible mistake. That is, until she ran up against an unexpected obstacle to her dream for an unencumbered life of free expression. She became a mother.

• • •

By the time the young couple reached California in the fall of 1887, Mary's pregnancy had progressed to the point that they realized that it was necessary to stop traveling for the sake of Mary's health and the health of the baby that would soon arrive. At an overnight depot stop near the California central valley town of Red Bluff, C.H. saw a sign in the window of a shop located across from the tracks. It read "Help Wanted", so he checked Mary into the rooming house where passengers were to spend the night and went to inquire about a job. He soon returned with the happy news that he had procured both a job as a butcher's assistant and a place for them to live rent-free in an apartment in back of the shop that the butcher, Mr. Johannsen, had once lived in before he was married to a woman who insisted on living in a proper house for their future family in town.

At first, Mary was much relieved that they would not continue traveling. By this time, she was quite large with child and she suffered horrid indigestion from the almost inedible fare available for rail passengers to purchase at various stops. In addition, her baby had settled onto her kidneys which made sitting long hours on a wooden, straight-backed coach seat hellishly uncomfortable. She found herself constantly dreaming of the day she would again be able to lie down any time she needed or wanted to. This lucky turn of events seemed to Mary to be a dream come true, and she greeted her husband's news with a heartfelt, tearful hug. That was until she was able to take some sober, clear-eyed stock of their new "home."

There was a reason the shop was located near the railroad, for this was also the area where cattle, hogs and sheep from California ranches were penned awaiting transfer to cattle cars for shipping to the large cities to the south. It was a natural location for a butcher shop since it provided easy access to a source of fresh meat for local tables. However, while the location was good for business, it was hardly an ideal place to live with its ever-present animal noise and stench. Mary was soon to realize that there was a good reason that their apartment was offered to them without cost. No one would have paid a cent to live in that area. Come every evening, the two of them were quite alone living at the edge of a sea of frightened animals.

• • •

Neither C.H. nor Mary knew anything about childbirth. Mary had been the youngest child in her family. In most other families, women often shared their own experiences, stories of friends and relatives, and passed along the vast accumulation of folk knowledge and superstition that surrounded this momentous event that has always been both a blessing and a rightly feared danger. Mary's family, even the Rhea's, believed it unseemly to refer to childbirth except as a sterile news item.

As for her husband, C.H. was raised like all men of the time without any real knowledge concerning what happened on the other side of a bedroom door that firmly closed out any male participation. When his own mother gave birth to her last child, a little boy who, like most of C.H.'s siblings did not live much beyond infancy, he had been sent away to the Shaw's for the three weeks it took for his mother to recover. Though childbirth remained a complete mystery to the young couple, both of them were well aware that it regularly killed otherwise healthy, young women.

C.H. was able to put aside his worst fears due to his punishing twelve hour days helping the butcher, Mr. Johannsen, cut, trim, bone, tie and grind meat in preparation for sale. His employer was a much older man and depended on his young assistant to also visit the slaughter house up the road several times a week to select and transport the huge carcasses back to the store for sale. By nightfall, C.H. barely had the strength it took to eat the usual bland concoction of meat and root vegetables Mary boiled together on the top of their tiny wood stove before falling into bed and instant slumber.

Mary, on the other hand, had plenty of time to think, and her thoughts became as hellishly bleak as the place in which she found herself living. Oddly, she began to miss her life in Arkansas where she had been surrounded by family and friends who cared whether she lived or died. She slowly realized that she had only herself to blame for her present circumstance. She began to believe she had committed a sin with her stubborn and ill-considered refusal to return to the place she now thought of as "home," a sin for which she was obviously being punished. She was certain that she was still to pay some horrible price for her sinful pride. Would she pay with her life or the life of her child? If her baby died, she would have to live the rest of her life knowing that this innocent child had paid for her own sin. She could hardly bare these fears that filled the lonely daylight hours but became so much worse once the sun went down.

As Mary entered her ninth month, she was nearly frantic with worry for her baby. She ate very little having no appetite and sleep alluded her efforts to calm the fits of panic that seem to attack most viciously at night. On one such wakeful night, her pacing about their tiny apartment woke C.H. who naturally wondered if it was time for the birth.

"If it was time for the baby to come, what would we do? We would be lost. We don't even have a midwife to help with the birth." Mary asserted with sudden, clear understanding of how unprepared they were. Then she burst into long suppressed sobs, "Our baby needs more than just us!"

. . .

"Are you telling me that there is a pregnant girl living in that hell-hole behind your shop!" cried the usually placid Greta Johannsen, when her husband informed her that his new assistant had a wife who would soon need a good midwife.

Within the hour, Mary was awakened from a fitful morning nap to the plump, smiling cherubic face of Greta. In her confused state, Mary thought that she was being visited by an angel since the woman's head was back-lit by the weak winter morning sun streaming through their bedroom window. Then the angel spoke and with a heavy Scandinavian accent said, "Good morning, dear girl. We'll dismiss with the usual pleasantries. Your husband is here to help you to my buggy. We're taking you to my home where we have a midwife for you to meet. She's a wonderful woman who delivered all six of my children. From the look of you, it will be none too soon!" As usual the butcher's wife was right. Within the week, healthy baby boy, Claude, was born to his proud and grateful parents.

. . .

In the following weeks, Mary and C.H. and their baby were welcomed into the local Swedish community which was made up of many immigrant families of men who worked for the railroad or in services supporting railroad workers. In addition to sharing common employment, these families all belonged to a church called, Swedish Mission Friends that, Greta explained to Mary, followed the teachings of "Mr. D.L Moody."

"Mr. Moody is our hero," Greta explained. "We follow his teachings because they rescue us from the grim patriarchy of most other churches. Mission Friends is a place where one's soul is warmed by

Christian love not frightened by cold threats of hell. You would certainly be welcome to visit. After all, Mr. Moody has never preached anywhere but in England and America, so his teachings are meant for everyone, not just Swedes. He began his ministry in the slums of Chicago where he believed that it was his calling to bring the word of God to those he said were 'the least, the last and the lost'. He did more than just preach at people. He gave all his personal savings to help the poor without any thought to his own needs!"

Mary at once became intrigued by Greta's description of her church. She had noted that all the women who visited Greta's home not only brought food and gifts to the baby, but also exuded the kind of warm interest that seems to immediately draw in the stranger as a beloved new friend. She also knew that she had certainly felt "lost" and was long overdue to have her "soul warmed."

Since C.H. preferred to stay home with his son on his one day off, Mary began to attend church with Greta every Sunday. From the first day she attended, Mary was swept away by how different Mission Friends was from any church she had ever attended. As Greta had promised, there was none of the usual talk of hell and damnation as the price one pays for not being "saved," though salvation was certainly the primary goal of these devote evangelicals. Mary also approved of the Mission Friends interest in the social reform movements that Mary had always worked for; prohibition and the vote for women. However, unlike the church fathers of most denominations, the Mission Friends did not just mouth platitudes about the need to empower women, then turn around and bar females from ministry. On that first visit, three women led the entire service, one actually preached from the pulpit. When Mary asked if it was usual for women to take an active part in their services, Greta informed her Mr. Moody had written that excluding half the human race from preaching the word of God was "unbiblical."

Mary not only found a new church but also a new understanding of how much she needed the comradeship of other women. If it were not for her new friends, she was quite sure she would have, at the very least, lost her sanity like some unfortunate pioneer woman unable to bear a life of bleak isolation in some lonely prairie sod house. For the first time, Mary began to fully understand the cause of her own mother's depression when war and her father's stubborn refusal to return to Rhea's Mill left her mother in fearful isolation. No, Mary thought, having a good husband was just not enough. Women absolutely need other women, or their lives can become unbearable. She vowed never to allow herself to be so isolated ever again.

...

Circumstances worked in favor of Mary and C.H. when his employer came to them with a proposition for opening a second butcher shop in Albina, Oregon, a small community just across the Willamette River from Portland. Mr. Johannsen explained his belief that this was a good business opportunity since Albina, like Red Bluff, became a transportation hub when the transcontinental railroad link was completed in 1883. The town was also the shipping center for Portland with large docks built along the river where the Willamette flowed into the mighty Columbia. As in Red Bluff, European Irish, German and Scandinavian immigrants found work with the railroad and on the docks and opened many small businesses to serve a rapidly growing population that was said would soon become annexed by the City of Portland.

Greta assured Mary that she would find a Swedish Mission Friends church in the area, and since the young family was already baking in the usual California Central Valley sweltering summer, it didn't take much to convince the couple to move to a cooler climate. C.H. was excited about becoming a partner with Mr. Johannsen and making a go of opening a new shop. He was surprised that even Mary seemed eager to begin this new adventure.

Mary kept to herself one big reason moving to the Portland, Oregon area suited her. She had kept up with the progress of those social causes close to her heart, primarily the progress toward women's suffrage and a legal ban on the sale of alcohol which she believed would never happen until women finally got the vote. She had come to believe that the sale of alcohol was a great evil that not only made good men into drunkards unable to provide for their families, but was also the ruin of family life since so many men spent what little money and free time they had drinking in male-only saloons. Since Mary knew that her husband did not share her hatred of whiskey, she did not tell him that she looked forward to their move primarily because Portland was an epicenter of female activism led by the famous suffragette, Abigail Scott Duniway.

C.H. and Mary both found that their new home in Oregon was all they had hoped it would be. Mr. Johannsen had certainly been correct that Albina was a vibrant, growing community and a perfect place to open their new butcher shop which would be located across from the railyard roundhouse in a new commercial building. C.H. purchased a lot a block away from his new shop which was far enough to suit Mary as the location for their new dwelling house. Mary was also pleased that the Swedish Friends Mission was walking distance from the new house too. Within a year of their move, the young couple was totally and happily immersed in the life of the Albina community.

C.H. loved being his own boss and took great pride in building his business that soon supported the families of two assistant butchers. His shop was twice the size of Mr. Johannsen's Red Bluff establishment but within a few months, C.H. realized that it was necessary to expand, so he bought an empty space between his shop and that of a green grocer at the opposite end of their building. This new space provided a larger storage area in the back for the sides of beef and pork he had to have on hand for the crowds of men who came every evening after work to purchase fresh meat for their families. Once he built a wall dividing the back storage area from a larger front room, C.H. was able to create a kind of delicatessen with a number of large round tables for working men to sit and enjoy a "ploughman's lunch" of sausages or cured meat they purchased from a glass case. These amenities, along with the winning personality of its proprietor, soon made Albina Meat the most successful business along what became known as Albina's "Produce Row."

For her part, Mary kept up a busy schedule of church and political activities connected with her membership in the local Women's Christian Temperance Union. Before her husband's business success made it possible for her to have a live-in housekeeper, she took her toddler everywhere with her. She was blissfully unaware of how unusual was little Claude's mild disposition and ability to entertain himself. Even at the age of four, he would sit quietly reading, drawing or working one of his many puzzles during the long, dull adult meetings that would have inspired rebellion in most children.

By the time Frank was born in 1892, Mary had full time help at home and was free to pursue her many efforts to change society. Mary felt strongly that gaining the right to vote was the only way for women to rise above the ignominious status of second class citizens. More importantly, gaining the right to vote, meant that women would finally have the power to put an end to what she saw as the source of so much female misery, the sale of alcohol.

At this same time, Mary's church was changing in a way that reinforced her own belief that prohibiting the sale of alcohol was the only way to save American society from the corrosive effects of this great evil. The Swedish Mission Friends of Albina began to embrace the teachings of an American evangelist, J. Wilber Chapman, who began preaching with the legendary D.L. Moody in 1893. Chapman was ordained by the Presbyterian Church and so were his "field evangelists" who were tasked with saving souls all across the U.S. either by becoming pastors of local churches or through "mass evangelical" campaigns that drew huge crowds. Mr. J.D. Crocker, an ardent Chapman follower, became the fiery new pastor of Mary's church that was then renamed, Albina Presbyterian.

Mr. Crocker brought with him all the highly charged elements that drew multitudes to the evangelical circuit. Chapman stressed the power of music to bring errant souls to God. Singing of uplifting gospel songs was an important part of every service as was the emotion-packed public confessions of sin and testimonies by the newly saved. From the pulpit, pastors preached the inerrancy of Scriptures where all Biblical accounts such as the creation story in Genesis and Jesus' miracles were to be taken literally and, therefore, powerfully reinforced the faith of believers. Heaven and Hell were viewed as actual places where the saved would be rewarded for their faith and the sinful would meet their eternal punishment. D.L. Moody had once said that he wanted to win souls through the word of God's love and that he did not "...want to scare men into the kingdom of God." Mr. Crocker made a weekly point of preaching what Moody called "the terrors of religion."

Such sermons week after week convinced Mary that her work to save the institution of the American family from society's sinful romance with alcohol was an important part of the evangelical calling to save the soul of the country one citizen at a time. Framed as a calling from God, Mary began to see her WCTU work as more important than ever. Still, her belief in the importance of the prohibition movement was largely an abstract notion and was not based on any personal experience. Then came the economic depression of 1893.

Portland was hit hard by the downturn that drastically affected lumbering, manufacturing and shipping. As these were scaled back, many men lost their jobs on the railroad and docks of Albina. Men with nowhere to go every day chased away fear of a bleak future in saloons where at least they could feel that they were not alone in their troubles. Some regulars took to hanging out at C.H.'s butcher shop, sitting for hours around the big round tables that had been put there for a lunchtime crowd when the men had been working.

When Mary occasionally visited the shop she saw the same men at the same tables, gossiping, playing poker and some drinking a liquid from mugs that was clearly not coffee. She finally decided that this "open house" had to end. Why, they might as well be running a saloon! What was going on at the shop was just as sinful, and it would be an unforgivable sin if she ignored it and allowed it to continue.

"My shop is a public place and the source of our income. I can't just shut and lock the door because it offends you that some poor unemployed souls have no place to go during the day." Responded C.H. that evening when Mary complained about the situation.

"Every one of those men have a wife and family. If they aren't working, they should be home with them!" Mary countered. "Instead you allow them to carry on at your shop; gambling and drinking. What you are doing is as bad as running a saloon. It's, it's an unpardonable sin!"

"Mary, it's a terrible thing for a man to be out of work. A man who has lost his job feels small and ashamed. It is hard for him to look his wife in the eye. Besides, I have an arrangement with the foremen on the railroad and on the docks to keep me informed about any job openings. Those men come every day with a glimmer of hope for some employment opportunity. Any God who would have me turn desperate men away is just not worth believing in!!"

"I cannot understand you, Charles. You would encourage men to sin, and break our Lord's first commandment, too!"

By then, they were both shouting unable to get through their obvious impasse. "Yes, Mary. I guess it is time that you finally know what an unredeemable sinner you are married to." C.H. said in a calmer voice as he turned toward their bedroom. Before he reached the door, a furious Mary flew past, then slammed and locked the bedroom door against her husband.

• • •

The next day, the usual regulars gathered around the butcher shop tables, while C.H. worked behind the counter to prepare orders for the occasional paying customer. He was careful to put scraps and bones aside that he would later wrap in packets for the non-working men to take home for the soup pot. As he worked, he listened to the banter around the table and chuckled over the good humored insults traded or the occasional off-color joke.

Then he looked up when the small bell attached to the shop's front door signaled someone new had entered. He was surprised to see his own wife come in and, without a word, she immediately sat down in an empty chair next to the table where eight men had begun a game of cards. The room was suddenly still. All eyes were on Mary as she smoothed her skirt, removed some knitting from a bag, and placed her leather-bound Bible on the table in front of her.

Within half an hour the shop was empty except for Mary and a very embarrassed C.H. "Do you plan to stay all day?" he inquired.

"I certainly do," she replied, ending all conversation between them.

• • •

Luckily, jobs on the railroad and on the docks were the first to return to Albina. At the same time, C.H. was approached by some city fathers to consider running for the position of Justice of the Peace for the Albina District. This idea intrigued him, so he agreed to run, and because he was well known and well liked, he won handily over the incumbent.

Though he still refused to attend Mary's church with her, and their relationship had remained icy for months, Mary was privately pleased that C.H. finally decided to sell his share of the butcher shop to his most able assistant and take the court job fulltime. Slowly things improved between them, that is until the day that their seven year old, Frank ran afoul of the law.

"Mary, you're his mother and you have a responsibility to be home and monitor his behavior," C.H. reasoned with his wife whose grim countenance betrayed none of the fear that had begun to constrict her breathing.

"I cannot do that. If I cannot attend Abigail Duniway's afternoon suffrage meetings, the Portland WCTU will not be represented in the final measure that must be presented to the legislature this year. I will have to give up my office, and all the work we have done to push for prohibition will be wasted!" she finished between clinched teeth.

"We are his parents, Mary. We owe it to him to guide him along the straight and narrow."

With that, Mary turned squarely to face her worried husband. "Charles, that's the most sensible thing you've said today! It is 'we' not just me who are his parents. Why can't you take some responsibility for guiding his behavior?"

. . .

By morning, C.H. had actually warmed to the idea. It made sense that Frank spend his after school hours observing the consequences people pay for breaking the law. Before the boy went off to school, C.H. took him aside and sternly explained that his punishment would entail a total loss of after school freedom. There would be no more running with his little gang of outlaws. Instead, he would end every day sitting in the Justice Court until it was time to go home for dinner. Though Frank hung his head while receiving his "sentence," C.H. was puzzled to see a small smile light the boy's face. He had no way to know that Frank had been wracked with worry that he would have to spend all his after school time alone with Mary and her Bible.

12.
Krann

In the months after Lawrence Kurt Krann was laid to rest in the Catholic section of Baker City's Mt. Hope Cemetery, the family managed to continue their long established daily routines though they were more like sleepwalkers operating under a dark cloud of grief. They were shaken from their stupor by the arrival of two hand-delivered letters.

One came from the letter writer for the local Chinese community informing August that the two men, Lo and Ping, who had worked side by side with Kurt and August at their placer claim for so long had returned to China to be reunited with their families. August had suspected as much since he had recently visited the claim and found it riddled with newly dug holes where the two men had apparently hidden their share of cash from their gold. He was especially glad that they had gone home, since he no longer had the heart to continue mining the claim without Kurt.

The second letter was delivered by a messenger from a new mining camp that had been established southeast of town. It brought the sad news that Miss Engel, the midwife who had safely delivered all of Marie's babies, had died of typhoid while tending a birth at the camp. Marie was both frightened and shocked by this news since the midwife had always stressed the need to keep herself, any woman she tended and the room where the birth took place as clean as possible. It seemed impossible that Miss Engel could die of a disease caused by unclean food or water, but then typhoid was the constant scourge of any mining camp.

Marie was in her last month of pregnancy and suddenly faced with the loss of her midwife whose abilities had earned the woman a justified reputation for performing safe, successful deliveries. Now Marie was filled with such a terrible sense of dread and fear for herself and for her unborn child that she finally shared her worries with Rosa and August who both suggested the same idea as a solution for the problem.

"I think we should talk to the nursing sisters at the hospital. The nuns would know of a good midwife to help you," coaxed August. "They have offered services to any miner who pays a dollar a month as a contribution, and the men I have talked to speak highly of how well they are cared for when they become ill or have an injury. Since our Archbishop Gross requested help from the Sisters of St. Francis of Philadelphia three years ago, their little hospital in the old school house on Second and Church has treated hundreds of miners, their wives and even their children."

"That's true," Rosa interjected, "And I have heard from some of my customers that women are very pleased with the hospital as a place for giving birth! You know how women gossip and talk about the most private things while hat shopping together. Recently they are all buzzing about the wonders of chloroform that women breathe in while in labor. Some say they just go to sleep and then wake up and it's all over. And practically without any pain at all!"

Marie was encouraged by these comments even though she was unhappy by the thought of giving birth anywhere other than at home in her own bedroom. Both she and Rosa were devote Catholics who attended mass every morning and had already met the three nuns who ran the little hospital next door to the church. Since one of them, Sister Mary Bruno, spoke German as well as English, Marie had spoken with her occasionally after mass and had been impressed by the nun's interest in their community and evident care for her patients. Marie also understood that they had no time to waste in finding a replacement for her beloved midwife, Miss Engel. She was much relieved that the good nun agreed to meet with her and Rosa the very next day.

• • •

"I wanted a chance to speak with the two of you before you meet our visiting doctor, Dr. Fielding," began Sister Bruno after ushering Marie and Rosa into the tiny hospital office where she beckoned Marie to sit in the lone chair stationed in front of a dusty desk, piled high with stacks of patient files. Rosa remained standing while Sister Bruno removed the empty chair behind the desk and brought it around to position it so that she could sit beside the pregnant woman while they talked.

"Marie, I can only imagine how upset you must be over the passing of Miss Engel, especially so close to the birth of your baby!" began Sister Bruno. " I hope that you will find that St. Elizabeth's is an acceptable substitute for that able woman. Should you agree to come here for the birth, I would be assisting Dr. Fielding in the delivery, and I have delivered hundreds of healthy babies."

"A man? I have never heard of a man delivering a baby." Marie responded with a look of undisguised alarm.

"We are told that doctors are now trained in newer methods for safer and less painful child birth. This is why we nurses are learning from a visiting doctor who has had this training..."

"Who moved my desk chair?" interrupted a man's voice from the office door as a flustered Sister Bruno jumped up and made an effort to drag the chair she had moved back behind the desk while attempting to introduce the man as the visiting Dr. Fielding. She also quickly explained why the two women wanted to meet with him.

"Well, I don't have the time right now to have some prolonged conversation about why it is a woman is so much better off delivered by a trained professional, a doctor, rather than by some backwoods midwife who will recommend a knife under the mattress to 'cut the pain,'" the physician barked as he quickly retreated and firmly closed the door on the three astounded women.

• • •

"Was the doctor angry with us or with Sister Bruno?" Marie wondered aloud as the two sisters walked home.

"Oh, he was not angry at all" Rosa answered, grateful for once that she had to interpret for Marie who had never even tried to learn English. "It seemed there was some emergency he had to attend to," she explained while vowing to find her sister a midwife who would deliver her at home.

. . .

But time had run out on their search to replace Miss Engel, for Marie went into labor that very evening and August took her back to the little hospital, grateful that Marie had told him how much she liked Sister Bruno.

As her contractions began to come close together, Dr. Fielding, without comment, clamped a chloroform mask over a startled Marie's nose and mouth. She did not regain consciousness until hours after her daughter, Anna, had been born and Sister Bruno had cleaned and dressed the infant and brought her to Marie's bed.

"What is wrong with her face? What is that red mark on her face?" Marie asked anxiously indicating a livid, red arch covering the infant's cheek.

"Don't worry. It will soon fade and she will be beautiful and perfect. The mark is from a tool the doctor used to help the baby out of the birth canal," Sister Bruno explained, without adding that such a crude tool is not necessary for an unobstructed birth like this one had been unless the woman is so heavily sedated that she cannot push to expel the child.

Sister Bruno also kept secret the on-going fight in which she was constantly engaged with this supercilious doctor who did not believe it necessary to sterilize the tools and gadgets he was all too eager to use even for uncomplicated births. The nun had been trained in Europe in Florence Nightingale's Environment Theory whereby nurses learned to manipulate all the variables in a patient's environment that might impeded recovery. Unnecessary noise, impure water or tainted food, putrid air, over-emotional visitors, unclean bedding and certainly the possibility of being touched or examined by unwashed hands or instruments were all to be avoided. Sister Bruno steadfastly refused to allow any instrument that she had not personally cleaned with rubbing alcohol to touch a patient. Even when she suggested the doctor wash his hands, he had rolled his eyes as though explaining to a dim-witted child, "Doctors do not have dirty hands."

Sister Bruno took Rosa and August aside when they came to take Marie and baby Anna home at the end of the usual two weeks of bed-rest. "As you can see, the mark on the baby's face has already faded and will soon be gone. I do need to warn you that the metal "forceps" which were the instruments the doctor used to extract the baby can also cause damage to the mother and, I know that this happened to Marie. She has an internal wound in the birth canal that has been closed and has thankfully not shown signs of infection. I do know that such a laceration is a permanent weakness and can reopen from the trauma of future births. Should such wounds become infected, most women do not survive the 'childbed fever' as I am sure you already know."

"What will you tell Marie?" Rosa wanted to know from August once they were home and Marie was asleep in her own bed.

"I will tell her there will be no more children. We are blessed with four and that is enough blessing for anyone." He stated with finality.

As Catholics, Rosa knew that Marie would need her husband's co-operation in abstaining from any activity that might put her in danger. But when she looked into his eyes, Rosa saw in August the iron deter-mination of a man who so loved his wife that he would do anything to keep her safe from harm.

• • •

For her part, Rosa was so busy building her own business that she had little time or energy to worry about Marie. She knew that she could not control the situation and felt lucky that she could completely trust August to keep her sister safe.

Though her hand-made creations were greatly admired by all the women of Baker City, by 1900, only the wives of the city's wealthi-est men could easily afford them. Women of lesser means had to save whatever they could for many months, sometimes years, before they could purchase a "Rosie hat." Only one other group of women had the means to regularly buy one of Rosa's hats, the city's high-end prostitutes.

After the turn of the century, Baker City was considered a place that had developed all the business and cultural amenities necessary to provide its citizens a measure of elegant living, but there still remained remnants of the once wild and wide-open mining camp town. Along with the many saloons, gambling houses and dance halls, the most colorful were thriving bawdy houses operating side by side with the banks, law offices, and department stores that filled the city's business district.

These employers of women involved in the "oldest profession" occupied every strata of a well-known caste system. At the top of prostitution's professional world was the "parlor house." In Baker City, only Jenny Duffy's three story mansion could be considered such a rarified establishment. It dominated the southeast end of Main Street's business district right before Main became tree-lined Dewey Avenue with its many lavish homes. These included the manse built by Mayor C.A. Johns who dreamed of one day becoming governor of Oregon and giving his acceptance speech from a window of the home's grand, four story turret. Though Johns lost his gubernatorial run, no one thought it was because he lived only a few doors down from Jenny's "house of ill repute."

Elite parlor houses, like Jenny Duffy's, employed only the youngest and most beautiful women who would meet and entertain men in a large, elegant parlor where these customers were expected to buy expensive meals and fine wines before retiring to a woman's splendidly furnished boudoir to be pampered and entertained for the entire night.

Only the wealthiest men could afford such fabulous treatment. Customers who could afford to enjoy what Jenny Duffy's had to offer were usually mining company magnates or rich men from Portland or Denver stopping over for an evening of pleasure where they could be sure to go unrecognized. They were invariably well-dressed and well-mannered. Should any man become loud, sloppily drunk, belligerent toward other customers or abusive toward any of the women, Jenny employed muscular bouncers to see that the offender quickly departed.

Across the street from Jenny Duffy's was Fanny Hall's establishment that could not be considered on a par with a parlor house, but was still a high-end brothel. The women were beautiful but usually older and never as expensively attired as those at Jenny's. An evening at Fanny's could include good food and liquor, but a man was not expected to purchase more than time with a woman which was by the hour, never the whole night.

Behind Fanny's and facing Bridge Street rather than Main, were several houses that were low-end brothels which were considered working men's whorehouses. They were shabby places that offered few amenities other than a short time with a woman often well-past her prime. A few of these women ran a volume business charging by the quarter-hour, but at least most cowboys, loggers or miners could afford a visit to one of these houses. This provided an important outlet for men living in a town where there were four men for every woman who was not a prostitute.

Baker City did not allow street walkers, so the lowest paid prostitutes worked out of "cribs" or tiny closet-sized rooms that were scattered about town and largely invisible since the women who worked in them rarely left their crib. They did not have to since men who could not afford a brothel always knew by word of mouth where the cribs were located. Most "crib girls" saw over twenty men a night. When the spring cattle drives were in town, a woman might see as many as seventy-five men a night. The women would often place a rubber rain cape over the end of their bed to protect it from the muddy boots of visitors.

Baker City's prostitutes provided a thriving market for Rosa's hats, but only women employed in Jenny Duffy's parlor house or one of the lesser high-end brothels could afford a made to order hat or who had the leisure time away from work to enjoy wearing one. Rosa had learned early that these customers favored large brimmed, elaborately trimmed hats. They had the practical advantage of providing cover for a messy hairdo when a woman wanted to venture out and about after an especially festive night. In addition, flamboyant, eye-catching trim could still attract male attention that might pay off later.

. . .

When Rosa first became the owner of her own millinery shop, she had enough money to invest in several hat trimmers and at least one sales woman besides herself to attend to the needs of customers. Unlike wealthy housewives who had servants to pick up a finished hat from Rosa's shop, prostitutes had no-one to do this kind of errand for them and preferred to have a new item delivered. Though Rosa had enough employees to send, she actually enjoyed doing this service herself. Over time, she developed her "parlor house trade" as a kind of boutique service where she brought samples of completed hats, various trim and drawings of the latest styles to Jenny Duffy's house for afternoon consults with the women.

The women were enjoyable to work with since they were actually far more adventuresome and knowledgeable about what was in fashion in the world outside of Baker City than were any of the married housewives in town. They were all very pretty, young and schooled in charm which made them quite good company. Additionally, their employer protected them from the kind of horrors experienced by the typical low-end prostitute. The house employed servants to do all the cooking and cleaning, so the girls could concentrate on pleasing their few clients. They ate the best food, drank the best wine, dressed expensively, made a lot of money and had free time for themselves every day.

It wasn't hard to understand why a girl might be drawn into this flamboyant and lavish lifestyle, though Rosa soon realized that they tended to live only for the moment. Few of them saved money and seemed to foolishly disregard the obvious signs that their circumstances could change at any moment. If a girl's looks slipped or she suffered a health problem or just failed to constantly please her clients, she was gone, and usually since she had already been cut off from polite society, her only choice was to take work at lesser establishments and begin an inevitable slide toward the gutter.

• • •

On one afternoon visit, Rosa sat with Madam Jenny Duffy sipping a glass of sherry. The two laughed and traded town gossip while a few of her girls tried on hat samples and consulted each other and Rosa about color, trim and style. Once the women had a chance to see and try on the samples, Rosa would consult with each individually.

Suddenly, they were all startled by the sound of Jenny's heavy front door crashing violently against an adjoining wall and a man's voice shouting, "Stand back ladies! Your prince has arrived!"

Then an obviously intoxicated young man in shabby work pants staggered through the parlor archway and immediately bumped into a small table knocking over a lamp that fell to the hardwood floor smashing its colorful glass shade to pieces. "Whoopsy daisy," he chuckled, surveying the resultant damage.

"Oh it's you again! I told you last night never to come back here again," an irate Jenny Duffy shouted bounding from her chair, "Jake! Jake! Oh Jake. Where, the hell is that man when you need him!"

Jake, Jenny's huge man servant and bouncer, could not have been too far away for he appeared almost immediately filling the room's doorframe with his bulk. He quickly assessed the reason that he had been summoned and strode to where the drunken man slouched against the opposite wall. Then Jake picked the drunk up by the shirt collar and seat of his pants and carried him to the open front door followed by the gang of women who crowded the front porch laughing and calling insults as the now thoroughly humiliated gate crasher was chucked unceremoniously into Main Street.

"Go to hell, all of you!" cried the young man, as he got unsteadily to his feet, though the women had already gone inside once the show was over. Only Rosa remained on the porch since she felt rather sorry for the young man who reminded her a little of her own brother, Matt.

"Are you hurt? Are you all right?" she called out.

"What the hell do you care? You whores are all alike! All you care about is a man's money!" he answered through clenched teeth.

"I, I'm not ...," she stammered, but realized he was already out of earshot and walking away, so she just shrugged and reentered the parlor house.

...

Unlike in most American towns and cities, Baker City's business district did not totally shut down every Sunday. Most of the larger stores in town were owned by European Jewish immigrants who closed their doors from sundown Friday night until early sun up on Sunday to celebrate the Jewish Sabbath. They would reopen to capture the Sunday trade from miners who needed supplies before they had to leave for a week of working their claims. Christian merchants who were closed on Sundays welcomed this lack of competition every Saturday and had no problem alternating weekend opening hours with over half the stores in town.

On Sunday morning, the day after the incident at Jenny Duffy's, as Rosa and Marie's family walked home together from Catholic Mass, Rosa began to worry that she might have forgotten to properly lock up her store after that day's unusual events. She explained to Marie that a quick check was necessary to put her mind to rest and then left the group promising to return home only moments behind them.

The day was mild and Rosa decided to walk to her shop down Main Street so that she could do a little "window shopping" on the way to her store. She especially wanted to see the window of the Heilner-Neuberger department store where she had consigned a few of her hats to be displayed for sale as an experimental alternative to the strictly one of a kind creations sold at her own store. She examined the display for many minutes and came away pleased with the presentation. The window dresser had placed the hats on a bed of rose colored satin surrounded by faux pearl jewelry which added a note of luxury and showed off each hat to advantage.

Rosa was surprised that for a Sunday, the north end of Main was very busy with shoppers piling into Heilner's and across the street she noted many large family groups crowding into the Geiser Grand Hotel for their fabulous Sunday menu. She thought to herself that it would be fun to take the family there on her birthday in a few weeks when she turned twenty six.

The South end of Main was much quieter since Rosa's store was located near a saddle shop and a brewery, neither of which was open on any Sunday. Once she arrived at the store, she immediately tried the door and was relieved that it was securely locked. It had not really been the door that worried her most. She just could not recall locking the side door of the shop which opened onto an alleyway where store deliveries were made. She hurried around the corner to check that door, and she found it had indeed been left unlocked. As Rosa retrieved the key from her purse, she perceived movement out of the corner of her eye, but when she stopped to look in that direction she was irritated to see a pile of empty packing crates that should have been removed by those making deliveries. Whenever clouds moved from in front of the sun, the boxes threw a long shadow across the alley.

Rosa made a mental note to pay Matt to break up the boxes and take the wood home for kindling. She always tried to find jobs for Matt who was in a deep pit of grief over Kurt's murder. She had been grateful that August had recently signed himself and Matt up for a double-jacking contest with a large purse to be held in Sumpter, a town named by some Confederate miners who thought Fort Sumter was spelled with a "p."

The two of them practiced their teamwork every afternoon until both of them fell into bed utterly exhausted. Rosa smiled to herself when she remembered Matt had told August that he didn't think he could live up to his father's drilling ability. August had looked the tall, skinny boy up and down. Anyone who had never seen this incredibly, strong tireless young man at work would chalk him up as a contest pushover. "Oh, I think you'll do every bit as nicely as your father," August had announced with a wink to Rosa.

Chuckling over the memory, she turned and bent to lock the door when a hand grabbed her at the elbow and jerked her backwards so hard that she nearly lost her balance.

"Well, well, well little lady. I do believe we have met before, you being one of the whores who had such a good laugh on me yesterday," purred the menacing voice of the young man who Rosa last saw walking away from Jenny's house. "Now that you aren't surrounded by your little friends and that muscle bound pile of shit who threw me into the street, we can take some time and get to know each other."

At first, in her rising panic, Rosa did not notice the knife the man was holding until she felt the point pressing painfully through the thin silk of her blouse.

"Wh, What do you want?" she muttered without taking her frightened eyes off the blade near her heart.

"Well, what do you think? I sure don't want no conversation. You may be from a fancy house, but you're still a tramp and you know well enough that a man don't plunk down a week's wage for no conversation," he growled and began cutting off the small pearl buttons of Rosa's blouse while his other hand covered her mouth before she could work up a scream.

His powerful arm had her head securely pinned against his sweaty shirt front. However, both of her hands were still free and she was just tall enough to claw at his eyes and stomp down hard on the arch of his foot which made him shriek and drop his knife. In the brief moment when he lost his grip on her, Rosa shook free and ran blindly down the alley, around the corner and toward the bustle of North Main Street.

As she turned the corner, Rosa was aware that her attacker had picked up his knife and was heading down the alley in her direction. She kept on running without looking back and tried desperately to remember which stores were likely to be open on Sunday. Rosa unsuccessfully tried several doors until she saw a woman enter Levinger's Drug Store. She grabbed the door before it closed and ran inside. The owner, Louis Levinger, saw the girl with her torn and bloodied blouse crumple sobbing to the floor just inside his door and ran to her side. His wife, Lyle, ran from the other end of the store and the two of them helped Rosa into a back office away from curious eyes.

By the end of that tumultuous weekend, Rosa finally rested safe at home. It did not take much in the way of argument from the Levingers and then from her own family to convince her that she must hire a man to make deliveries for her.

As for the angry young man, she would not see him again for three years. By then, his name had become known throughout the county, and his story would claim front page news coverage for months in Baker City.

13.
McColloch

C.H. sat alone in his Portland firm's law library staring at a letter laid flat on the table before him. It was from Eugene Bartholf, general manager of The Constellation Mining Company of Sumpter Oregon. For such a short letter, it had certainly packed an emotional wallop. After reading it twice, C.H. knew that he faced a crossroads in life that required the kind of decision that could easily determine what was left of his future.

The content of the first part of the letter was what he had expected it to be, a newsy update about a new mining company in the Cable Cove District near Sumpter in Eastern Oregon. He had done some work over a two year period to provide legal guidance in its incorporation, so this letter thanked him for his service. He thought wryly that he should be the one expressing thanks.

The work had actually been the most exciting thing he had done since passing the bar and securing a job in corporate law. It had provided him a chance to leave the confines of the firm's musty law library for the first time in the three years since he had been hired. As a newly minted lawyer, he was never allowed to consult directly with clients, nor did he ever see the inside of a courtroom. Instead, he was relegated to dull, library research day after day to provide the firm's partners with information concerning legal precedent that would support their various cases.

Since Oregon's economy was based on the state's wealth of natural resources, most of C.H.'s research centered on issues of law surrounding the logging, fishing, and mining industries. He had been most interested in mining, but he feared that the closest he would ever come to an actual mine would always be the hours spent reading mining law. He did not fully realize that all his research was making him quite knowledgeable on the subject and his expertise had not gone unrecognized by his superiors.

Occasionally, C.H. would be asked to sit in on a meeting one of the senior partners would have with a client. At first, he had been told that he was not to speak in such a meeting but to just quietly take notes as directed by any of the meeting participants and later look up the information needed for their next meeting. However, the younger lawyer's level of expertise in mining matters became clear, when he began to provide written answers within the context of an initial meeting without the need to run to the law library or mining archives. Finally, all the firm's attorneys began to ask C.H. for oral comment rather than continuing the cumbersome note-passing during their client meetings. For this reason, he was asked one day to attend a meeting with J.E. Reed, president of the board for the Constellation Gold Mining Company. C.H. saw, at once, as he walked into the room, that this must be a meeting the firm felt was of the highest importance because every senior partner was seated around the table.

That meeting ended with the decision that C.H. would travel to Eastern Oregon to help a group of men in Sumpter, form a corporation holding ten lode mine claims and three stamp mills they claimed had great potential for future earnings. In addition, to providing legal consult, the senior partners of the firm were very interested in the project as a possible investment opportunity as individuals, since there had been much recent news that a renewed gold rush was on in the area around, Sumpter, the little boom town in the Elkhorn Mountains.

...

Within a week, C.H. was on a train headed east along with Mary and ten year old Frank, since it was the boy's summer break from school. Claude, who was now in high school, could not join them because he had landed a coveted summer job as a junior reporter with Portland's nationally recognized newspaper, *The Oregonian.*

C.H. was amused watching his son take in the wonders of the Columbia River Gorge from the window of their private room. The boy had been a feverish ball of excitement since the day he found out about this trip to a place he had learned still held the promise of Wild West adventure so lacking in the large, settled cities west of the Cascade Range.

Mary, on the other hand, was less enthused about the trip, but agreed to go along, since C.H. explained that the work would take over a month to complete. She also had less responsibility with her Temperance Union group because she had been voted out as president over her inability to get along with the erasable, stiff-necked Abigail Duniway. The situation had put her in a foul mood for months, and C.H. hoped that a change of scene would help her cope.

Mary had been pleasantly surprised that Baker City turned out to be a rather civilized place. They stayed three nights in the Geiser Grand Hotel and Mary was amazed at the hotel's sophisticated appointments and the gorgeous suite of rooms they were given in the building's clock tower. She was further impressed by the dining room's fantastic menu that even featured such extravagant selections as Atlantic Blue Point oysters, turtle soup, prime rib, and roast pheasant. Frank was especially partial to the offering of English ice cream and assorted cakes which his father allowed him to order as a main course one night.

After C.H. had time to examine the many records of lode mine claims housed in Baker City, the family purchased tickets on the Sumpter Valley Railroad passenger train. Frank eagerly accepted an invitation from the engineer to sit up in the engine cab for the twenty five mile trip as the single gage locomotive chugged up a steep track that seemed to hang without support over sheer cliffs carved by the Powder River far below. Frank leaned so far out the open side window of the slow moving train trying to see the bottom of the deep canyon that the laughing engineer had to hold the back of the boy's belt to keep him from toppling out.

As they reached the Sumpter Valley plateau, Frank was entranced by a line of two dozen boys fishing along the banks of the fast moving

Powder. He watched and waved at ranch-hands harvesting the summer Eastern Oregon grass to use for feeding stock all winter. He gave a loud "whoop" at the sight of three cowboys on horseback riding herd on a few cows that threatened to try crossing the rail tracks ahead. The engineer reached out and placed Frank's hand on the train's whistle cord and the boy pulled blast after blast of the horn, long after the stray cows had been frightened away. By the time the train reached Sumpter station, Frank was deeply engaged in weighing whether to pursue a future career as a cowboy or as a railroad engineer.

As the family disembarked the train, they were met by J.E. Reed who introduced all three to Eugene Bartholf, the general manager of the Constellation Co. He explained that Mr. Bartholf would be their guide for a trip around Sumpter in his open carriage and then they would be taken to the Sumpter Hotel where they would be accommodated during their stay in the town.

"I believe that you will be impressed by our little town," Mr. Bartholf began with evident pride, as the carriage proceeded down Granite Street, "Why just ten years ago, our population was a few hundred people and now we have 3,500 citizens according to the last census not counting women, children and the Chinese, of course."

"The women don't count, of course." Mary whispered into her husband's ear.

"Back then, there were only saloons, one market and a few rooming houses," their guide continued apparently without noticing the looks that passed between the couple. "Now, you'll be surprised to learn that we have seven hotels, six fine restaurants, seven general stores, two banks, five cigar stores, six law offices, an opera house that provides wonderful entertainment, a dance hall, sixteen saloons and a handful of churches!"

"A little heavy on the saloons..." C.H. heard Mary mutter and squeezed her hand in a rather tight grip that he hoped, in vain, would shut her up.

"We also boast the most modern electric light plant, a much needed new saw mill due to our booming house construction, and a very busy telephone and telegraph office." he explained, while pointing out each imposing structure.

"What's down that street?" C.H. inquired just to make conversation as their carriage continued past a street without turning.

"Oh, ha, ha! That's just Cracker Street. You won't want to walk down there." Mr. Bartholf answered rather nervously, then added, "It's the red light district. We're working on that. You see the miners complain whenever the town fathers vote to clean it up. We are surrounded by thirty-five area mines that extracted $8.9 million last year alone! So, when the miners speak, we listen. You can bet on that!"

"I guess the sixteen saloons, the dance hall and the opera house don't provide enough 'entertainment' for them?!" Mary put in and quickly removed her hand from that of her husband before he could possibly break one of her fingers.

...

In the weeks to follow, C.H. was caught up in daily meetings of the Constellation group and the resultant paperwork in the office provided him on the second floor of the First National Bank. In addition to this activity, he was interviewed frequently by reporters from the Sumpter Miner, a newspaper that filled its weekly twelve pages with stories meant to highlight the robust mining economy of this fast growing town. Naturally, the paper devoted a lot of space to such an important concern as the Constellation, especially since the directors of the company planned to purchase expensive half-page ads on the paper's front page meant to trumpet their upcoming stock offering. C.H., at the center of all the enthusiastic cheerleading, was totally swept up and energized in a way he had never experienced before.

As for Frank, the town was also working its magic on the boy. Almost immediately, he had made friends with other boys of the town. In turn, they introduced Frank to exciting daily adventures in the wild forests of the Elkhorn. He had learned to shoot a gun and found he was a pretty good shot. When he knocked over three of four tin cans lined up on a fence, the other boys slapped him on the back and called him "a natural sharphooter." So, whenever the group was not exploring a cave, fishing the Powder River, or peeking in the windows of Cracker Street, they took their guns to the woods in search of small game. In short, Frank was sure that he had died and gone to heaven.

Mary remained the only family member who was not thrilled with Sumpter. "Appalled" was a more accurate word. There really was little about the place she approved of. The women married to mine owners and other business types dutifully entertained her and C.H. in their homes and they were nice enough, to be sure. However, when she attempted to discuss anything that was not related to children, new recipes for pie, or the next church social they seemed to quickly change the subject. Only once, she mentioned national politics and the suffrage movement and was met with blank stares. What bothered her most was that none of these fine folks seemed to care much about the sinful underbelly of Sumpter represented by the overabundance of saloons with their whiskey, gambling and "upstairs girls."

Mary managed to keep her negative feelings to herself. In truth, her husband and son were far too busy having a great time to even notice that she was not. After that first day, she never criticized or complained. She figured that she could manage her plastered smile for a few more weeks to keep the peace. She did well with it too. That is until Sumpter's big Fourth of July celebration.

...

Frank was quite excited by the roundup of usual Sumpter July Fourth activities described by his new friends. There would be a parade in the morning, an afternoon town picnic, and various races and contests throughout the day and plenty of fireworks come evening. Even Mary looked forward to the holiday since it all seemed more wholesome than the gambling, drinking and whoring that usually took place every Saturday night when hundreds of miners with a little gold dust to convert into cash descended on the town.

The family joined the onlookers that lined Granite Street early in the day and waved tiny American flags as horse drawn floats passed by representing the Red Men, the Woodmen and the Knights of Pythias lodges that provided the social life for Sumpter family men and their wives. The Sumpter Orchestra converted itself into a fairly decent marching band and was greeted by cheers as it played rousing John Phillip Sousa tunes. Frank was wowed by an eighteen-horse team pulling some huge piece of lode mining machinery.

The parade was followed by speeches and a performance by the Catholic Church choir given from a high temporary platform that had been erected in front of the Sumpter Bank building on Mill Street. At noon, it was announced that the contests would commence and Mary was beginning to notice that the crowd had changed once the speeches were over. As the families left for home, young men began piling out of nearby saloons in various states of inebriation.

Since C.H., Mary and Frank had gotten there so much earlier, they had secured a prime spot close to the platform, but the new arrivals began pushing and jostling for a position as close as possible to better see the mining contest event. The family was soon fairly smothered by sweaty men who so wreaked of whiskey that Mary had to press a scented handkerchief to her nose to keep from fainting.

Mary tugged at her husband's sleeve to get his attention in the melee, "I think we should leave. This is just awful!," she shouted over the crowd noise.

But, C.H. shook his head, "I really want to see these single and double-jacking contests between miners. I need to have some knowledge about this if I am to represent mining companies. Why don't you take Frank back to the hotel," he said, bending close to her ear.

She took Frank, who did not want to leave the excitement, by the hand and attempted to lead him through the crowd just as a fight broke out near the back of the crowd which surged in the direction of the combatants. This allowed a path out for Mary to drag her unhappy son.

As they wormed their way to the hotel, Mary noticed that men were lined up to place bets inside the bank. Many others were making informal bets between themselves. As though public drunkenness and street brawling was not shocking enough, now the city was also encouraging sinful gambling on a national holiday!

"Mother! Look at those beautiful ladies!" Frank shouted over the din and pointed toward a group of women that were conspicuously dressed in a rainbow of form clinging, low cut satin dresses. Each was painted up with bright red lip rouge which was calculated to draw attention. This ploy was apparently effective, for Frank stared in gaping appreciation of this feminine array.

Mary turned in the direction Frank was pointing and was horrified to see an obvious group of Cracker Street denizens infiltrating the crowd of miners hoping to pick up a few new customers. She swirled back and grabbed her son's arm with a force he had never before experienced.

"Frank! Stop gawking at those, those women! And they are certainly not 'ladies', young man!" she cried and continue to drag Frank, who was mystified as to what had made his mother so angry.

C.H. was also puzzled when he returned to the hotel room and was met at the door by a fuming Mary. He was completely taken aback by her mood since he had totally enjoyed the day.

He had already concluded that the double-jacking contest was the highlight. He had not done any betting himself, but wished he had made a bet on the team that won the grand prize money. Like most in the crowd, he had badly underestimated the fifty-something older man paired with a gangly youth who looked as though he would be unable to lift the heavy sledge hammer let alone able to drive a spike through solid rock to form a competitive hole. He noticed that many of the drunks were laughing at the team.

But when the two began to work with perfect rhythm and obvious power, the derisive laughter faded away and the crowd actually began to cheer. In the end, no-one was surprised when the bank president took up the megaphone to announce that the grand prize winners was the team of "Gritty Gus and The Kid." C.H. who stood just below the contest platform, was amused to see the team handed two envelops by the banker. He thought to himself, that these two must have certainly won a lot of additional money bet against them.

C.H. was sorry that Mary had missed the excitement of the contest and was about to propose that they take Frank to the town picnic and fireworks when he was met at their hotel room door by Mary with obvious fury in her eyes.

"I never thought that I would live to see a more sinful place than Hot Springs, Arkansas! But this, this place ranks right up there with Sodom and Gomorrah!" was Mary's surprising answer to the picnic suggestion. "This whole trip has been a revelation to me," she continued in an odd, chocked whisper which was an apparent effort to keep Frank, who had been sent to his own room, from overhearing what she had to say to her husband.

"I don't understand. Towns all over the country celebrate the Fourth just like they did here with parades and picnics. What has you so riled up, Mary?"

"That attitude of yours is exactly what has me 'riled up'! You so apparently see nothing wrong with public drunkenness, wanton gambling and traffic with whores in the public square!" She fairly spit out the words in the same horse whisper which by now was no doubt audible in the next room. "It is finally clear to me that your acceptance of the sin in others is just as sinful especially because it teaches the worst kind of lesson to your son! Do you know that he was actually ogling prostitutes in the crowd today and even said they are beautiful!"

"For heaven's sake, Mary. He's never before seen women who dress as colorfully. He has a ten year olds taste which I am confident he will soon outgrow."

"He won't outgrow liking the look of whores or the drinking and gambling sinful men take part in as long as his own father just shrugs his shoulders over all the sin around him, as though such behavior is nothing to care about."

"What are you saying? Because I don't chose to chastise strangers for behavior I don't participate in makes me a bad father and a sinner too?"

"It certainly does. And don't even try to tell me you never have a drink of whiskey." she countered.

"I won't try to tell you that. If I have a friendly drink with another man it's an adult activity in an adult place far from the eyes of my son. So far as I know, your prohibition friends have not yet succeeded in making such a pleasant form of human interacton illegal." C.H. responded with more than a measure of hurt anger in his voice.

"You believe that whiskey consumed with other men in a saloon is not sin? Well, maybe you should try a little time in church if that's your twisted thinking on the subject. Reverend Crocker would tell you that 'whiskey is all right in its place-but that place is hell!'"

"So, now all I need to cure my 'twisted thinking' and sinful nature is some church time with the circus tent revivalist crowd you follow. Well that group with all their breast beating and sanctimonious hosannas and halleluiahs will never convince me to join their merry band! If I have a choice, I have to go with Twain who advised, 'Heaven for climate, Hell for company!'" C.H. called after Mary who had retreated behind their locked bedroom door leaving him seething and alone in the small parlor.

...

For months after their return from the fateful trip to Sumpter, C.H. and Mary maintained an icy distance. For his part, C.H. had been sorry that he had allowed himself to be provoked to the point that he had said some very hurtful things out of anger. He could think of no way to end their stand-off except one. He must make an effort to do some of the things Mary most wanted of him and at the top of that list was to attend her church with her. There was really no choice in this since he knew from long experience that her stubborn will would not allow her to give in and come to him first.

Mary's reaction to this concession was far better than he had expected it to be. When he suggested that he would like to attend her church on the following Sunday, the ice melted and she flew into his arms nearly knocking him off his feet. He thought to himself that a little church-going was worth it if it meant that he had his wife back.

...

Mary's Presbyterian Church had changed since in the year she first attended. It was no longer the homey little Swedish Mission Friends because the pastor Reverend Crocker had taken on the trappings and preaching style of the very successful revivalist crusades that drew thousands in attendance across the U.S. As a follower of D.L. Moody, and John Wilber Chapman he had always stressed saving souls and leading his flock to salvation. But his preaching had been most influenced by a new comer to the crusade circuit, the popular baseball player turned evangelist star, Billy Sunday. Crocker no longer just gave a quiet weekly sermon from the pulpit, but now engaged in the acrobatic antics and colorful language that was typical of a Billy Sunday revival. He was in constant motion, pacing back and forth on the speaking platform, at times jumping into the audience to embrace someone or running down the aisle to continue his address from the back of the room. He was backed by a retinue of choral performers that punctuated Crocker's disjointed sermon with spirited selections that always brought the audience to their feet, clapping and swaying to the music. All this participation seemed to electrify the audience, but it just embarrassed C.H. who cringed each time Crocker appeared to head in his direction.

C.H. also noted that the preacher's message was generally anti-sin but specifically was anti-alcohol and the moral necessity of setting a temperate example for one's children. Crocker borrowed liberally from the "Echoes of Glory" tracts written by Billy Sunday. He said, "Be careful, father, or while you are taking one lap around the devil's track your boy will make six." And, "To train a boy in the way he should go, you must go that way yourself." C.H. was beginning to think Mary had ordered up this sermon just for him when Crocker said, "Whiskey is all right in its place-but its place is Hell."

"Now where have I heard that before?" C.H. said to Mary who pretended not to hear him.

Once the sermonizing was over, a special choir selection seemed to be the signal for those is the audience who felt especially moved by the Holy Spirit to prove it by flinging themselves onto the steps of the altar platform. When that group returned to their seats and the choir quieted, Crocker came to the center of the stage and looked right at Mary and C.H. seated several rows back.

"We are privileged to have a new visitor today that we will take into our hearts. Sister Mary has brought us her husband, Charles, to join our congregation. Will the two of you come forward to be recognized," the pastor announced in a voice loud enough C.H. was sure could be heard on the street.

"He just wants to give us his blessing", Mary coaxed her reluctant husband forward with her.

Once they stood as directed beside the pastor on the alter platform, Crocker produced a Bible which he held out and intoned, "We are all of us eager to share your rebirth in the love of Jesus Christ. It is not enough to have a Christian wife. That alone will not save your soul. You have to be more than a brother- in- law to the church. Your salvation rests here in the holy words of this book and in your sacred promise to renounce sin and therein receive God's eternal grace. Are you ready, Charles, to place your hand on the Bible and take the vow to renounce the evil that most threatens our society, namely demon rum and all the animal behavior and destruction of the soul caused by this tool of the devil?!"

C.H. was stunned and totally unprepared for what this preacher was asking him to do. He looked at the Bible as it was pushed closer to him and he looked at Mary who mouthed the words "go on." Then, without a word, he turned and walked down the aisle, picked up his hat from his seat and continued out the door.

The next day C.H. reread the letter sent to him from the Constellation Group of Sumpter Oregon. The second part of the letter was now of primary interest since it contained an offer to join their board of directors and to take a more active role with the company which would require him to spend several months living and working in Sumpter. Several months? After a moment's reflection, he took out a clean sheet of paper and wrote, "Dear Sirs, I am happy to accept a position on the Constellation Group board of directors..."

14.
Krann

Rosa Krann particularly loved the Christmas season in Baker City since, as a business owner with a Main Street location, she would join the rest of those in commerce along that wide thoroughfare to decorate for the season. She had always thought it interesting that all the store merchants, even the large number of Jewish merchants, took extra pains to fill their windows with the evergreen boughs and other symbols signifying the season. In truth, these symbols were never religious in nature but rather the more secular array of snowmen, decorated evergreen trees, candle lit wreaths, candy stuffed stockings and piles of brightly wrapped presents tied up in big red bows which, of course, carried a not so subtle message that December should include lavish gift giving whether one's family celebrated Christmas and the birth of Jesus or the Maccabees' rescue and rededication of the Holy Temple in Jerusalem commemorated by the Hanukkah Festival of Lights.

For Rosa, the season was one time that she could pull out all the stops and instead of a window presentation meant to convey elegant sophistication, she could indulge in the kind of extravagant ornamentation and whimsy that would be considered garish or childish any other time of year. For 1902, she had created a faux sky of gauzy white tulle covered with patches of sequins that flashed brightly even in the weak December sunlight. Between the ample folds of the material, she hung on various lengths of pink satin ribbon a large number of cherubic angels fashioned out of tiny identical baby dolls purchased from the toy department of Heilner's to which she had added tulle wings and silver wire halos. These hovered above snowy hills of cotton batting that displayed, along with her collection of tree ornaments, some of Rosa's flashier seasonal hats.

As Rosa stood on the walk outside her store checking the effect of her work, she did not notice that someone was standing behind her until she heard a small appreciative laugh.

"Oh Rosie! You have outdone yourself this year. What a fun, adorable window creation!" cried the onlooker who, Rosa realized, was Mary Henner a long time customer who only visited the store a few times a year since the woman lived with her husband, a wealthy rancher, thirty miles north of Baker City near the community of Haines.

"Why thank you, Mary! I always wonder if people will think I have lost my mind around Christmas time, but I just love thinking up these seasonal windows and I have noticed that even some of the more conservative store owners have become a little more daring in their window displays over the years."

"I have noticed that too, though I imagine that it is the wives not their crusty husbands who have taken a hand in the decoration," Mary laughed. "At any rate, that is a reason that I make a point to make at least one of my few trips here a year at Christmas. But, this year I have a reason more than for just Christmas shopping and that reason involves you, Rosie."

"Really? Then I think we should go inside where we can warm up with some tea and you can tell me what I can do for you. We aren't open for business for a while, so it will be quiet and we won't be interrupted."

Once seated over their tea, Mary got right to the point for wanting to speak alone with Rosa. She explained that two of her sisters, Blanche and Minnie, had accompanied her on this particular trip and that she had left them eating breakfast after the three had spent the night at the Geiser Grand. Mary said that she and Blanche had cooked up the trip as a way to help Minnie get over a break up with a young man who their parents and Minnie's ten siblings all believed was, in her words "completely unsuitable."

"It was nothing more than a 'crush', really. My sister, Minnie, is something of a romantic and doesn't have a practical bone in her body. And this man, I have heard, is charming. I have never seen him but my sister, Blanche, met him a year ago when a bunch of miners working west of the Elkhorns attended a dance at the Haines Grange. She told me that he is quite handsome, but that certainly can't make up for the fact that he is just an uneducated, common laborer and a drifter to boot. Even Minnie admitted that he has no family, was orphaned at age four and has been on his own since he was only thirteen. Minnie is educated, well read and anyone will tell you, is simply beautiful. She teaches school at Muddy Creek which is where they met since he was digging ditches there for the Maxwell Mining Company. I can't even imagine what they have to talk about. They have absolutely nothing in common, but Minnie has spent most of her life with her nose in a book and has never had a real-life romance. She cannot know that what she is feeling is no more than infatuation and that without more basis, never lasts. Finally, our parents took charge of the situation when they found out from a young woman who is a confidante of Minnie's that this man had actually proposed marriage and, worse than that, my sister was considering the idea! Our father put his foot down and convinced Minnie to write to this person and end the relationship. As a dutiful daughter, she wrote the letter, but now is understandably heartsick. Blanche and I hope that a dose of cheer that you and your ladies here always bring to any shopping trip will help poor Minnie get past this sad episode!"

"Oh dear," Rosa responded to this unrealistic expectation. "I know from experience in this business that a new hat can do wonders for a woman's mood, but I don't know if a hat can fix a broken heart."

As it turned out, Rosa felt that she and her sales ladies had at least met with a measure of success in their efforts to cheer Minnie. By the end of the afternoon, the girl had even begun to smile in response to her reflection as she tried on a series of hats and a new line of removable lace collars that Rosa had created to dress up a plain gown for any special occasion. When she showed the women pictures of the hats and collars that were fashionable in New York and in Europe they all agreed that Minnie would be gorgeous decked out in Rosa's creations on a European trip she would soon make with her parents right after Christmas.

Rosa already knew that Minnie's parents, Mr. and Mrs. Ensminger, were wealthy and owned one of the largest ranches in the Haines/Rock Creek area. "It must be nice to be able to give one's daughter a grand tour of Europe in order to help her get over a broken heart!" she told August and Marie over dinner that night.

"If she's smart, she'll have a broken heart every year!" observed ten year old Betty with a wry smile, as the adults all turned to stare at the usually very serious little girl before bursting into fits of laughter.

...

Christmas was always an exceptionally joyous time for the Krann/ Meyer family and the celebration traditionally began on Christmas eve when the entire family would attend midnight mass at the little Mission Church of St. Francis de Sales. The children loved the yearly telling of the Nativity story and would sit in perfect quiet not to miss a word about the night that the baby Jesus was born in a Bethlehem sta- ble. As they walked home afterwards, the younger children would be full of questions about this miraculous event. On the night of Decem- ber 24, 1902 it was the youngest, Anna, who began the usual analysis of the Biblical account.

"Wasn't Mary worried that a horse might step on her baby? What if they all fell asleep and a horse accidently stepped on the baby?" fret- ted the four year old.

"That would never happen. The shepherds were there to watch out for the horses, remember?" Instructed seven year old Harry. "And if the shepherds fell asleep, then the angels would always start singing real loud to wake everyone up," he told the girl who nodded at her big brother's evident wisdom about that holy night.

Once home, Marie immediately served everyone dinner since they would all be famished from fasting before receiving Holy Communion. Their tradition was to have a meal of wonderful Apfelpfannkuchen. Marie could produce these light and airy apple pancakes hot from the oven in only minutes since she had prepared the batter ahead of time. Then, just before midnight, everyone would turn in to rest up for a new day of special treats from the candy filled stockings and gifts left under the tree by Father Christmas in the morning to the evening when the family would sit down around Marie's a candle lit dinner table groaning with succulent roast goose, cheesy potatoes and pickled red cabbage.

...

While one family peacefully slept and dreamed, another family, thirty miles away, was leaving an annual dance party held at Joseph and Mary Henner's ranch just as the clock struck one o'clock Christmas morning. Mary Henner had continued her campaign to help mend her sister Minnie's broken heart, and had invited several unattached young men to the party figuring that the best cure for Minnie's present unhappiness would be to enjoy the company of some attractive local bachelors.

When the party started, Mary kept a sharp eye on Minnie and was gratified to see her sister sitting with two young men and, miracle of miracles, Minnie was laughing! It seemed to Mary that Minnie fairly glowed and appeared to be far happier than she had been in weeks. Mary could not help but be proud of her own splendid plan, but as she was lost in quiet self-congratulation, her sister Blanche interrupted.

"Mary! That man is here!" Blanche whispered with obvious agitation. "The fella who wanted to marry Minnie is here!"

"What are you babbling about, Blanche? I assure you that my guest list did not include Minnie's former beau!" countered Mary.

"You didn't invite him! You hired him! Look at the musicians. The man playing the fiddle. That's him. That's Pleasant Armstrong! He's the same man I saw playing the fiddle at the Grange dance! And he's the same man who asked Minnie to marry him!" Blanche explained breathlessly.

Mary turned to look closely at the handsome young man playing the fiddle. She immediately noticed that he was staring at Minnie who sat, with her back turned, across the room laughing and surrounded by admirers. "My God, Blanche! You never told me that the guy played the fiddle! How could this have happened! We have to do something before he makes a scene!"

The two women realized that they had to act fast because the musicians had finished their number and announced a short break. But just as they were telling their father and brothers of the problem, Mary saw, out of the corner of her eye, the fiddle player cross the room to the group where Minnie sat unaware. Before Pleasant Armstrong could speak to Minnie, the Ensminger men surrounded him and began pushing him toward the door.

"You are not welcome here, sir," announced Minnie's irate father.

"We think you need to tell your music group over there that you have a headache and want to leave," added one of Minnie's brothers. "Ah, here is my sister, Blanche, with your coat."

"I just, just need to talk to Minnie." Pleasant replied weakly as he struggled against the group "You, you people made her write me a letter that I know she never meant. She loves me! We love each other and want to be together as man and wife! Minnie, tell them what I say is true!" he called out when he saw that the girl was standing by her chair watching in shocked disbelief. Then, without a word, she merely responded by turning away.

"Never! I will never love anyone but you Minnie!" he cried, wiping tears with his coat sleeve. Then he turned and left the house and ran into the gloom of a moonless night.

Though most of the party guests were unaware of the drama that occurred at their party, poor Minnie had lost her festive glow and sat alone brooding over the disturbing events. Since the dance melodies were primarily provided by the fiddler, the other two musicians stopped playing altogether and decided to leave without payment, so the party broke up earlier than usual. Minnie and Blanche walked with some of the last guests into the barnyard to bid them "goodbye" before boarding their parents' sleigh for the short ride home.

Just as Minnie began to climb aboard, Blanche shrieked at the sight of a dark figure bounding out of the trees. Before Minnie could turn to look, Pleasant Armstrong fired two pistol shots into her back and she crumpled to the ground in front of her horrified family. Then, Armstrong turned the gun on himself firing a shot at his own forehead.

The remaining party guests carried Minnie who was still conscious into the ranch house and placed her carefully on a couch. She would lay there intensely suffering from one of the bullets that punctured her left lung and then penetrated her diaphragm while Haines doctor, Charles Francis attended her around the clock. After two days barely able to take a breath and in horrible pain, she mercifully died.

As for Pleasant, they left him in the barnyard, lying on his back alive but unconscious with blood trickling into the snow from his minor self-inflicted head wound. Within a few hours, Jess Snow, the Baker County Sheriff's Deputy arrived to escort Pleasant to the Baker City jail. When Pleasant heard of Minnie's death he hung his head and declared, "I'm sorry that the last shot was not sure."

...

No-one in Rosa's family heard of the happenings on the Henner ranch as they quietly enjoyed their Christmas festivities. Since Christmas fell on a Thursday, only a few Baker City merchants decided to open their stores the next day. Many, like Rosa, who did not sell items people might need over the weekend, did not open until Monday, December 29th. By the time Rosa returned to unlock her shop door on that Monday, it seemed the entire town buzzed with the news that Minnie Ensminger had been murdered by a jealous lover.

Rosa's saleswomen all knew that she had been visited before Christmas by Minnie and her sisters. They did not keep this information to themselves and by noon the shop was packed with Baker City citizens wanting to hear about the visit. Try as she may, Rosa was unable to convince anyone that she had no inside knowledge about Minnie's romance with her killer. Finally, she hid out in a back room and instructed her employees to tell anyone asking for her that she had gone home with a headache.

As they were closing the store for the day, Rosa emerged from hiding only to find her trimmers and saleswomen still chattering about the crime and about the preliminary hearing scheduled for the next day at the Baker City Courthouse.

"Will you be going to the hearing, Rosie?" one wide-eyed girl wanted to know. "The papers say this Pleasant Armstrong is very handsome."

"That's right. They call him 'an Adonis," put in another.

"Of course not." Rosa responded with some irritation. "If you all want to give up your lunch time to go, that's fine, but I have a business to run."

...

Seeing that Rosa was not interested in their talk, the girls turned to each other to share whatever snippets of exciting gossip they had heard about Minnie and her murderer while Rosa went through the motions of closing up.

Though she tried to ignore them, Rosa was suddenly stunned by one girl who said, "I heard that he already had a bad reputation before this thing happened, which is one reason her parents refused to accept him. They said he showed up drunk once to a Haines church supper and acted so bad they threw him out! And another time he actually chased some poor girl with a knife, because she would not go out with him! I guess he has a very dark side to his nature."

To this another girl barked a derisive laugh and added,"Yes, Sarah, as a rule of thumb most men who kill their girlfriends have a 'dark side to their nature."

"What was that you said that he did?" Rosa asked trying not to sound too interested.

"Oh, he was thrown out of a church supper and came back with a gun and shot it at the crowd but was too drunk to take aim, so no-one was hurt. He was arrested for it and put in jail, anyway."

"No, not that. The thing you said about a knife and chasing a girl. Who was the girl?" Rosa questioned, trying hard to sound casual.

"I asked about that too, but no-one I asked seemed to know."

"It sounds like the kind of rumor we should all write off as idle gossip." Rosa cautioned.

"Well, we all now know what this man is capable of, so I for one, think the rumor must be true," the girl, Sarah, stated with certainty.

Suddenly, the import of what this girl had heard sank in, and Rosa knew that she just had to attend the hearing and look closely at the accused murderer. So, as she began to turn down the lights and lock up, she turned to the other women, who were still flushed with excitement and said, "I can see that none of you will have your mind on work tomorrow. Maybe we should all go to this hearing and get it out of our systems."

...

The Baker City Courthouse was filled to the rafters with curious citizens who wanted to get a look at the man who had killed Minnie Ensminger. By the time Rosa and her employees arrived, the crowd had expanded to hundreds milling about on the street outside unable to even push their way into the building. When her saleswomen and trimmers eagerly joined friends gossiping on the lawn, Rosa broke away and approached a court bailiff standing by the open doorway.

"Excuse me sir. I am Rosa Krann and I am a good friend of Mary Henner's here to offer her support at this terrible time," she explained.

"Yes ma'am. I know who you are. I can take you in to sit near the family. I am sure they will be grateful for your support."

Once inside, Rosa was taken to the front of the room where she greeted a tearful Mary sitting with her husband in the third row. The family members had no sooner made a small space for Rosa on the bench, when the judge entered followed by Sheriff Harvey Brown and two of his deputies who each held an arm of a man whose head was wrapped in a large white bandage. Since the crowd had been asked to stand for the judge, Rosa's view of the defendant was completely blocked by taller men in the front rows. By the time the crowd was again seated, the bandaged man sat with his back to Rosa who could not see any of his face.

At one point during the proceedings the defendant flanked by the two deputies was asked to stand but he was still turned away from Rosa's view and she began to despair that she would not ever be able to get a look at the man's face. Even as Pleasant was being escorted out at the end of the hearing she could only see the side of the white bandage and just the tip of his nose, not nearly enough to make an accurate identification. Then, just as the three men got to the door from which they had initially entered, a man in the back of the courtroom shouted out, "There he is! String him up now! String him up now!"

It was at this moment that the two deputies and the bandaged man all turned to look out at the crowd and Rosa finally saw the face of Minnie's killer. It was the face she remembered well. The face that had haunted many a nightmare. The face of the angry young man who had menaced her in the alley next to her shop three years before! Now he had a name. And that name was Pleasant Armstrong.

...

By morning on the next day Rosa awoke from a fitful night's sleep with a slow burning panic from an idea that took root deep in her psyche, an idea that she could not shake off or rationalize away. She had become certain that she was somehow to blame for Minnie's death at the hands of a man whose capacity for violence she should have reported three years ago. But she had told no-one but her family and the druggist, Louis Levinger and his wife, when she had fled her attacker by hiding in their store.

It was true that Mr. Levinger had immediately run into the street to seek the man, but had seen no-one on the street early that quiet Sunday morning. He had even rounded the corner of the alley only to find it empty as well. When he had returned to his store he comforted Rosa with the idea that the man had sensibly left town rather than risk facing the law.

Later that same day, Rosa had sent August to Jenny Duffy's "rooming house" to see if anyone there could provide a name of the man who her bouncer had ejected into the street. He reported back that none of the women there knew much about him other than the fact that he had been asked to leave once before for being drunk and disorderly as well as having no money to pay for "entertainment." August had also bought into the idea that the man had wisely left town and probably for good.

None of these memories served to quiet Rosa's guilty feelings by the morning following the preliminary hearing where Pleasant Armstrong was indicted for first degree murder, so she quickly dressed and left to attend morning mass as usual. After mass, she stayed to offer her confession to Father Olivetti, the parish priest.

Instead of her usual confession of small errors such as feeling too much pride in her work or feeling irritations with difficult customers, Rosa surprised her confessor by blurting out the fear that her silence over the attack years before contributed in some way to Minnie Ensmiger's murder.

"I was ashamed that I had personally and foolishly visited Jenny Duffy's which led this man, Pleasant Armstrong, to believe I was a prostitute. I never reported his attack properly because I just wanted the whole thing to go away! If I had reported it, he could have been arrested right then!" Rosa explained while wringing her hands.

"And what, exactly, would you have reported, Rosa? You did not know his name or where he might work or where he lived? You tried to find out, but no-one seemed to know him. We now know he was a drifter who rarely spent much time at any one job or place. Why you, yourself, did not see him on our streets for years, so we can be certain he left town soon after your run-in with him."

"I know who he is, now! So, I at least should tell Sheriff Brown about what he did to me. I might be the one rumored to have been chased with a knife."

"I very much doubt that. The rumor had to be based on his behavior with someone who knew his name. You did not know who he was at the time he attacked you, so how could your experience be the basis of this rumor. And there is another thing I want you to consider before you make an official complaint against this man. I understand that the official charge against him is first degree murder which means premeditated, cold blooded killing and is a capital crime for which he would probably be executed. Everyone knows he killed poor Minnie, so his only defense will be that he did not plan the act, but instead shot her in a fit of great emotion which would not be a capital crime but would surely lead to a long prison sentence or even life in prison."

"Oh, I would not want to be even partially responsible for someone hanging!" Rosa replied nearly in tears over this thought.

"And another thing, my dear. Feelings among many of the men from Haines and even here In Baker City are running high. There has been talk about a lynching. If these men hear of his attack on you, a well-known and respected local woman, well, it might just be the spark to end in a mob killing."

"I know this is true. A man shouted out to hang him right there in the courtroom yesterday! I don't honestly think I could live with myself if my story started something like that. It is almost as if I have no good option in this situation," Rosa sighed wiping at her tears with a handkerchief she fished from her purse.

"You are not at all responsible for the 'situation'. Never think that. He created it himself, and he will be punished by the court for it. It is best, I think, for your own spiritual and mental health to remain quiet about what happened to you, through no fault of your own. If it will make you feel better, I will go and see if I can't help him find peace as he faces what is to come," the priest said as he put an arm around the trembling young woman.

Father Olivetti was as good as his word and became a frequent visitor for Pleasant Armstrong who brought with him the "peace" he had promised as he instructed the young man in the Catholic faith. The good priest was also right about one other thing, for even without "the spark" Rosa's testimony might have produced, the men of Haines and Baker City grew impatient over the slow wheels of state justice, and formed a lynch mob that did march on the Baker City jail.

15.
McColloch

Frank McColloch raced through the Albina streets and back alleys until he came to his front door which he threw open with such force that it banged against the wall knocking bits of plaster to the floor.

Then, with a loud "whoop!" he did a little celebratory dance about the room before breaking into strident song.

"No more homework, no more books, no more teacher's dirty looks!" he called out to the walls.

"Frank, what on earth! Can't you just enter a room like a normal person?" Mary suddenly interrupted the boy's exultation.

"Well, I'm just happy. Stupid baby school is finally over! Next year it's high school for me!"

"Please, try to be 'happy' without destroying the house," his mother cautioned. "Just settle down and I'll make you some lemonade."

"Yeah, I guess I should settle down and start packing for my trip," Frank called as he started for the stairs to his bedroom.

"What trip?" asked Mary, knowing full well that her son expected to spend summer with his father in Sumpter, Oregon.

"I'm going to Sumpter right away. I wrote Dad and told him I would be there in June. I told you that weeks ago," Frank answered carefully, hoping that Mary had just forgotten his plans.

"Yes, you did tell me that. But, since then I have decided that it is best for you to stay here for the summer just until it's time to take

Claude to school. You will be able to go with us on the train to Palo Alto when he enrolls at Stanford. Won't that be fun?" reasoned Mary who was fairly sure that Frank would reject the idea, but also sure that on this point she would not back down.

"No! No! I don't want to go to California with you. I promised Dad I would visit him and I wrote all my Sumpter friends that I was coming back for the summer just like last year! I even told my boss that I quit my paper route. You, you can't change everything just like that!" wailed the stricken boy.

"If your father wants to see you, he can always come here for a visit."

"You know he can't do that! He is still Mayor of Sumpter and his term isn't up for another year. And anyway, why would he want to come here? Every time he comes, you treat him like poison! You never even say as much as 'hello' to him and you make him sleep on that lumpy couch!" Frank added pointing an accusatory finger at Mary and then at the worn parlor sofa.

"Did your father tell you that?"

"No, he did not tell me that! Remember, I live here too and I have eyes. He always tries to make up with you, but you won't have it!" shouted the boy from the depths of an anger that had smoldered for some time over the obvious rift between his parents.

"Perhaps, you should go to your room until you can speak to me with more respect, young man! This outburst is not convincing me to buy you a train ticket. Quite the opposite. And you will not be going to Sumpter, that most unholy town, and that is that!" Mary called after her son who was already retreating upstairs to his room.

Mary stood trembling with fury which was aimed more at herself than at Frank. She knew that she should have spoken to him earlier about her decision that she could not allow him to visit Sumpter again. After all, her own mind had been made up concerning the wicked influence the place might have on her sons since the year before when Frank and Claude had returned from visiting C.H. for the entire summer.

At that time, she had begun to mellow about her belief that her husband must join her in a vow to fight the evil sale of alcohol as well as the other sins such as the gambling and prostitution that every saloon seemed to offer morally weak men. She knew in her heart that C.H. would not have spent such long stretches of time away from her and their home if she had not made that home so coldly forbidding to him. She also knew that he could well have divorced her due to her treatment of him, but in the three years since that fateful day at her church, he had never legally moved against her. He had even promised in writing to always support her and their sons and to remain her husband unless she, herself, demanded an end to their marriage.

Mary had missed her boys that summer even though she still had a very full schedule of church and temperance union work which so occupied her time that, when Claude and Frank were home, she rarely saw them. Since her boys both had jobs and got good grades in school, she had believed that they didn't need more from her. Even Frank had not gotten into trouble since the Killingsworth Avenue Station incident. But now, with Claude going off to school, she did not relish having an empty house all summer.

However, Mary's decision to keep Frank from visiting C.H. was based on more than a selfish wish to avoid loneliness. That decision was made after the boys had returned from visiting Sumpter during the prior summer and she was unpacking their suitcases when she found several copies of the Sumpter Miner newspaper all dated from the preceding year and all containing articles about their father. One of these articles dated December 10, 1902 was published just after C.H. was elected mayor and carried the headline, "Our Mayor-Elect: C.H. McColloch Outlines a Portion of the Policy to be Pursued." Mary had sat down and read this article with interest.

Mayor-elect C.H. McColloch amidst his many other duties, is taking time to formulate the policy which he will pursue when inducted into office the first Monday in January. Up until this morning he had not perfected all his plans, but had no hesitation in stating that the present city marshal would be kept in his responsible position, as the incoming mayor considers him to be an efficient and capable man.

Speaking of the tough element which appears to be heading towards the lively towns of Eastern Oregon, our next mayor is of the opinion that they can be handled properly, and if necessary thoroughly subdued should they commit any wrong acts.

Mr. McColloch takes a very broad view and has quite liberal ideas on the gambling question. He thinks that if ...such games that give a man a reasonable show for his money are allowed to run that the sporting fraternity will be of the better class in their line and will lend their aid in upholding law and order...

At this point, Mary furiously threw down the paper, "So the only thing 'the Mayor-elect' planned to do about the sin of gambling was to make sure the games aren't rigged!" she shouted out loud. " I just bet that he is very popular with all those 'liberal ideas!' How nice of him to share his 'broad view' with his sons!" At that moment she renewed her decision to keep her children far away from their father's influence before they were completely corrupted.

Claude had his summer job as a cub reporter with *The Oregonian* and would soon be safely in California, but Frank had counted on a summer trip to Sumpter. Mary realized that she should not have sprung on him at the last minute the fact that she was not going to allow him to go. The only sensible thing to do after she had made that mistake would be to wait until morning when Frank had time to cool off and then she would go to him and explain her reasons which she was sure would convince him that her decision was in his best interest.

The next morning, Mary knocked on Frank's bedroom door and waited a few moments before entering. The first thing she saw in the empty room was a note on top of the boy's unmade bed. In shock, Mary picked up the piece of paper and read, "I have gone to see my father." Then she saw that Frank's closet was empty of clothing and the jar that had held the boy's paper route money was empty as well.

• • •

For Frank, his summer arrival in Sumpter always felt like coming home. He knew everyone from the station master at the Baker City depot to Mr. Hotchkiss, the engineer who drove the Sumpter Valley Passenger Train thirty miles up the mountain twice a day. They all greeted him by name and expressed an interest in how his year had gone while he had been away.

He had arrived several days before the date he had written to his father, so he did not expect to be met at the Sumpter station. He rather liked the fact that a parent would not be meeting him like they would for a little child. It reinforced his feeling of being a "man of the world" traveling on his own.

As for C.H., he had spent days worried about Frank's visit. He very much looked forward to seeing his son, but he realistically knew that Frank would be just as excited about seeing the boys who had become his friends over the years as he would be to see his father. His worry centered around the changes he had seen in Frank's friends since an older boy had moved into town a few months before.

George Patterson was the son of a wealthy mine owner who always seemed to have plenty of money to spend on his new friends. Athletic and good looking, George had almost immediately become a leader for that gang of kids who happily followed him into one illegal or dangerous activity after another.

C.H. knew that his own son would probably find George Patterson as beguiling as had the other boys who were his smitten followers. He had decided that he would have to sit Frank down from the start and tell him what his friends had been up to and his own expectations concerning his son's behavior during his summer visit. There would be no petty theft from the general store and no pranks against the citizens of Sumpter. Should Frank weaken and be drawn into such activity, C.H. would promise to send him back to his mother and her Bible for the remainder of the summer.

After that talk, C.H. began to relax as the weeks passed and Frank seemed to avoid doing anything that would threaten to send him back to Mary. C.H. had not just blindly trusted in Frank to automatically do the right thing. He was wise enough to engage several key adults around town to keep an eye out for any trouble Frank might get into and report back to him. It was not difficult to convince the shopkeepers who had already been burnt by the little gang's activity that his concern had merit. Luckily, he had not heard from anyone that Frank had done anything he had been warned not to become involved in.

By July, C.H. was sure that Frank had been involved in nothing more sinister than the usual romps with his friends hunting small game in the Elkhorn forests or long, lazy days fishing for trout in the Powder River. That is until near the July Fourth holiday when a man visited the mayor's office and told the receptionist that he needed to speak to the mayor about "his son, Frank." C.H. was surprised when he saw that the man who asked to speak with him about Frank was not one of his shopkeeper spies but was, instead, John Simmons, the bouncer at Sumpter's largest Cracker Street brothel. He was shocked beyond words when he actually heard what the man had to say about his thirteen year old son and his friends. John Simmons got right to the point after C.H. closed his office door and they were alone.

"Mr. Mayor, I stopped in at the Sumpter Hotel for a little lunch yesterday and was telling Jake Walters, the bartender there, a funny story about that George Patterson kid and his friends. Seems that the Patterson kid with all the money his dad gives him to throw around has worked out a deal with May Robbins, the madam I work for, to give his little pals a July Fourth special treat with some of her girls, if ya know what I mean. An' Jake says to me that you have the word out to folks to keep an eye on your kid, Frank. An' he said that I should tell you right away."

After catching his breath at this news, C.H. thanked the bouncer and added, "I'm going to have to do some fast talking with my boy, I see. But if he shows up at May's place, I would ask you to bring him right here to me. That is before he indulges in any 'special treats.' You can be sure that I will show you my appreciation for that kindness, sir."

...

The next day at breakfast, C.H. told Frank that there were a couple of people he wanted the boy to meet. When the boy asked who they were, his father answered with only a slight tremor in his voice that it would be a "surprise"

C.H. had spent a sleepless night trying to think of how best to handle the situation with Frank. He knew better than to try to turn his son away from pleasures of the flesh with the kind of moralistic lecture his mother was so fond of. In the end, he had decided that what the boy needed was a more graphic lesson about the wages of sin. And he also knew that the best person to teach such a lesson was Doc Bradley since the most common complaint brought to the good doctor by the oversized and undereducated Sumpter male population concerned symptoms they called "the pox" and medical books called "syphilis."

Doc Bradley was the kind of physician that most people immediately trusted with their various ailments. A good listener and quick with a joke, he was no ordinary frontier doctor, but had gotten his medical training in Bellevue Hospital in New York City and had seen and treated every scourge that plagued mankind in those decades before the miracle of antibiotics.

"Your dad tells me that some of your friends are planning a visit with the girls at May's place in a few days. He is worried that you might join them," the doctor began without any preliminaries and looking the shocked and suddenly frightened boy straight in the eye. "He wants me to explain what happens to many men who visit those places, so you'll know what you're in for. That is, if you're thinking of joining your friends at May's."

Before Frank could choke out an answer, Doc Bradley continued as though lecturing a medical school class. "There are many diseases one can pick up from a prostitute, but the one I treat most often, almost every day I might say, is 'the pox' or syphilis which has four stages and each stage takes a different treatment. The first stage is when a man notices sores on or around his penis. The usual treatment is through cauterizing the sores."

"Cauterizing?" asked Frank.

"Yes, that is the best way we know for killing the germs inside the sore," the doctor continued as he walked over to a woodstove, took up an iron poker and shoved it deep into the fire, then withdrew it to display a red hot tip. "We cauterize, or burn away the infected skin." He instructed Frank whose face had grown ashen and who could not suppress a shuddering wince at the thought of such a treatment.

"This doesn't usually work, though, and the patient goes on to suffer the second stage. This is when a rash of more weeping sores cover the person's whole body. It looks a lot like chicken pox which is why people call it 'the pox'. The worst part of this stage is the awful headaches a person will get. They can feel like a person has his head in a vice! Now, the doctor who had this office before me used this to drill into a man's skull to try to relieve the terrible pain," Bradley said taking out a small hand drill from a drawer, But I don't hold with that."

"That's good," Frank whispered to himself, as he eyed the evil-looking drill held out for his inspection.

"No, I believe the only hope is to use mercury at this point. Now, some will cover the patient with mercury then wrap him in blankets to make him sweat out the poison. But, in my practice, I have observed that this usually kills the patient. I usually administer mercury directly to the private parts with this special syringe." He explained about the very long needle he held close to the boy's bulging eyes and who appeared likely to faint at any moment. "Sometimes it seems like a person is cured because this disease kind of goes underground in the body, but even if it doesn't show up again for years, it is still attacking all parts of the body; the bones, the heart and especially the brain and nervous system. That is why, when it shows up again, it causes many to go insane."

"Do only men get this disease?" Frank wondered.

"No, women too, if they have sex with a man who is already infected. Women who are prostitutes have sex with many men and that is why many of them get this disease. Then they turn right around and spread it to all their customers. And so it goes. The only way to be sure that a man won't catch it is to stay far away from prostitutes. That would save you and that nice, innocent girl you'll want to marry some day from both dying of this awful disease or the many other diseases a man who traffics with prostitutes is likely to get. That would be my recommendation." The doctor finished. At that point he turned to C.H. and handed him a folded piece of paper.

"His name is Bub Hanks and he is expecting you."

"Bub?"

"I am sure it's a nickname but he's been a miner here for years, and it's all anyone ever calls him," Bradley said as he waved good bye.

...

The address on the paper given C.H. led father and son to a shack at the edge of town. C.H. knocked on the door held on its hinges by bailing wire then heard a soft voice call out, "Come in."

Inside the room was so dark it took moments before the two could see anything, but finally could make out a shadow moving about. "I know it's purty dark in here. I'll have ta light a candle sos ya can find a chair ta sit in," said the voice.

After some shuffling, a faint light glowed from a lit candle on a nearby table. As C.H. and Frank moved toward the table, they could more plainly see the shack's inhabitant sitting across the table from two empty chairs. The two also noticed a distinct, nauseating smell as they moved closer to the seated man, though C.H. continued on into the room and introduced himself and a reluctant Frank who he dragged forward and then pushed into one of the chairs.

"Ya can call me 'Bub'. My real name is Bertram Hanks, Mr. Mayor, but Bub's what most know me as." As he said this, the man shifted a bit closer to the light and his guests saw immediately a face so ravaged by disease that it barely passed for human.

While C.H. maintained his composure, Frank could not suppress a sharp intake of breath at the sight of the skin covered with pustular eruptions so huge that they nearly swallowed the man's eyes and mouth.

"Sorry about the way I look. That's why I never go out any more. Doc calls it 'Syphiloderm'. It happens to folks who are in the last stage o' the pox. But ya already know why I'm sick. Doc says ya want me ta tell your son how I got this way, sos he won't be a fool like me and go with the whores."

"I appreciate your seeing us, Bub. It takes a big man to do this for us." C.H. acknowledged. "Doc sent us here so my son, Frank here, wouldn't think Bradley was just making up some story to scare him when he told him what could happen if he wasn't careful."

"Well, it can happen all right. An' I know a lot o' fellas over the years that died the same way I am, sores all over, head aches that make a guy nearly blind with the pain and some go crazy to boot. I was on the mercury for a while, but it just ate out my stomach so bad that now I can't eat nothin' but porridge or plain oatmeal without vomiting. It's just as well 'cause the mercury took out all my teeth so I couldn't eat no steak even if I wanted to. Son, I sure hope you take my advice an' stay away from the fallen doves. You will, if you're smart."

"Oh, I would never go near the doves, sir," Frank mumbled, as C.H. ventured a slight smile.

"I'm here to tell you the God's honest truth. A fella might have a moment of pleasure, but it is just not worth a lifetime a pain! You are lucky that you have a smart daddy who loves you enough to try to get through to you before you do something stupid. I wasn't so lucky. I just never really believed the stories I heard. All young men are kinda dumb, I guess. They have to see it to believe it, but guys who end up like me stay home to die, so no one learns a lesson about how dangerous goin' with the whores really is."

By the time this interview was over, C.H. walked with an uncharacteristically pale and quiet Frank back to his office. He was fairly confident that their visit with Doc Bradley and his patient had been an effective deterrent to foolish youthful transgression. He had also decided, at the good doctor's suggestion, to clue in the parents of Frank's friends before the day the boys planned their visit to May's brothel. C.H. was gratified that on the morning of July Fourth when he overheard a conversation between Frank and the Patterson boy who rang their front doorbell.

"No, I can't go with you today. I, I'm not feeling well. I might have the flu or something," Frank was saying.

"What the hell! Is there some kinda plague goin' around?! Everyone's sick with somethin'. Mick, Ron, Sam an' Joe, too. Everyone!" railed George Patterson. "Well, I guess I'll be the only one havin' any fun this Fourth!"

"Yeah, I guess you will," Frank said as he closed the door.

16.
Krann

Father Olivetti let himself in the side door of the Baker City jailhouse as he had done every day after morning mass for nearly a year. Two sheriff's deputies sat just inside the door playing cards as he entered and nodded to the men.

"Hi ya, Father. Is it hot enough for ya?" remarked Deputy Jess Snow referring to the unseasonably hot October weather that had the two sweating in their starched uniforms.

"How is he, today? He seemed so keyed up yesterday that I was a bit worried for his state of mind," the priest said, motioning toward a closed door that led to the jail cells.

"Well, who wouldn't be nervous in his shoes? The Supreme Court sure took their sweet time getting' around to hearing his case. My God, here he was braced for bein' hanged in May and they go an' announce they'll consider his appeal just ten days before the execution. But they won't meet on it until October! It's enough to give a guy a heart attack," Snow exclaimed shaking his head in disgust.

"Yeah," Snow continued, "We seen how upset he was gettin' last night so we got him to play cards with some of the boys who come around every evening. They're the same ones Sheriff Brown hired last March to guard Armstrong after that lynch mob tried to take him. I still get a laugh when I think of their dopey looks when they broke in here only to find an empty cell. That dumb bunch all liquored up and talkin' big at the bar down the street gave the Sheriff plenty a time to get Pleas outta town. We're all real glad that they didn't get to him, now. All the fellas agree he's a real nice guy when ya get to know him, aside from bein' a murderer that is.."

"Yeah, a real nice guy," confirmed the other deputy. "He even plays his fiddle for us once in a while. We're all hopin' they change his sentence to life, that's for sure."

"Yes, that would surely be a blessing we all pray for. I don't even think the Haines folks who all loved poor Minnie want to see him die any more. Whatever way it goes, the boy has made his peace with God," added the priest as he moved toward the room that held the cell of Pleasant Armstrong waiting to hear his fate from the Oregon Supreme Court.

...

After his morning visit with Pleasant Armstrong, Father Olivetti made one of his usual stops by Rosa Krann's millinery shop where he could count on a nice cup of spiced tea and a one of her sister, Marie's, superb butter cookies. If the shop was not too busy, Rosa might sit with the priest in her sunny back office and enjoy the tea with him.

As he entered the shop ringing the overhead bell, Rosa rushed up to Father Olivetti and quickly ushered him into her office. "How is he today?" she inquired with obvious concern over the man whose fate the entire town of Baker City knew was in the hands of a few men who sat on the state's highest court.

"He's making an effort to hide how frightened he is about the possible outcome of this appeal. He told me to pray for the lawyers who have taken on his case as part of their campaign against the Oregon death penalty. I assured him that our congregation prays daily for their success."

"I pray for him, too, and I think about him every day as only you would know," Rosa put in referring to Olivetti's singular knowledge about her former run-in with Armstrong.

"I am so grateful that you stopped me from telling anyone about how he … he accosted me once. Why, if I had stepped forward, he might not have had grounds for this appeal. I truly get a chill when I think about what might have happened! I also think about what kind of life he had that brought him to this end. I understand he bounced from foster home to foster home and was on his own, penniless and alone at a very young age. I remember how humiliated he looked when he was thrown out of Jenny Duffy's house. He probably had never known love until Minnie and then her rejection was just too much for him," Rosa continued as she poured two steaming cups of tea.

The priest nodded confirmation and said, "Yes, he has always stood by his testimony at trial when he stated that he took the gun to the party to use only on himself if Minnie continued to reject him. He still says that he never meant to shoot her. But in the moment he tried to talk with her and she turned her back on him, he lost his already weak grip on sanity. And I believe this is true and that he did not commit premeditated murder. I sincerely believe that he does not deserve to hang and that belief is not just due to the fact the Church teaches that the death penalty is immoral."

For many minutes the two sat silently lost in their own thoughts as their untouched tea grew cold. When Rosa turned to speak again to Father Olivetti, she saw him looking at her with what could only be described as a sly smile.

"Father?" she questioned.

"People tell me that you have begun stepping out with LeRoy Collins." He chuckled as Rosa immediately reddened at the idea that people were talking about her.

"I wouldn't call it 'stepping out.' You know I first hired Mr. Collins to do deliveries for me so that I would not be putting myself in danger as I promised my family and the Levingers who helped me that, that terrible day. Of course, he still works for Carl Adler selling music and instruments in his store, but the store is so close he occasionally stops by and we go to lunch together that is, if there are no deliveries to make that day," she finished hoping to sound like their relationship was purely business related.

"Mr. Adler tells me that his ability to play any instrument and to sing so beautifully has nearly doubled his sales since he started work there," Olivetti remarked then added, "Really, Mr. Collins does possess a formidable talent. Since he began singing at mass, I have noted the pews are full of new faces. I would like to think that this increased attendance is due to my inspiring sermons, but I know better. It is most certainly due to that amazing tenor voice of his."

. . .

Yes, Rosa thought, that voice was certainly the first thing she noticed about LeRoy Collins especially since the Catholic mass had never included music before the tenor had been hired by Father Olivetti. The priest loved music and when Pope Leo XIII had named Baker City the seat of the Archdiocese of Oregon for all the lands east of the Cascade mountains that encompassed three fourths of the state, Olivetti and the new bishop, Charles O'Reilly, had decided that some beautifully sung classic hymns would add grandeur to any mass. Bishop O'Reilly was especially eager for this addition since he had immediately created a fund for the building of a new cathedral where he planned to install a huge pipe organ capable of sending its powerful notes soaring heavenward to the rafters of a fifty foot ceiling and beyond.

The second thing Rosa had noticed about Mr. Collins was his looks. Many parishioners had noted that the singer was "handsome," but Rosa thought that with his white blonde hair and sky blue eyes that "beautiful" was a better adjective in his case, though she never voiced this opinion aloud.

After Carl Adler sent his wife, Laura, to Rosa's shop to suggest hiring LeRoy Collins to make deliveries to the more unsavory parts of town, Rosa had felt immediately drawn to him for much more than his good looks. Within weeks of their meeting, they began to have lunch together every day. Though ostensibly LeRoy came to the shop daily at noon because of their business arrangement, they were both delighted when no deliveries were waiting for him.

Within the first few of their lunches together, Rosa and LeRoy realized that they had much in common due to their particular backgrounds that were very different from those of most Baker City's citizens.

LeRoy was an only child raised and educated in Boston by wealthy parents who recognized early their son's musical talent and sent him for his advanced training to the Lowell Mason Boston Academy of Music. Though Rosa lacked this kind of formal musical education, she had learned much at her grandfather Joseph's knee about the famed classical greats, Mozart, Brahms, Beethoven, and Strauss whose timeless compositions became the foundation of Viennese culture.

Both young people especially loved opera and had been exposed as children to many of the great live productions of the time. Rosa recounted how her grandfather had taken his granddaughters to operettas when they were so small they sat on special cushions in order to see over adult heads.

"Marie and I loved going to the Theater an der Wien where the audience was as entertaining as the performers," Rosa recounted. "I remember once when we saw Strauss' Die Fledermaus the whole audience stood begging and shouting for an encore, and when the performers began to sing everyone remained standing and joined in. Grandfather lifted us up to stand on our cushions so we could take part with the rest!"

"I did not see Die Fledermaus until I was much older than you and already at the Academy of Music," LeRoy put in. "When a troupe from the New York Metropolitan came to Boston, we students were invited to a rehearsal which led to our decision to put it on ourselves. I ended up playing Dr. Blind. I still remember the part," he said and, to prove it he burst into song which ended with them both in fits of laughter.

Rosa had seen Verdi's Rigoletto in Vienna while LeRoy had been lucky enough to attend its 1885 U.S. premiere at the Metropolitan Opera in New York. They agreed that with opera, it did not matter that the entire story was sung in Italian because the emotion infused in the music made the meaning clear.

Rosa said, "I thought that I would really like Beethoven's Fidelo just because it was performed in German, but I had to admit later that I did not like it as much as many Italian operas. For example, the power of Mozart's Don Giovanni gave me chills I have never forgotten. It helped, I am sure, that Grandfather Joseph explained to us before the play that the evil Don Giovanni dies and is taken to hell because he refused to repent his sins when he had the chance," she finished with a shudder thinking of Pleasant Armstrong who still waited in his cell for the Court's decision on his case and, like most condemned men, must surely worry about what was to come in this life and in the next.

Their mutual love for classic music and for the opera inevitably led to dates for many evening performances at the magnificent Baker Opera House. Because Baker City was the usual stop between Portland, Oregon and Salt Lake City, Utah for traveling performing troupes, LeRoy invited Rosa to every ballet, stage play and opera that appeared in the sumptuous surroundings of that theater. Because Rosa was small in stature, LeRoy purchased season tickets for two in one of the upper boxes so that she would have an unobstructed view.

"I can't have you standing on a cushion to see the stage," he explained as they took their expensive seats.

In time, the couple felt comfortable enough in their relationship to include their respective families. Leroy's parents had moved to Baker City several years before when his father made several investments in the booming mines of the remote Cornucopia region in the wild Wallowa Mountain foothills in north eastern Baker County. They bought a large stone Victorian house with a distinctive turret just down the tree lined street from the block where the Italianate house of Carl and Laura Adler stood on one corner and its twin, the house of Sam and Sallie Baer, Laura's sister, stood on the opposite corner. Sadly, soon after the family moved in, LeRoy's father had a heart attack and died leaving his estate to wife, Ethel, with LeRoy as executor.

It seemed to Rosa that LeRoy was somewhat reluctant to introduce her to his mother, so she decided to take the first step in sharing more of her own life with him and invited him to dinner with her family. Mathew was particularly excited to meet LeRoy because of his involvement with the mines at Cornucopia. Matt had long wanted to finally put to use his youthful energy and formidable hard rock skills and join the underground mining activity in the region where it was rumored that gold nuggets literally tumbled out of the rocks where impossibly rich veins had been discovered. But whenever he had tried to convince August to go with him, his brother in law argued against the idea, repeating the list of dangers involved for miners working far beneath ground.

Since Rosa had invited LeRoy for Sunday dinner when her shop was closed, she was able to help Marie prepare the meal featuring her sister's fabulous sauerbraten with baby carrots, turnips and plump tomatoes from their own garden followed by one of her buttery strudels filled with apples and wild huckleberries. As the house filled with the succulent aroma of braised meat, Rosa was sure that this meal would top even those served to LeRoy by the French cook in his mother's employ.

Marie insisted that it would be prudent to feed her children early so that the adults could enjoy a quiet dinner getting to know one another free from the usual childish chatter.

"Why should the children be locked away when they are used to eating with us?" Rosa wanted to know.

"I know you think that I never leave the house, but I do. And I know that other people raise their children quite differently than we," Marie calmly explained. "Their children are not allowed to speak when adults are conversing. They would find our enjoyment of what the children have to say quite unsettling, and the fact that we even encourage them to make their comments at the dinner table they would think is, at the very least, inappropriate."

Later, Rosa reviewed the evening and judged it a total success. Even Mathew was happy with the result of the conversation he and August had with Rosa's new beau as they sipped sherry in the parlor before dinner. He had carefully planned to steer the talk to what was happening with the mines in Cornucopia by showing LeRoy an article he had clipped from the Oregon Daily Journal some months before that claimed, "...The Cornucopia group of gold mines contains what is probably the largest ore body in the Pacific Northwest, if not in the United States."

After Matt finished reading, LeRoy nodded and said, "It is true that this area has proven to be incredibly rich which has drawn some 700 miners from all over to work for the Cornucopia Mines of Oregon, the company in which my father had the good sense to invest. It is now, I understand, the sixth largest mining operation in the United States. I have to go there soon before November when the snows will begin making travel difficult, why don't the two of you join me and see for yourselves," he said as Mathew, eyes glowing, turned to August who could not bring himself to argue against the trip.

...

Before the day the men planned to make their trip to the mines of Cornucopia, LeRoy surprised Rosa and invited her to dinner with his mother. Nervous as she was, she was curious to see if his mother's reaction to her was one of acceptance or if there were any signs that the woman felt threatened by her son's new relationship. As a widow and having LeRoy as her only family it would be understandable if she wanted to keep him to herself.

When they first arrived at the massive Victorian and a maid had taken their coats, the couple was told that Mrs. Collins would be down shortly and would meet them in the small drawing room. This gave Rosa a chance to take in the grandeur of the home with its sparkling leaded glass windows and staircase winding in a half circle inside the impressive turret toward a second story landing. The "small" drawing room turned out to be far larger than the parlor in her family's crowded rental house across town. She wondered what the "large "drawing room was like. Before she was tempted to go exploring, an unsmiling woman with piercing blue eyes and amazingly erect posture entered the room, walked straight toward Rosa and offered her hand in greeting.

"I am very pleased to finally meet the woman my son talks so much about. I hope it is all right to call you Rosa and please call me Ethel," the woman said without looking all that "pleased" in Rosa's estimation.

LeRoy's mother motioned the couple toward a silk covered divan and took her seat on a matching one directly across from them and proceeded to ask Rosa a series of questions that seemed to the younger woman to be more like a grilling than an attempt at conversation. In question after question, Ethel probed for knowledge about Rosa's family background, their reasons for coming to Baker City, how Rosa got started in business, and so on with absolutely no reciprocal information offered about herself.

At one point, Rosa attempted a query of her own only to be thwarted. "How do you like living in Baker City, Ethel?" Rosa tried.

"Oh enough about me, I would be more interested to know how you find Baker City after living in a city like Vienna?" The woman countered.

Enough about her? What has she said about herself? Rosa wondered as LeRoy's mother ushered the couple into her dining room.

The dinner was delicious, though Rosa found it hard to concentrate on enjoying her food as she continued to be peppered with questions by Ethel who hardly touched her own plate. Finally, the exhausting meal came to an end and Ethel sent her son out to "bring the carriage around."

Once alone, Ethel Collins turned to Rosa and smiled broadly for the first time all evening. Then she embraced Rosa with a hug that so took Rosa by surprise that she nearly lost her balance.

"I am so sorry to have behaved rudely, my dear. You were so kind to tolerate all my questions but I just had to get to know you quickly. You see, I greatly miss Boston where all my friends and family are and my sister has begged me to come live with her. I have not even told my son about my decision to go. That is because I had to know if you are the kind of woman that would be good for him or not. I had decided if you were not right for him, I would just stay here to do whatever I could to...protect him."

"And, may I ask what the verdict is?" Rosa wondered.

"I will start packing my things tomorrow for the move. I have decided he'll be safe in your hands!" LeRoy's mother laughed.

. . .

On the Monday of the last week in October LeRoy arrived on horseback early in the morning the three men had planned to travel to Cornucopia just as August was hitching his two horses to the family's open wagon.

"Do those take a rider," LeRoy called motioning toward the horses meant to pull the wagon.

"They do when we need them to," August answered turning to greet LeRoy then quickly suppressing a laugh when he saw the other man holding a riding crop, dressed in coat and jodhpurs, sitting top his English style saddle like nobility ready for a fox hunt.

"Oh, they'll need to all right. That wagon will make it to Halfway sure enough, but from there it will be almost useless."

To this August shook his head, "This wagon has never let me down not even on the rocky ruts they call a road from Cracker Creek to Sumpter."

"Better to take along some saddles just in case. In the 5 miles from

Halfway to Carson we'll gain a thousand feet in elevation on the only road up the mountain. It's so narrow and steep that it takes ages for wagons to make that trip. Then after that, it is almost straight up another fifteen hundred feet to Cornucopia. Most of the miners never even try to take a wagon up, they pack all their supplies on mules instead."

"Thanks for the advice, we'll take some saddles to use if necessary," August agreed, still not convinced that the wagon was a bad idea.

...

On the same morning the three men left for Cornucopia, Father Olivetti entered Rosa's shop after his usual trip to the jailhouse to see Pleasant Armstrong. One of her sales women ushered him back to Rosa's office where she sat at her desk considering her need for more inventory due to increased sales before the holiday season that would soon begin.

"Father! You're just in time for tea. I just put a new kettle on," she said, then lost her wide smile when she saw the priest's grim, ashen expression. "Whatever is the matter, Father? Please, you look like you should sit down!"

"Yes, I had better sit. Thank you, and I'll take some of that tea. It has been a perfectly terrible morning," he began as Rosa poured out a steaming cup and handed it to her guest, noticing the man's trembling hand as he guided the china cup to his lips. Then he took a breath and continued, "As you know I always visit the jailhouse before coming here to visit with you, my dear. Well, today, when I arrived there, Jess Snow warned me that they had some news from Salem concerning the Supreme Court's decision on the Armstrong case. It seems he lost his appeal and a new date has been set for his execution!"

"Oh no, the poor man. After he had such hope for a change of sentence!" Rosa breathed.

"It's true he had hope and now all hope has been dashed. That's not the worst of it, though. He has decided that it is evidence of God's decision about his fate as well! He believes that since the society of man has turned against him, that heaven has also turned against him. He is more afraid than ever to die. He reasons that since he is locked up and unable to make any true amends to those he has wronged, God will have no proof of his heartfelt contrition. He truly believes that the fires of Hell await him! He rejected all my arguments that God reads the heart of man and always forgives the truly penitent."

"How terrible! You have worked so hard to give him hope in God's grace, and now..."

"I know now that I cannot help him face his death alone. On the way over here, I thought about who might help him more than I can, and...my thoughts kept turning to you, Rosa."

"Me?! How could I possible help him. He would know as soon as he saw me who I am and what he did to me."

"That is exactly why you would be the best one to talk with him. I know that you have forgiven him as has been indicated by our many conversations about Mr. Armstrong. I believe that he should hear this from you, so that at least he will know my promises about the many people who pray for him are not just empty words."

. . .

The next morning, Father Olivetti entered the side jailhouse door and then turned to hold the door for Rosa Krann who entered behind him. A puzzled deputy let the two visitors in to see the prisoner housed in the first cell.

"Well, he might as well have some company since he didn't touch his breakfast," the deputy remarked as he unlocked the cell door to retrieve the untouched tray of food.

"Can you please bring us another chair, deputy?" Olivetti asked clearly indicating that the two visitors intended to sit inside the cell with the condemned man. Once the second chair was provided, the deputy left closing and locking the outer office door. As he left, Pleasant Armstrong who lay on his cot facing a brick wall turned slowly to see who had entered.

"You?!" was all he said when he saw Rosa sitting beside Father Olivetti.

"I have brought Rosa here because she has something she would like to tell you," the priest explained.

"Go ahead then. Considering what I did to you, I deserve to hear whatever you want to say to me," Pleasant mumbled hanging his head.

"Mr. Armstrong I am not here to chastise you, I am here to confess how I wronged you." Rosa began.

"Wronged me? I attacked you in an alley! You were the victim of my sin, just one sin in quite a pile I have created against my soul, I might add."

"Sin doesn't occur in a vacuum, I believe. I made a contribution of some sins of my own that I think you need to hear from my lips. You may know by now that I am not what you originally thought. I am not a prostitute employed at Jenny Duffy's bordello. You would not have made that assumption, if I had not been there sitting with Jenny and the other women who do work there. If I had not been there you would not have attacked me later. For one thing, I was foolish to go there in the first place, but I went often as a lark, I enjoyed Jenny's company and the wine she always offered and the delicious feeling of doing something a little naughty."

"Well, maybe you are guilty of using bad judgement, but it's probably not a sin."

"The sin lies in what went through my head when you were humiliated by being thrown into the street... into the mud while everyone laughed and taunted you. I did nothing to help you. I just stood on the porch hoping that none of the wealthy Baker City citizens who live in those fancy houses along the same street as Jenny's place would see me involved in that unseemly affair. I was only selfishly worried about myself and my own precious reputation."

"Well, so what, why would anyone try to help a drunken bum like me."

"It was only later that I thought about how that event must have affected you, and how differently it may have turned out if I had only come off that porch to help you out of the dirt. If I had proved that I was not like them and that I cared about you even enough to help dust off your clothes, that might have been enough to diffuse your understandable rage, the rage you exhibited in that alley. But I didn't do any of that. I just left you seething and believing yourself worthy of being an outcast. And,...from what I know of your background, the cruelty of that group on Jenny's porch was just part of a lifetime of cruel humiliation that must have seemed to change when you met Minnie. It had to have been intolerable for you when her family convinced her to turn her back on you."

"Yes, her back! It was her back turned against me at the party and later again as she walked away refusing to talk to me," Pleasant Armstrong said in a low, haunted whisper.

"Mr. Armstrong, I think that it is important for you to see why my sin is especially grievous and why you should believe that God will, probably has already, absolved you of your sins. I want you to have this rosary which was given to me by my dear grandfather who lovingly taught me beginning when I was very young all the tenants of our faith." Rosa said pulling out a worn rosary of blue and white beads. "I have always known what the Church teaches about the sin of pride and lack of charity, but I committed those sins anyway which I believe led to some terrible consequences for both of us. You, on the other hand, had no-one until Father Olivetti to teach you about a God who loves us and always absolves the truly penitent of their sins. You will pay for what you did in this life, but on the basis of everything I have ever been taught, I know that you will not pay in the life after this one ends. I believe that every time you say the Prayer for the Rosary, you will be more and more convinced that what I am telling you is true."

As Rosa handed the rosary to Pleasant Armstrong, Father Olivetti suggested they bow their heads while he recited the Prayer of Contrition as he would do every day until the cold, gray dawn of January 22, 1904 when the priest would walk with Pleasant Armstrong up the thirteen steps of the gallows that had been built outside the Baker City jailhouse.

After receiving a last benediction, the condemned man turned to the crowd of 500 men gathered below and gave a speech that ended with, "I am sorry for the things I have done. I sincerely repent of all my sins, especially the great crime I must now suffer for ... Into thy hands O Lord, I commend my spirit."

Then, after his hands and feet were bound, he cried out, "Did you ever see a brave man? Look at me. I forgive you all."

When Rosa Krann heard of how Pleasant Armstrong, who had been baptized "Samuel Armstrong" the day before, had so courageously met his end, she cried. She knew that he would be buried in the Catholic section of Baker City's Mount Hope Cemetery. She also knew that his grave would forever be unmarked, but she took comfort in the fact that he would be buried with a rosary of blue and white beads.

...

The crime, trial and execution of Pleasant Armstrong had consumed Baker City for over a year. When it was over, the town's people expelled a great sigh of relief that they could finally turn again to the mundane affairs of daily life.

Rosa had been too absorbed by worry over Pleasant Armstrong to notice how excited August and Mathew had been when they returned from their trip with LeRoy Collins to Cornucopia. Matt had always wanted to try hard rock mining for real instead of only exhibiting his mining skills in some miners' contest. While August had never been tempted to seek riches underground, he had taken note of an interesting possible business opportunity.

On the way to Cornucopia, LeRoy had explained that his reason for needing to visit the remote region was to see why his father's investments had stopped yielding their prior dividends. When the three men had traveled as far as the little town of Halfway they stopped to buy a few supplies before starting the uphill climb to the Cornucopia mines. While Mathew and LeRoy loaded their goods into the saddle bags of the horses they would ride the final difficult miles to their destination, August talked with the store owner about a "For Sale" sign he saw tacked to the store's door.

"It's true, mister, I have decided to sell the place," the man had answered and then went on. "It's not that this little ol' store hasn't seen some real good days. For one, this here is the last place that the miners heading up hill can buy the supplies they'll need. Then, once the snow flies and all but buries Cornucopia, most of the miners winter down here in Halfway so business is normally real good year round."

"I don't get it. Why sell the place if it is such a good business," August wondered.

"Lately, things have changed up hill. Seems that the mine owners haven't paid some disputed big engineering bill they owe an' now because of the liens the engineers slapped on 'em, the bank is foreclosing on the mines! Work has all but stopped now and most of the men have gone elsewhere."

When the three men reached Cornucopia, August saw that the store owner had told the truth. The few inches of new snow on the ground was clearly not enough to have slowed mine activity, but the town seemed to be nearly abandoned.

After they checked into the town's one hotel, LeRoy headed straight for the Cornucopia Mines of Oregon office to investigate the situation and to find out why he had stopped getting a return on his father's investment. When he returned, LeRoy seemed inexplicably upbeat and the other men wanted to know what he had learned.

He told them over dinner, "The owners are holding out on an engineering bill. They are determined to get a better settlement in court and their case will be heard this spring. I was actually able to talk with the company president about all of this and he convinced me that the whole thing will be settled and the mines will be hot again by summer!"

By the time the group had returned to Baker City, August had a solid plan to buy the store in Halfway while its owner was eager to sell at a discount. He figured that his insider knowledge about the region's future made it worth the gamble he was taking that Cornucopia would soon be booming again.

Later, August was gratified when his sweet Marie became as excited by this idea as he was after he explained his plan to her. She had long worried silently about how despondent August had been ever since selling his Cracker Creek operation. She knew that a vital man like her husband needed the stimulus of work for his emotional well-being as much as he needed food for the well-being of his body. She was also extremely happy that this plan would allow her and the children to live in Halfway with August instead of seeing him only on weekends as in the past.

Within a week, August took Marie back to Halfway, so that she could see the kind of town it was and approve of it before he offered to buy the store. At once she was impressed by the place which had all anyone would need to live comfortably including a school for their children and several church sponsored social clubs including one for Catholic couples. So before they returned to Baker City, August made an offer on the store and the sale was finalized in the office of the town's one lawyer. Now all they had to do was wait until April when the mine operators would go to court.

By the end of April, LeRoy had still not received the promised telegram from the mining company board of directors, so he sent one to them himself. The disheartening answer came a few days later that the plaintiffs' lawyers had filed for a continuance and the court had granted it with a future court date set for the following November!

"Well family! Looks like we are not moving for a while," August announced at dinner.

Then, as he surveyed their crestfallen faces, he added. "But, I think we all need something to do while we wait. In fact, Rosie gave me an idea that should just fit the bill."

"How smart of me to do that!" Rosa put in as August laughed over her puzzled expression.

"Well, it was you who said you needed a trip back East to buy new stock of hat trim. You mentioned Chicago, I believe. But I know another big city with great hat trim to sell you that is also, I have heard, having a really great fair. Not just a county fair or a state fair but a world's fair! And I thought that it is high time my children learn more about the big, wide world outside of Baker County Oregon! So I bought rail tickets for all of us and for Mr. Collins too. We will go early in the Fall when the weather is not so hot in St. Louis and before the court decision on Cornucopia!" he finished as everyone broke into cheers at the news.

17.
McColloch

When Claude McColloch walked onto the Stanford University campus, he felt the delicious thrill of a young man who experiences total independence for the first time. He thought to himself that everything was in place for a successful beginning for four years of college where he could finally be on his own.

Claude had expected that his mother would accompany him when he enrolled at the school, but after Frank had gone to Sumpter against her wishes instead of joining them on the trip to California, Mary seemed to lose all interest in going with him herself. He hadn't really understood that she had changed her mind about going until the day a messenger came to the house to deliver his train ticket. When he opened the packet he realized that it held only one ticket.

"Mother, there seems to be a mistake here," he said waving the packet to get her attention as she worked at her desk. "They only sent my ticket and there is no ticket for you."

"That's right. I'm not going. I intend to be here when your brother decides to come home!" she answered in a tone that made him shudder.

...

Claude felt sorry for his brother. Poor Frank had never known how to keep the kind of low profile Claude had always adopted in order to stay clear of his mother's wrath. He had learned an early lesson from watching Frank slam himself against the wall of Mary's will. Of the two boys, Claude was known as the "quiet, studious" one. Because of this, his mother had always been way too busy trying to corral and control her husband and younger son to pay him much attention. Only he knew that this was just a façade behind which he hid as the only way to negotiate the pitfalls of their tumultuous home life.

Now that he was on his own, he felt somehow lighter much like a horse that has been freed from bridle and rider.

Claude felt especially blessed to be admitted to the young university as part of the class entering in fall of 1904. The school had only been in existence since 1885 when Senator Leland Stanford and his wife, Jane, had made a grant of the land and most of their fortune in memory of their son, Leland Jr., who had died at age 15 from typhoid fever the year before. The two had stated that they wished to use their wealth to help "other people's" children to become "cultured and useful citizens."

Claude was also exhilarated to be part of this campus because it was untraditional; coeducational and non-denominational when most private universities were all male and associated with a religious organization. He immediately felt inspired by the words in the informational booklet he had received that stated the university's mission; "... to qualify students for personal success and by so doing enable them to promote the public welfare by exercising an influence on behalf of humanity and civilization." He definitely wanted to do much more with his education than just make money. He wanted to be able to influence society for the better, and the people he knew who were in a position to do this were either journalists or held public office.

Without having his mother tagging along, Claude could take his time exploring the campus that in his estimation was the most beautiful place he had ever been. The land itself had been Leland and Jane Stanford's 8,000 acre Palo Alto Stock Farm located thirty-five miles south of the founders' home in San Francisco which was the reason that the school was often referred to by a nickname, "The Farm."

The Stanfords spared no expense when they engaged famed landscape architect Fredrick Law Olmstead who was well known for his design of Manhattan's Central Park, the sumptuous grounds of the Biltmore mansion in North Carolina and the Capitol Mall in Washington D.C. Claude thought that Olmstead's design of a cloistered quadrangle with the Memorial Church as its focus was truly breathtaking. He was even more impressed by the entrance to the main quad marked by the enormous Memorial Arch with its frieze that depicted Leland and Jane Stanford on horseback mapping a course over the Sierras for their Central Pacific Railroad. The frieze was inscribed with the stirring words, "The Progress of Civilization." From the main quadrangle the campus expanded laterally to a series of quadrangles dotted by beautiful sandstone California-Mission inspired buildings with their pretty red-tiled roofs. By the time Claude finished his tour, he was truly grateful to be part of such a wondrous place.

• • •

While Claude enjoyed his first taste of freedom, Frank sat miserably on the train as it traveled ever closer to Portland and to what he felt was sure to be his doom. He knew his mother would be waiting at the station for him because C.H. had telegrammed the day and time of Frank's arrival. When the train finally pulled into the station, Frank was the last to depart the car fearful that Mary might make a humiliating scene right there in front of strangers. When he finally stepped onto the platform, he immediately spotted his mother standing with her very erect posture several cars down but turned away from him which made it possible to quietly approach her from behind. He reasoned that if he got close at least she would not have to shout at him from some distance away.

"Hello, Mother," Frank nearly whispered.

"Oh there you are!" she said in a tone that anyone would describe as "joyful." Then he was completely astonished when Mary grabbed him in a rather suffocating embrace and said, "You can't know how much I missed you this summer, Frank!"

Once they were on the Albina Area trolley headed home, Mary kept up her happy babble which only reinforced Frank's opinion that his mother must have lost her mind since he was away. He had certainly never seen her behave this way before. This stranger looked just like his mother, but that was where the likeness ended.

"Claude has settled in at Stanford and he writes that he actually got a job on the *Palo Alto Daily* newspaper! I guess they were impressed with his prior experience on *The Oregonian*. He says that he might join a fraternity since he will be making extra money at the paper. Isn't that wonderful?" she gushed. Then without even taking a breath, the stranger turned to Frank and continued. "When we get home, I'll make us a nice cup of tea and over a plate of cookies you can tell me all about your summer and all the fun you had with your Sumpter friends!"

"That will be nice," Frank mumbled, looking down at his hands, but he thought, "I'll just bet she'd love to hear about my new friend, Bub, and his little pox problem!"

Once the two arrived home, Frank braced himself for the confrontation he knew was sure to come when their front door was closed and Mary no longer had to keep up this motherly display meant for public consumption. To his surprised, there was no change in her at all. As the days passed, his mother stayed so nice that Frank worried that she must have fallen and hit her head while he was away. He even visited the library to read up on the effects of concussion, but he found nothing to explain Mary's very odd behavior. It was unnerving; like waiting for a second shoe to drop. But, when Mary did not revert to her old lecturing, disapproving self, Frank concluded that she acted this way because she was sorry that she was the reason he had left town without her blessing.

Finally, Frank gave up trying to find a logical reason for this radical change in his mother. He really liked all the little niceties she continued to shower on him, and he didn't want to say anything that would bring up any subject that might start a fight with her.

When school started, Frank was way too busy to continue to wonder about Mary. In the first week he signed up to run for freshman class president. When the votes were counted he had tied with his best friend, Freddie Welsh. When Freddie won their run-off, the students decided that Frank should be made class vice president since he had received more votes than anyone who had run for that office. Frank enjoyed serving on the student council so much that he vowed to run again for office as a sophomore.

In December, Frank tried out for a part in the school's pick for the winter play, Charles Dickens' "A Christmas Carol." He was thrilled to get the part as the ghost of Scrooge's dead business partner, Jacob Marley. Mary seemed to enjoy watching him practice his few lines over and over as he lurched about the house rattling his paper mache chains and moaning so loud the neighbors could probably hear, "Scrooge, bewaaare! Bewaaare! I forged these chains in life!"

The days seemed to fly by, and soon it was spring when Frank made the baseball team. He had always loved playing any sport. The coach believed in trying all the freshmen in all the positions in order to see what best fit their individual talents. At the end of spring practice, the coach took Frank aside and told him that the boy was sure to make the varsity team as a sophomore. However, this ego boost was nothing compared to what happened to Frank mid-season.

Not many students turned out to watch the freshmen team play, so Frank noticed that a girl, Katy Douglas, always attended their games and sat prominently in the middle of the bleachers' first row. Whenever he looked in her direction, she would give a small smile and sometimes even made a little wave at him. He had thought that Katy was pretty, but even better, she was the kind of girl who seemed reserved and much more dignified than most of the giggling, gum chewing, gossiping girls in his class. He began to think about taking a chance and asking Katy to go for ice cream with him sometime, but he suffered the same insecurities of all young boys who had never before had a date with a girl, so he held back.

It was after their fifth win in a row. Frank's team was ahead by only one point and the team they played was at bat with runners on all the bases. When the batter hit a pop fly to center field, Frank dove to catch it for the out that won the game. As his teammates gathered around him in jubilation, Katy broke through the group of boys and presented Frank with a rose bud and kissed him lightly on the cheek. Frank finally took Katy for that ice cream following their next practice and he didn't even mind that his friends called him "Lady Killer" for weeks after that.

All was perfect in Frank's world and then, the other shoe dropped.

It happened on an unseasonably warm day in May when Frank was walking home from baseball practice. He was engrossed in oiling his fielder's mitt, so he did not see the man standing in their front yard holding a clipboard and making notes.

When Frank did look up and spot the man he shouted in his surprise, "Who are you and what are you doing in our yard!"

"Ain't your yard much longer, sonny. When our office sells a property they send me around to make notes for our files," answered the man as he turned away in irritation.

"Wh, what do you mean 'sells a property?'" Frank asked with some trepidation.

"Ya had ta know your mama put yer house up for sale some months ago and we were able ta sell it for her! That's what I mean," the man mumbled and turned away since he did not intend to go on being given the third degree by some kid.

With that, Frank dropped his glove and ran into the house looking frantically for Mary. He finally spotted her sitting on their back porch reading a book.

"What's going on! There's some guy in our yard who said we sold our house!" Frank shouted as he rounded the corner.

"Good Heavens, Frank! You could give someone a heart attack yelling like that," Mary cried as she bent to retrieve the book she had dropped. "That's right, I sold our house. We'll be moving as soon as school is out," she added without additional explanation.

"We'll be moving? Did you find some better house in town?" Frank asked hopefully.

"No, I think we'll have to rent for a while. I was lucky enough to find a nice house in Palo Alto to rent. It's near the Stanford campus, so when we move there, your brother can easily walk from our home to his classes," she answered with a sidelong glance at Frank, knowing full well the impact that this statement would have on him.

"Palo Alto?! Stanford?! We can't live there! We have to live here! MY school is here! I have big plans for next year! I'm running for the school council and I'll be playing baseball on the varsity team!" Frank cried nearing hysteria.

"You'll adjust. They have student councils and baseball teams at the high school there, just like any other high school," Mary scoffed.

"You can't do this to me! You can't always change things on me! You can't make me go! If I have to, I'll go to Sumpter and live with my father and you can't stop me!"

"You won't have to run away again just to spite me. Your father is on his way here. He'll be here in a few days to help us with the move," Mary stated calmly turning for the first time to face her son. It was then that Frank saw her small smile and raised eyebrow, an unmistakable look of triumph.

It slowly sunk in as Frank backed away from that look in horror. All those months filled with "nice cups of tea" and other special treats and all the time, his mother was plotting this cruel vengeance against him! At that moment of recognition, Frank turned and ran away from their house.

He ran and ran with no final destination in mind as long as it was as far as possible away from his mother. When he could run no more, he stopped to sit down on a patch of grass to catch his breath and was shocked to realize he was sobbing in great, loud gulps. He rubbed at his wet cheeks with his shirt sleeve as he began to calm down.

Frank realized, with grim finality, that he had no power to fight his mother. He was just a kid and a kid has to do whatever his parents want him to do. Before he began to cry all over again, he remembered that it was only one of his parents who was out to give him grief. He had a potential ally in his father!

Frank was certain his father would believe him when he told C.H. about Mary's double dealing. Hadn't his mother done this kind of thing to his father too? She had caused his father to be publicly embarrassed in front of her whole church with one of her tricks which was the reason his father left for Sumpter. After that, she had been so mean to his father whenever C.H. tried to return home that the poor man had just finally stayed away. And it was not lost on Frank that C.H. loved his sons since he had continued to stay married and to financially support his family despite his banishment. Feeling a bit better, Frank wiped his face with his sleeve again and decided to visit Freddie Welsh who was his best friend precisely because he was a good listener and always made Frank laugh.

True to form, Freddie listened soberly to Frank's story, then slapped his friend on the back and said, as he as motioned Frank to his bedroom , "I've been savin' something to show you and I think it might be the answer to your problem."

...

Frank was not the only one who hoped that the rift between his parents could somehow be mended so things might go back to the way they once were. C.H. also held such hope for them. He had actually first heard of Mary's plan to move to Palo Alto from a frantic letter Claude sent to his father begging him to stop Mary's move. Claude stated that he had no intention of living with his mother and little brother, since he now lived in his fraternity's house near campus. He argued that because of his job on the Palo Alto Daily, he could afford to finance his own independence.

Actually, C.H. had hoped to establish peace with Mary for some time. He was saddened by the pain their estrangement caused his sons, and after the George Patterson incident over the prior summer, he realized that Sumpter was not a healthy place in which to raise a family. He had begun to agree with his wife who never mentioned Sumpter without adding the words "evil" or "vile." He decided that he would try to convince Mary to stay in Oregon in exchange for his promise to resume his law practice in Portland when his term as mayor of Sumpter was up in a few months. He was sure that her desire to move close to Claude was born out of loneliness and the desire for the family life they once had. He admitted to himself that he had also been lonely and that he dearly wanted to live with his family again.

The small seed of C.H.'s hope that he could actually reunite his broken family began to blossom in the moment Mary greeted her husband as he walked through the door of their Albina house. He was sure that he saw her smile in a way that indicated she was happy to see him. Though their front parlor was cold, dark and littered with packed boxes, he noticed the homey aroma of chicken roasting as Mary led the way into the warmth of their kitchen. He thought it a good sign that she had taken the trouble to make his favorite meal.

As they ate, both C.H. and Mary were careful to keep their conversation light and newsy. Neither one seemed anxious to broach any discussion that might touch on the differences that had kept them apart so long. Finally, after they had exhausted talk of the weather and their children's accomplishments, their conversation turned to Mary's reasons for wanting to move to California. Since this move was the reason she had asked him to return to help, C.H. thought it was another safe subject and might give him an opening to make his offer to come back permanently to live and work in Portland. But he was wrong.

"I know Claude does not want to live with Frank and me! He has made it very clear that he only wants to live at his precious fraternity. Where he lives is of no concern to me! It certainly does not change the fact that we are moving and that's that!" Mary snapped in a sudden rage that took her husband by complete surprise.

"I, I thought that Claude was the reason you decided to make the move," C.H. protested.

"Claude?" she said vaguely, as though this was the first time she had considered him at all. She made a little hand-wave as though brushing away that subject as one of no interest to her. Then C.H. saw the storm clouds gather again behind her eyes. "Did it ever occur to any of you that I might have needs too?! Claude insists on having things his way! You insist on living and working in a godless town I hate! Frank runs away to Sumpter when I forbid him to go! And now..."

"Hold on a minute! What was this about Frank running away?!" C.H. cut in, as Mary stopped mid-sentence realizing that she had never intended to tell him about Frank's disobedience because it demonstrated that the boy had so wanted to visit his father that he would defy Mary and risk her wrath.

"Yes, he ran away, like a thief in the night. He's a big reason we need to move far away, so it'll be harder for him to pull that stunt again!"

"Oh Mary, Mary. Look what we have done to our lives and our children," C.H. whispered. "This just shows how much we need to mend the mess we have made of our marriage. Can't we at least try to end the pain we all feel?"

When she didn't answer, he continued though this was not the opening he had hoped for. "Look, Mary. I have been thinking a lot about this. I agree with you that Sumpter is not the sort of place a sane person would choose to live, especially one with a family. As soon as my term is finished, I want to move back here and work as I had before in our Portland firm. Then there will be no need for you to move. Don't you see? We can stay in Oregon and buy a new house, maybe one of those palaces in the West Hills. We could start over and get back the happiness we once felt."

When he had finished this little speech, Mary just sat there staring at her husband as though he was a total stranger who had spoken to her in a foreign language.

"No need to move? Start over? Stay in Oregon?! ... I hate this state! Why on earth would I want to continue to live in a state that, election after election, has denied women the same full rights of citizenship that every man just takes for granted!"

"Mary, last time I checked, women have yet to get the vote in California," C.H. muttered wishing that they were not going to go through the same old political quarrel that always seemed to drive a wedge between them.

"Well, they are a lot closer than we are, and the California women working for suffrage have not sacrificed their principles like all the blind followers of Abigail Duniway who are willing to just turn their backs on our push to ban the sale of alcohol once and for all. Abigail continues to preach that the vote is lost if women insist on Prohibition along with the vote. Really? It doesn't seem to matter what we say, suffrage continues to go down in defeat in this state because of Oregon liquor and business interests!"

"I'm surprised that you are willing to give up on Oregon so easily, just because one woman doesn't agree with you. I would think that you would want to stay and fight," C.H. cut in hoping to appeal to Mary's usual combative nature.

"Well, for your information, I have fought! I have put up with Abigail's constant efforts to sideline my Christian Women's Temperance Union group. She has made it very clear that, in her opinion, all the failed suffrage votes are mostly due to WCTU's desire to pass a ban on the sale of alcohol, which as you so well know, is not popular with the men of this state!"

"Why don't you give her ideas a chance, Mary? Why can't you just work toward getting the vote in Oregon and wait until that hurdle is cleared before you tackle the alcohol question?"

At this, Mary jumped to her feet in what C.H. believed to be the worst rage he had ever witnessed in his wife. "I'll tell you why I won't work with Abigail! It's because she won't let me!! She doesn't want any of my group around next month when they hold their national convention here, in Portland! That's why!"

It took over an hour for C.H. to get the whole story from his fuming wife. Once she had calmed a bit and stopped pacing about the room, Mary explained that Oregon suffragists had successfully convinced the National American Suffrage Association to hold their summer 1905 convention in Portland. National leaders, Susan B Anthony and Anna Howard Shaw were coming to aid in creating the strategic campaign for the 1906 Oregon election. Not only was Mary's WCTU group not allowed to be among the sponsors of this event, her frequent arguments with Mrs. Duniway had led to Mary and the other leaders of her group to be banned from attending the convention.

"Abigail said that Mayor Lane and Governor Chamberlain will be speaking in support of the women's vote and she doesn't want any of us to mess it up by marching around singing 'Onward Christian Soldiers' and waving our 'Down with Whiskey' signs! And now the women in my group blame me for getting us banished! They even ordered me to resign!" Mary finished, finally breaking into sobs and running from the room.

C.H. sat stunned at Mary's story. He realized that she had suffered a crushing failure and betrayal in the one area of her life that had given her a feeling of importance and even power to change a society that so often treated women as unpaid maids and baby factories. Susan B. Anthony! Anna Howard Shaw! How awful that Mary had been denied any part in this momentous occasion. And worse yet, women who had been her closest friends had turned against her. He could readily see why it would be futile to try to convince Mary to remain in Portland, even in a West Hills palace!

· · ·

For the next few days C.H. quietly helped Mary pack boxes for the move to California. Neither of them mentioned the suffrage convention debacle again, but C.H. was grateful that they had come to an understanding and had fashioned a compromise concerning the future of their family. Mary agreed that it was unreasonable and unfair of her to keep the boys from seeing their father. C.H. was hardly a deadbeat father and, since he continued to support them all, he had a right to expect visits from his children. It did not escape Mary that, if they ever divorced, he could easily take the boys from her. Privately, she decided that she would never push her luck that far. C.H. calmed her fears about the boys' visiting Sumpter when he promised that he would move to Baker City where he could continue with the clientele he had already built. By the end of the week, the two were ready to sit down with Frank as a united front and explain to him what they had decided.

Mary hardly spoke as C.H. laid out to their son what the two had decided.

"So, Frank, after my move to Baker City next January, both you and Claude can visit me every summer without any problem from your mother. But, since your mother and I agree that Sumpter is not a healthy place and I still live there, you will have to stay in Palo Alto this summer."

Then C.H. and Mary both fell silent and stared at Frank who sat quiet and motionless on the porch swing across from his parents who were braced for what was sure to be his emotional explosion. But it never came.

"I'm sorry, that just won't work for me," Frank finally said, shaking his head back and forth. "Freddie Welsh and I joined the Oregon National Guard this week and my summer training boot camp starts June first."

Then he went inside the house leaving his two astonished parents mutely watching the empty porch swing rock back and forth.

18.
Krann

"Papa, why are we going on such a long trip? We have been on this train forever!" whined Anna who sat between her brothers, Gus and Harry across the aisle from their parents and older sister, Betty, as their railway carriage chugged along through a rather bleak stretch of Midwest prairie.

"Not quite 'forever,' Anna. We've been traveling for only two days now. And, I believe when we reach our destination even you will think it was well worth the trip. We will have a grand time because a fair is always fun. Isn't that right, Harry? You and Gus have been to fairs. Why don't you two tell her about the fun you had." August suggested resisting the temptation to use any of the hyperbole mentioned in every news account he and Marie had read or heard about the Louisiana Purchase Exposition in St. Louis which was popularly known as "The 1904 World's Fair."

It was fine that his sons' account of small town events featuring arcade games, booths filled with prize pies, jams and other homemade treats, the usual judging of locally raised livestock and the occasional rodeo events managed to enchant little Anna enough to reinforce her patience with travel boredom.

"Harry said he saw a baby lamb at a fair. Will we see a baby lamb at this fair too, Papa?" the child asked and without waiting for an answer added, "I surely hope that we see a baby lamb."

"I'm not sure about lambs, but I did read that they have baby elephants at this fair," August laughed when his wide-eyed daughter's mouth flew open at the thought of such a wonder.

"Anna, why don't you let me read to you? That will help the time pass," suggested Betty who had been reading one of the many books she had brought with which to entertain herself.

"Oh, I wish Rosie was sitting with us. She always tells great stories that are really fun to hear! Why does she have to sit in that other car so far away?" questioned the petulant youngster.

"Why Anna, your auntie sat with us and told you a story just last night about King Arthur and his court with that round table. We can't pester her all day for more stories," Marie cautioned.

"She doesn't mind. She loves to tell us stories. Mama why don't you invite her to come and sit with us?"

"No, Anna, that's a really bad idea," broke in Harry while giving the little girl a slight poke with his elbow. "She'll bring Mr. Collins with her and all they ever talk about is ballet or opera. It's sooo boring!"

"Yeah, boring!" whispered Gus in her other ear.

"Well maybe we should invite them both in. You children could do with a little culture," laughed August.

"I think I have a better idea," said Marie reaching for the large carpet bag under her seat she had nicknamed her 'first aid kit'. "Oh look what I found! A brand new puzzle! We'll just pull down the table and you children can work on it together! What a coincidence. The picture is of a knight in armor and he's fighting a fire eating dragon!" she exclaimed to her suddenly enthused children.

...

When LeRoy Collins was first invited to accompany Rosa's family on their trip to St. Louis, he was very glad to have a long uninterrupted time period to get to better know Rosa. They already knew that they enjoyed each other's company and that they had much in common. In fact, after every short lunch the two enjoyed together during their busy work days or evening dinner outing or to attend some show at the Baker City Opera House, LeRoy felt he was falling more in love with this young woman. He had looked forward to the trip that would allow the kind of time couples need to really learn about each other. When LeRoy had suggested to August that he wished to purchase tickets for himself and Rosa and that he would request seats in a car next to the one in which the rest of the family would travel, August winked and slapped LeRoy on the back saying, "I think that is a fine idea, my friend!"

Additionally, LeRoy knew that his mother had a dear friend, Pamela Smyth, who had married a St. Louis financier and presently lived on a private street, Waterman Avenue, which was only a few blocks from Lindell Boulevard and the main entrance to the fairgrounds. His mother had written her friend and had secured an invitation for both Rosa and LeRoy to stay at her friend's large manse. He felt very good about this idea since August had secured rooms for his family at The Inside Inn, the only hotel actually inside the fairgrounds. In LeRoy's mind, this was a perfect setup since the hotel was located on the other side of the fair from Mrs. Smyth's home. That would make it impossible for Rosa's nephews and nieces to constantly seek her attention as they tended to do at home.

For her part, Rosa was not enthused by the idea of staying so far from Marie, August and the children. She had looked forward to attending the fair with the children so that she could experience such a grand event by seeing it, in part, through a child's eyes. However, at the same time LeRoy had told Rosa about the invitation to stay with his mother's friend, he told her that Pamela had promised to introduce Rosa to Louis Ackerman, a close neighbor who was President of the Louis Ackerman Millinery Co. Rosa could not ignore the fact that this represented a great opportunity for her to gain inside knowledge about the workings of the millinery trade and current fashion in the country's biggest cities. She had to remind herself that this trip was primarily a buying expedition and the fair visit was of secondary importance.

In truth, Rosa realized that she needed to establish contacts with people who she might later rely on to provide her with the supplies she would need for her growing business. If she had such contacts, it might not be necessary to personally travel to the Midwest to buy stock in the future. She also felt a bit guilty for having felt peeved when LeRoy first mentioned the idea of their both staying with Pamela, when this was actually turning out to be a great business opportunity. She would just have to put off visiting the fair with the children until after she had finished with her supply purchases.

...

Since the travelers arrived on a Sunday, the only day the fair was closed, Marie and August had a chance to settle into the Inside Inn and let their children finally sleep in a comfortable bed for the first time in several days. The children were much too tired to fully appreciate the amazing ten acre structure built by the great hotelier, E.M. Statler, the first of its kind located actually inside the grounds of a world's fair. This alone was a great luxury for visitors to the St. Louis fair since any other hotels were over a mile away.

But the luxury did not stop at the convenience of the hotel's location. This building not only housed over five thousand guests in its 2257 rooms, their every need would be met by a staff of two thousand. Additionally, there were two large restaurants, one of which could seat 2,500 patrons, a drug store, a lounge, clothing stores, a newsstand and a barbershop.

As the family, walked to the hotel's main entrance from the trolley stop, even the children gaped in wonder at the view of the fairgrounds below the hill on which the hotel stood. The group was mesmerized by the sight of the impressive avenues of the Plateau of States beginning with the elaborate building for Indiana on the left and Utah on the right. Through the shade of oak trees, they could even see the looming dome of the Pennsylvania building.

Once they had all eaten dinner, the family hurried outside at the suggestion of their waiter for what he explained had to be seen to be believed. As they walked through the large front doors everyone stopped to stare in renewed wonder at the fairyland created by thousands of electric lights on every building below. As he looked at the astounded faces of his four children, August smiled at Marie and whispered, "Well no-one is sleeping tonight!"

The next morning when the family gathered around one round table for breakfast, August handed out small booklets that described the various exhibits, concessions and events for fairgoers to enjoy. Once everyone held their own booklet, August explained, "I got each of you a booklet of your own because I want each of you to decide on the one thing you most want to see during our week here. This fair is much too big for us all to see and do everything. Your mother and I brought you here because we wanted you to learn more about the big, wide world that exists outside of Baker City. It will be fun, but it will be educational as well. But there are also many other things one can do here that is only for fun, so each of you must decide on one thing that we will make sure you get to do."

With that, each child fell silently to work examining the booklets, but it wasn't long before they began to chatter about those offerings that caught each youngster's eye.

"Wow, I want to see these battles they put on!" Harry said excitedly. "Look here, father. They put on the Boer War every day, twice a day!"

"Now, that is something I would also like to see. A whole war that is over in half a day!" laughed August.

"This 'Creation' ride looks interesting," remarked Betty. "You ride in little boats and pass scenes showing man's history on earth and also the creation story about Adam and Eve in the Bible. It says here that…"

"Does that ride have a baby elephant? I want to see a baby elephant." Anna interrupted her sister as Betty began to read aloud from the book.

"No, it doesn't mention baby elephants, Anna. You keep looking in your book for one."

"Look at this!" Gus nearly shouted waving his book with a two page picture of the Observation Wheel. "It's a giant wheel with thirty-six cars and each car holds up to sixty passengers. It goes around and, at the top, people can see the whole fair at once because it's almost three hundred feet high!"

"Well, children I think you are making a good start picking your favorite activity." Marie said.

"I don't see any baby elephants in this darn book," Anna mumbled as she flipped through the pages of her book. But just as the little girl got close to tears, their jovial waiter began laying out several platters groaning with pancakes, eggs and sausages which brought out the child's biggest smile.

As they ate, August continued the discussion of fair events. "Children, you probably will not be surprised that your mother's choice is to see the Austrian Pavilion."

"We will probably never see Austria as a family, so this is a chance for everyone to learn something about the country Auntie and I are from," explained Marie.

"And you are probably not going to be surprised that I choose to see the Palace of Mines and Metallurgy," put in August as Harry sighed unhappily.

"Oh, you think that will be boring, Harry?" August laughed. "The book says that this mining display covers twenty-two acres! That has given them lots of room for a gigantic miniature railroad, and a ride that takes you in cars down inside a coal mine. And, hmmm, there is something else there called 'The Crystal Cave' to see... What do you think?"

"I think we should hurry up and finish eating so we can see all that!" cried the suddenly excited boy.

• • •

On their first day after arrival, Pamela Smyth made some suggestions to Rosa over breakfast in her sunny conservatory about how to make the most of her short buying visit. Their hostess had set up a visit to Louis Ackerman's millinery company where he planned to introduce Rosa to some wholesale vendors of millinery supplies. However, after seeing how Rosa was prepared with a small sketch pad for drawing styles she would see on the women attending the fair, Mrs. Smyth said," I think that you should not buy anything until the end of your trip. I have noticed that women visiting from out of town are dressed to the teeth in the latest fashions. This will give you a chance to make a comprehensive list of hat trim items that you cannot get in Oregon. After your tour of vendors, today, you will know from your sketches exactly what materials you will want to purchase."

Pamela had been correct to suggest Rosa put off actual buying until after she had seen for herself what women visitors at the fair were wearing. Her tour of St. Louis vendors proved to be a wonderful new experience for a "country milliner" who wanted to bring current millinery fashion to the women of Baker City.

As she and LeRoy toured both the Ackerman and the Sonnenfeld businesses, Rosa wrote page after page of notes about the amazing array of trim available. Since the well-dressed woman in 1904 considered the hat to be an essential element of any ensemble, those who could afford hats trimmed with exotic plumes and the eye-catching artistry of beadwork and artificial flowers would spare no expense for a well-made hat.

Rosa was shown whole rooms with bins of every possible bird feather. At home she could rely on a supply of local pheasant feathers, but it was quite difficult to find those of the osprey, egrets, herons, peacocks, birds of paradise and the most popular of all, the billowing plumes of the ostrich that women prized.

 She was also intrigued by the various use hat trimmers made of velvet ribbon, and she was even given a gadget that allowed trimmers to turn a length of ribbon into a fabulous flower. As she held what looked like a large empty thread spool topped by a series of nails, a female worker guided Rosa in the way to wind the ribbon into a perfect velvet rose.

Another item that Rosa found very intriguing was what trimmers called the "pompadour frame" which once placed on the head acted as a base for styling a woman's hair into a high pile of curls. The structure of this hairdo with its firm base gave any hat a support on which to rest. Women could also add flare by securing a hat with a long decorative hat pin. The finished creation produced the illusion that the hat magically floated on the wearer's hair. Rosa was eager to incorporate these frames into her business by demonstrating to Baker City women how they, too, could adopt a "big city" look.

In addition to hat trim, Rosa was shown finished hats of all shapes and sizes. By day's end, she could hardly wait to see how actual fair visitors wore the various wide brimmed 'picture hats', the brimless velvet toques, the turbans, and light, straw boaters she saw displayed on rows of hat stands. She was especially glad to note that she did not see one horrid bonnet all day which she had always believed made even a very young woman look like a dowdy matron.

Both Rosa and LeRoy were surprised that, by the time they were leaving Mr. Ackerman at his building's door, the sky was already dark and street lamps had been lit for the night. Though it had been a very long day with much to take in, Rosa felt assured that her business would greatly profit in the future because of the new contacts she had made that day. Her head was swimming with new ideas and she carried a purse full of business cards from St. Louis milliners and vendors that promised to provide her with the materials she so needed to take her brand beyond the limits of Baker City.

"I think that you should begin your survey of well-dressed women fair visitors. Why don't we take the streetcar to the main entrance since the most of the grounds are closed by now, but the restaurants and concessions on the Pike will be open until midnight? We can find an outside table where we can eat and also watch people," LeRoy suggested as though reading Rosa's mind.

The streetcar ended only steps from the Lindell Street entrance and the east end of the Pike, the closest thing to a carnival midway that the fair offered. The crowds at this entrance were daunting, but the couple was in luck and found an empty table in one of the beer garden restaurants in the "Tyrolean Alps," a section featuring German style food vendors operating next to a huge medieval castle replica and painted "snow-covered" mountain backdrop. The "castle" held many inside restaurants but were less amenable to "crowd watching."

After ordering, LeRoy spotted a "World's Fair Bulletin" on their table that featured a list of "Odd Things on the Pike" and began to read from it.

"What should we do after dinner? We could see the 'Indian Rubber Man' tie himself into knots at 'Mysterious Asia' or listen to a band of '60 Sober Musicians' from Ireland. We could also ride a submarine and an airship on a ride called 'Under and Over the Sea,' or talk to 'Jim, the Educated Horse.' I myself am leaning toward the 'Dancing Girls of Madrid'! Don't laugh, Rosie! These are definitely the kind of cultural experiences we have been missing at home!" LeRoy exclaimed with mock seriousness.

Then he put the book down and took Rosa's hand, "I was so proud of you today. I saw how you completely won over those crusty businessmen with your enthusiasm and obvious desire to learn from them," he said in a tone that was both sincere and intimate.

"I guess they don't often get a visit from an unsophisticated hat maker from the Oregon backwater," Rosa muttered.

"No, no, I mean that you impressed them! I know that you really surprised them with marketing ideas that I bet they never thought of before. Did you see how Mr. Ackerman turned to his secretary and directed her to take notes when you told them that, for lack of trim, you often have women bring you some bauble from home that they are fond of to incorporate into a hat that then becomes a very custom creation! I'll bet anything he begins that practice right away. I will also bet that the old man had planned to meet with us briefly and then pass us off to some assistant. Instead, he was pleasantly surprised by you. So much so, that he spent all day with us and even walked us to the building's door!"

As LeRoy talked of the day's events, Rosa felt embarrassed at first since she had never been particularly comfortable being complimented. But as she looked into the young man's eyes she began to believe he was sincere in this praise. She also could not help but notice how, as he spoke with such animation, LeRoy looked even more handsome than usual. His blue eyes had actually darkened with a burning intensity that she had never seen before, and as he leaned closer to her, his very nearness made her tremble. Such feelings were so totally new to the girl that they were a bit frightening, and she was relieved when the waiter interrupted this moment by bringing their food.

After they finished a delicious but decidedly rich dinner of fried schnitzel mit spätzle, LeRoy suggested they walk a bit to "help digestion." By then, the crowds had left the main fairgrounds though the closed buildings were still lit with row upon row of electric lights which added an ethereal element to the majestic palaces lining each side of the wide plaza leading up to the Grand Basin. On a hill just beyond the lake, Festival Hall stood like an impossibly ornate wedding cake ablaze with thousands of electric "candles." More incredibly, a continuous cascade of water, lit by bulbs of constantly changing color splashed between the two long staircases leading up to Festival Hall.

The magnificence of this sight was undiminished by the usual crowds of people, so the couple could sit on a bench and view the fairyland around them without distraction. They sat quietly for several minutes. Then Rosa heard LeRoy softly speak her name. As she turned, he leaned into her and she felt him softly kiss her cheek and then, less softly, kiss her lips. Then, incredibly, he pulled her into his arms and whispered, "I hope you know, I am in love with you. Rosie, I also have come to believe that I should marry you. That is…if you would have me."

· · ·

By the next day, the one thing Rosa most wanted was to talk to Marie about LeRoy's proposal. She had not slept and had realized that this was a more complicated decision than it is for most young women when a man they love proposes a lifetime commitment. She was nearly thirty, that looming border that society had drawn for women between the proper age of a debutant and the age when a woman is suddenly known as an "old maid."

She was surprised to even consider her age as a reason to marry since she had never thought much about it before. Her self-concept had never involved worry over being an unmarried woman. After all, she had always thought of herself as a business woman, and as her success grew, she knew that is how others saw her as well. If she married, she wondered, would she be pressured to give up her shop? Even if she wasn't overtly pressured by a husband to close her shop, would the new responsibilities as a wife require so much of her time and energies that she would have to end her millinery business?

Marriage usually meant children. As a devote Catholic, Rosa fervently believed that marriage was a covenant a couple makes with God to procreate and educate children in the faith. In truth, Rosa loved helping Marie with her children. Her nieces and nephews were probably her greatest source of joy. But, even having one child of her own would mean an inevitable and drastic shift in her adult responsibilities. She would just have to face the reality that marriage was certain to mean giving up a career as a milliner. How bad would that be? The more she considered the implications of being a married woman the more she realized that what made her happiest was not fashioning women's hats but was being a part of a bustling family complete with the needs of children. She also had to face the fact that her present home life was about to change. When August and Marie moved to Halfway, she would no longer enjoy their family life as her own. In the final analysis, Rosa decided that what LeRoy was offering was exactly what she, herself, most wanted.

Suddenly, Rosa knew that she was actually ready to become someone's wife. To make things even more perfect, that "someone" was a fine man whom she had grown to love. She was certain that LeRoy would make a wonderful husband. At the end of her sleepless night, Rosa had firmly decided to accept LeRoy's proposal.

...

Rosa and LeRoy found August, Marie and their family eating breakfast at the Inside Inn and planning another big day of sightseeing. The couple had already decided not to tell the family about their marriage plans until Rosa could speak to her sister alone first, or at least before the adults dined together that night once the children were in bed.

As they arrived at the hotel dining room, Rosa and LeRoy found the children in animated discussion about what they had decided to do that day. As they joined the group, Marie quieted the children.

"Yesterday while everyone was inside the Palace of Electricity, Marie decided she needed fresh air and left to take a short walk outside," explained August. "When she returned, she was full of excitement about the Jerusalem exhibit nearby. We all followed her around a corner and were astounded by high walls and buildings that looked very much like pictures we have seen of the holy city complete with sites like the Dome of the Rock, the Western Wall and the Church of the Holy Sepulcher, if you can believe that!"

Betty handed LeRoy a folded brochure and said,"Mother got us this booklet that says that the exhibit is ten acres and presents the stations of the cross along the Via Dolorosa. You can also take camel or donkey rides and shop in a bazaar where actual natives of Jerusalem have been brought here to wear period clothes and work in artisan workshops and booths. It would be like actually being there!"

"We all decided that was the first thing we want to do today!" Harry added. "Then we are going to the Austrian exhibit and then to the Pike to go on the Observation Wheel! You should come with us, Auntie!"

"I am more than ready to see something of this fair now," laughed Rosa in response to the children's evident excitement.

...

By noon, the adults felt a need to rest from the morning's sightseeing, so LeRoy suggested that they all eat lunch on the Pike at the same outside restaurant where he and Rosa had dined the night before. It proved to be a good choice since the wait staff was able to move two tables together to accommodate the unusually large group of eight.

Since they were eating out of doors and at a table placed well away from other diners, neither August nor Marie felt a need to caution the children to keep their voices down, and in their over-stimulated state the younger Meyers all began talking at once about what they liked most from their morning experiences.

In spite of the chaos, Marie and Rosa quietly discussed their impressions of the Austrian Pavilion. When speaking to her sister, Rosa always spoke in German as did August since they knew Marie was not comfortable with English.

It was not long before the children's chatter and the many shifts of language usage managed to completely leave LeRoy out of the group interaction. As the only child of rather staid, Boston parents, he did not enjoy such familial chaos. In fact, he thought, he did not like it at all. He had been raised to believe conversation at mealtime must be hushed and infrequent in order to aid one's digestion. He was also raised to believe that one should never correct someone else's children. So, he sat uncomfortably mute through the entire meal at the end of which he took notice that not one child had taken more than a few bites of food. This so offended his sense of Bostonian frugality that he was tempted to suggest that everyone should wait while the youngsters finish eating what was still on their plates.

Since their next planned stop was to be the great Observation Wheel at the other end of the Pike, the group began to weave slowly through the thickening crowd toward that ride. On the way, August stopped to buy a folded crisp waffle "cone" topped by balls of ice cream for each child as LeRoy silently shook his head over such flagrant overindulgence.

While the group paused to buy the treats, a sign across the wide walkway caught little Anna's eye. It bore a definite picture of an elephant! As she strained to see it, Harry dropped her hand when he was given his cone, so the little girl moved a bit through the river of fairgoers toward the sign that drew her like a magnet. When she moved to a spot just below the sign, she saw that it displayed a delightful picture of a smiling elephant sliding down a steep slide into a lake of water. She couldn't read all the words, but she certainly recognized "circus."

"Hey, there's a circus here, and it's with elephants!" she exclaimed as she turned to tell Harry who was no longer right beside her.

"Harry? Harry? Mama? Auntie? Papa?" Anna cried turning in all directions for a glimpse of her family. No-one. Only a sea of strangers. These strangers all kept surging past her in their constant search for more wondrous entertainment never hearing the small voice that rose ever more stridently in growing panic.

· · ·

Meanwhile, at the bottom of the impossibly gigantic Ferris wheel the family gathered as August went to buy their tickets. Marie surveyed the group silently counting heads. Then she stepped closer to Harry who was intently licking the last of his ice cream. "Harry! Harry! Wo ist Anna?!" she asked, grabbing him by both shoulders to get his full attention.

At this, the boy just held up the hand that had held his little sister's all day and looked at it in total confusion. Then he mumbled while still staring at his empty hand, "Ich weiss nicht. I don't know!"

With that, Marie turned to run and fetch August from the ticket line. Together the two sat the children on a nearby bench with instructions for Betty to watch them, while the four adults waded through the crush of people frantically looking from side to side for a small girl wearing a lace dress and pink hair ribbons. Occasionally, they stopped some stranger to find out if anyone had seen such a girl. As they neared the elephant sign, a portly man with a red face heard them questioning random people.

"I saw her! I saw that little girl because I was tired and hot and had to sit down over there." He pointed to a bench beside the ice cream stand. "I saw her crying, but before I could do anything, her father came and took her by the hand and they walked that way," he said pointing in the direction of the Pike side entrance.

"Mein Gott, August!!" Marie cried in alarm at the notion that they now faced a parent's worst nightmare. A stranger had taken their child!

...

After a few minutes of questioning the red faced man, August and Marie had a description of the person who took Anna and led her away. He had not been dressed in any kind of uniform, so they concluded that he was not a policeman or a fair worker, which seemed a far more sinister situation than if Anna had been taken somewhere by an official.

"Well, then we need to involve the police," concluded August.

"Rosa and I passed several stationed around the main fair entrance off Lindell Avenue," LeRoy informed the distraught parents, so the group hurried in that direction.

However, once they arrived at the crowded front gates, they could spot no man in uniform, so without explanation, August cut through the line for tickets to talk to the man behind the ticket window.

"You want a policeman? That's bad timing. All our officers are gathering at the foot of the Grand Basin for a parade, but it should be close to the time for it to end," remarked the man with a shrug as the four turned in that direction to continue to weave through the thick crowd.

Within a block of the entrance, however, it became impossible to continue forward. No-one in the press of people appeared to be moving since they were held back by the rows of stationary parade watchers lining the parade route. As the minutes ticked by in this immobile state, the parents' panic grew nearly intolerable, yet they could do nothing but wait for those in front to begin moving.

Finally, they could move a bit sideways which they did while holding hands so as not to become separated. Still, progress was painfully slow until the group finally found an opening as the mob holding them in place began to break up. This allowed August, the tallest member of the group, to see a small knot of blue uniforms moving in their direction, so he advised that the group remain motionless until the police arrived at their position. When the crowd finally parted for the men in blue, August and Marie wriggled close enough to speak to one of them, and he directed them to a quiet spot behind one of the great columns at the entrance to the Palace of Varied Industries.

"Any report of a lost child needs to be made to the Bureau of Lost Children here on the fairgrounds, so I will take you there," the policeman explained once he heard the story of Anna's disappearance.

The walk to the office dealing with the constant problem of children who become separated from their parents at the fair seemed interminable to the group following the kindly policeman through the midday throng. Finally, they could see over the heads of people pressed in front of them a high chain link fence that surrounded what appeared to be an empty children's playground next to a low building with a sign "Bureau of Lost Children."

Once inside, they were shown to an office where several women at a row of desks interviewed groups of parents describing their lost child. At the end of each interview another woman in a nurse's uniform led the parents out through a double door. After Marie and August were interviewed they, too, were taken through the door which they believed led outside where they feared they would be left with nothing much accomplished in their search for Anna.

The door did not lead outside but, instead, it led into a large carpeted room, sun-lit by a row of tall windows. In every corner of the room children sat at little tables drawing and painting or scooted around the floor playing with an assortment of colorful toys.

"See if you can identify your daughter because a child brought in earlier said her name is 'Anna Meyer'," encouraged the woman who opened the door for Marie and August.

Before August had a chance to translate, Marie gave a cry of joy at the sight of the pink hair ribbons and lace sundress that Anna had chosen to wear that morning. With that, the child turned to see her parents and dropped a doll she had been holding.

"Mama! Papa! You found me!" she called out and ran into their arms.

Once both parents had had a chance to determine that no harm had come to Anna, August wanted to know who had brought his daughter to this safe place.

"I don't know the man's name. I just know he is really nice." the girl answered nodding her head.

"Anna, don't you remember the rule about talking to strangers?

You can't tell by looking at someone that they are nice. Now, can you?" August reasoned feeling that they had not done a very good job of counseling their brood about the dangers lurking in the world waiting to ensnare the innocent.

"Oh, I know he is nice because he brings me pancakes for breakfast every day!" Anna stated as August stared in stunned disbelief.

When he had regained composure, he picked up the little girl, kissed her on both cheeks and whooped, "I think our waiter is going to get a very big tip!"

19.
McColloch

"**D**on't worry, Mary. Our son will not turn his back on our home or fail to finish his education to permanently join the Oregon Guard. For one thing, as a kid in high school, their rules require that boys his age be trained only in the summer, so they can return to school in the fall," C.H. explained to calm Mary after Frank's announcement that he would be attending military boot camp instead of moving to California with his mother in June.

"Well, the whole thing makes me nervous. I really don't think we should allow him to rebel in this way just because he isn't always getting everything he wants! I'm sure, Charles, if we inform these people who let him join up that it was totally against our wishes, as a minor, they would have to let him go." Mary grumbled through gritted teeth as she paced the narrow floor space between the packing boxes piled in their parlor.

"I think that would be a big mistake. Knowing Frank, I believe such a move would only increase his desire to rebel against our authority. I also feel that he will hate the military because he tends to resist anyone giving him orders. You'll see, he will get his fill of marching to someone else's tune very quickly."

...

In fact, C.H. could not have been more wrong about how his boy would react to the military. Frank absolutely loved it without reservation, though he would not have been able to fully articulate why. From the first day, military life began to satisfy his long repressed hunger for stability. It was as though he had been finally fed a satisfying meal after his chaotic home life had left him close to emotional starvation.

He loved everything about this new experience. It offered the simplicity of male camaraderie free from female complexities. It offered the relief of a totally predictable routine free from fear of being blindsided by the ever changeable goals of his mercurial mother. It offered strong, sure guidance from steady male role models in the place of his largely absent father.

In addition, the military demanded from recruits the exact abilities and skills that Frank already possessed. He immediately demonstrated to his superiors the same physical dexterity that had already proven his worth on any sports team. Frank's hours of shooting tin cans from a fence post and hunting small game in the woods of Eastern Oregon made him a standout among the city boys in his cohort. He had always embraced any physical challenge finding great joy in pushing himself. So, without even knowing it, he set the pace for less committed recruits. Yet, he escaped any resentment from peers due to his easy manner and keen sense of humor.

By the end of the summer, Frank vowed to make the military his life. He knew, however, this decision would have to wait a bit longer. He still needed to finish high school and probably college, since he did not want to just become an infantry grunt. He had been greatly impressed by the Army commissioned and non-commissioned officers who, not only trained the youth volunteers, but fulfilled many of Frank's needs that should have been met by his own parents.

Certainly, his parent's difficulties had left Frank nearly alone to figure out for himself how to manage growing up. Of course, Mary and C.H.'s physical separation removed the kind of day to day support a boy-child needs from a loving father in order to successfully negotiate the challenges presented by the world outside the home. For her part, Mary's constant involvement in her many political and religious commitments took her away from home nearly every day. Even when physically present at home, Mary was always so distracted by her outside interests that she paid attention to Frank only when he annoyed her. Even worse, her duplicitous manipulation of him had nearly destroyed his trust in her. He had grown certain that he could not count on her for much of anything beyond the bare necessities of survival. It is little wonder that, by the end of three months, Frank's respect and admiration for his commanding National Guard officers had grown into a glowing hero worship.

In short, he wanted to be just like them, and he did not want to do anything that would limit his newly chosen career. He would just have to join Mary and enroll in school in California. He had to face the fact he had nowhere else to go since his father had made it clear that Frank could not even visit until C.H. had completed his term as mayor of Sumpter and had finalized the move of his law practice to Baker City.

The move to California did have one saving grace in Frank's mind. He would finally be closer to his brother Claude who he had missed terribly once Claude entered Stanford. He was especially delighted when he received a letter from Claude while at boot camp. It read:

Dear brother,

I have thought often about you and about the difficulties you must have faced with our mother this year. I know things have not been easy and that you must be very disappointed by being made to leave Portland High after your first year! I have heard from James Sullivan that you were a real plus for the baseball team and that you were to be put on the varsity team next season. I am sure that you will prove to be just as valuable to the Palo Alto High varsity team when you come here. I have covered their games for the Palo Alto Daily and so I know that they could really use your talent.

As for me, I have told mother that I will not be moving in with the two of you because my bill has been paid for another year of residence at my fraternity. Just between us, I paid it the moment I got her letter about moving here. I did, however, promise to eat dinner with you both on Sundays. I also want you to know that I can give you a job at the paper if you want to make some spending money. Just know that I miss you and am glad that you are going to be here soon.

Yours,
Claude

By the time Frank reached Palo Alto, Mary had purchased a house close to the Stanford campus. Both she and Claude met the train when Frank arrived and he surprised himself with how glad he was to see both of them waiting on the depot platform. He also liked the little house with its cozy parlor that was kept warm by a small brick fireplace surrounded by shelves lined with his parents many books. He noted with satisfaction that his own upstairs bedroom was tucked under the eaves and that the brick chimney that ran up one wall easily warmed this room as well.

The next day, Claude took Frank to see his "office" at the Daily Palo Alto newspaper which was actually just a tiny nook located next to a hall leading to an archive reference room where old copies of this newspaper run by Stanford University students were housed in rows of wooden file cabinets. Claude proudly pointed out his name plate with "associate editor" printed beneath his name.

"Wow, I guess you're pretty important around here," Frank remarked running one finger lightly across the name plate.

"Hardly, but it's a job I have always liked because it keeps a person in the thick of things. It's a job that constantly forces you to learn all the facts about any situation and to constantly challenge your opinions about what is going on in the world based on facts not just popular gossip. I was hoping you'd want to help us out here when you're not in school, that is."

"Yeah, I can see that would be something you'd like to do, but I know that I could never be able to sit for long at any desk. School is hard enough without doing it after school too." Frank said shaking his head at the idea.

"I know you well enough to never offer you a desk kind of job. No, I have a better idea for you. Come on, I have something to show you," Claude said as he took Frank by the arm and steered him toward the door to outside and around the corner of the building.

"It's over there," Claude motioned toward a solitary bicycle chained to a bike rack, while retrieving a key on a leather strap from his jacket pocket.

"What a great bike! I've never seen one like it. Is it yours?" wondered Frank as his brother freed the bicycle from its lock and rolled it away from the rack for Frank's inspection.

"No, a guy in my fraternity owns it. It's a new racing bike made by a company called "Schwinn." The guy, Sam, is willing to sell it to me for a fraction of its original cost. I looked it up and it sells for $150! Can you believe it?! " Claude explained as Frank gaped at the idea of such a luxury.

"Sam has rich parents and terrible grades. They want him to finish school back home, in Chicago, where they can keep an eye on him," Claude added as Frank admired the bicycle's sleek lines and tested its light weight. "The drop handlebars and high seat makes the rider more aerodynamic for fast racing."

"What about these?" Frank asked pointing at what looked like saddlebags slung over the bike's top tube.

"Oh, Sam bought those so he could carry his books while riding. Apparently he rarely took the books out of those bags," Claude laughed. "But, I think this bike with those bags will do just fine for you when you deliver your papers."

"Me!? This bike is for me?" Frank whispered in disbelief. "This is just too much! But ... I could really use a job, so I'll just have to take this, this really great bike, so I can do the very best job I can for you."

"I will forever be in your debt, little brother. Maybe you should ride it back to the house to get the feel of it." Claude had to shout this last part since Frank was already peddling away.

• • •

When school started the next week, Frank was quick to find out just how lonely life can be for "the new kid at school." He had grown up with the kids at his old school, so when faced with the treacheries of high school social life as a freshman, he had been protected by his large circle of friends. However, his first day at high school in Palo Alto quickly taught him that a high school sophomore without friends is probably the loneliest person on earth.

If it had not been for Claude who invited Frank to his fraternity house for dinner several times a week, Frank would have had no social life at all. Every school day began to seem like an endless prison sentence in solitary confinement. Frank moved through each day in somnolent depression where not a soul, with the exception of an occasional teacher, ever spoke to him. To avoid the ignominy of eating alone at an empty lunch table, he began to pack his own sandwich and eat by himself on a bench outside the school building.

One sunny day as Frank sat alone as usual eating his lunch of a butter and sugar sandwich, he began to get angry. Of course, it was natural for him to be angry with his mother who never acknowledged how hard starting over in school would be for him. But, he surprised himself when he realized that he was really very angry with himself.

"I'm better than this! I'm no shrinking wallflower!" he said right out loud, then looked around to see if anyone heard his embarrassing announcement. Regaining his composure, Frank began to analyze his situation. The reason he had no friends in Palo Alto was because, unlike in Portland, no-one at his new school knew that he could be of value to a group. In Portland he had joined many groups; student government, drama club, and a sports team and he had always tried hard to be a valuable member of the group. He had never thought it necessary to be the best at everything, but he knew instinctively that everyone has to contribute to a group, even if that contribution is just a well-timed joke. No, especially if that contribution is a well-timed joke.

By the end of the day, Frank had joined the cross country team. After all the running he had done with the National Guard during the summer, he figured that this was as good a place as any to begin "fitting in." By the end of the month, Frank was regularly invited to various team members' homes and he never had to eat lunch on his lonely bench outside again.

. . .

After his epiphany concerning the age old mechanism people use to build a social circle, Frank began to love his new school. He found his teachers to be inspiring and well-versed in their various subjects, which was not always the case at his old school. For the first time in his life, he felt really challenged by public school academics.

He also found many new extra-curricular activities to try. He joined the chess and debate clubs. Then chose to try out for the debate team since he found that he was very good at supporting any side in an argument.

He took an art class as an elective and enjoyed drawing and painting so much that he joined the school art club which, like debate, was not typically populated by athletes, so his social circle began to expand beyond his cross-country teammates. Because of his town's close proximity to the cultural offerings of San Francisco, the art club frequently traveled by rail on weekend field trips to enjoy the art museums and gallery shows in that largest city on the West Coast and the ninth largest in the U.S.

By spring, after the final tournaments for both debate and cross-country, he could work baseball into his busy schedule and still have time for his morning paper deliveries. He tried out for both the junior varsity and varsity teams and was picked as a varsity outfielder, so he reasoned that he lost nothing there with his change of schools.

Meanwhile, his mother knew very little about Frank's many new friends and activities, but not because he refused to share his personal news with her. She was ignorant about what was happening with her son because, as usual, she was just too distracted by her own interests and activities.

Upon moving to Palo Alto, she had quickly found that the women there were a provincial group of homebodies interested far more in trading recipes than in any of the feminist issues of the day. Soon, however, she had found that in the city to the north there existed a large crowd of like-minded women who lived and breathed advancing the twin causes of women's suffrage and prohibition. This discovery led Mary to make many, many overnight trips to San Francisco for meetings and marches while Frank came home to a dark, empty house.

Whenever Mary was home, the two spoke little. It seemed to Frank that the only words he could always count on hearing from his mother were, "Did you put your bicycle in the shed?"

It sometimes seemed to Frank that his mother worried much more about the fate of his expensive bicycle than about what might happen to him.

Nothing about the evening of April 17, 1906 was any different than any other night when Mary was home. As Frank, carrying a load of school books, elbowed the front door closed with a loud crack, Mary called out from her desk upstairs asking if his bicycle was safely in the shed.

"Yeah, I put it away in the shed!" he called back with some irritation and a tiny twinge of guilt since he had actually leaned it against the side wall of the house so he wouldn't have to carry his books so far. But, after he laid the books down, he decided to eat the sandwiches laid out for him and to do his homework and get it out of the way before putting the bike in the shed. Somewhere between his second sandwich and his Geometry assignment, the bicycle was forgotten.

...

At 5:12 am the next morning, Frank was thrown from his bed by such violent shaking that it seemed his bed had come alive and no longer wished to accommodate a sleeping boy. Jarred awake and finding himself on the floor with his room so quiet and still, Frank reasoned that he must have had some wild nightmare that made him roll out of bed. But within seconds, as he began to climb back in bed, Frank was again thrown to the floor and this time the intense shaking went on and on as the Pacific Tectonic Plate rumbled northward slipping over its boundary with the North American Plate. The violence of the earth's movement was felt from Oregon to Los Angeles and lasted only 47 seconds but seemed an eternity to the frightened boy lying on his room's undulating floorboards.

...

The tremendous tectonic movement along California's San Andreas Fault that runs south to north 810 miles was so powerful that it permanently diverted the Salinas River in Monterey County six miles south of its prior channel. It certainly caused great damage to many California communities, but the event quickly became known as The Great 1906 San Francisco Earthquake, because it was that great city that suffered nearly complete destruction, not only from the quake itself, but also from the resulting fires that raged for days and ultimately leveled whatever buildings had been left standing when the intense shaking had stopped.

These fires were initially started by ruptured gas lines but were exacerbated by citizens who actually set fire to their own buildings knowing that their property insurance did not cover earthquake damage but did cover damage from fire. It was primarily fire that left 300,000 people homeless and living in a makeshift tent city for months before "relief housing" could be constructed.

Palo Alto avoided the horrific fires of San Francisco thanks to the quick thinking of one brave man, Robert McGlynn, an engineer who was at the city's power plant when the quake hit. When he saw the plant's sixty foot tower begin to tilt and sway, he had the presence of mind to shut off Palo Alto's power supply which assured the town of continued water and electricity in the days after the quake. This allowed many relief efforts aimed at helping beleaguered San Franciscans to be staged and carried out by the people of Palo Alto.

Throughout the first day after the quake, Claude and the other staff of the Daily Palo Alto ran about campus to gather information concerning damage to buildings and any victims of the disaster. Then they worked feverishly with a hand press in order to put out a paper by evening. Their lead article titled, "Magnificent Structures Razed and Two Lives Lost," explained that one student, Junius Hanna, was crushed to death when a chimney fell through the ceiling of his residence hall and that a campus fireman, Otto Gerdis, who was on a utility tower attempting to turn off the University's steam and electricity circuits had died when the tower collapsed.

The following day David Starr Jordan, the University's President, closed the campus and sent all the students home. However, many of the students including Claude and his fraternity brothers decided to head to San Francisco to participate in Camp Stanford in the City, a project to provide food and build shelters for the displaced people there.

Before leaving, Claude wanted to check on some things that had aroused his curiosity while gathering information about the damage to the Stanford campus buildings for the Daily Palo Alto news article. He also swung by Mary's house to check again on her well-being and to ask Frank if he wanted to come along with him when he was ready to leave for San Francisco. Claude already knew that neither of them had been injured in the quake, because he had checked on his family the day before. It was then that Frank had taken Claude aside to admit how careless he had been about leaving his bicycle outside.

"I left it by the house around the corner. I forgot to go out and take it to the shed," Frank had confessed.

"You must have put it in the shed today. I see the shed is still standing, so your bike is fine now," Claude surmised as he leaned to look around the corner of the house.

"No, it's still by the house. It's under all that!" Frank said, pointing to a pile of bricks that until that morning had been their chimney. "Mother nagged me a hundred times to put it in the shed so it would be safe."

"Well this just goes to prove, even nagging mothers can be right one out of one hundred times," Claude laughed.

...

Frank was thrilled with being asked to tag along with Claude while his brother toured the various damaged buildings on campus. Claude explained to Frank that President Jordan had given the news staff a copy of a preliminary engineer's report that estimated the costs of reconstruction. Claude had seen immediately that the report suggested something odd about the damage. The report estimated the cost of the damage to the older buildings of the inner quad to be no more than $50,000 while the cost estimates for the newer buildings in the outer quad was in the millions of dollars. What could be the reason for such a wide disparity of costs, Claude wondered.

As the brothers toured the ruins of once great buildings, it became clear that the huge costs attached to reconstruction of the outer quad buildings was due to the inordinate amount of damage to those buildings compared with the relatively minor damage to the older buildings of the inner quad. In fact, much of the new construction, like the huge domed men's gymnasium, had completely collapsed and would not be able to be restored at all. The estimates concerning the cost of rebuilding the outer quad didn't even include the astronomical sum it would have cost to rebuild those piles of rubble.

As the two continued to walk about the outer quad, they met a group of engineers taking measurements, weighing debris and making notes, so that Claude had a chance to ask the burning question he most wanted answered. "Why are the newer buildings of the outer quad so much more damaged than the ones over there that were built ten or fifteen years ago?" he asked an official-looking man nearby who was making notes on a clipboard.

"Well, for one thing, those older buildings were the pet project of Leland Stanford himself who knew something about construction and was on site every day to personally oversee what was going on. He made sure that those buildings still standing were built of concrete, reinforced by metal rods anchored in the concrete. These newer buildings were built of brittle materials like stone, brick and cast iron that were poorly anchored to each other without metal reinforcement. It's very odd that the builders did not reinforce the concrete at all with metal rods like they did with buildings built a decade or more before," the man explained then picked up two bricks held together by some mortar and held them out for Claude's inspection.

"Look here, we think there is also something wrong with the composition of the mortar, too. See how powdery it is? You can actually dig it out from between the bricks with your fingers. Also, these buildings like the gym, the library and Memorial Church were designed with big open spaces that just do not offer enough support to their heavy roofs in a quake. It's not like everyone didn't know that we have tremblers from time to time around here," the man snorted, shaking his head in apparent disgust.

Inspired by the clues offered by this man as to what went wrong in the construction of so many Stanford buildings, Claude and Frank interviewed several more people that week. Since there were no students or classes, they found it very easy to converse with teachers, finance office personnel, a board of trustees' member and even President Jordan, who was surprisingly open and approachable when questioned about the future of the University. To Claude, the man seemed particularly clueless when it came to having any knowledge of the ins and outs of building design and construction.

At the end of the week, they talked with one of Claude's favorite professors who showed them a copy of the San Francisco Examiner newspaper that contained editorials offering criticism aimed at the architect and contractor responsible for designing and building the outer quad buildings that had so spectacularly failed during the quake.

"This is unbelievable, Frank," Claude exclaimed as the two boys poured over their notes and the newspaper editorials. "I'm going to put it all together for a story that calls attention to the facts that show the destruction on our campus was not just caused by one natural event but was probably helped along by some very greedy, foolish people!"

"You're just a kid, Claude. Who's going to publish an article like that from a kid? Maybe you should get your teacher to put his name on it?"

"It is true he has been angry a long time about what he believes is the school's mismanagement of building funds. He also knows that if he did that he would surely be fired. He has a family and can't risk their livelihood. I'll just have to write it and hope for the best," Claude concluded.

• • •

By the time the brothers left on the next wagon of volunteers wanting to help out in San Francisco, Claude had filed his story with *The Portland Oregonian* newspaper. For weeks the two worked along with other Stanford students to clear block after block of rubble so that the stricken city could finally start rebuilding.

Since all means of communication with San Francisco had been badly compromised by the quake, Claude was unaware that his article was featured on the center front page of *The Oregonian* on May 7th. The editors of the paper had found the article's thesis fascinating and very newsworthy and chose to highlight the most inflammatory content in the headline: "Mortar Crushed by Finger's Touch." This was followed by several lines also in a bold font which read: "Fine New Buildings at Stanford Shown to Have Been Poorly Constructed, Trio Under Suspicion." Finally, the trio was named and identified boldly on three separate lines, "C.E. Hodges, the resident architect: C.G. Lathrop, who handled the funds: J.D. McGilvray, who got all contracts."

The body of the article correctly pointed to research by the news organization of the San Francisco Examiner that had already publically suggested that the three men had conspired to enrich themselves by charging the school more than some buildings were worth and offered evidence that actual costs were cut by using substandard materials. Specifically, Claude wrote that the Examiner had uncovered "… that certain buildings were very poorly and improperly constructed, and that specifications had been tampered with and cheaper material substituted by the contractors than their contracts called for." Though both the architect and contractor were implicated of wrongdoing, Claude went on to quote the Examiner's suspicions connected to the actions of Charles G. Lathrop, the brother the late Mrs. Jane Lathrop Stanford. It was Lathrop, Stanford's official treasurer who was responsible for handling the University's building funds and who directed a bidding process that seemed to ignore more competitive bids in favor of McGilvray's contracting firm which had gotten all the outer quad construction jobs. Though the Examiner had clearly suggested that the actions of the three men pointed to a possible conspiracy between them, Claude took pains to note "Not an iota of proof can be brought to prove that there is and has been a deal between them."

Finally, Claude wrote that members of Stanford's faculty expressed the same concerns as the city newspaper. He stated, "A prominent professor, ... a man known the country over ... took one of the student correspondents into his confidence and enlisted his services to attempt disclosure of the situation. This man said that he thought the university had been managed badly and that now was the time to clear up certain misunderstandings."

The efforts of major news organizations and one Stanford student reporter were successful in exposing the poor workmanship that led to the catastrophic destruction of so many Stanford buildings. A June 10th article in the New York Times discussed the reasons that Charles Hodges, who designed the faulty buildings, ultimately resigned: "It is believed that his resignation is due to criticisms that have been made as a result of the immense damage caused to the university buildings by the earthquake and the inferential suggestion that the architect was at fault."

In addition, another Times article pointed to an announcement by President Jordan that the school would not be making McGilvray's construction mistakes in the future. He firmly stated, "The buildings of the future will be provided by steel frames and be built of concrete and will thus be earthquake proof."

· · ·

While Claude might have felt some pride in his small part in Stanford's announced policy changes, by writing his article, he had also managed to ruffle the feathers of arguably the most powerful person connected to Stanford University in 1906, Charles Lathrop. When the brothers return to Palo Alto in August, Mary grimly, and without a word, handed Claude an opened letter from President Jordan advising him not to attempt to register for the fall semester until he had "… come to an amicable understanding with Treasurer Lathrop…"

Since classes were soon to begin, Claude immediately began his crusade to be allowed to register, a crusade that would continue for months. It no doubt complicated Claude's efforts that every step of his campaign to reenroll was documented by the San Francisco Call newspaper in cooperation with the San Francisco Examiner. One of their articles published September 11, 1906 with the headline, "McColloch Causes Ire by Criticizing C.G. Lathrop," began with a reconstruction of Claude's offending *Oregonian* article followed by a detailed account of how the "… prominent sophomore from Portland has been forced to dodge from pillar to post in a vain attempt to register for the semester."

On October 20th, The Caduceus, the official magazine of Claude's fraternity Kappa Sigma published an article explaining, as the title indicated, "Why Bro. McColloch Isn't In Stanford." Like the San Francisco paper, the writers described the content of Claude's *Oregonian* article and "the merry chase…" the student continued to make in his quest to attend Stanford classes. It read in part:

… Upon his return to the campus this semester, McColloch went to Professor Rufus Lot Green, chairman of the student affairs committee, and the chairman of this committee seemed in favor of allowing McColloch to register. However, the chairman referred him to Dr. Jordan, as the request to refrain from registering had been a personal request from Jordan, and the committee had taken no cognizance of the objectionable article. When McColloch appealed to Jordan he was referred to the board of trustees, who…decided that it was strictly a matter for consideration by the student affairs committee. McColloch again visited Professor Green, and again he was passed up to President Jordan, and was no nearer registration than at his first visit to the president …

The entire first semester, Claude continued to be rebuffed in his attempts to register for his junior year at Stanford. He was never officially expelled, but still faced the frustratingly passive aggressive campaign to deny him the registration paperwork that would allow him to attend any classes. As January 1907 and a second semester began, Claude went to see the professor who had encouraged him to write his article after the quake to see if the man could help him in his quest to reenroll.

"I have been very grateful that in your writing and in all your dealings with the University, you have never mentioned me by name, and understand that I have done whatever possible to help you behind the scenes," the teacher had said.

"I always thought that if I had identified you, it would only hurt you and would do nothing to help me get back in."

"Well, by now I am pretty sure that you won't get your way with them, Claude. I can, however, be of some help if you would consider changing schools. For example, my alma mater, University of Chicago, has a strong journalism department. I could recommend you to them."

"Journalism? I think I have given up on any future as a muckraker, thanks. My father is a lawyer and I have decided to study law," Claude concluded with finality.

...

As Claude struggled with the complications that *The Oregonian* article had caused to his life, Frank was thoroughly enjoying his junior year in Palo Alto High. He had reluctantly given up cross country because his participation on the varsity debate team took him away for out of town tournaments which conflicted with track and field obligations. However, he had found that he had a real gift for argument especially when that argument was controlled by the rules and structure of Lincoln-Douglas debate.

By the time Claude had been accepted by the University of Chicago and was packing to leave for the Windy City to attend a summer catch up semester in May, Frank was completely immersed in his campaign for a seat on the next year's student council as well as his weekly games as the varsity baseball team's catcher. He was not too busy to realize that he would really miss his brother who was great company and the only family member to regularly attend his games. Frank had quite gotten used to the long talks the two had had every night in their shared bedroom, while Claude waited for his life to start again. Frank had not known how much he would miss Claude until he happened to look up during his team's final game to see that his brother's usual seat behind the catcher's position was empty.

Frank was especially sorry that Claude would not be able to come with him to visit their father in Baker City over summer break as they had planned. Some of that disappointment was mitigated by a letter from C.H. informing Frank that two of his Sumpter friends had moved with their families to Baker City to work at the lumber mill since several mines in Sumpter had closed.

Compared to the tumultuous prior year in Palo Alto, Frank's first summer visit to Baker City was filled with long, lazy days of pleasant pursuits with old friends. The same Powder River that he had fished so often during other such summers in Sumpter, ran right through the heart of town and was much handier, not only for a quiet afternoon of fishing but also for a refreshing dip on a hot day. There were other forms of entertainment that were never part of a Sumpter visit; the high school baseball diamond, long soaks in a natural hot spring, and best of all, three weeks when a traveling circus set up their "Big Top" just outside of town.

When the circus traveled on in August, it was time for Frank to return to California. On the trip back, Frank could think of little but all the plans he had for his upcoming senior year. He had long ago admitted to himself that he was glad that he had been forced to leave Portland as upsetting as that move had initially been for him. He was sure that the year ahead would be the best year he had ever had and he could hardly wait until it actually began.

Frank was even excited about seeing his house and his room and when he saw his mother standing on the depot platform, he was even glad to see her! On the ride home, he fairly bubbled over with all the things he had to take care of before school began, the classes he planned to take, what the debate team schedule would be, the possibility of running for class office... Then the taxi rounded the corner and he saw it. A sign stood in the middle of their lawn that read "For Sale."

Suddenly, Frank realized that his mother had not spoken a word all the way from the depot.

As a gut-wrenching feeling of déjà vu washed over him, Frank walked to the sign and stood just staring at it. He could barely hear his mother clear her throat behind him because of the rush of blood in his ears.

"Frank dear, I thought of writing to you about all this but then I decided it was probably better if I waited and told you about everything in person," she began, then cleared her throat again and, in a rush of words she went on. "Well, I realized that with Claude gone and with all my ... my work being in San Francisco that it is ... is just silly for us to live here. So ... I am selling the house here and was really lucky to get one of the really cute cottages they are building in the city ..."

Frank vaguely knew that his mother was still talking as he walked into the house and closed the door.

20.
Krann

After the Meyer/Krann family returned from their St. Louis adventure, every member faced a life-changing event, and there had been much discussion of plans on the train ride home. August and Marie expected that they would soon be moving to Halfway to begin their future as storekeepers for the population of miners that would fill the town to await the opening of the Cornucopia mines after the engineer's lawsuit was heard and settled. Mathew would go along to help and then move on to Cornucopia in the spring to satisfy his dream of using his formidable hard rock skills not just in a contest, but in an actual mine. Rosa planned to get right to work on some stylish new hats using some of the exotic product she had purchased in St. Louis for the holiday season. And, of course, everyone knew Rosa and LeRoy had a wedding to plan since they had set a tentative date for late the next year in order to give LeRoy's Boston family time to attend.

However, almost as soon as these plans were made, fate stepped in to alter them. August and LeRoy soon learned that the Cornucopia mine owners had not settled with the engineers suing them in November and that another court date had been set for later in the spring.

Though she kept it to herself, Rosa was pleased that her sister would not be moving her family as soon as had been expected, since that plan had also meant that they would give up their rental house and Rosa would have to move to one of the non-brothel women's boarding houses in town. Besides, she also knew how much she would miss all of them, especially Marie who was needed to help her plan the wedding.

Without the pressure of an imminent move, the family was able to enjoy a happily uneventful Christmas. This alone was a welcome relief after the prior two years when the holidays were marred by the tumult surrounding Minnie Ensminger's murder and then the execution of her murderer, Pleasant Armstrong.

Their usual Christmas celebration was made even more festive by the wild success Rosa enjoyed when she placed two high fashion hats in the center of her holiday window, each trimmed with the most exotic beadwork and feathers any Baker City woman had ever seen. In order to take advantage of the season for giving, Rosa supplied any man wishing to give his lady such a wonderful gift at Christmas with a small gold foil box secured by a red bow. Each box had a handwritten gift certificate for one custom-made hat tucked inside. Rosa soon realized that the gift's popularity would keep her busy for months.

· · ·

When early summer finally arrived and it was announced that the Cornucopia mines would open as soon as the deep snows at that high elevation cleared, Marie's family finally began their preparations for the move to Halfway. The lease on their house had expired, but their landlord was happy to allow a month by month arrangement, since the snows that year had been especially deep which might delay the family's move well into the summer.

By mid-July, August deemed the roads passable enough for him along with Mathew's help to take their wagon with some of their belongings to Halfway in order to begin setting up their store for the business that was sure to begin in earnest once the steep road from Halfway to Cornucopia became passable. Marie and the children would remain in Baker City to pack the rest of their things until the men returned with a second wagon August had purchased along with the store.

The two men returned as promised after two weeks preparing the store to find that Marie had organized and packed everything. She had even sold their furniture to their landlord who was happy to advertise a "furnished house for rent." The prior owner's house behind the store in Halfway had been part of his deal with August and it was already furnished.

As the group began loading the wagon, Marie gave each child directions, but when she instructed Anna to help Betty take down and fold some of their last minute wash, the little girl complained that her head hurt.

"I think I got Harry's cold, Mama," she said as Marie felt the child's forehead and noted a touch of fever. "He coughed and coughed all night and I couldn't get any sleep."

With that news, Marie called Harry and felt his head which also seemed overly warm. She then ordered the two children inside to lie down and rest on their beds which would not be stripped until the next day, while the older children and adults continued to load the wagons.

The next morning, the family gathered for a light breakfast before their trip to Halfway. As Marie cut pieces of apple cake she looked around noting that her youngest two had not left their bedroom, so she instructed Betty to go hurry the children along.

"Mother, something's wrong with Anna and Harry," Betty whispered quietly in her mother's ear when she returned to the kitchen. "Anna says her head really hurts and Harry has a bad nosebleed. They're both coughing and say they have sore throats, too."

When she saw them, it was clear to Marie that both children were very sick and sent Betty to get Sister Mary Bruno, the one medical person in Baker City who Marie thoroughly trusted. Sister immediately dropped what she was doing to go with Betty knowing that neither Marie nor August had ever been the type of parent that panicked over a child's every sniffle.

After examining the children, Sister Bruno, met with the worried adults. Though she did not want to frighten them more than they already were, Sister Bruno felt it necessary to lay out the facts they needed to know to keep the rest of the family as safe as possible.

"Both children have fevers and exhibit the white patches in their throats typical of diphtheria which several children in town have come down with," she began, but continued even though Marie gave a small strangled cry at these first words. "I also saw that both have definite neck swelling and the barking cough associated with that illness. Also, the bloody nose that Betty told me Harry had this morning is another sign."

"Sister, what should we do to help them and to keep the other children safe?" Rosa asked when she saw that both the children's parents were white and trembling and in great need of some practical plan of action.

"You need to isolate both children because diphtheria is very contagious. Any object the children have touched will need to be boiled in soapy water, and everything in their room should be washed down with a carbolic acid solution I will bring you. I will also bring you cotton face masks I make for myself to wear in hospital. These, too, must be boiled daily after use. The doctors laugh at me, but I do not get sick when I wear my mask around coughing patients. Try not to touch the children, but do a lot of hand washing whenever you visit their room. Remember diphtheria spreads through the air, but also by touching objects that patients have coughed on."

Marie and August stood in silence at the foot of their sick children's beds after Sister left to fetch the items she had promised to bring to them. Neither of them spoke, but somehow knew that they had the same thought. Was this their turn for the sorrow so many families around them had to bear? Children died all the time. Most died in infancy, but many, many older children died too. They were well aware that they had been incredibly lucky that none of their four healthy children had ever contracted a serious illness. In fact, they were the only parents they knew of who had not lost at least one child to the scourges of childhood; measles, mumps, small pox, bacterial meningitis, influenza, whooping cough, pneumonia, tetanus and on and on.

They also knew many parents whose children had survived some virile or bacterial condition only to live forevermore with some terrible after effect. One family had a child left blinded by measles and another family had a child who was deaf as a result having had a case of mumps. One family had a boy whose legs were withered and paralyzed by some mysterious epidemic that had killed and crippled many children in Boston, a city where they had once lived.

Marie and August had wondered why they had been spared this

kind of parental nightmare. It had even been Marie's first thought when Anna had gone lost at the St. Louis Fair. As they had frantically searched for their child, she had actually thought that this may be the time they would finally pay for all their years of luck.

...

For three weeks, Marie and August took turns sitting and praying in their children's sick room, always hoping for some sign that the children were recovering. But during these vigils, all they heard was the barking cough and high whistle emanating from the two small forms under their blankets as they strained to draw breath. Their poor little necks were so swollen that they could barely swallow the chicken broth they were fed whenever they awoke from sleeping.

Sister Bruno visited often just to give the parents moral support. She had talked more openly with Rosa about possible permanent effects that could remain even after a patient's fever and cough abated. The worst of these complications were permanent heart damage or nerve damage that resulted in permanent paralysis. Though she did not want to alarm Rosa, she did want to inform at least one of the adults in the children's lives just how important it was for the family to keep the patients isolated and to be vigilant in the cleaning ritual she had prescribed. She also warned Rosa not to enter the sick room herself, even while wearing a mask, because none of her precautions was foolproof and Rosa could end up infecting her millinery customers since it might be days before she showed any symptoms of infection.

Sister did explain to the parents that patients with diphtheria did not usually recover before five weeks just so that they would not despair because it was taking so long for the illness to run its course. By the beginning of week six, Marie and August did begin to feel desperation over their little ones plight. Marie was grateful for the cotton mask she wore around the children since they would not be able to see the tears that bathed her cheeks.

One night as Marie prayed by the foot of Anna's bed, August over heard her whisper, "Dear Lord do not, I beg you, take my children. Take me instead."

At those words, August hurriedly picked his wife up from her knees and threw his arms around her. "No, no my love. Don't even think such words!" Then he cupped her face in one big hand and looked deeply into those sky blue eyes. "I would die if I lost you," he breathed and then led her into their own bedroom where they stood together and finally allowed their tears to freely flow.

The pain and the fear lasted only four more days when, as Marie brought a bowl of broth to the sickroom, she heard a heavenly sound, children's laughter coming from behind the door.

"Mama, Harry makes the funniest faces. I told him to stop or his face might freeze that way!" Anna called out giggling as her brother tossed his pillow at her.

Astonished by seeing both her children sitting up in bed for the first time in weeks, Marie dropped the bowl of soup and ran to get August.

"What is wrong with Mother?" Harry wondered aloud. "She dropped her bowl. It's broken and there's soup all over."

"Oh, who wants some old soup," Ann laughed. "I want pancakes! I'm starving!"

After the health scare with the children, August and Marie were anxious to complete the packing and make their move to Halfway while the fall weather allowed passage on the rocky, steep Cornucopia Road. They had hoped to make the trip before any snowfall that usually occurred before the end of September though the hearty Cornucopia miners often continued to work the mines in the upper elevations through October. August and Mathew had wanted to finish setting up their store before most of the miners moved downhill to Halfway to spend the winter safely without the constant threat of deadly avalanches.

By the time the Meyer family left, Rosa and LeRoy had changed their wedding date twice and had settled on a date in early summer of the next year, to be sure that the roads would be clear enough for Marie's family to return for the ceremony.

Rosa was too busy with the abundance of new custom hat orders to worry much about their many wedding delays. She had a move of her own to make after Marie's family left and moved out of their rental house for good. LeRoy still lived alone with two servants in his mother's large house and suggested that Rosa could live there. She, however, had no intention of doing anything that would so easily invite gossip and scandal.

Instead, Rosa happily took up residence in a rooming house where several single women, mostly teachers and two of her trimmers lived. She had often visited friends who lived there and noticed the clean and lovely chintz filled rooms with approval. In addition, the owner was a plump, good-natured woman who was an excellent cook, so that the evening meals were always a pleasant, social affair. Rosa knew that she was going to miss Marie terribly, but at least her new landlady would match her sister's skill in the kitchen.

...

As the holiday season drew near, the population in the town of Halfway more than doubled with so many miners and their families moving downhill. Miners who had children were the first to arrive and the Meyer children were especially happy that there suddenly were so many new playmates among the students who attended their one room school.

The season was made even more festive for the adults when the uphill miners arrived, since these men and their wives were used to working seven days a week in twelve hour shifts for months. In winter they were finally free to rest and to party. Marie was pleased to see that the men really seemed to enjoy dressing up for social events. In addition, many men and women played musical instruments, so the town held dances every Saturday night. One group even enjoyed putting on amateur theatrical productions, which tended to be hilariously over-acted melodramas with plenty of slapstick humor.

During the week, the Meyer Store became another social gathering place for both men and women. Marie enjoyed baking special treats for anyone who dropped in to shop and then to stay to take part in some harmless town gossip. This life surrounded by new adult friends suited Marie who had spent so many years as an isolated housewife in her own home while all the adults in her family were off working. August was amazed at how his wife, who had always seemed to him to be so quiet and shy, had suddenly become so happily outgoing. It helped the situation that so many of the miners and their wives were new

German immigrants who, like Marie, were more comfortable speaking in German than in English.

"I'm glad that you are so happy with living here," August remarked to Marie one morning over breakfast. "I was worried that you might miss Rosa too much, especially at Thanksgiving and Christmas when the weather will not allow us to travel back to Baker City."

"Of course I miss my sister, but I am far too busy to be sad. You are right, though, I will be happy to go back next summer for the wedding. I will be excited to see everyone," Marie began, then looked down at her hands and said in a voice so soft that August could barely hear her. "and, and I will be excited to show off our, our new baby."

"What was that? Did you just say something about a new baby!" August cried, knocking over his coffee cup in startled attention. "My God, Marie. I thought you had gained some weight from all those parties we have gone to! I thought it looked good on you after the strain of having sick children! But, this?"

Marie looked up in time to see the kaleidoscope of emotion registering on her husband's face. At first there was the flush of joy and then a shadow of stark fear.

"Marie, we were told it isn't safe for you! I promised to keep you safe and I, I failed," he whispered suddenly remembering the one terrible night when the two of them had been so sure diphtheria was about to take one or both of their sick children. That was the one time that they had forgotten themselves and had found solace in each other's arms.

"Darling, I needed your touch at that moment more than anything I have ever wanted! I don't call that 'failure', I call that 'love'. Remember, we had known that most children die of diphtheria, and God allowed our two to live. We will pray and put ourselves in God's hands. I can't believe that He would save our children just to leave them without a mother!"

August found these words of some comfort, but in a few days the fear returned. If there was any chance he could lose Marie, he was sure he would not survive the loss. But he vowed to himself to put on a brave face and remain quiet about his own doubts about their future.

As the weeks passed and Marie became heavy with their unborn child, August was almost driven crazy with concern for her. He found himself praying under his breath nearly every minute of every day. The only thing that saved his sanity was work when spring arrived along with hundreds of miners eager to try their luck in the Cornucopia mines that had finally reopened.

One such busy morning, as August was filling a long list of orders for mining tools and provisions, Mathew entered the store flushed and breathing so hard that he could hardly speak.

"What kept you? I needed your help an hour ago!" August grumbled as the young man struggled to catch his breath.

"It's Marie! She sent me to get you. She's in labor," Mathew wheezed as August paled at the news. Within seconds, the two had pulled down the store's window shades and locked the front door turning the sign that hung outside from "open" to "closed."

When they arrived at the house August had rented for his family, the midwife attending Marie was already inside with the bedroom door firmly closed. The men were met by Betty who had been instructed to tell her father and uncle that it would be hours to wait.

"Mother said for you to go back to the store. She said that it would make the time go faster for you, Father." But the girl could see that August was not about to leave, though he told Mathew to go on back and open up and finish with the many unfilled orders. Then, the expectant father began his hellish vigil that would last until evening when finally the tired midwife emerged to tell him that he had a healthy baby boy.

August could barely see through his hot tears when he beheld his sweet Marie sitting up in bed, alive and well, gazing with rapture at the tiny being she held in her arms.

"Thank God, thank God!" he sobbed over and over as he sank to his knees seemingly too weak to remain standing beside the bed.

"Come look at how beautiful our son is," Marie whispered holding the blanketed child out for her husband to see.

Then, as August looked with wonder at the infant's wrinkled, red face, Marie said, softly, "I think we should call him 'Francis' after the saint who loved all living things. I just know that name will suit him."

She is never so beautiful than when she has an infant in her arms, August thought.

...

With Marie out of danger and the delivery of a healthy baby, August turned to the pressing matters of his business. He had put off a needed trip to Cornucopia to bring supplies to miners who could not spare the time in their short mining season to go to Halfway and buy fresh provisions. This trip, though not very far as the crow flies, involved the steep and rocky terrain of the last five miles which made it impossible for any wagon. August and Mathew would have to make several hauls up the mountain using their two horses pulling a wheeless sled. This, they knew could take days to complete but the aggravation paid very well.

August had left Marie in their daughter Betty's capable hands, and past experience had taught her parents that the twelve year old could cook, clean and run a household full of active children as well as any housewife in Halfway.

After August and Mathew left on their trip, Betty and Marie established a routine that satisfied them both. Betty would bring her mother breakfast and then give her baby Francis to nurse while Betty fed the other children. Since school had let out for the year, the children would disperse to various friend's homes for the day except for Gus who kept shortened hours managing the store. Then Betty could attend to light cleaning and cooking for the evening meal while occasionally bringing the baby for Marie to nurse.

Betty noted that her mother seemed to need more rest than she had after the birth of Anna, but Mrs. Conrad, the midwife who had helped with the birth of Francis, reminded the girl that seven years had passed since Anna had been born, so Marie, now in her thirties, was just not as strong as she had been in her twenties. Mrs. Conrad also told Betty that she played a vital role by making it possible for her mother to get the rest she needed to recover far more quickly than those wives who had no one to help with the normal arduous tasks required of most wives and mothers.

Calmed by the notion that everything she did would allow her mother to better recuperate, Betty continued their established routine without worry for her mother's well-being. That is until one morning she entered Marie's room and found her mother sitting up in bed with a stricken look.

"Betty, you will have to wash these sheets today. I seem to have soiled them in my sleep. I don't understand this. It never happened before! Get Gus from the store to help you build a fire in the yard to boil water in the big kettle. You will need to boil them stirring often to get them really clean."

After starting the fire, Betty helped Marie out of her soiled night gown, and put the extra sheets on her bed. It bothered Betty that the small amount of exertion required just to change clothing and return to bed appeared to exhaust Marie who immediately fell asleep and remained sleeping for most of that day.

•••

By the first of June, Rosa and LeRoy had finished with all the plans for their mid-month wedding. They would be married at the temporary rectory home of Bishop Charles O'Reilly, because the new Cathedral, a gothic wonder inspired by this first Bishop of the Catholic Diocese of Baker, had not yet been completed and the old Mission Church had been removed from the building site the year before. Rosie had wished that their wedding could have been held in the completed Cathedral, but she was not about to wait until 1908, its completion date.

After the wedding, the couple would travel to Boston to visit LeRoy's extended family and to attend the many parties planned in their honor. On the return trip, they would stop in St. Louis and Kansas City to buy supplies for Rosa's store.

Early, on a morning just a week from her wedding day, Rosa sat in her little office making notes as to exactly what items she needed to purchase back East for the store. She always enjoyed the hour of quiet before opening the door for business, so she was surprised and a little irritated when she heard a loud rapping on her door's glass insert. Peeking under the shade, she was astounded to see that it was her brother, Mathew, at the door.

Breathlessly, Matt managed, "August sent me to get you, Rosie. It's Marie. She's real sick and we brought her to the hospital."

Without a word, Rosa wrapped her shawl about her shoulders and quickly followed Matt in the direction of St. Elizabeth's Hospital. Once inside, Rosa was relieved to be met by Sister Bruno who always seemed to know exactly what to do in any medical emergency.

"Wh, what is wrong with Marie? Is she ill?" Rosa blurted out before the nun could explain why her sister needed a doctor.

"Rosa, come into my office. We can talk better there," Sister Bruno motioned the frightened woman through a nearby door. Once inside she drew up two chairs while she suggested to Mathew that he go tell August that Rosa had arrived.

"Marie is running a very high fever and, according to Betty, she has had this fever since shortly after her baby was born," Sister began, then faltered, when she saw Rosa's confused and shocked look as she wordlessly mouthed the word, "baby."

"You didn't even know she was pregnant. Did you, dear."

"She can't have had a baby. We were told she couldn't have any more children!" Rosa nearly shouted, shaking her head at news she just couldn't accept.

"Not exactly. You were told that she 'shouldn't' have any more children. That she had suffered a vaginal tear with Anna's birth and that it would be dangerous to give birth again. It seems with this birth, that wound reopened and is now infected causing the fever. We are preparing her for surgery to close the wound. The best thing that you can do for her right now is go to the pharmacy and get laudanum for her. She is in great pain and will need it after her operation."

When Rosa returned with the pain medicine, she was told that the surgery on Marie had been performed and that the patient had asked for her. Rosa was directed down the hall where a row of chairs had been placed outside Marie's room. Mathew motioned for her to sit next to the room's closed door as he explained that August and the Bishop were inside with Marie.

"The Bishop is with Marie?!" Rosa questioned with alarm, fearing that this meant he was performing "last rites" and that her sister was near death. But before she could ask for more information, the door opened and the two men walked into the hall. The Bishop's arm was around Augusts' slumped shoulders and Rosa caught only a glimpse of the grieving husband as they passed. Before the two disappeared into the hospital chapel, the Bishop turned toward Rosa and said in low tones, "Marie has asked to see you, dear."

The room was so dark that Rosa could barely make out the small motionless form that lay under a thin blanket, but as she quietly approached the room's single bed, Rosa saw Marie turn her head and manage a weak smile. "Rosie, you're here...good. I must talk with you... I was afraid there wouldn't be enough time..." she barely whispered, then appeared to lose the strength to go on.

"Marie? Marie? What is it you want to tell me?" Rosa prompted with a slight squeeze of her sister's small hand.

Finally, Marie opened her eyes and seemed to muster the will to focus again on speaking. "Rosie, my children...they think of you as their other mother. Now...now they will need you more than ever. I fear I will not make it...back to health. Promise...promise me that you will be their mother...in my place and, and that your home will always... always be their home," Marie whispered these words and was asleep before hearing Rosa's choked reply.

"I promise, I promise."

$\cdots$

Marie was buried in the Catholic section of Mt. Hope Cemetery. Her funeral was a simple mass held in the Bishop's rectory attended by August and their children, Mathew, LeRoy, Rosa and Sister Bruno holding baby Francis.

"Last week I believed that this would be a gathering of celebration for our wedding. What a difference a week makes," Rosa thought as she gazed at the devastation that marked the faces of every family member.

As the small group walked away from the cemetery's newest grave, Sister Bruno approached Rosa and LeRoy, "Your sister, Marie, was her family's heart and soul. They will need you now more than words can describe. God bless you, Rosa, for your promise to make a home for them. I know you and LeRoy will provide a haven that will comfort all of them once the sharpest pain of loss subsides."

"What was that Sister said to you about a promise you made to Marie?" LeRoy whispered pulling Rosa off the path as the rest of the mourners continued on toward town. "Did she say that we would make a home for Marie's five children? Did Sister forget that they already have a father who should be the one to 'make a home for them!'

LeRoy's peculiar emphasis on the word "we" stopped Rosa in her tracks. She turned in time to see an unmistakable flash of anger pass over LeRoy's face which he managed to hide a bit by turning away to take a deep breath.

"It's true. I did promise and I wish that there had been time to discuss it with you, but there just wasn't the opportunity. I guess I just had faith that what was so very right for me would be right for you too. Isn't that part of the vows we will take?"

"Rosa, I don't think that the vows say anything about promising to raise someone else's four children and an infant to boot!"

"'Oh, I think the 'for better or for worse part' probably covers this situation, LeRoy," she gasped through a sudden shock of the hot tears she had fought for days to keep at bay.

"Look Rosie, you are right. There was no good time for us to talk about this. I was just taken by surprise is all. It is like all of this turned my life, my plans upside down. Please forgive me for coming on like a selfish idiot," he said as he took her in his arms. This made her feel slightly better, but for a small alarm bell that sounded deep in her psyche. When was it, she wondered, that for LeRoy, "our life and our plans" became "my life and my plans"!?

. . .

Rosa didn't have much time to ruminate over LeRoy's state of mind because that very evening when Rosa returned to the room she shared with Betty and Anna at the Bishop's rectory, she saw at once that Anna had fallen into an exhausted sleep, but Betty was awake and sat in a hard chair in a shadowed corner. The girl was not crying, but Rosa could clearly see that she was very agitated.

"Betty, sweetheart, do you want to talk? Let's go outside so we don't wake Anna," Rosa suggested as she took the girl's cold hand in hers and led her out the door and onto the rectory porch.

"Betty, I can see how upset you are and it looks to me like, on top of the horrible sadness we all feel, that you might have some special worry. Am I right about that?" Rosa prompted as they sat side by side on wicker porch chairs.

"Rosie, God forgive me. It's all my fault." Betty sobbed and wrung her hands.

"What? What on earth could you believe is your fault? What fault do you have that is so bad you need to beg heaven's forgiveness?"

Betty took some deep breaths and began. "When Mama took sick after the baby, no one was home but me to take care of her. At first ... at first she was fine. Oh, she slept a lot, but she got up to nurse the baby and she ate the soup and things I made for her. But ... but one morning, she said for me to boil her sheets because ... because she had messed the bed. I changed the bed and boiled the sheets and everything seemed fine and she went back to sleep. But, the same thing happened again and again and, and ..." Betty stopped to catch her breath but instead broke into ever more pronounced sobs until she finally quieted and went on with her story.

"Oh, Auntie, I just couldn't keep up. I tried and tried, but I couldn't keep her clean! There was so much to do and she got weaker and weaker with the fever and ... and I heard Sister say that Mama had a cut inside that got infected. I knew right then that I was the one who let it get that way and that same infection is what killed Mama," and Betty began her bitter sobbing all over again even as Rosa held the shaking girl and tried to reassure her that no one could have done any better.

From Betty's frightened confession, Rosa knew that the source of the girl's guilt was a general misunderstanding about the cause of Marie's death. There was only one person who would be able to set Betty's fears to rest; Sister Bruno. So, Rosa took Betty to see Sister the very next day.

Sister Bruno, aided by graphic drawings of the female anatomy, did provide the child with a complete understanding of what had taken her mother's life. The nun explained how the doctor who delivered Anna had over-medicated Marie with chloroform so that she had been unconscious and unable to push and help expel the baby. That doctor had been over-anxious to show off what he thought were wonderful new tools and techniques that made the "modern" delivery by a trained medical professional far superior to delivery by some backwater midwife. Sister then showed Betty a picture of the metal forceps he had used to turn the baby and to pull her down the birth canal.

"This particular design is now banned in most hospitals because of the harm this tool can cause to both child and mother," she told the wide eyed girl. "In so many cases and in the case of your mother, this kind of tool welded by a … a less than skillful doctor can actually puncture the wall of the birth canal that separates the vagina from the bowel or the urethra, which, if not closed, leads to the kind of infection that Marie had. I want to be clear about this. It was the botched delivery by that foolish doctor that created a wound that reopened during the birth of Francis. It certainly was not the midwife's fault or your fault. You, dear girl, did all that any person in your place could have done to help your mother. In my opinion, you are the hero of this sad tale," the nun said softly as she took the sobbing girl into her arms.

After several minutes, Betty sat back and rewarded Sister Bruno with a shy smile and a whispered "Thank you."

• • •

Rosa was immensely relieved when she finally talked with Betty and was assured that the girl was no longer haunted by undeserved guilt. "You know that Sister is right about you. And I will definitely need your capable support what with working at the store and doing all the things involved with running a house full of children including one tiny infant! Why, you won't just be my assistant. You will actually be my teacher! You already know what I have to learn because your wonderful mother taught you so well."

So Betty would be all right, as all right as could be expected under the circumstances. But Rosa still was not sure about the future of her own life. It was clear that LeRoy would need time to adjust to her new responsibilities. He still could not understand why she would not just marry him and walk away from the rest of her family. Yes, the children had a father and LeRoy should know that no-one, least of all August, wanted LeRoy to take over the fatherly role. But children very much need a mother, too and LeRoy would have to accept that she was the one those children grew up with and already loved in much the same way they loved Marie.

But there was another problem that had actually bothered Rosa for some time. She was perceptive enough to realize that LeRoy did not approve of the way the children had been raised. He had been an only child raised in a strict, home of the sort that dominated family life in the era of Victorian tradition. "Children should be seen and NOT heard." Certainly he was quite appalled by the lively dinner time conversation of the Krann-Meyer clan where everyone's opinion from adult to the youngest child was welcomed and encouraged. He actually believed that children are best raised for the most part out of sight by their nannies only to be presented to their parents once a day when they were expected to be well-scrubbed and quietly polite.

Yet, LeRoy had been so contrite over his initial reaction to Rosa's promise to raise Marie's children, that she knew he was trying hard to accept the new situation. She knew that he loved her, but had definitely imagined a different future for themselves than the one that was now unfolding. It would be very unfair, she decided, for her not to understand how hard this was for him. It would be just as unfair not to give him the time he needed to make this rather huge adjustment.

A month later, Rosa and LeRoy received news that would automatically provide the time he needed. It was at their usual daily lunch in Rosa's office that LeRoy told her that he had received a telegram from his mother. She was an asthmatic and had had another attack and wanted to know when they were to make their visit, because she especially missed her son whenever she was ill. Though there was no possibility for Rosa to leave with him, she encouraged LeRoy to go and he seemed very pleased with her thoughtful suggestion.

Rosa and Mathew took LeRoy to the station on the day he was to leave. While the couple said their goodbyes, Matt ran to get a handcart for the baggage.

"LeRoy, you sure must own a lot of clothes to need all these bags," Mathew remarked as he piled the suitcases on the cart.

"Well they are a formal lot in Boston. They all dress for dinner every night, tuxes and gowns are required just to eat, if you can believe that!" LeRoy chuckled.

After the passengers were told to board, Rosa and Mathew started to walk back to their buggy, but the way was blocked by several huge crates that three husky men were wrestling onto a flat wagon. Rosa was shocked to see the name "Collins" written on each crate.

"When is Mr. Collins coming back, Rosie?" Matt asked as they drove away.

"I don't think he'll be coming back." She answered softly and quickly looked away.

21.
McColloch

The years 1908 and 1909 amounted to an epic contest of wills between Frank and Mary with C.H. the hapless bystander without the power to stop their constant clash which he feared would ultimately devastate his younger son's future.

As soon as Frank learned that Mary intended to move him to San Francisco for his last year of high school, he began planning his escape from the unpredictable, chaotic world his mother had created for her miserable son.

Luckily, their Palo Alto house was not immediately sold, so Frank had some time to think through his options. Running to Baker City to live with his father was just too risky, he decided. He was fairly certain that his father would send him home again once Mary was settled, since he knew that C.H. harbored the notion that women are better suited to raising children than are men. Unless the mother of a child is involved in immoral activity or addicted to drugs or alcohol, C.H.'s consistent opinion had always been that a child belongs with his mother.

In late November, the Palo Alto house was finally sold, and Mary began packing for the move. As soon as the sale was complete, Mary traveled to San Francisco in order to enroll Frank in school, happy that he had only missed one semester which could possibly be made up in summer semester classes. As he saw his mother off, Frank decided that this was the very best opportunity for him to execute his plan of escape. As her train pulled away from the station, he turned and marched over to the ticket window and bought a ticket to Portland for late afternoon giving him plenty of time to fetch the packed suitcase stashed under his bed. By the next evening, he stood on the porch of his friend, Freddie Welsh, who had received a telegram the prior morning that his friend would arrive for a "short visit."

True to his word, the visit with Freddie ended December 3rd when Frank bid "good by" to his friend who believed that Frank was headed back to Mary in Palo Alto. Frank waved to Freddie and his father as they pulled away from the Portland depot, but instead of entering the depot to purchase his ticket, Frank walked four blocks to the National Guard registration office.

The registrar looked up frowning slightly from Frank's carefully worded application and said, "It says here you're only fifteen years old, son. We have rules now that restrict Guard service to young men who have at least finished their junior year in high school, so I'm afraid that you don't qualify except for summer training."

"I have finished my junior year before our family moved up here from Palo Alto last May after my father started his new law practice in Baker City," Frank countered, handing the registrar his excellent school record from California along with the announcement for the opening of C.H.'s law practice in Baker City which provided the proof that Frank had, in fact, finished three years of high school and supported Frank's contention that he lived with his family in Oregon and until December had been enrolled in high school in Baker City.

"With these grades, you should finish up and maybe even go on to college," the man suggested.

"Your records will show that I have Guard experience, and this is where I want to be. I know the military gives a fella a better education than any high school classroom and my dream is to serve my country while I learn things I really need in life," Frank explained, knowing full well that this little speech was just the thing any military man loves to hear.

"Good luck son. We need more men like you, that's for sure!" the man announced as he stamped Frank's application and passed the new recruit on to the medical checkpoint.

...

Frank was assigned to Company A of the Third Infantry Regiment after his boot camp and gunnery training. He had been a stand-out among the new recruits not only displaying the skills that had served him well in his prior summer camp with the Guard but also for the positive attitude he brought to every challenge.

At the end of his training period, he was promoted to the rank of corporal which gave him some leadership responsibilities in the regiment. By then, Frank was confident that the military still represented the perfect life for him, and that his decision to leave home had been the right one. He already knew that the regulated military routine suited him very well.

Even more importantly, the Militia Act of 1903 and the act's amendment in 1908 allowed men to serve beyond the original nine month limit and also dropped the ban on Guard units serving outside the United States. As a full time member of the Guard, it was exhilarating for Frank to know that he could be sent anywhere to aid and defend the people of his country. Increasingly, rumors pointed to a growing cloud of trouble with a brewing rebellion in Mexico that threatened the southern U.S. border.

As rumors of a possible border war with Mexico grew, Frank's regiment was told one morning that they would begin training for duty in Arizona to support the U.S. Marines on border patrol. This news was greeted by loud "whoops" after the group was dismissed.

Frank was as excited as any of the men but stood aside thinking it would probably be unseemly for their corporal to join in the celebration. Turning away from the group, Frank nearly ran into a messenger from the command office who shoved a note into his hand advising him to report immediately. He thought that perhaps he would be told that his regiment was to be called to the border sooner than expected.

Flushed with anticipation, Frank knocked on the door of Colonel McDonell, the base commander, and went in when he heard the command to enter. Coming into a darkened room from the bright autumn sun of the parade ground, Frank blinked to help his eyes adjust to the dim light while he saluted and announced his name.

"At ease, corporal. It has come to my attention that you may not qualify for service in the Oregon Guard," the Colonel stated, waving some paperwork in Frank's direction.

"Sir, I have explained that I have finished three years of high school as required by rules," Frank began shakily.

"Are you aware that you must also be a resident of the state of Oregon? And it is this part that may disqualify you from our service. Your application says that you were a student of Baker City High School, which would indicate that your home is in Oregon. However, we now have evidence that you were never a student at that school, and that your home state is, in fact, California. This paper I have here indicates that you were enrolled in high school in San Francisco the very month you joined the Guard in Portland. Can you explain this discrepancy, so I can be sure you did not lie to us?" the man asked in a softer tone, clearly hoping that Frank could adequately put these concerns to rest.

"No, sir, I can't prove I didn't lie," Frank mumbled hanging his head in humiliation. Then he jumped when suddenly startled by a shout that cracked like a whip behind him.

"Of course he can't prove he didn't lie! Because he did lie!" Turning in the direction of the shout, Frank saw his mother, red-faced with fury, leap from a chair to stand in front of him. Then, turning toward the shocked man behind the desk, she continued in a slightly lower tone, "I demand that you sign his discharge papers, so I can take him home. To his real home!"

With that, the Colonel sighed and bent to work, though in a moment of rebellion against being ordered about by this strident woman and with sympathy for her unhappy son, he wrote the discharge to indicate that Frank C. McColloch ... "is hereby honorably discharged from the Oregon National Guard by reason of his removal from the state ..." He also pointedly wrote that Frank's former occupation was "student of Baker City High School" and "No objection to his reenlistment is known to exist." Under "CHARACTER" the Colonel wrote "Excellent" with a flourish.

"This isn't true! You need to change this!" Mary demanded, pointing at the parts that most offended her. "A boy who lies to his mother certainly does NOT possess 'excellent' character!'"

"Madam, it stands as written. Now, if you'll excuse me, I have work to do." And the Colonel turned away from the fuming Mary.

• • •

Mary had a reason to visit Portland other than to collect her wayward son. She very much wanted to attend a meeting put on by her prior Albina church that featured the wife of colorful evangelist and supporter of the Prohibition movement, Billy Sunday. For this reason, she and Frank would not return to California for a week, so Mary could attend the speeches and parties surrounding Helen "Ma" Sunday's visit.

Feeling triumphant in her quest to prove her authority over Frank, Mary had no fear that he would try any of his rebellious tricks since she had so thoroughly thwarted his last attempt. She had no qualms in leaving him stranded in their hotel room while she attended her meetings and social events.

However, on the morning of their second day in Portland, Frank left the hotel minutes after Mary and headed to the nearest bank to cash his final Guard paycheck and then continued on to the Portland depot for a ticket to Baker City. He felt sure that once he told his father that he would fight any effort to return to his mother, C.H. would have to let him live and attend school in Baker City.

As it turned out, Frank had been correct to assume that his father would understand his son's position on the matter of Frank's wanting to live far away from his mother. Though C.H. never spoke any ill word about Mary, he did not refuse to help Frank enroll in school.

Baker City, however, refused to allow Frank to be placed in the senior class without a transcript from his school in Palo Alto that would show that he had earned enough credits to enter as a senior. The National Guard had Frank's prior report cards, so C.H. tried a request to Guard headquarters to send Frank's file. Finally, after a month of waiting, Frank received a letter explaining that his file had been "closed out" and returned to his mother.

Mary had Frank's school transcript and all his past report cards. C.H. had no choice but to write to his wife for her help in this matter, though he knew that she might stubbornly reject this request.

After two months of writing without one word from Mary, she finally sent a terse letter stating that the only way Frank was going to get his school records would be for him return to California and to agree to finish his senior year in San Francisco while living in her home. C.H. had to face the fact that he could not enroll Frank in school at the level the boy deserved. He decided that there really was only one realistic course of action for his son to take. Frank would have to return to California to attend school for only one more year, so he could graduate.

"Frank, I know this will be horribly hard for you to do, but it is the only way to finish school in the shortest period of time," C.H. had reasoned.

"Father, you can't believe that I can do that after all I've been through with Mother!" Frank pleaded.

"You must finish high school, so you can go on to college. Without an education, you face a life as nothing but a common laborer. I can't let you do that. As hard as this sounds, I refuse to let you turn your back on school," C.H. emphasized.

"You aren't a common laborer and you said, yourself, that you only ever went to school for one semester." Frank countered.

"Well, I grew up in a very different time than you have. A man needs the credentials that an education provides today in order to advance in any profession other than those that require a life of low pay and hard labor. I must be adamant on this point. I can't just sit back and watch you chose a path you will surely regret later."

After another hour of back and forth with his father, Frank realized that he wouldn't be able to convince C.H. not to send him back to San Francisco. Finally, a compromise was reached. Frank could stay in Baker City and get a temporary job, but would return to California by August and finish high school by enrolling for school year 1909-10.

. . .

By September, C.H. was convinced that Frank had finally resigned himself to another year with Mary in California especially when the boy boarded the train south without any argument. As it rolled slowly out of the station, C.H. went inside to telegram Mary. He was fairly certain that this news would give his wife a moment of gleeful pleasure thinking she had so thoroughly won the stubborn war of wills with her son. If ever there was a woman who never should have had sons, C.H. thought, it was his wife. For that matter, he decided ruefully, Mary was a woman who most probably should have spared all males and remained single.

Frank's demeanor further convinced Mary that she had so defeated him that the boy would certainly offer no more resistance against her authority. Though he barely spoke to her for the week following his return, Frank nodded agreement when Mary told him that she would be enrolling him the next day in school. When asked if he wanted to accompany her, he just said, rather bitterly she thought, that she could handle the details by herself since she had had so much prior practice.

The next morning after Mary left for her appointment at the school, Frank ate a hurried breakfast and then retrieved his packed suitcase from under his bed. "And I am pretty good at this from all my prior practice", he thought.

Before Mary had finished her school enrollment chore, Frank stepped off a trolley car at its stop in front of the U.S. Marine Corps recruiting office. A few young men were ahead of him in line so, he could hear the questions and answers in a few of their exchanges with the recruiting officer as they stood in front of his desk. One fellow just ahead of Frank made the mistake of saying that his age was seventeen and was told he should come back when he was at least eighteen.

Before Frank could plan his response for this age question, he was ordered forward knowing only that he could not let on that he was only sixteen years old. When the officer filling out the enlistment form barked "birthdate!?" Frank was not prepared and said "August 25th" which was true. But the man then barked "year of birth!?" and Frank, at a loss as to what else to say responded "1888," which was the year Claude was born. This would make Frank twenty years old which he was sure no one would believe. He was much relieved when the man wrote everything without looking up once, so Frank turned quickly away to hurry on to the next station.

"Hold it, guy!" yelled the officer as Frank was almost through the next door. "One more question! What is your present occupation?"

Without turning around, Frank replied loudly, "common laborer." And retreated to the next room.

...

Frank's battle with Mary landed him in a military boot camp for a third time in his young life, and as a new Marine, he found this to be the toughest training period yet. However, his prior experience served Frank well and he again proved able to meet every challenge.

After Frank began his life as a full-fledged Marine, he was soon to learn that the exciting possibility of being sent to protect the U.S. border with Mexico had become a probability because of the rebellious activities of the bandit turned revolutionary, Pancho Villa. Villa's banditry in Northern Mexico near the U.S. border that had once been purely for economic gain, became a political tool in support of anti-government revolutionaries, after Villa met Abraham Gonzales and Francisco Madero who convinced him to join their fight against the corrupt Mexican President, Porfirio Diaz.

The Mexican Revolution officially began when Madero challenged Diaz in the 1910 elections. Diaz arrested Madero and staged rigged elections. Madero called on his many pro-democracy supporters to stage revolutionary action to end the Diaz regime. Because most of the fighting took place along the northern border of Mexico with the U.S., federal troops were deployed immediately to Arizona and Texas border towns to protect American lives and property.

Frank's U.S. Marine unit had actually been among the first troops deployed to the area. They were among some 4,000 U.S. and Mexican troops sent to the West Texas border town of El Paso in late 1909 when William Howard Taft was to meet in a summit with Mexico's President Porfirio Diaz. This historic meeting would be the first time a U.S. head of state would meet with his Mexican counterpart. Meetings between the two leaders were to take place both in El Paso and in the Mexican town of Ciudad Juarez just across the border with Texas. As the time for the summit drew near, however, tensions on both sides of the border including assassination threats against both leaders required a high level of security which included agents of the FBI, Secret Service, and U.S. Marshalls as well as the heightened military presence.

Frank was thrilled to be a part of such an important international event which would take place in El Paso, one of America's most colorful towns often referred to as "The Six Shooter Capital." As his Marine officers frequently reminded their troops, he knew his country needed him. For the first time in his life, he did not feel like a wayward child struggling to free himself from the reigns of parental control. He was filled with a vast relief that thousands of miles separated him from the constantly shifting demands of two parents who could never agree on their goals for his future. He knew with certainty that neither his mother nor his father really understood that their goals for him were far removed from the future he dreamed of for himself. Suddenly, he realized that he had arrived in the exact future he had always wanted, one filled with the adventure of exciting new places and new circumstances where brave men of integrity and accomplishment expressed belief that he, Frank, had the talent and training to meet the considerable challenges of this shared commitment in service to their country.

Since he was so far away from home, this deployment also brought with it the freedom to finally communicate with his family. They might guess based on past behavior that he had, once again, joined the military. He did owe them some reassurance that he was all right. At least he thought he owed his father that much, knowing that his father would be worried about him, that is, if his mother decided to tell C.H. that he had run away. He knew that it was entirely possible that Mary might not want her husband to know that Frank had again been able to thwart her efforts to make him bend to her will.

In the end, he chose to telegram his father that he was alive and well. He felt certain that his father had been so angry with his mother over the stalemate Mary had imposed concerning where Frank went to school, that he would not tell her any details about where the telegram came from and what her son was doing in that place. He felt fairly sure that he would not be called again to a humiliating meeting where his mother called him a "liar" in front of his commanding officer. After the telegram was sent, Frank was freed of guilty worry and turned to the task of defending his President and his country.

Military patrols along the Rio Grande continued to be uneventful during the run-up to October 16, the first day of the summit. However, as the presidential procession prepared to make its way through the streets of El Paso on opening day, Fredrick Russel Burnham, a celebrated scout and C.R. Moore, a Texas Ranger, found a man holding a palm pistol standing along the parade route. The two captured and disarmed this assassin just as Taft and Diaz passed within feet of his hiding place.

Within a few months, due to Diaz's illegal election tricks, the Mexican Revolution was in full swing, and even more troops were sent to protect Americans all along the border with Mexico. Frank's unit, which had been among the first to be called up, remained in El Paso.

Though the rebels planned several attacks to Mexican towns at the border, most did not involve action on the U.S. side much to Frank's disappointment. Throughout 1910 and into 1911 his day involved hours of boring guard duty and marching patrols along the Rio Grande.

If it had not been for disagreements concerning the goals and strategy between those forces loyal to Madero and those under the command of the colorful Pancho Villa, American troops might never have seen anyl action. At one point, Madero called off the rebel siege of the strategic Mexican town of Ciudad Juarez fearing that fighting so near the border with Texas might draw intervention from the U.S. forces. Villa, however, ignored this order and continued to attack Juarez which put the troops in El Paso on high alert.

The danger to American interests intensified when Mexican saboteurs bombed the barracks of the Mexican Army stationed across from El Paso. A huge nitroglycerin explosion was seen on the American side of the border and a large cannon was stolen by rebels from the town square of El Paso.

A few months later Villa's forces attacked Juarez again, and this time the American garrison in El Paso was charged with using any force to keep the rebels from crossing the border. This led to an exchange of fire between the Mexican rebels and the Americans that ended in minor casualties on both sides.

* * *

After Frank was involved in his first exciting taste of actual combat, he could not stop himself from writing to his father about it. When C.H. received this letter, he realized that he had to take some immediate action to protect his prodigal son. In fact, C.H. had already taken steps to lure Frank home. First, he had visited Mary and told her face to face that he would not continue to economically support her if she did not release Frank's school records to him and agree to allow their son to complete high school in Baker City. He had also spoken with Baker High School officials and had gotten them to agree to allow Frank to enroll for his senior year as long as he completed it before turning age 21. Finally, he approached the Marines and received permission to purchase an honorable discharge for Frank.

By January 5th 1912, Marine Private Frank C. McColloch was released from duty and was on his way back to Oregon after his father paid the Marines in full the agreed upon sum of $14.96.

22.
Frank and Betty

From the beginning, U.S. mass circulation magazines relied on the popularity of human interest stories about the lives of the ordinary Americans who make up the reading public. A staple of such stories involved celebrating one small town or another as a wonderful place to live. Invariably, the selection of such a town was based on similar criteria such as a thriving economy, moderate climate, natural beauty, good schools and a well-developed cultural scene. Because these articles were usually authored by writers living and working in some big city hundreds, even thousands of miles away from the subject, the characteristics under discussion rarely involved insightful examination of what really makes a place a great one in which to live. No one from the outside can ever know if, at its core, any place is what it seems to be. This would take a much closer look and involve the caliber of people who live there. In all probability, only the people who live there can really know if theirs is the kind of town that readily rallies to support any neighbor in times of need. Such a test came for Rosa Krann when her sister, Marie, died leaving behind five young children. Soon after, it became clear that the only person in Baker City who turned their back on the grieving family was LeRoy Collins.

...

"What are you going to do now, Rosie?" Louis Levinger wondered when Rosa Krann remembered several months after Marie's funeral that she had not paid the druggist for the laudanum pain medicine she had gotten during her sister's last days. By then, the entire town knew of Rosa's determination to make good her promise to Marie. They also were aware that LeRoy Collins had returned to Boston and had informed Rosa in a subsequent letter that he could not return to marry her under the present circumstances. Any doubt about this was erased when a "For Sale" sign appeared in front of the house belonging to the Collins family.

"I have decided to bring the children here and to enroll the older ones in St. Francis Academy."

"Such a big family! My wife informs me, that you live with your millinery assistant in a small apartment. You will need a much bigger house for all those children and three adults if you are including Mathew and August as well," the druggist said nodding sadly over the overwhelming problems facing such a young woman.

"I believe Mathew plans to stay in Halfway and continue working in the Cornucopia mines during the warm months. But August is my biggest worry right now. The poor man is so despondent I can't get him to make a firm plan for himself, though I know that eventually he will want to live with his children," Rosa explained, glad that she was able to share some of the concerns, the burden of which had been on her solitary shoulders for months.

"He has always been so devoted to his family. Of course, you are right that if they live here, he will want to also. I hope that you will forgive my prying, but rent for such a big house and school tuition as well would be a shock to anyone's bank account," Levinger replied shaking his head at the thought.

"These are certainly worries that keep me up at night, but I am grateful to be able to talk with someone about the situation."

"I am not alone in wanting to help you and Marie's family. Since so many of my customers have asked about you and how they can help, I began to get an idea. Would you make me one of your hats? I will need one of your fanciest creations to make this plan work. Please include some of those wonderful ostrich plumes all the ladies seem to covet."

"I can have a hat like that for you tomorrow evening. I am sure your wife will enjoy it," Rosa promised assuming the hat would be for Louis's wife, Lyle.

Rosa returned as promised with a beautiful spring hat the next evening. "I forgot to go to the bank today. I hate to inconvenience you. I will come to your shop tomorrow straight from the bank. This hat is certainly worth every penny of your thirty dollar price!" Louis said turning the gorgeous hat this way and that in admiration.

Late the next afternoon, as Rosa and her assistant, Gertrude Brubaker, were going over the day's receipts, they heard a soft knock on the office door that led to the side alley. When she answered the door, Gertrude was surprised to see Louis Levinger standing outside. Embarrassed that the lady might wonder why he was at the store after hours, Louis quickly said," I hope I am not interrupting your work Miss Brubaker, but I promised to pay Rosa for the hat I bought yesterday and I could not get away from my store any sooner."

"We are always glad to open our door for anyone who wants to pay a bill, Mr. Levinger," Gertrude laughed as she ushered the druggist into the little office, "Actually, I was just leaving myself for the evening," she added as she wrapped a shawl around her shoulders and passed him through the open door.

"Well now, Rosie, I am here as promised to give you this," Louis said, and stepped forward and laid $300.67 on the table in front of the startled young woman.

"Wh … what on earth!?"

"I lied. Or rather, I lied by omission. I let you think that I bought the hat for Lyle. But instead I visited my lodge, The Elks, and raffled it off. It was so easy! Every man there bought a ticket hoping to be able to take such a lovely gift home as a surprise for his wife!"

"I, I don't know what to say. This is a princely sum! It's way too much for one little hat," Rosa gasped.

"Every man who bought a ticket wanted to help you with your new family, I assure you. I have also spoken with Lyle about your situation and she had a wonderful idea. As you know, we have just finished building a new house and we were planning to rent out our present home. She said that we should rent it to you as long as you might wish to keep it. Our plan is to help you with the rent by raffling off the occasional hat. I figure why not let the Knights of Pythias, Masons, Kiwanis, Optimists, and heck, the whole darned Chamber of Commerce in on a chance to impress their wives!"

"I don't know what to say. This is so, so unexpected." Rosa mumbled through her tears.

"It shouldn't be. This is Baker City and we take care of our own. It's a wonderful thing you promised Marie and the town is grateful for the chance to help with that promise. So, bring those children home. It's a big house with room for everyone!" Louis exclaimed as he backed out the door.

. . .

The Meyer children arrived in Baker City to move into Rosa's rented house the last day of May with August driving one wagon filled with their things and Mathew driving a borrowed wagon loaded with goods they would need in their new home purchased from their store in Halfway. It was the first of June when the family began to actually move in, and it was also Betty Meyer's thirteenth birthday which she was sure had been totally forgotten by everyone what with all the upheaval of moving day. However, that evening, when Lyle and Louis Levinger brought sandwiches and fruit to feed the hungry group, they also brought a decorated cake that August had purchased that morning with Betty's name on it.

"This celebration of the day of your birth is very important, my daughter," August began by raising his glass of sweet cider while Rosa began to cut the cake. "It is special because it marks the day you leave childhood behind. You are no longer a little girl but are becoming a woman, and one I am very proud of."

Betty had no idea during that little party, how much truth was behind her father's words. In the weeks to follow, she and Rosa fell into a routine that would require the girl to grow up fast taking on very adult responsibilities. Luckily, it was summer and schools closed so students would be free to help with the spring planting, calving and branding necessary on the small farms and larger ranches that dotted Baker Valley.

So every day, after morning mass, Betty followed Rosa to her shop to go over their marketing list and discuss what other tasks Betty was to accomplish at home. In short order, the girl proved to be capable of all the normal housewife responsibilities from laundry to cleaning to cooking due to the solid training she had received from Marie. It was even apparent that the younger children were used to depending on Betty to help or advise them every bit as much as they had their mother.

Though Rosa realized that her household would definitely run smoothly because of her niece, she felt guilty that, because she herself had to work at the shop every day, Betty could not enjoy her summer freedom from school like other children.

Rosa was unaware that Betty did not feel put upon at all. In fact, the girl was quite proud of her adult status. She had always loved to cook and bake even though she felt that she would never be the culinary genius her mother had been. She also enjoyed taking a motherly role with her siblings. But, it was in the area of cleaning where she truly excelled. Perhaps it was a subconscious desire to banish the last vestige of guilty memory from the terrible time when no amount of Betty's ardent sheet-boiling saved her mother from infection and death. There was no doubt that Betty clearly considered any kind of filth to be her mortal enemy and would fight it with a vigor that would never weakened in all her living days.

In addition to actually liking household tasks, Betty was quite aware that most children even younger than she in Baker City filled roles that in later decades would be considered too adult for youngsters. For these children, summer "vacation" would not be filled with lazy days at a swimming hole. Those who did not have to work sun up to sunset on a farm or ranch, worked long days in their father's shop or even became little entrepreneurs in business for themselves.

Betty was especially amused and impressed by one nine year old who visited Rosa's shop one day while she and Rosa were reviewing the day's marketing list. Both of them looked toward the door when they heard the ring of the small bell that signaled someone had entered.

"Leo! Come in, dear. Betty and I are just finishing our grocery list," Rosa called out from the back of the store, then she turned to Betty and said in a quieter voice, "It's Carl and Laura Adler's boy, Leo."

"I don't want to interrupt, but I wanted to speak with you before business hours when you would probably be busy with customers," the boy explained as he set down a heavy bag next to Rosa's chair. "I am trying to get to every store and office in town where customers have to wait to be served. You see, I have started working for the Curtis Publishing Company selling their magazines and I am taking orders for The Saturday Evening Post and The Ladies Home Journal "

"I thought that you have a newspaper route like your friends, Francis Leipzig and Norris Poulson. Have you stopped doing that, now?" Rosa wondered.

"I still deliver *The Oregonian* but I want to try something new, Miss Krann. I don't really like to compete with my best friends, anyway. I saw a letter that the Curtis Company sent out to convince boys like myself to become 'magazine specialists.' So I filled out their coupon for ten free copies of their magazines to show prospective customers. I already have orders from all the barber shops, doctors and lawyers in town who mostly wanted to take the Post which comes every week. My mother suggested I show you a copy of the Journal because it is for ladies, and she said that you have a lot of lady customers, who would probably like to have something interesting to read while they wait their turn to try on hats."

"Why that's a very smart idea you have there, Leo. Can I buy one copy to look over and show my customers to get their opinion?" Rosa responded.

"I know you'll be impressed, Miss Krann. The Journal has a lot of real good stories by famous authors like Mark Twain. See. Here is a story by Rudyard Kipling. And there are lots of articles with tips on how to keep a nice home that ladies always like to read about. And your customers would really like to see these drawings that show what's fashionable to wear in the big cities," the boy pointed out as he flipped from one sample page to another.

"My you are certainly selling me on the idea of providing this magazine for my customers to read. Why, many will probably want to take it themselves each month, don't you think so Betty?"

"Yes Auntie. I'm sure the ladies will like reading it," Betty nodded.

"It does seem to work that way, Miss Krann." Leo put in. "A few months ago I sold a subscription for the Post to one of the big law offices in town and after the first month, Mr. McColloch, one of the lawyers there, bought his own subscription. He said it was one of the finest magazines he's ever read. He said he read it cover to cover the first time he opened it."

"Say Leo, is that your little dog looking in our window?" Betty asked pointing at a small furry face peeking through the glass.

"Oh, that's my dog, Prince. In a way you could say he's my business partner. He gets me up at 5:30 every morning for my delivery route, without fail. He keeps me on track, too. If I change the route he'll whine until I return to my normal route. You'll see, in a few minutes he'll give a bark that means we need to move on to keep our schedule," then both women laughed when the little dog looked straight at his master and gave the described bark. "Well, I'd better be going. It seems my 'board of directors' does not want me to dawdle in my rounds," Leo said, nodding toward the little dog that had turned and was already walking with purpose down Main Street.

As they watched the nine year old lug his heavy bag down the street with Prince in the lead, Rosa turned to Betty laughing, "There is a boy who will go far, I believe!"

Rosa had been right that her customers would enjoy Leo Adler's magazine idea. Most of her customers enjoyed the periodical so much that they quickly contacted the boy to start their own subscriptions. And a year later, Betty showed Rosa an advertisement in that same magazine that featured a picture of ten year old Leo standing holding his bag of magazines with Prince beside him. The ad read, "Getting a Start as an Agent for The Ladies Home Journal, Leo Adler, Oregon, Sells 250 Posts, 110 Journals."

"Look at this, Auntie! Leo is four years younger than I am and he's already making his mark in the world," Betty groaned.

Rosa turned the girl to face her and looked straight into her eyes. "Whether you know it or not, you are also making your mark . The children are all happy and thriving because they had you when they lost their mother. And I am able to continue to run the shop which would have been impossible if I didn't have you so capably running our home. And I am amazed that you do so well in school with all the other responsibilities you have taken on. Sister Bruno told your father that you are first in your class at St. Francis, and he was nearly bursting with pride. I so rarely see him smile that this news was a real blessing for him, Betty."

...

It was true that, though his children had seemed to adjust to the loss of their mother, were doing well in school and had many friends, Rosa continued to worry about August who she knew was still living life in a depressed fog of grief. She was also aware that the man suffered an acute sense of guilt for his beloved Marie's illness and death. She remembered well how her own father, Kurt, had suffered when her mother, Marta, had died. She remembered, too, how her family had been so afraid that Kurt, who was not eating or sleeping, might actually die from his grief that they had considered taking him across Europe to the foot of the French Pyrenees where it was said many people had been cured by the Virgin Mary at the little town of Lourdes.

But then Rosa knew that it had not been a visit to Lourdes that had helped Kurt, but a change of focus provided by the chance to finally experience his lifelong dream of traveling to America. Poor August had closed his shop in Halfway and seemed to have nothing to fill his days but hour after bleak hour of depression. If any man needed a source of distraction it was August Meyer.

Finally, a small source of healthy distraction did help to refocus August when a friend encouraged him to join their group of Civil War Veterans. These men did much more than march in a few patriotic parades each year. They functioned like any one of the many men's social-service lodges in Baker City. Every week the group was involved in community events and fund raising activities that helped support those vets who had fallen on hard times. Such work did for August what it does for all people in pain, it released him from the prison of his own despair. And no man was more proud when he put on his Grand Army of the Republic uniform to join the others marching down the streets of town.

...

During Betty's senior year at St. Francis Academy, the school got a new head mistress, a very strict teaching nun who decided that the children missed too much school because school was not only closed for weekends and summer but also for many holidays marked by several Saint's days. So, in March of that year, she announced that school would not be closed as usual for St. Patrick's Day.

This move was not happily received by the student body, but Betty Meyer was particularly sad because this was the holiday when her father would march in the St. Patrick's Day parade for the first time and he had been so proud to tell his children about it. He had certainly expected that the family would all turn out to see him marching in his GAR uniform.

The day after the announcement, several students surrounded Betty and some of her senior friends on the school playground to implore them to go to Bishop O'Reilly to protest the principal's decision to hold school on St. Pat's Day. It was not lost on most of the students that the Meyer children were favorites of the Bishop who enjoyed Rosa Krann's delectable fried chicken at Sunday dinner any week that he was not out of town on archdiocese business. Betty was only too happy to join her friends for a visit to the Bishop.

"What? She said what?!" Bishop O'Reilly sputtered when the little group met with him later that day and told him of their head mistress' decision. "Not close school on St. Patrick's Day?! Well, we'll just see about this!!" And with that, the girls watched from the open door as the Irishman clumped down the street splashing mud on his ecclesiastical robes with every step.

The Meyer children and every other child in town happily wore their Irish green and cheered the marchers in the big parade that St. Patrick's Day. It was a very proud moment for August seeing all his cheering children lined up as he marched by decked out in his GAR uniform.

• • •

By 1913, all the Meyer children with the exception of little Francis, were out of school and working in Baker City. August Jr. found well-paid work at McKim's Foundry and Harry became a pastry chef whose dessert creations were enjoyed nightly by diners at the Geiser Grand Hotel. Anna went on to college and earned an elementary teaching degree. Betty, who had excelled in math, got a job as bookkeeper for the Basche-Sage Hardware Company.

Because she enjoyed having the children live at home, Rosa purchased a large, five bedroom two-story home on tree-lined Grove Street across from the city park where everyone would be comfortable. Each evening, dinner was a lively affair with much laughter and teasing among the young people while Rosa and August were frequently called on to give advice or settle some disagreement.

On one such evening, Gus turned to Betty and said, "Do you remember Peter Ward from school, Betty? He asked about you the other day. I think he wants to ask you out or something."

"Or something?" the girl smirked. "Has he grown a chin yet? I don't remember him having much of one when we were in school."

"Such high standards you have!" Harry put in. "You're going to end up an old maid if you insist on a man having a chin. Poor Gus keeps trying to help you out, but you'll have none of it."

"Well he can just save his efforts for Anna, then. I can find a man on my own. As a matter of fact, I met someone very different and very interesting just today."

"Oh, I didn't know the circus was in town," Harry scoffed. "I can't wait to hear what sister thinks makes a man 'very different and very interesting.' I once saw a show with the Fantastic Rubber Man who could tie his arms and legs in knots right before your very eyes. Now, that's interesting!"

"No circus was involved. He came into the store with a broken lock and Mr. Basche asked me to help him find a replacement in the catalog. His name is Frank McColloch, and he moved to town a few months ago to live with his father, he said."

"Wow! I know about him. He played varsity football for Baker High this year. He was really good, too," exclaimed Harry.

"Oh dear. He's out. If he was in high school this year, he's got to be several years younger than I am. Too bad," the girl muttered, clearly disappointed.

"Nope," Harry said shaking his head. "I read in the paper after the team beat La Grande that he had been in the Marines for the last three years or so. Saw action on the Mexican border. And he's headed for Stanford next year. He's around twenty years old. Oh no, now she has to get serious! This Frank is back in the running!"

...

The next day, while Betty sat at her desk in the hardware store, Frank returned with a broken door hinge. "A hinge, now?" she said. "Someone is hard on doors."

"It's the door to the law office where my father and brother work. You know, it's the place that the lawyers call 'Robbers Roost'. People seem to keep slamming doors around there, I guess," Frank remarked with a laugh.

"Oh dear, then maybe we should order you a box of door hinges. Just to be safe."

"I don't think that would be a good idea. I rather like visiting you on a daily basis," Frank whispered as he leaned over her desk ostensibly to look at the hardware catalogue she had opened in front of her. "You know I just realized that it's nearly noon. I hope I'm not keeping you from your lunch break."

"I usually have a sandwich I bring from home right here at my desk. They give me an hour, but I rarely need more than ten minutes," the girl explained.

"Well, I think for once you should use your whole hour. How about joining me at the Cattlemen's Café?" And, before she could even answer, Frank had retrieved Betty's coat from the rack by her desk, helped her into it and took her arm steering the startled but pleased girl toward the door.

For the three months of that summer Frank and Betty were together whenever she was not working. Both their families were especially pleased with the match. Of course, Rosa had insisted on meeting the young man before the two ever "stepped out" together, so she had Betty invite Frank to dinner. Betty's brothers were both very glad that finally, finally Betty had found someone who actually lived up to what they considered to be her impossibly high standards. Rosa was pleased that Frank was older and more worldly than any of the local boys who were all incapable of interesting conversation according to Betty. Rosa was very proud that this boy's father was Baker City's new City Attorney. It very much mattered to her that Frank came from a family of professional men who were able to make a good living and that he aspired to go to college to study law like his father, C.H. and his brother, Claude, who had joined his father's practice after graduating from the University of Chicago.

Frank had no qualms about how his family would accept Betty who was everything his father would approve of. She was very pretty, certainly. Her flawless complexion and high cheekbones would withstand the ravages of time that so often seemed to turn a blushing debutante into a dour matron almost overnight. More importantly, there was not even a hint of guile in those big brown eyes and a man could be sure that she was a girl who spoke with thought behind her words or, if those thoughts might bring hurt, could be trusted to keep them to herself. But best of all, Frank soon learned that Betty had a very keen mind and a quick wit and was well able to see the humor in any situation which made her very good company indeed.

After Frank had Betty to his home for dinner for the first time to meet C.H. and Claude, he asked the two men what they thought after he took her home. Claude teased that Betty obviously must be very nearsighted and also one of those girls who is vain and refuses to wear her prescription eyeglasses if she agreed to step out with Frank. But C.H. remained uncharacteristically quiet while the brothers traded insults. Finally, he spoke and said, "She is exactly the kind of girl you should marry. She's nothing like..." then stopped himself, but both boys knew that he was about to say that Betty was nothing like their mother.

• • •

After Frank went off to Stanford in the fall, Betty worried that because the school had female students, Frank would quite naturally find a replacement for her. Yet, without fail, he returned to her during every school break and was devoted to her throughout the next summer. And as Frank was about to leave for his sophomore year, the couple had some plans for Betty to visit Palo Alto during the school year.

Stanford had banned the dangerous game of football by 1914, so Frank joined the drama club, Masquers, and he landed a small part in their fall play. He wanted Betty to see him perform his three lines, and to meet the many friends he had at Stanford especially a boy from

Portland, Andrew Koerner, who was also a pre-law student. The two were to be roommates in the coming year. This effort on Frank's part to make Betty more a part of his life served to quell any doubts Betty might have had about his serious intentions.

Like most Americans in the summer of 1914, Frank and Betty were fairly oblivious to the tumult going on in Europe. Neither of them would have taken much interest in an assassination that took place in the little Balkan city of Sarajevo except for the fact that the man and wife killed by Serb nationalists was the Austrian Archduke Franz Ferdinand and his wife, Sophie. As a former citizen of Austria, Rosa still took a German language newspaper to keep up with events in that country.

"He is the heir to the throne of the Austrian Empire, so this is no small event," Rosa explained to the family at dinner after Frank had asked her for her opinion about the assassination. "Austria has already declared war on Serbia."

"Such a little country won't be able to put up much of a fight. That war should be over soon." Harry put in.

"It's not Serbia I worry about. It's Germany!" Rosa retorted. "Kaiser Wilhelm is a fool for war. He will see this event as an excuse to attack other countries besides Serbia. For months he has been making speeches about the danger of Slavic countries like Serbia and Russia and even their ally, France. He says they want to attack Germanic countries out of racial envy. He says that Germanic countries should strike first to crush the Slavs and their allies."

"You think that the Kaiser wants to actually attack a country like France without some aggressive action on France's part?" Frank wondered.

"Yes! Last week a few days after Austria declared war on Serbia, Germany declared war on Russia and two days later Germany declared war on France and at the same time invaded Belgium which the paper assumes is the route they plan to use to invade France!"

Frank looked down at his hands for a moment of thought and then looked at the group and said, "Then I would say that you were right about the Kaiser being 'a fool'. The Kaiser is foolish to start a two front war like that. Anyone who studies military history knows that a two front war is unwinnable. This whole thing will surely be over soon when Germany cannot defend its borders against attack from all sides."

These events were certainly worrisome to Rosa's family and most other Americans who were aware of world events. Still, Europe was far away and across a wide ocean, so worry about wars over there for most people was usually momentary and easily shrugged off.

Frank, however sure he was of his analysis of Germany's military chance for success, continued to worry about the developments in Europe. When he left active duty in the Marines, he had remained a member of the National Guard which could be called up if the U.S. should become embroiled in this European mess. As distracted and excited about college life and his budding romance with Betty, he always kept one small part of his attention on world news.

23.
Frank and Betty

As Frank McColloch kissed Betty Meyer "goodbye" and boarded the train eager to begin his second year at college, other fresh-faced young men were boarding trains in Germany eager to take part in the recent glory of their country's September 1914 invasion of France that had begun a month earlier just as the war was beginning. German troops had swarmed in and quickly taken the Argonne Forest and the land above the Meuse River, two areas of great strategic importance to France. Then they marched into the east and took over two hundred square miles of the Woevre Plain which cut off the transportation route to France's industrial center from Nancy to Verdun.

All this was reported to the German people as an unmitigated German victory with no mention of the fierce resistance made by French soldiers to stop this unprovoked assault on their country. In fact, when Kaiser Wilhelm had started what Frank correctly labeled an "unwinnable' two-front war, he had believed that France was too weak to put up much of a fight and that he could take what he wanted from them and then put most his armed strength on the eastern front with Russia, leaving only one front to contend with. Even as he addressed his troops heading toward France in August 1914, he probably believed his own words that these men would "... be home before the leaves fall from the trees."

In reality, German high command soon realized that holding the lands they had taken in France would not be an easy task and ordered the building of defensive trenches throughout the two hundred square miles of occupied French countryside. These were not at all like the cold mud trenches held up by logs built in haste by the French army. The German system was made of concrete with drainage pipes, sniper's towers and machine gun shelters. They built impenetrable bunkers fitted with periscopes from which they could safely watch for any advancing enemy. They built concrete underground towns with barracks, kitchens, and armories In addition, there were many "rest camps" that piped in fresh, clean water for tired or wounded troops during any break from battle.

Such preparations were proof positive that the Germans meant to stay. And stay they did. Month after month the Germans perfected their defenses especially in the Argonne where they took advantage of the natural terrain. They made the most of the many rocky outcroppings, densely wooded narrow valleys and steep hills bordering open meadows which could so easily be swept clean by the German machine gun nests that topped every high spot and were constantly fed with fresh ammunition by a vast rail network safely ensconced in tangles of barbed wire.

By the end of the war's second month, trench warfare dominated the Western Front. Even after Britain joined France in their effort to break through Germany's defenses, the Allied forces made no headway, and stalemate marked by periods of ferocious battle became the norm for the area year after bloody year.

• • •

With every year of a war that had engulfed Europe, much of the Middle East and Russia, Frank became more concerned that he would soon be called up. Finally, during his senior year at Stanford, when Germany escalated unrestricted submarine warfare which directly threatened U.S. shipping and finally led to an official U.S. declaration of war with Germany, he decided to put his college education on hold and join many Stanford students for officer's training at the Presidio in San Francisco. Before his training was completed, he was commissioned as a Captain due to his prior military experience. His first act as a newly minted U.S. Army officer was to send a telegram to Betty that read: "Sweetheart new officer needs a wife please use rail ticket to follow." They were married August 15, 1917 in Palo Alto.

For Betty, the next few months would prove to be a constant, silent battle with a number of her long-held, black fears. Of course, there was the ever-present fear that the war Frank was sure to join would leave her a very young widow. Even on their honeymoon in Santa Cruz, during Frank's leave from the Presidio, she could manage little more than a nervous smile as they walked the beach boardwalk or ate dinner in one of the many outdoor cafes beside the lovely palm-lined boulevard above the roaring Pacific surf.

While Betty worried over the looming darkness that seemed obvious to her to be their future, she was in constant wonder over Frank's high spirits and apparent enthusiasm for what he saw as his part soon to be played on the world stage.

Additionally, the word "honeymoon" itself had always seemed to Betty to be a cruel, ironic joke meant to trap love-blind women before they truly understood the ominous danger of this traditional beginning to wedded life. It meant sex and sex meant childbirth, and for too many women, childbirth meant death.

War meant death, too, but Frank could be happy about going to war because it just wasn't real to him, she knew. He had never seen the ravages of war up close. Even the skirmishes his unit had had on the Mexican border, he had reported to her as being quite the exciting adventure.

But she had seen what could happen to a woman from giving birth. From those horrible days caring for her mother who lay in such pain and mortification from the stench caused by her condition, to the moment she would also risk such a fate, herself, Betty had been deeply, implacably afraid. But, there was no way that she could share her fear with the man who loved her and was also about to go off to war. That would be truly cowardly and besides, she thought, it wouldn't really help her in any way.

So, Betty remained smiling throughout the few days they had together before Frank had to return to San Francisco. She managed this feat primarily because she kept telling herself that in such a short time together, she probably could not become pregnant. But by the time

Frank had completed his officer's training and received his orders to travel to Camp Lewis in Washington State for training and deployment to Europe with the newly formed 91st Division, Betty knew with complete certainty that she was indeed pregnant. Very soon anyone else who had eyes would also know of her condition, so she would have to tell Frank about the baby before he left for Camp Lewis.

Betty fervently hoped that her pregnancy would mean that she would soon have to return to Baker City. She had already lived for months in a strange town, far from Rosie, who she needed now more than ever for reassurance in the face of her greatest fear. Rosie would completely understand why she was so afraid, and that understanding would make the months of waiting for the birth more bearable.

However, when she finally told Frank, he was so excited and happy about the news that he never once thought it possible that Betty did not share his unmitigated joy. In addition, he believed that she needed to be with him during this delicate time, so he immediately wrote to Rosa and to the Catholic Bishop in Baker City about the situation begging for help in finding a safe place for Betty to live in Tacoma close enough to Camp Lewis so that they could be together occasionally. He did not tell her about this request, because he did not want her disappointed if she had to return to Oregon.

When Frank received the Bishop's response that arrangements had been made for Betty to live with a family in Tacoma near Camp Lewis, he was overjoyed and anxious to surprise Betty with this happy news.

" 'Mr. and Mrs. Mike Giblin of Tacoma are a nice Irish couple of my acquaintance who have agreed to have your dear wife as their guest until your child is born and mother and child can safely travel back to Baker City,'" a grinning Frank read aloud from the Bishop's letter as Betty listened in mute horror.

"Isn't that wonderful, sweetheart?!" Frank nearly shouted as he put down the Bishop's letter. "Now we can be together and you won't have to go through this alone!" He added, misreading Betty's shocked expression as thrilled disbelief over their good fortune.

Three very lonely, very fear-ridden months passed and Betty finally gave birth to a healthy baby boy. Though she had not wanted to live with "strangers," the Giblins had proven to be exceedingly kind, thoughtful people who tried to do everything possible to give comfort to a poor pregnant girl who was about to be separated by war from her loving husband. Unfortunately, their idea of "comfort" meant feeding Betty many, many delicious, fattening meals. She gained weight in their care, but so did the baby who weighed a whopping eleven pounds at birth making it a long and difficult delivery.

When she saw tears in Frank's eyes as he repeated for the third time how much he loved her and how "simply beautiful" was their baby, Betty finally and for the first time felt it might have all been worth it. "Let's name him after your father," she suggested.

"I hoped you would want to call him 'Charles'. And for a middle name, would you like to use 'August' for your father?" Frank offered. "But, really, we should save that name for when we have our second son, don't you think?"

"Dear God! He's already getting me pregnant again!" She thought but said in a tired voice. "Why don't you chose a middle name and surprise me with it, darling."

It wasn't until Betty was on the train to Baker City with little Charles sleeping in a basket beside her, that she actually opened and looked at the baby's birth certificate, and laughed right out loud. "Charles Koerner McColloch" it read on the line for the baby's name. She leaned over the sleeping baby and whispered, "Your daddy is certainly a man's man. He 'surprised' us by naming you after his best friend, Andrew Koerner!"

...

The men of the 91st "Wild West" Division under command of Major General William H. Johnston assigned to General John Pershing's American Expeditionary Force (AEF) arrived in France in August 1918 after their training at Camp Lewis was cut short in order to provide fresh troops to relieve the war weary French and British who had been fighting the Germans without success for nearly four, long years. They were told that they would continue their training for the next three months behind the lines until they were ready for battle.

Yet, in early September, after only one month of behind the lines training, the AEF high command curtailed their training and ordered the 91st into battle at St. Mihiel as a reserve force. The men of the

91st, so totally lacking in experience and training for war, showed their spirited eagerness for battle with the cry, "Powder River let 'er buck!"

For his part, Frank was glad that the men of the 363 infantry were so eager to prove themselves in actual battle, but was greatly relieved that their first test would be as reserves since he knew that they all were sorely lacking in the training needed to meet the challenges of real war. What he did not know, was that very soon the 91st would be thrown into the front lines of the Meuse-Argonne Offensive that became the second-deadliest battle in all of American history.

When the 91st Division was moved without any further training to the Meuse-Argonne area, they were tasked with conducting the initial attack. Frank knew that none of the men under his command had ever had any battle experience. He ruefully had to admit to himself that he had so quickly been made a captain after completing the officer's candidate school instead of graduating as a second lieutenant as was usual because of his brief battle experience. However, he also knew that what he had faced before in the bandit attacks on the U.S./Mexican border was really only a series of minor skirmishes. Now he had real responsibility for a large number of very young, untried soldiers who were completely unready to face the seasoned forces of a well prepared, well positioned German army that had already seemed to have convinced much of the Allied forces fighting them, that they were invincible.

As time passed before the offensive would officially begin, Frank found that there was so much more he had to worry about besides the inexperience of his men. He was aware that his 363rd infantry regiment was ordered to be part of the first line of attack and would march forward on the far left abreast of the 361st in the center and the 362nd on the far right. They were to be supported by the 35th Division on their left flank. However, he was shocked to learn just before the battle started, that the commander of the 35th had relieved both his brigade commanders and all four of his regimental commanders just five days before because he "couldn't trust them."

"And he picked the eve of battle as the best time to get rid of all his top officers?" Frank cried in exasperation when told of this. "I wonder how much 'support' we'll get from our flank now?" he muttered to himself.

There were more immediate concerns bothering Frank on the morning of September 26th when they were to go "over the top." The weather was proving to be uncooperative because a heavy fog refused to lift after the early morning hours. The artillery barrage that had begun six hours before the 5:30 H-Hour added thick smoke to the foggy terrain which made it impossible to see more than 50 feet throughout the morning.

Just an hour before they were to begin their charge, Frank was frantic. He had requested a compass which had still not arrived to his position in the trenches. He knew that the smoke and fog would make it impossible for him to rely on using visual clues from terrain features to guide their attack. Also, they would not be able to communicate with other groups with hand signals in the usual way. So, without a compass they would really be operating blind.

When the final command came to start their charge, and still he had no compass or even a map to rely on, Frank could only order his men to keep an eye on the man on each side of them as they made their way slowly through the fog. Yet, he was afraid that as men were shot and fell away, any semblance of order could quickly turn into chaos.

And the sounds! The crash of the continued artillery was punctuated by the fearsome rattle from enemy machine gun nests which seemed to be coming from everywhere. Yet on they went, hoping that they were pushing forward in the general direction of the villages of Eclisfontaine and Epinonville the first step toward Kriemhilde-Stellung, the initial Army objective in the campaign.

In the crushing fog, none of Frank's regiment knew that they were actually making an advance that was far quicker than their High Command had reckoned was possible for the first day. Since no-one could see the advancing troops, the American artillery gunners aiming to hit the German held French towns ahead of the infantry could not see that their shells were falling short and hitting their own troops.

It was also impossible for the American troops on the ground to see that the Germans were falling back from their lightly held first line of defense and that groups of Americans were being surrounded by retreating enemy soldiers. The American troops nearest Frank comprised one of these smaller groups and, as the fog began to lift a bit mid-morning, he soon realized that they were cut off from the main part of their regiment by the enemy, an enemy that was now fleeing in their direction and would soon surround them on all sides

He could also see that they were surrounded by huge shell holes and that many of these were filled with the bodies of dead U.S. soldiers. Very quickly, he ascertained that their best shot for survival until the retreating Germans passed would be to take cover in one of these holes. It would be hard in the fog for any passing enemy soldiers to see if a man laying down in a hole was alive or dead. Frank could only pray that the retreating enemy would not stop to investigate or even long enough to spray the dead with bullets.

After giving the order to take cover, Frank ran about pushing bodies close around his hiding men. And just as he saw the darker colors of some German uniforms coming toward them through the white haze, Frank jumped into a hole full of bodies himself. Hours passed as German troops continued to make their way through the eerie fog passing close enough to Frank and his men lying motionless among the dead for them to hear snatches of German that seemed to float out of the foggy soup around them from all sides.

"Gunther! Sind Sie das?" (Gunther, is that you?}

"Ja, ich bin heir. Ich kann nichts voraussehn!" (Yes, I am here. I can see nothing ahead)

"Ich sehe etwas!" (I see something)

"Was ist es, Herman?" (What is it, Herman?)

"Feind! verwundet oder tot." (Enemy! wounded or dead)

"Wir mussen weitermachen..." (We must keep moving)

By late afternoon, the blinding fog remained covering the field like a musty blanket. Besides the continued stream of German soldiers, sporadic machine gun fire that seemed to come directly ahead of the men hiding in a shell hole, convinced Frank that as long as the fog persisted, he could not safely allow his men to leave their positions.

"Please, Lord. Help them to stay still!" Frank prayed silently. But, as time passed, Frank began to realize how horribly hard this would be for them.

After the initial adrenalin from battle wore off, Frank first noticed the stench rising like a steamy cloud around him. Without moving, he could peripherally see some of the bodies nestled around him. These men had died from shell blasts that had torn off limbs and disemboweled those unlucky enough to be hit by "friendly fire" coming from their own side. Inches from his own face, lay a man missing most of his face and Frank had to choke down the bile that threatened to cause him to cough or vomit.

Frank also began to notice just how frigid the fog was on the skin and in no time the cold seemed to pierce his body to the bone. Then, he began to suffer violent cramps that gripped both legs in horrendous, vice-like spasms. His men had to be suffering as he was, and yet they remained stolidly silent as the enemy walked by within yards of them.

• • •

Throughout the night, German forces gave up their lightly held first line of defense and moved back into the towns of Eclisfontaine and Epinonville which would make the American objective of taking those towns impossible without a deadly fight. Miraculously, small elements of the 91st had made it into the village of Epinonville by the end of the first day, but in the face of a heavy German presence, they were unable to secure the town and had to give up the day's gains.

By the morning of the second day, Frank's group was able to leave the shell holes and join the troops that had made it to Epinonville as they all withdrew back to their starting point. Frank had been correct when he predicted that the American troops in the first line of attack would not be well supported by the poorly led 35 Division on their flank. The 91st suffered incredible losses in their first attack on the German positions, so further attack plans were stalled while unit leaders tried to reform their units as small groups of soldiers arrived throughout the morning of the second day.

• • •

"Take your men and join that group down field, Major McColloch." an officer barked at Frank after he had reported in.

"It's Captain McColloch, sir." Frank corrected.

"After our assault yesterday, we are short officers, and you are now a Major." The man explained over his shoulder as he walked away from the startled Frank.

Within the hour, Frank would learn that the American infantry,incurred thousands of casualties on that first day, but also had made more progress than had been made by the French and British in four years of trench warfare. Frank would also be advised that his own brigade commander, Brigadier General Foltz of the 182 Brigade, had been relieved of duty by Johnston for ordering a retreat on the first day, because he had rightly ascertained that the risk to his men was just too great considering the conditions that morning. This move made it clear to all junior officers that Johnston would not allow a retreat mentality in his division. From that first day on, the attack orders for the 91st read "push forward at all costs." And that is what they did with 26,277 Americans giving up their lives to maintain a battle momentum that finally broke German morale.

In the face of all their battlefield challenges, Frank realized that, as an officer directly responsible for maintaining the discipline of his men while carrying out extremely risky orders, his most important duty would be to do whatever necessary in order to maintain the morale of those brave men. Early on, he had demonstrated that he would "lead from the front" and stay close to his men acting with their welfare firmly in mind.

On September 28, the third day of fighting, the Americans were able to drive the Germans out and to secure the towns of Eclisfontaine and Epinonville. It was the seemingly unstoppable men of the 91st that were first to reach this objective. At this point, officers were tasked with trying to continue to motivate their men to continue their fight under the worse conditions imaginable. They were being fired upon from all directions, yet the High Command sent orders for the 91st to push forward and attack the town of Gesnes. The order specifically stated, "...divisions will advance independently of each other pushing the attack with utmost vigor and regardless of cost," which was no less a desperate attempt to maintain the momentum in the battle.

It would be in Gesnes that the 91st would have its deadliest fight. Germans surrounded the town on all sides and the Kriemhilde-Stellung, a German intermediate line of defense, was just north of the town. Additionally, the men on the ground were either hectored by poorly coordinated artillery fire or were required to proceed with no artillery support at all. They would be forced to attack two times without artillery support, suffer great casualties and be repulsed. Finally, the artillery arrived and was successfully employed which allowed the infantry to move in and take and secure the town.

Miraculously, the Wild West division had captured Gesnes and was first to reach the Army's 1st objective, Kriemhilde-Stellung, but at great cost in lost lives. One company of 179 men reported only 18 men at roll call after the battle. The brave men of the 91st whose training was cut radically short and had only been tested in five days of battle, managed to distinguish themselves as a significant force for the German army to reckon with. Their successes managed to severely damage German morale and helped to bring an end to a war that had all but stalled in the trenches for years.

Even without much specific training the men of the 91st learned quickly to use the tactics of "open warfare" to their advantage which has been credited with ending the trench stalemate. The combat Instructions manual issued just twenty days before the Meuse-Argonne offensive detailed how the infantry would proceed. Instead of being micromanaged by higher headquarters, junior officers could use their own initiative and were encouraged to employ innovation on the battlefield. There would be, the manual stated, "…little regulation of space and time by higher command, the greatest possible use of the infantry's own firepower to enable it to get forward, variable distance and intervals between units and individuals, and use of every form of cover and accident of ground during the advance."

These smaller, irregular formations became known as "gangs" and were especially effective in taking out the German machine gun nests that seemed to top every Argonne hill. When attacking such a nest, the 'gang,' using any available cover, would bound in short rushes towards the gunners and use flanking maneuvers to take out the enemy and put the guns out of service. Without such innovations, the war could have continued far longer in stalemate. Instead, by October 30, the German army had retreated to Belgium where a hastily re-organized 91st and 37th Division joined the French VI Army under King Albert I of Belgium with the common objective of pushing the German army back beyond the line marked by the Scheldt River. The 91st reached Audenarde on the Scheldt November 1 where they found the bridge over the river destroyed and the enemy occupying a commanding position southeast of the town.

Despite blistering artillery fire from the German camp, the men of the 91st began immediately to rebuild the bridge across the river. Frank worked side by side his men of the 363 Regiment throughout the night of November 1st and 2nd, but their efforts to rebuild the bridge were finally judged to be futile since every new plank was immediately destroyed by enemy fire.

At the first morning light on November 2, Frank received orders to discontinue their effort and join the 37th the following night since they had made more progress on another bridge. As he turned to speak with his second lieutenant, Frank was knocked to the ground by an exploding German shell. When he regained consciousness, he found that he had been evacuated to the rear and was being treated by a French doctor who spoke to him as he wiped a great amount of blood from Frank's side.

Frank did not understand what the Frenchman said, but when the doctor handed him an evil-looking piece of shrapnel, Frank understood that he had been wounded in the abdomen. When the doctor finished dressing his wound, Frank tried to sit up but was too dizzy to manage this for long.

By that evening, Frank could sit up and saw that a tag had been tied to his toe which read "evacuer an Angleterre." He knew enough French to realize that he was soon to be evacuated to England.

"That is out of the question," he mumbled as he removed the offending tag and tied it to a sleeping man with a head bandage in the bed next to him. "You look like you need a trip to England more than I do," he whispered, then turned to leave and rejoin his Regiment.

On November 10, the 91st and 37th finally crossed the Scheldt. At that time, they did not know just the day before, Kaiser Wilhelm had abdicated the throne and Germany was about to sign an armistice with the Allies. When the Armistice took effect, on November 11, the two American divisions were well east of the Scheldt advancing in pursuit of the retreating Germans.

On November 14, 1918 Frank wrote a letter to a wounded comrade, Lieutenant Hydn O. Duke:

My Dear Duke,

... Of course you know the glorious news and know how happy we are that it is all over. You asked about the fight...We arrived on the heights overlooking Audenarde and the Scheldt River at 3:00 pm the afternoon of the first of November. The next morning a piece of H.E. gouged me in the abdomen and took the top two buttons off my breeches. They sent me back to evacuation hospital and almost got me to England, but I escaped and hiked back to the outfit...On the tenth we moved up and crossed the river at Audenarde at daybreak and attacked the heights beyond. Well, the Bosch had pulled out the night before leaving only a few pieces of artillery and a few m.g.s. We made nine kilometers that day as front line battalion. Just before dark we ran into the most perfect hail of m.g. fire we ever faced. Old man McColloch wasn't going to go to hell the last day of the war, so we halted and dug in for the night. We were ordered to attack at 10 am next day. At 9:50 a message came declaring cessation of hostilities. Some dramatic finish wasn't it?

Anyhow, the old battalion saw the thing to the end. Since then we have moved into billets, established our outpost line and here we lie waiting for orders. We don't know where we go from here but we hope it is toward the nearest seaport ...

It would be several months before Frank would see that "seaport" he wished for. On March 15, 1919, he was one of the officers Pershing ordered to Paris to take part in a conclave tasked with forming a veterans association in order to provide veterans of war with the political clout needed to fight for veterans' benefits and support. This organization, The American Legion, would play a vital role in drafting the Servicemen's Readjustment Act of 1944 better known as the "G.I. Bill."

On July 1, 1919, Betty finally received word that Frank had arrived in New York and soon she would have her husband and their son, Charles, would have his father home to start their interrupted life as a family.

...

As his train moved slowly through the Eastern Oregon hills turned golden by the late summer sun, Frank strained to pick out any familiar landmarks that would indicate how close he was to his final destination. But it was not until they rolled into the depot, and he saw the people gathered beneath the Baker City sign that he felt a punch of overwhelming joy that was evidenced by tears he quickly wiped away on his sleeve. There they all were, C.H. and Claude, Rosa, August, Mathew, Harry, Gus Jr, Anna, Francis and his beautiful Betty. But it was the sight of little Charles standing proudly by his mother and waving a tiny American flag that made the unstoppable tears come again. His family. His home. It was what they had fought for and for what so many had died.

That night, at his father's insistence, Frank allowed C.H. and Claude to see the decorations he had received in France. After he read the certificate that accompanied the medal of which Frank was most proud, C.H. embraced his son and murmured, "The French Croix de Guerre. Well deserved. You boys gave them back their country. Do you think the French will ever forget what you all did for them?"

"No, Dad. Not even in a hundred years."

Post Script

In 2014 to commemorate the hundred year anniversary of the start of World War I, Richard Rubin of the New York Times wrote of his trip to Northern France to see the battle sites of that bloody war in and around the Argonne forest and the Meuse River territory. He was particularly interested in, "sites linked to the 91st Division known as the 'Wild West' Division because ... they saw some of the heaviest fighting ... and took a great many casualties." But he was most impressed by "the old German fortifications that have decayed hardly at all over the last century, the ones that make you stare in wonder and ask yourself: How did the Germans lose that war? Ask the French that same question, and, if your experience is anything like mine, they will always, always give you the same succinct answer. Les Americains."

Afterward

Charles Henry McColloch (C. H.)

C.H. continued to practice law in Baker City first serving as City Attorney 1906-1924 and then as Circuit Court Judge of Baker County 1924-1942 when he retired and moved to Portland to be closer to his sons and their families. For a number of years he took a leading part in the Oregon National Guard at Baker City where he was captain of the local unit. He also served as chief of engineers under Governor George Chamberlain. He and wife, Mary, continued to live apart throughout their lives though C.H. always supported her and provided for her to be buried at Riverview Cemetery in Portland in a plot next to his own. C.H. died Sept. 7, 1950.

Mary Woody McColloch

Mary continued her work in support of women's suffrage and prohibition throughout her life and lived to see the day when both became the "law of the land" shortly after World War I. In her later years, she lived with her mother in Los Angeles after C.H. accompanied Mary back for a visit to Hot Springs to collect her mother and bring the old woman west. Mary died in 1947. She is buried next to her husband and nearby her sons in Portland's Riverview Cemetery.

Claude C. McColloch

Claude graduated from the University of Chicago in 1909 when he failed to reenter Stanford due to his flamboyant news article in *The Portland Oregonian* following the 1906 San Francisco earthquake.

He was admitted to the Oregon Bar in 1909 and practiced in Baker City where he married Erma Clifford in 1912. He served in the Oregon Legislature in the 1911 and 1913 sessions then served 21 years as associate and chief justice of Oregon's Federal Court. He was appointed by Franklin D. Roosevelt due to the efforts of James G. Farley, Roosevelt's campaign manager. Later in his book, "Notes of a Federal Judge," Claude wrote that C.H. had written Farley to thank him for Claude's appointment, and said, "Because he encouraged me as a boy, I always regarded James G. Blaine as the greatest man I ever knew. Now, you have first place in my affections." Claude died Sept. 30, 1959 just months after his wife.

Frank C. McColloch

Frank studied law and was admitted to the Oregon bar in 1919 and practiced in Baker City until 1935 when he was appointed public utility commissioner for Oregon. He also served as Baker's City attorney, and circuit court judge for Jackson and Josephine Counties. In 1937, he became a partner in the Portland law firm that became Koerner, Young, McColloch and Dezendorf until 1973. In his later years, Frank enjoyed traveling to Europe, the Middle East and Asia with his Betty. He and Betty lived in Portland's Arlington Heights next door to Frank's longest friend and law partner, Andrew Koerner, until Betty's death in 1964.

Betty Meyer McColloch

After Frank returned from war, the two settled down in their own house in Baker City where Betty happily took on the household responsibilities of the typical housewife, the "job" for which she was so well suited. In 1937 they moved to Portland to be close to the doctors who were treating their son, Charles, for osteomyelitis, a ravaging bone infection. They were warned he would not survive beyond age 30. She was much loved and revered by her extended family, but especially by her husband who wrote in his diary after her death, "She was clean in spirit and person. Both men and women were attracted to her—not because of personality because she did not "sparkle." It must have been her quiet sincerity and an aura which radiated quietly and naturally...God! How I miss her!!"

Charles K. McColloch

As he grew, "Little Charles" endured the agony of over 24 surgeries to "dig out" the unremitting bone infection that coursed through his body until the boy was over twenty years old. Despite his ongoing medical condition, the young man attended Stanford and Willamette School of Law to become an attorney like his grandfather, uncle and father. At Willamette, he met Beverly Nordean, a willowy beauty ironically from Baker City, whose family moved there soon after Charles' folks moved to Portland. Despite his dark prognosis, the two courageously decided to marry and to live in Baker City. Soon after the wedding, two Baker City doctors close to Beverly's family, Palmer McKim and Robert Pollack, conferred over Charles' condition and suggested they try a course of a new medicine called "penicillin." Within weeks, the constant pain and the seepage from the man's many open wounds vanished. He was pronounced cured! Charles did not die before age 30. Instead, he went on to represent Baker County in the Oregon Legislature, to serve at the Oregon Tax Commission, practice corporate law in Portland for two decades, and finally to serve as Oregon's Real Estate Commissioner under the legendary Governor, Tom McCall. He and Beverly had four children, and when they were grown, the couple was able to realize their dream of retiring in Hawaii. Like for so many others, the miracle of antibiotics made possible a long, productive life for Charles who died peacefully in his own bed, surrounded by family, at the age of 88!

Rosa Krann

Rosa, would be affectionately known by all as just "Rosie" throughout the over fifty years in Baker City where she continued to provide stunning head ware for the lucky women there. Her renown as a milliner reached beyond that small town and even impressed Mamie Eisenhower who so admired the "Rosie hat" a Salem woman was wearing at a Republican fundraiser, that the first lady ordered several custom creations from Rosa to make and send on to Washington D.C. Additionally, Rosa was especially successful raising Marie's five children. She saw to it that they all attended St. Francis Academy except for Marie's "baby", Francis, whose exceptional academic prowess convinced her that he should go to Mt. Angel, a respected Benedictine-run Catholic boarding school, where he attended from sixth grade through college. He then married a Portland girl, they had nine children and later moved to California where Francis worked for Lockheed Aircraft Co. A deeply religious man, Francis became president of the California Knights of Columbus and Rosie's proudest moment was when she went to a banquet in his honor where the Cardinal of Los Angeles conferred on Francis honors as "the outstanding Catholic layman in Southern California." Rosie died after a very short retirement in 1962 and was buried in Baker City's Mt. Hope Cemetery.

August Meyer

August lived out his life near his children in a cottage behind Rosa's large house on Grove Street across from the park in Baker City. He took much pride in all his children's accomplishments. His happiest moments were spent at dinner in Rosie's large kitchen warmed by its wood stove while listening to the gentle teasing and good-humored argument between the siblings gathered around their huge table. August also took great pride as a member of the Grand Army of the Republic Joe Hooker Post #20 where he served Baker City along with good friends, who were four other Civil War Veterans. He died in 1922 at the age of 74 and was buried in Mt. Hope Cemetery next to his beloved Marie and a plot later housing her sister, Rosa.

Photos

Charles Henry (C.H.) McColloch

August Meyer, 1914

Frank McColloch age 7

Frank and Betty 1917

Frank at Stanford 1913

Rosa Krann Active in Local Millinery Store 52 Years

MARIANNE G. SHURTLEFF
Democrat-Herald Society Editor

Miss Rosa Krann, local milliner, located in the Antlers Hotel Bldg., has been in business in Baker for 52 years. The small, gentle mannered lady with the rich Austrian accent arrived in Baker in 1882 with her mother and grandfather. Her father had arrived here earlier. Miss Krann had studied the art of hat making in Austria and had worked there for five years in Vienna, her home, while attending high school.

The circumstances surrounding the family's decision to come to America w e r e unusual. Miss Krann's father har invested money in the Baisley mine which he had learned about in Austria. He was a man who wanted to own property which was his own without strings.

In Austria his grandfather had operated a brickyard for the government, then his father had operated the same business which in turn would have passed on down to him. The government of Austria owned the property and businessmen could obtain 99 year leases on such businesses. This was all right but it did not satisfy Mr. Krann, consequently he bought the mining stock.

When he began to wonder what was wrong that he did not receive any returns on his investment, the family came to investigate. He was told that in blasting operations the gold vein had been lost and so was Mr. Krann's money. Mr. Krann then took up other mining property in the area, some was in Griffin Gulch, and Prairie City.

The family seemed doomed to misfortune. Within a period of 10 years Miss Krann had lost her parents and grandfather and her brother. Then her sister who was married and had been living at a mining camp, became ill and was operated on.

The day following the operation Miss Krann went to see her sister in the hospital and she asked Miss Krann to care for her children as she felt she was not going to recover. She died soon after, leaving Miss Krann with five children to raise, the oldest being a girl of 12. The other youngsters were 9, 7, 5, and the youngest was 18 months.

At that time Henry Levinger's father was operating a drug store here and when Miss Krann entered his store to pay a bill for medicine her sister had needed, he asked her what she was going to do. Miss Krann said, "What else? Put the children in school here and take care of them." She was not quite 21.

Mr. Levinger studied for a moment and then said "Rosa, make me a real pretty hat with a lot of plumes on it, I'll get it this evening." He came for the hat at about 6 in the evening and Miss Krann had a lovely hat made for him. He left with it and came back in about two and one-half hours. He said, "I sold your hat, Rosa, and here is the money." In her hand he placed $300 dollars and 67 cents. He had raffled the hat off so that there would be funds for Miss Krann's new family. He also rent-

MISS ROSA KRANN

ed his home to Miss Krann. He was building a new home here.

Miss Krann was able to keep the family together and kept on making hats. She employed several ladies as hat makers and trimmers until the manufacturing firms started making hats and it no longer was practical to make them by hand. Her business now consists of carrying a good stock of well-known hats and she also does the hand work on bridal veils and other lovely bits of finery.

In the earlier days of Baker Miss Krann sold her hats for as high as 65 dollars. When asked who bought the most hats she smiled and answered, "well, Baker was a wide open town, then."

On her buying trips she would have to go to Chicago and Kansas City as there was only one small wholesale house in Portland. Fancy feathers were in demand and hats were elegantly trimmed.

Of course, the question of when she will retire was asked, and again the gentle smile appeared as she said," on the days when I feel cross and grouchy, I think I will sell out, and then the next day when I feel happy, I don't want to sell."

With a wistful air Miss Krann stated that the city now seemed very different from the early days in Baker when the livery stable stood where the Hotel Baker is now, and mud and sagebrush lay between the main streets of the town and the little shack that was the depot at the time. Miss Krann thinks that she would enjoy going on a trip just to visit and see the country. Perhaps she will, one of these days.

TO SEE JOHANSSON

NEW YORK — (UPI) — Promoter Jack Fugazy of Feature Sports Inc., leaves for Madrid next Tuesday to meet Ingemar Johanssen and his advisor, Edwin Ahlqvist, for talks concerning the world heavyweight champion's title defense next summer. Johansson has been appearing in the Gaza Strip this week in exhibition matches for U. N. troops.

Baker Man Made Army Captain Then Promptly Gets Married

The news reached Baker today that Frank C. McColloch, son of Attorney

Frank McColloch.

Former Baker resident who has just been appointed captain in the United States Reserve Corps.

C. H. McColloch had been given a commission as captain in the United States Reserve Corps. The appointment was made in San Francisco where Captain McColloch and the other new officers of the corps will soon take up their duties at the officers training camp at the Presidio. Unlike the officers' commissions in the new national army which are for three years, the appointment of the officers in the reserve corps is for five years.

Evidently believing that the right way to start on his career as an army officer was to get married, Mr. McColloch was joined in wedlock at 6:30 o'clock last evening with Miss Elizabeth Meyers in San Francisco. Mrs. McColloch, who is also a resident of Baker, was formerly employed as bookkeeper by the Basche Hardware company and has many friends here. It is understood that Mr. and Mrs. McColloch will make their home for the present in San Francisco.

Although Mr. McColloch's appointment has just been announced, he received his commission on June 22. At present he is taking a 12 days' furlough which the government has granted to all the officers who were recently appointed.

Mr. McColloch is well known in Baker where he formerly lived and received his early education. After attending the Baker high school he enlisted in the United States Marines and served four years. While in the (Continued on Page Eight)

Registration Retarded

palo alto news claude mccolloch   Find   cancel

McColloch Causes Ire by Criticising C. G. Lathrop.

Brightness: 0

Contrast: 0

STANFORD UNIVERSITY, Sept. 10. Because he wrote a vivid and trenchant account of the damage wrought upon the buildings of Stanford University by the earthquake, implicating Charles G. Lathrop, treasurer of the institution and a member of the board of trustees; C. E. Hodges, former university architect, and J. D. McGilvray, head of the large San Francisco contracting firm, Claude C. McColloch, a prominent sophomore, registering from Portland, Or., has been forced to dodge from pillar to post at the request of the authorities in a vain attempt to register for the semester.

The young collegian has taken an active part in the university journalistic field and has also been a writer for metropolitan dailies. His name is included upon the staff of the Daily Palo Alto, the official daily of the university, as an associate editor.

PRESIDENT JORDAN'S STAND.

President David Starr Jordan says no official action has been taken regarding the matter, but admits he communicated with McColloch during the summer vacation requesting that some amicable agreement be reached with the trustees before he attempted to register. This request was based upon the stand which was taken by Charles G. Lathrop, who believed the article to be vicious in character and radically wrong. Although the trustee has no hand in the discipline of the students, the matter has been held up pending action upon the part of the authorities.

McColloch has not interviewed the angry trustees, his stand being that as a member of the board of trustees Treasurer Lathrop has no power to intervene in the affair.

HAS A MERRY CHASE.

McColloch has had a merry chase in the attempt to find the right place to file a protest. He has been referred from one official to another until the entire system has been traversed. As is the custom under the university, he first applied to the chairman of the students' affairs committee, Professor S. L. Green, who has charge of such

CLAUDE C. McCOLLOCH, THE STANFORD SOPHOMORE WHOSE REGISTRATION IS DELAYED BECAUSE HE CRITICISED TREASURER LATHROP.

WORKMEN TO COME BY THE SANTA FE

San Francisco Newspaper

Article about Claude McColloch

Betty at Seaside, Oregon

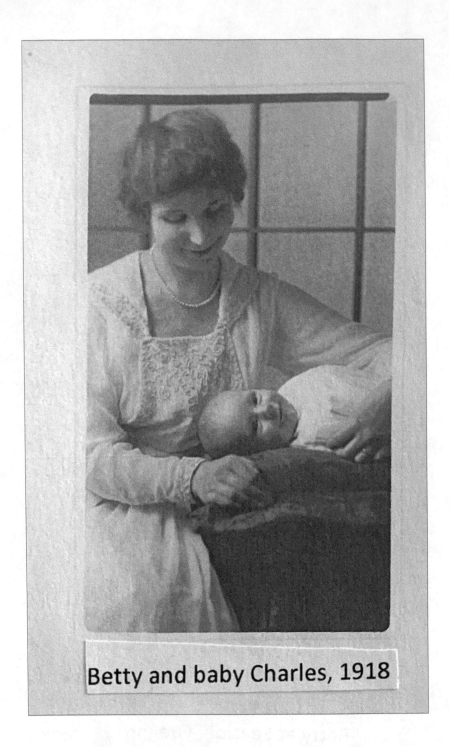

Betty and baby Charles, 1918

Charles Koerner McColloch

Age 4

Viva Nordean (author's maternal grandmother) wearing a Rosa Krann hat

Sources

Bianco, Juan Ignacio. "First Public Hanging-Pleasant Armstrong." Murderpedia. Web. http://murderpedia.org/male.A/a/Armstrong.

"Civil War through Reconstruction 1861 through 1874."Encyclopedia of Arkansas. Web. http://www.encyclopediaofarkansas.net.

Dielman, Eloise. Baker County Links to the Past. Baker City Oregon: Baker County Historical Society, 2006. Print.

Dielman, Gary. Essays on Eastern Oregon History. "Tenderloin District: Prostitution was illegal but Condoned until 1906, "1904 Hanging of Pleasant Armstrong," and "1700 Block of Main Street: It's Burning and Subsequent Rise from the Ashes." Web. http://www.bakerlib.org/photoarchive/dielmanlocalhistory.

Fox, Timothy J. and Sneddeker, Duane R. From Palaces to the Pike: Visions of the 1904 World's Fair, St. Louis: Missouri Historical Society. 1997. Print.

Friedman, Ralph. Tracking Down Oregon. Caxton Press, 1997. 95-103. Print.

Hiatt, Isaac. Thirty-one Years in Baker County. Baker Historical Society. 1997. Print.

"Historical style show at regional museum," Baker City Herald. 17 Feb. 2005. Web. htpp://www.bakercityherald.com.

"James G. Blaine." Encyclopedia Britannica Online. 2016. Web. 12 April. 2016. Web. http://www.encyclopediabritannica.com/biography/James_G_Blaine.

John, Finn J.D. "Mountain Town of Bourne was the Site of a Magnificent Swindle." Offbeat Oregon History. 2010. Web. http://www.

offbeatoregon.com.

Knowles, Brenna. "Wind rips façade off building." Baker City Herald. 20 June 2002. Web. htpp://www.bakercityherald.com.

Lancaster, Bob. Jungles of Arkansas. University of Arkansas Press. Print. P.121.

Law, Adair. The Spark and the Light: The Leo Adler Story. Leo Adler Trust, Print. 2004.

"McColloch Causes Ire by Criticizing C.G. Lathrop." The San Francisco Call. 11 Sept. 1906. P. 16.

McColloch, Claude. "Mortar Crushed by Finger's Touch." Portland Oregonian, 7 May 1906. P. 1,4.

McColloch, Claude. Notes from a Federal Judge, Portland, Oregon: Press of Stevens-Ness Law Publishing, 1949.

McColloch, Charles Henry; McColloch, Claude and McColloch, Frank. "McColloch Family Papers." Unpublished. The Oregon Historical Society.

McColloch, Charles K. "Family Memoir" unpublished: 1988.

Potter, Miles F. Oregon's Golden Years: Bonanza of the West. Caldwell, Idaho: Caxton Press, Print. 1982.

"Rhea's Mill Ledger-1871." Web. http://ozarkscivilwar.org/archives/3535.

Rutter, Michael. Upstairs Girls: Prostitution in the American West. Farcountry Press, Print. 2005. Pp 1-26 and 29-77.

Shurtleff, Marianne G. "Rosa Krann Active in Local Millinery Store 52 Years." Democrat Herald.

Starr, Alexander. "Vienna: Trapped in a Golden Age." The American Scholar. Web. http://the americanscholar.org/vienna_trapped_in_a_golden_age.

"Traveling on the Emigrant Train."1879. Web. http://eyewitnesstohistory.com/emigranttrain.

"Why Bro. McColloch Isn't in Stanford." The Caduceus of Kappa Sigma. 20 October 1906.

"Woman Suffrage in Oregon." Oregon Encyclopedia. http://oregonencyclopedia.org/articles_suffrage_in_oregon.

Woodcock, Bryan L. The 91st Infantry in World War I-Analysis of an AEF Divisions Efforts to Achieve Battlefield Success." Fort Leavenworth, Kansas. 2013.

CPSIA information can be obtained
at www.ICGtesting.com
Printed in the USA
FSHW021711250819
61379FS